Hello Again,

from The Land Of Morning Calm

A Cara Youngblood Moon novel

BOOK 2

R. L. Lee

Crag View Publishing

Cover Photo
Photograph of Mount Shasta - "Eye of The Storm"
by Cindy Diaz Photography - Shastaphotografix
Mt. Shasta, California

Cover Design
R. L. Lee & Eva Long/Long On Books
RLLeeWrites.com
www.longonbooks.com

Interior Book Design & Book Production
Jeff Duckworth
www.duckofalltrades.com

Print edition: 978-0-9907263-2-6
eBook edition: 978-0-9907263-3-3

Printed in the United States of America

Prudy,
This one is for you, kid.

—————— **ACKNOWLEDGMENT** ——————

To my cherished readers
who inspired me to continue the saga of
All My Love, from The Land of Morning Calm.
To those who could not wait.
To the helping hands
who brought this sequel into the light.
My humble thanks.

CONTENTS

MICHAEL

MADAME CHANG

Dear Readers,

Hello, and welcome back. There are a few well-chosen song selections in this sequel to the first novel, *All My Love, from The Land of Morning Calm.* Enjoy them as lyrical expressions of the prose—or, you may eschew them. As always, your preferences will be respected. Whatever you choose, however, it is my fervent hope that you enjoy the continuing adventure.

With kindest regards,

"Love looks not with the eyes, but with the mind,
And therefore is winged Cupid painted blind."

A Midsummer Night's Dream – Act 1, Scene 1
William Shakespeare

Home and Family

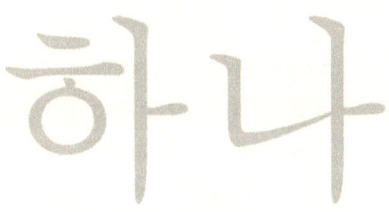

1
Peace And Comfort

June 2006
Northern California – North Country

Cara Moon sat outdoors on the gracefully sweeping redwood deck that adjoined the back of her home, feeling the soothing warmth of the afternoon sun on her back.

The dormant volcano of Mount Shasta, haloed with a lenticular cloud and shrouded in mysticism and legend, provided a spectacular panoramic backdrop. The larger of its two peaks was still resplendent after 249 inches of winter snowfall that mantled the mythical lovers defining its topmost ridges—a Native American warrior and his sleeping princess.

Cara smiled contentedly, enjoying the life-sustaining current of her family ebb and flow around her. It was as if all the planets in the galaxy were in perfect alignment—with everyone healthy and happy, and peace and prosperity reigned throughout the realm.

Her son, Regalo, happily bounced on her friend Michael's lap, pulling on the ears of his battered and much beloved stuffed gray bunny.

Jezebel, Cara's Golden Retriever, was laying at Michael's feet, never too far away from Regalo.

Cara's father, Vincenzo Antonacci, was standing before the gas grill wearing a chef apron and oven mitt, waving grilling tongs in the air like a maestro while sharing with his grandsons, Franco and Gio, his years of wisdom on barbequing the perfect steak.

Her mother and sister, Angelina and Annabella, were bringing plates and silverware from the kitchen to set the patio table for Sunday dinner. Aldo, with a beer in his hand, affectionately patted his wife's ample fanny—or as Annabella breezily referred to it, her "largest asset"—as she walked by him.

Cara drew a blissful breath of sweet azalea-scented air into her lungs. She closed her eyes and captured this precious snippet of her life behind her eyelids, like a photograph. She savored the moment, committing it to her memory—when the existence she now took for granted would retreat to the past, taking with it the people she loved.

"Cara, are you all right?" she heard Michael ask with a light touch on her forearm.

Her eyes popped open. She grinned at him. "Perfect. It's all just perfect."

WAS IT JUST SIX MONTHS ago that Michael came to her after she had said goodbye to her life in South Korea and her husband, Moon Hyo? More accurately, when Moon sent her away shortly after they had returned to his family estate in Seoul. When Michael confessed he had been in love with her since the first day they met six years earlier. When she surprised him with the birth of Regalo, Moon's son, and he unwaveringly asserted that his feelings for her were unchanged. When they mutually agreed to take their time to explore the possibility of a life together.

It was like a pleasantly recurring dream, having Michael so close once again—his bedroom just down the hall from hers—just as it once was in Seoul seemingly so long ago.

She basked in the serenity of his company—his unfailing steadiness and affection—flourished in the peace and comfort he inspired with his presence.

If, as the mysterious fortune teller in the café at Sinsa-dong had predicted, this was her much needed respite from a whirlwind of frustrated love, betrayal, and heartache, Cara determinedly pushed from her mind any thoughts about when it would end—and what was to come next.

REGALO WAS STRAINING TO REACH Jezebel. Michael plopped him down on the deck to sit next to her. Jezebel nuzzled Regalo and he captured her muzzle in his little hands, crying out with delight.

Michael exchanged satisfied smiles with Cara.

He doted on Regalo, and the baby thrived under the influence of his serene nature and quiet strength.

Over the past months, Cara had come to rely more and more upon Michael.

When they were shopping at the local chain pharmacy one afternoon, Regalo began to fuss in Cara's arms. Without a thought, she passed him to Michael. The baby settled immediately, his little head burrowing into Michael's chest.

"Well, look at that!" exclaimed the cashier who was checking out their items. She winked at Michael and cooed, "He does love his daddy, doesn't he?"

The misunderstanding was justifiable. Michael, like Regalo's father, was Korean—except he had been born and reared in the United States.

Cara shot Michael a conspiratorial glance. He purposefully ignored her.

Depending upon the impatience of her customers or their mood at the time, the well-meaning and gregarious older woman behind the checkout counter could be either charming or annoying.

Cara smiled kindly at the cashier, choosing to be charmed. "He does love Michael, that's for sure."

REGALO GRIPPED TUFTS OF JEZEBEL'S ruff in his fists and pulled himself to a wobbly standing position. Nearly nine months old, it was something he had been experimenting with lately.

Jezebel patiently indulged her helpless human fledging and remained motionless.

"You're being very understanding, Jez," Cara fondly praised her. "Thank you."

When Regalo attempted to chew on Jezebel's ear, Cara cautioned him, "Be gentle, Regalo. Don't bite."

Jezebel swiveled her head toward the baby and knocked him on his well-padded butt.

He was startled, looking to his mother for reassurance—perhaps some sympathy or solace.

She exclaimed gaily, "Ooh...boom!"

His cupid bow mouth began to quiver.

Jezebel ran an apologetic and consoling tongue over the crown of Regalo's head, creating a soggy and comical cowlick.

It made Cara giggle.

She sang a cheery tune from a favorite Fred Astaire and Ginger Rogers movie she thought appropriate under the circumstances. "Pick yourself up...dust yourself off...start all over again."

Regalo responded with a pathetic and rather shrill wail, crocodile tears squeezing from his eyes and tracking over his chubby cheeks.

The focus of the family pivoted accusingly on Cara.

"What?" she demanded, casting a bemused and evenly distributed glance among them. "I didn't do anything."

Michael eyed Cara with disapproval. He collected Regalo, wrapped him in his arms, and resettled him on his lap.

The baby promptly stopped crying. He thrust his index and middle fingers in his mouth and laid his head against Michael's shoulder.

"Really, Cara," Michael chastised her. "At times, your mothering skills are a little too laid back."

"Is that right, Regalo?" Cara inquired of her son with feigned seriousness.

Regalo gazed at her unblinking, in that unsettling way babies have of staring you down.

Although she spoke to Regalo, Cara slyly baited Michael. "Is your *Zio* Michele trying to make a sissy out of you?"

Regalo pinched the flesh of Michael's arm between thumb and forefinger and smiled up at him. Michael smiled back.

Cara often spoke to Regalo in Italian. He understood very well that his mother was referring to his Uncle Michael.

Michael was usually beguiled when Cara called him by his Italian name, by its affection and intimacy. It was so lyrical—Mee-keh-leh.

Today, he could not set aside his annoyance with her. "I think your Mama could use a good spanking," he murmured to Regalo.

The baby extracted his fingers from his mouth, laughed, and joyfully patted his hands against Michael's forearm.

Cara gasped in mock offense. "Are you boys ganging up on me?"

She made Regalo shriek in surprise when she growled and nipped at his tummy.

"You're going to make him poop his pants, Cara," her mother cautioned, placing a basket of freshly baked and sliced Italian bread on the dining table.

When Vincenzo loaded a serving platter with steaks still sizzling from the barbeque, Angelina Antonacci announced with authority, "Wash up, everybody! Time to eat!"

Baby Moon

Nine months earlier, Cara's water broke at the Antonacci family home during a Sunday rigatoni and meatball dinner.

She peered under the dining table at her wet skirt and legs and heaved an exasperated sigh. "How undignified."

Angelina Antonacci barked out orders to her husband to get the family's four-door sedan, Annabella to call the doctor, and her son-in-law to get Cara's bag—which she now toted with her everywhere she roamed—and put it in the car. It was like a slapstick comedy, family members jumping up from the table and flying off in all directions.

Franco, quiet and composed—perhaps the most intelligent one in the bunch—regarded his aunt with a droll expression from across the dining room table. "You ready to do this?"

Cara smiled fondly at her sensitive and scholarly nephew. "I sure am ready to lose twenty pounds," she replied dryly, gazing with consternation at her swollen belly.

"Gio," Angelina Antonacci addressed her grandson, "let Jezebel go potty, fill her food bowl, and make sure she has plenty of water before we leave."

"Bring Jezebel," Cara commanded.

Her mother was skeptical. "But…"

"Ma, she's a registered therapy dog. She is allowed in a non-sterile patient room."

Most everyone had cleared the premises, and Cara affectionately patted Jezebel's head as she protectively stayed at her side. "No worries, Girlfriend. We will all get through this just fine."

Her mother had a grip on one arm, Franco the other. They made their way down the walkway just in time to see Vincenzo Antonacci peel off in the car down the driveway.

Cara directed a bewildered glance at her mother.

Angelina Antonacci stoically shook her head, watching the sedan reach the main road. "Look at this, will you?"

It reminded her of the morning she was ready to deliver Annabella. Never known to stay calm in a crisis, Vincenzo had jumped in their '56 Ford and sped away, leaving a strained and irritable Angelina standing on the curb in front of the cramped, two-bedroom house they had purchased after they were married.

Angelina's papa—high-strung and humorless—ran down the street waving his arms like a lunatic trying to catch Vincenzo, cursing him in Italian.

This evening, Vincenzo Antonacci turned around in the driver's seat to pass along encouraging and soothing words to his daughter, but it was Annabella who stared at him with an expression he had seen many times before on his wife's face—one of stony exasperation.

He stomped on the brakes. Once the car came to a full stop, he exclaimed, "You're not Cara!"

Annabella made a wry face. "Great, Pop. I was waiting for you to notice."

"When were you going to speak up?" he blustered. "When we got to the hospital?"

Gio took a post at the end of Cara's bed with the new video camera his mother and father had gifted him upon his graduation from high school—poised to capture the magic moment.

Cara regarded him with a face flushed with Italian temper. Holy Mother of God, there were just certain parts of her anatomy she did not want digitally captured for posterity—bad pun acknowledged—thank you very much.

"Gio, I swear if I get my hands on that camera, you're going to have to glue it back together with spit and chewing gum."

Annabella patted Cara's shoulder to pacify her. *"Calma, Sorella. Calma.* You need to stay tranquil and focused."

Cara huffed in irritation. "I don't know at what point in our culture childbirth became a spectator event," she hoisted herself up on her elbows and shrieked at the top of her lungs, "but I don't like it!"

Her clamorous outburst echoed off the walls of the cheerfully decorated birthing room, causing everyone in the family to freeze, wide-eyed. Jezebel's head swiveled toward Cara, ears alert, as she too gaped.

The nursing staff came on the run.

Cara's father and brother-in-law beat a hasty retreat to the visitor's lounge as Angelina took Cara's hand and murmured soothing Italian endearments to her.

"Everybody up here," Annabella ordered, gesturing for her two sons to join her at the head of Cara's bed. "Come on. Let's allow *Zia* Cara some dignity, please."

A LITTLE LESS THAN THREE hours later, mother and newborn were freshened up and comfortable, and the family sitting in the lobby waiting patiently to visit them.

The attending nurse brought Cara's son to her and placed him in her outstretched arms.

"Jeez, they've got you wrapped like a little burrito." Cara looked up at the young nurse. "Can we give him a little breathing room here?"

The nurse smiled indulgently and loosened his swaddling blanket. Cara took her son's tiny hand with its perfect little fingernails in hers and curiously read the blue plastic bracelet they had circled around his wrist. It read, "Baby Moon" with the day's date printed beneath it.

"Hey, buddy," she crooned to the little hitchhiker she had been toting around for three trimesters. "Happy Birthday."

The little guy blinked drowsily at her, lids puffy and heavy.

"Hey, you," she said, gently bouncing him. "Wake up. You've been floating in a warm pool for nine months. I'm the one who should be tired."

Jezebel rested a muzzle on the side of the bed and gazed at them with soft brown eyes. She sniffed the little package that Cara held in her arms.

Cara acknowledged her with a wry comment. "He doesn't smell bad now, Girlfriend, but just wait."

She spoke in hushed tones to her newborn son, allowing him time to adjust to the cacophony of his new world. "I thought this might be a good time to square away a few things between us. First, and perhaps most importantly, I don't know much about being a mom. Nothing, actually."

She pursed her lips. "But I'm pretty good at taking care of Jezebel, huh girl?"

Jezebel shifted on her paws and licked her chops.

Baby Moon's small face puckered.

"I know what you're thinking…you're not a dog. But I want you to know that I am a responsible person. I will never let you go hungry…in an Italian family that is practically impossible anyway…especially with *Nona* and *Nono* Antonacci. You will meet them shortly.

"I'll never let you sit in a wet or poopy diaper, or dress you in silly undignified clothes, or embarrass you by taking a picture of you naked on a fur rug. By the way, I much prefer that the original owner of the fur retain all rights." She gently stroked Jezebel's head.

"I won't talk baby-talk to you or force you to eat everything on your dinner plate before you can leave the table." The edge of her memory lifted and Cara assured him, "Oh, and I will never say, 'because I said so!' when you ask me why. I always hated that," she grumbled in fresh annoyance.

"Lord knows, I won't be perfect. I will be learning new things along the way. But I will always try to be fair and patient, and give you my full attention."

She ran the back of her index finger against his fuzzy, ruddy cheek. "I can promise you one thing…you will always know that you are loved."

Maybe it was her imagination—it probably was—but Baby Moon actually appeared to smile.

"But you have to do your part, too," she advised him. "You have to be strong and brave, and kind to animals, and respect your elders."

She studied her son's sweet face and ruminated, "I think it's too early to tell who you resemble. I'm not very good at recognizing that anyway." She grinned and smoothed down the wild tufts of black hair on his tiny head. "But you do have your father's unruly hair.

"On that subject," she murmured, feeling a bit melancholy, "I'm sorry your dad isn't here to welcome you. That is partly...mostly...my fault. We can talk about that another day."

Her eyes misted with emotion. It did not take much to bring her to tears lately. She sniffed and impatiently swiped at them with the back of her hand. She hated being a crybaby.

"But I will make sure you know who he is and, one day...when I am braver...I will make sure you meet him.

"He is from Korea, you know. How exciting that will be for you, coming from two cultures, learning about your Korean heritage and your father's family." She thought of Moon's mother and shuddered. "You can visit your dad anytime you want. I promise you that."

Baby Moon burbled, or gurgled—whatever it is that babies do.

"What's he like, you ask?" Cara looked off in the distance, collecting her thoughts, wanting to use exactly the right words. "Well, he is very dignified. At times, he can be a little intimidating and stern. He is honorable, intelligent, and accomplished." She sighed, smiling wistfully. "When he is dressed in his hand-tailored suits, he is very handsome. At least I think he is."

She got back on track, attempting to spare her newborn son from her feminine reveries. "He takes his responsibility to his family and country very seriously, and works tirelessly to please them both."

Which brings him little happiness, Cara thought sadly, but did not share with their son.

Above all, she was adamant that the predestined future of the father would not be visited upon their son. She nodded with determination. "I want you to be your own person. To define your own life and do what brings you happiness."

The little guy yawned. Cara followed suit, her eyes drooping. "Yeah, I'm pooped, too. Maybe we can take a little nap." She rang for the nurse. "You can let the hordes descend," Cara jokingly advised the young woman as she relinquished her son.

Satisfied that all was well, Jezebel curled up at the side of Cara's bed and settled her muzzle on her paws with a low growl of contentment.

All in all, a good day.

A Lighted Candle

T HERE WAS A BIT OF a brouhaha when it came time to baptize
Regalo.

Cara had acquiesced to her parent's appeal to baptize him in the
Catholic Church to mollify their ever-faithful convictions. In truth,
she was not opposed to the baptismal rite, or the spiritual precepts that
would teach her son right from wrong. The form of religion Regalo chose
to accept as an adult, if any, was something he would be free to decide.

Cara stubbornly insisted that Michael serve as godfather to her son.
However, in the eyes of the Church, Cara was a divorced woman who
no longer practiced her faith. Michael resided with Cara under the same
roof—no matter how innocently—without benefit of the sacrament of
marriage and, more importantly, was not of the Roman Catholic faith.

Faced with this unconventional predicament, the young and
unseasoned parish priest had mumbled in mounting anxiety that he
might require the counsel of the bishop in the Sacramento Diocese.
Maybe the archbishop in San Francisco. Perhaps the cardinals of the
Vatican. Even the Pope himself.

The family gathered around the Antonacci dining table over coffee
and dessert early one Friday evening to discuss this dilemma.

Michael quietly tried reasoning with Cara, proposing that he remove
himself from the baptismal ceremonies.

She was staunchly resistant to his suggestion.

After much debate about Church dogma, possible alternatives and
concessions, the Antonacci family conclave digressed into a free-for-all
with everyone talking and no one listening.

Vincenzo Antonacci pushed back his chair, threw his napkin on
the table, and muttered, "I've had just about enough of this nonsense."

He glanced around the table, his determined gaze falling on his youngest daughter. "Leave this to me, Cara."

He marched out of the dining room, climbed into the family car and proceeded down the driveway—in greater haste than normal—toward town.

"Should we go after him, *Nona?*" Gio asked his grandmother with a deep frown of concern creasing his fine forehead.

Deadpan, Angelina Antonacci looked around the table at her tensely silent family and inquired dryly, "After we are excommunicated, what are your thoughts about becoming Lutherans?"

A calmer Vincenzo Antonacci returned to the house later that evening. He never hinted about what he had said to the parish priest, but every member of the family privately speculated and put forth his or her own theory.

Perhaps there was mention of the indisputable fact that Vincenzo's father, newly arrived from a dirt-poor village in southern Italy, built the church in which the local faithful continued to celebrate Mass.

Furthermore, several years ago, after vandals set fire to the celebrant and tabernacle altars, Vincenzo devotedly recreated and donated them to the Church.

Lastly, the generous contributions to the collection plate, passed around the congregation on Sundays and Holy Days, ungrudgingly pledged by three generations of their family.

"This is how it will be," Vincenzo firmly stated to the attentive family gathered around him as he sat on his recliner in the living room. He fixed Cara with a hawk-like glare that defied argument. "Your mother and I will stand as Regalo's parents."

Cara opened her mouth to speak and Michael silenced her by placing his hand over hers.

"We must profess our faith and loyalty to the Church," Vincenzo reminded his blithely independent daughter. His tone became gentle. "Can you do that, Cara?"

Cara lowered her eyes. "What else?"

"Annabella and Aldo will stand as his godmother and godfather."

Cara's head snapped up.

"For the same reasons your mother and I must act as his parents," Vincenzo explained patiently.

Father Bannon had read, for the benefit of Vincenzo Antonacci, the text of the baptismal sacrament.

The celebrant asks for the threefold profession of faith from the parents and godparents:

Celebrant: Do you believe in the God the Father, almighty, creator of heaven and earth?

Parents and Godparents: I do.

Celebrant: Do you believe in Jesus Christ, his only son, our Lord, who was born of the Virgin Mary, was crucified, died, and was buried, rose from the dead and is now seated at the right hand of the Father?

Parents and Godparents: I do.

Celebrant: Do you believe in the Holy Spirit, the holy Catholic Church, the communion of saints, the forgiveness of sins, the resurrection of the body, and life everlasting?

Parents and Godparents: I do.

"What about Michael?" Cara asked.

Vincenzo nodded at Michael, grateful for his stability and sound judgment that grounded his daughter's impetuous temperament. "Michael will hold the baby throughout the baptism. You will stand at his side."

Cara smiled with relief at Michael, content that he would participate. She regarded her father with love, gratitude, and pride. "Thank you, Papa."

On a windy, early spring Sunday afternoon, the family gathered around the baptismal fountain where each of them had been christened, to bring into the light, Regalo Michael Moon.

He remained sleepy-eyed and peaceful in Michael's arms. He started when the celebrant poured holy water over the crown of his head, little fists threshing the air, but did not cry. When the priest put his thumb over his eyes and ears, and anointed him with holy oil, the baby stared at Michael, taking comfort from his tranquil and unwavering gaze.

Then Father Bannon passed Michael an unlit candle, motioning him to light it from the Easter candle that flickered on its nearby stand in the sanctuary. "Receive the light of Christ."

When Michael had performed the task and jointly held the candle with Cara, the priest concluded the baptismal rite. "Parents and Godparents, this light is entrusted to you to be kept burning brightly. This child of yours has been enlightened by Christ. He is to walk always as a child of the light. May he keep the flame of faith alive in his heart. When the Lord comes, may he go out to meet him with all the saints in the heavenly kingdom."

CARA HAPPILY PULLED MICHAEL WITH her to the life-sized statue of the Holy Blessed Virgin at the front of the church. He knelt by her side on a padded kneeler as she prayed quietly. "Thank you, Holy Mother, for giving me a healthy son, for my sweet Michael, my loving family, and my many blessings."

Michael's heart swelled with tenderness and the pleasant sensation of belonging to something greater than himself. He smiled at Regalo—his head cradled on his broad palm—and made him a silent promise. He pledged to watch over him and keep him safe, as he previously had sworn for his mother. That he would guide him, if asked, through the often bumpy and emotionally depleting misfortunes of life. That he would believe in him, speak only the truth to him, and set a solid, honorable, and respectable example for him to follow.

Michael gazed into Cara's expressive eyes, warmed by the radiance of their adoration.

He heard a faint, cautionary rumbling from the depths of his consciousness. *Be careful, Michael. They are not yours. Not yet. Be careful.*

Papa Mia

May 2006
Northern California – North Country

O N A MILD AFTERNOON IN May, in the meadow by the pond,
Michael was demonstrating martial arts exercises to Cara's
nephews who, once they discovered he was a Taekwondo master, relentlessly
badgered him to teach them some movements. He was running them
through some disciplines, which they soaked up like sponges, eyes tracking
his every graceful and deliberate motion—revering him.

Cara was at the kitchen island washing lettuce for a tossed salad, her
father slicing tomatoes by her side.

Vincenzo glanced past the deck, where his grandsons were laughing
with Michael. "He's a good man," he ruminated, a thoughtful frown
creasing his brow.

"Yes, he is, Papa. He made me well…want to live…after I was injured
in the car accident."

Cara had wisely spared her parents the details of her physical assault
that had resulted in a broken collarbone, collapsed lung, two orthoscopic
surgeries to mend torn ligaments in her knee, and a traumatic lapse in
trust in police officer Kang Dae Ho, a man who attracted Cara from
the first moment they met.

"You got something against American men?" Vincenzo asked, more
out of curiosity than disapproval.

Cara was amused. "He is an American, Pop."

"You know what I mean," he huffed, a bit testy.

Cara grinned. "I was married to one of the first Americans,
remember?" she reminded her father of her former husband, Tay
Youngblood, a member of the Oglala Lakota Sioux tribe from South
Dakota. "You didn't approve of him, either."

"Don't get smart with your father," Vincenzo Antonacci warned, although without much starch. He always said that when he felt his daughter was getting the best of him.

"Pop, do you remember my favorite ice cream flavor when I was a kid?"

Her father's hazel eyes lost focus on the present to look back in time. A light came on in their depths. He chuckled softly. "You didn't have one. You said you wanted to try them all before deciding."

Cara grinned. "That's right."

Vincenzo glanced around to confirm the whereabouts of his wife. She was visiting with Annabella and Aldo around the patio table on the deck, Regalo filling her petite lap.

He dropped his voice and asked skeptically, "How many have you tried?"

"Not as many as I hoped, that's for sure," she admitted with lighthearted chagrin.

Vincenzo blanched and made a tsk-tsk sound with his tongue. "Don't let your mother hear you talk like that."

"Okay, Pop," Cara complied fondly.

"That's because you're a good girl," her father affirmed with quiet conviction. "We raised you that way."

Cara kissed his cheek. "Yes, you did Papa." She muttered with a shake of her head, "I was good...but so restless."

"He's wonderful with the baby," Vincenzo praised Michael.

"Mmm," Cara conceded distractedly. "Regalo loves him. And he loves Regalo."

Vincenzo fixed her with a worried stare. "What about you?"

"What?"

"Your son. Do you love him?"

She hesitated, surprised by the question—surprised by her hesitation. "I would die for him."

"That's not what I asked."

"He's so new. So...helpless." She shrugged lamely, uncomfortable with the neutrality of her answer.

She read the disappointed in her father's expression. "I never imagined myself as a mother. A career...lovers...those were my dreams. A child..." she shook her head broodingly, "that I never imagined."

Vincenzo took his daughter's shoulders in his strong hands. "Thank you for giving us Regalo, Cara. To welcome him and love him as a part of our family." He confirmed quietly, "I know you could have made other choices."

Cara assured him gently, "Even though Moon and I are estranged, I wanted to give our son life."

She confessed her shortcomings to this simple, devoted man who knew them all—forgave them all. "So typical of me, isn't it? Trying to cope with a situation that caught me off guard...that I didn't even anticipate." She said with mild disgust, "I keep hoping I will get wiser with age."

"You will," Vincenzo soothed her with sturdy assurance.

She smiled wryly. "In my lifetime?"

Her father shot a speculative glance at Michael. "Have you two..." He made the *you-know-what-I-mean* gesture.

Cara watched Michael correct some arm and hand positions with Gio. "No, not yet," she replied absently.

Vincenzo frowned, somehow sensing that his question had been misinterpreted. "What are you talking about?"

Cara gave her father her full attention. "What are you talking about?"

"Marriage."

"Oohh." She laughed lightly. "I was talking about sex."

Her father shook his head. "You are nothing like your mother, I can tell you that."

Regalo riding on her hip, Angelina Antonacci carried to the table a platter of chicken that Aldo had just removed from the barbeque grill.

"Salad!" she demanded of her youngest daughter and husband.

Cara scooped the condiments on the cutting board into the greens, picked up the salad bowl, and headed outdoors. "We're in no hurry, Pop. I guess if it's meant to happen, it will."

The Doe And Her Fawn

June 2006
Northern California – North Country

Michael and Cara were enjoying a glass of wine, sitting side by side in lounge chairs on the shady side of the deck. Jezebel was sprawled at their feet—dozing—her shiny coat ruffled by a soft breeze.

"Oh, look, Michael," Cara said in a hushed voice, pointing to the meadow where a graceful, long necked young doe appeared, a tiny spotted fawn trailing behind her. "She finally gave birth."

They had been watching her for weeks, belly swollen with her unborn fawn, browsing in the meadow, laying perfectly still in the overgrown, wheat-like grass in the warmth of a late afternoon sun.

Michael smiled.

The doe stopped and looked back in confusion and annoyance at the tentative fawn who was trying to keep up with her.

"Look at her expression," Cara marveled with a grin. "She may have given birth to this little one, but you can tell she doesn't know what to do with him now…or why he keeps following her."

Having said that, the doe sprang away at a full gallop, attempting to rid herself of the nuisance that had attached itself to her. His mother's sudden departure startled the sweet fawn. Distressed and determined to keep up, he bounded on his long, spindly legs to chase after her. They disappeared in a copse of evergreens.

"Oohh," Cara commiserated with the newborn. "The poor little thing!"

She turned to find Michael pinning her with a pointed and purposeful stare, a message for her in his eyes.

She laughed sheepishly and shrugged. "Well…at least I haven't run yet."

As if on cue, Regalo awakened from his nap and cried for attention from his crib in the house.

Jezebel snapped awake and sat up, alerted to the baby's cries.

When Cara remained seated and looked expectantly at Michael, he challenged her with raised brows.

Although Michael was always first to jump up and fetch the baby, she took the hint. "Why don't I go this time," she offered, rising.

"Yes, why don't you," Michael murmured sardonically.

They were heartened two weeks later to observe the doe back in the meadow with her fawn, greedily suckling while his mother arched her long neck and methodically swiped him clean with her tongue.

"Well, new mama," Cara murmured benignly, "I guess there's hope for us yet."

CARA SKIPPED DOWN THE STONE pathway from her house to the mailbox, gaily waving to the departing postal carrier who had just delivered the day's mail. Jezebel barked her usual greeting.

Among the stack of advertisements, catalogs and bills, Cara was pleased to discover a letter from Lena Bright Star, an educator and administrator at the Red Cloud Indian School on the Pine Ridge Reservation in South Dakota.

In honor of Youngblood and his proud family—whom she had met on a road trip to the reservation with Tay before they were married—Cara had been a regular contributor to the Red Cloud School since she began working for the Chang Agency.

After Tay died in an automobile accident nearly ten years earlier, Cara periodically wrote to his mother, Winona. Receiving no word back from Winona after a handful of years, Cara surmised that her letters only served to provoke painful reminders of the loss of her son. She ceased her efforts to keep in touch, with the exception of a remembrance at Christmastime.

Now, Cara depended on Lena Bright Star for news about the state of the reservation and, of course, Winona.

Cara promptly opened Lena's letter.

I am grieved to report, the letter began in Lena's slanted script, *that the spirit of our sister, Winona, has departed this earth. I do not believe she ever recovered from her son's death. She now lies beside him and her father, the Old Chief, in our sacred burial ground. We will miss her kind heart and healing hands.*

Cara closed herself in her bedroom and wept bitter tears for the loss of the courageous, enduring, and accomplished Winona; the family who had so warmly welcomed her into their home; Tay whom she had loved passionately and without hesitation; and her blissfully naive youth that once made everything seem possible.

The L Word

June 2006
Northern California – North Country

CARA RESTLESSLY SHIFTED IN BED—ADJUSTING the covers then her pillows—trying to get comfortable. She heaved a frustrated sigh, threw off the duvet, and sat up on the side of the bed.

It was useless—this attempt to still her thoughts and unwilling body.

Although it was officially summer, the evening mountain air was cool. She retrieved her silk wrap, slipping it on as she made her way down the hall.

She quietly entered the nursery to check on Regalo. His diaper was dry. Feathers of silky black hair clung to his perspiring forehead. She gently blotted his sweet face with a cool washcloth and smiled when his cherubic mouth began to suckle.

His crib was awash in light.

Had she forgotten to turn off the outside security lights?

She peered out of the bedroom window.

The moon strained to clear the rim of the mountains, its broad and clearly outlined face pitted by craters, shadowed by mysterious lava seas. A fiery, orange glow radiated from its ripe, full surface—seeming to pulsate from deep within its core.

Cara stared at it in awe. Its frosty luminescence, eerily brilliant, blanched her skin blue-white and turned her eyes the color of quicksilver.

The moon. A study of contradictions. So much like the man Moon Hyo—the man she had loved—whom she believed had loved her.

Although she had not let on to Michael or her family, Cara had been stunned to learn about Moon's engagement less than seven months after they had separated. She had not allowed herself to dwell on the fact that Moon so quickly and easily replaced her in his heart. It was too hurtful.

Evidently, he found his fiancée—a young woman just graduated from university—more suitable for his traditional lifestyle. Undoubtedly, his family—most particularly his mother—happily embraced her.

Cara slid back on the seat of the oak rocking chair Vincenzo Antonacci had lovingly handcrafted for his daughter and new grandson, and placed in the nursery next to Regalo's crib.

She observed the child that she and Moon had created—his little chest rising and falling—envious of his peaceful and unmindful slumber.

She rocked back and forth, back and forth, back and forth—burning up the restlessness that prickled under her skin.

Since her pregnancy, her hormones were raging. Tormenting her. How she yearned for the satisfying embrace of strong arms, the whisper of soft, sweet kisses upon her lips, the pleasurable touch of warm hands caressing her body—the primal rhythm of two bodies seeking relief from the lust that provoked them into thoughtless pursuit.

She felt as though she would burst out of her skin with the ache, the longing, for lovemaking.

Hot pants, her mother would call it with a shake of her head, her mouth compressed into an adamantly disapproving line.

Cara gazed at the framed photograph of Moon displayed on the chest of drawers.

She had captured his pose when they were enjoying a rare, warm Sunday afternoon in the neighborhood park near their San Francisco townhouse. The photo was taken with the camera he had gifted her on their only Christmas together.

Cara focused the lens on him, waiting for just the right moment to snap the picture—teasing him, coaxing him to smile.

He was reclined on a plaid picnic blanket on the lush green grass, propped on one elbow, seducing her with teasing, smoldering eyes.

It was her favorite photograph of him.

She remembered, without a word spoken between them, their shared urgency to reach home. They had barely closed the front door and released Jezebel from her leash, when they began exchanging hot, wet kisses—hastily scrabbling to remove each other's clothing—awkwardly stumbling toward their bedroom.

They never got that far.

Cara uttered a strangled oath and flipped the photograph face down on the surface of the chest. The evocative reminiscence was not helping matters.

She laid her head back against the headrest of the rocking chair and closed her eyes. Was it sex that she missed, or sex with Moon? Or, was it just Moon?

She smoothed Regalo's blanket before softly closing the nursery door behind her.

Once in the hallway, she stopped and gazed at the closed door of Michael's bedroom. She had no idea what time it was. He could be asleep.

She walked to his door and nervously stood there, debating whether to chance waking him. She held a fist up to the door, ready to knock, but checked herself. She turned to leave, stopped, and then swiveled to stare at his door.

She released an impatient rush of air. This was ridiculous.

Michael was lying in bed, reading the latest John Lescroart Dismas Hardy novel. He looked up from the print on the page and frowned when he heard movement outside his door.

"Cara?" he called quietly.

Cara hid her eyes behind her hands, cursing herself for waking him. She had forgotten about his extraordinary sense of hearing.

Michael imagined her dancing in indecision on the other side of the door with a rare reluctance to disturb him. "Cara?"

A hesitation. "Yes?"

Michael removed his tortoise shell reading glasses. "What are you doing?"

"I don't know," she admitted sheepishly.

He smiled. "Come in."

"What?"

"I'm awake," he said a little louder, mindful of disturbing Regalo. "Come in."

After a moment's pause, Cara pushed open the door and peered into the bedroom.

Lamplight burned brightly on the bedside table. A stack of pillows supported Michael's back, a book opened on his lap, his body bare to the waist.

Cara had always admired his tall, lean and finely defined muscular frame.

Michael observed Cara—lovely in a silk, floor-length Asian-print gown and matching robe—fluttering before the door like a colorful and skittish butterfly.

Anxiety tensed her features and clouded her eyes.

"What is it, Cara?" he coaxed gently.

She deliberated whether to follow through with her resolve to speak with him about a very delicate matter. A very personal, unsettling matter.

She walked to the center of the room, closer to Michael's bed, and apprehensively broached the subject. "Once, I was able to say anything to you...to confide in you. I could throw my arms around you and hug you, or sit on your bed and talk with you. You used to sit on my bed. Remember?"

Michael tilted his head and studied her—unsure if he was ready for this discussion.

Cara rushed on in a frustrated tumble of words. "Since we mentioned the 'L' word, I feel...awkward...not as free to...do those things anymore."

Michael held her gaze while he processed her comment. He put aside his reading on the nightstand and laid his glasses on top of the closed book. He rearranged the pillows, slid toward the center of the bed, and peeled back the corner of the covers.

"Come here," he invited softly.

Cara's footfalls were silent on the carpeted floor as she tentatively approached him. She kicked off her slippers and slipped into bed beside him.

He covered her with the duvet, took her in his arms, and cradled her head in the curve of his shoulder.

"You gave up your warm spot," Cara observed timidly.

Michael chuckled, stroking the crest of her shoulder with a comforting hand. "I don't mind."

Cara burrowed closer to him.

Michael enjoyed the pleasurable, pillowy pressure of her breasts against his side, her small hand lightly resting on his chest.

"I imagined us like this once," she recalled dreamily.

"Like what?"

"Just as we are...lying in bed together, me in the circle of your arm, your hand stroking my shoulder." As an afterthought, she revealed to Michael, "I felt ashamed."

Michael was disappointed—puzzled. "Why?"

"Because I was still married to Moon."

Michael's hand stilled its caress of her arm.

"I shouldn't have, Michael," she announced with conviction.

"Shouldn't have what?" he asked hesitantly. Imagined him?

"Been ashamed."

Cara felt the release of his tense muscles.

She freely shared her disputable thoughts. "The longer I live, the more I believe it's not only possible but natural to love more than one person. All these strict social and religious mores that force us to suppress our desires, deny our feelings...suffer in silence...till death do us part." She shook her head at the pure absurdity—impossibility—of defying human nature. "We can love many people in our lifetimes for different reasons...for the way they make us feel, or what we admire about them." She gazed up at Michael. "Or the way they complete us."

Although Cara's revelation did not surprise Michael, he was not so willing to embrace her theory of polyamorous relationships. Especially as they related to him. He had shared her long enough.

"I think couples who live happily ever after are truly blessed with good fortune," she murmured philosophically. "They should try their luck in Vegas."

Michael chuckled.

Cara eased into the conversation she had debated having with Michael for a long while. She had even practiced its content, inflection, and timing.

"Apart from Regalo, do you enjoy being here, Michael?"

As always, Michael focused her thoughts. "What are you really asking me?"

Cara anticipated his response. "Do you enjoy being here with me?"

Motivated by his significant silence, she attempted to elicit enlightenment from the depths of his eyes. "What are we doing, Michael? You have been here almost eight months, and we…we are…" She sighed helplessly. "I can't seem to put my feelings into words without sounding needy."

"Cara…"

"It's as if you made the gesture, said the words, but aren't invested in them. What are your plans, Michael? For us…for you and me? Because if you do have plans, why are you waiting? And if you don't, why keep up the charade?"

She proceeded cautiously, lightly—filling in his persistent silence. "If you are gay, Michael, you know that's okay with me. I will always love you. You can be free to be who you are, and we can still be best friends."

Michael looked away from her, releasing a frustrated gust of air from his lungs. That is not what he wanted—needed—to hear.

Cara strived to ease what she perceived to be his reluctance to admit the truth. "If that is the case, it's fine. Really."

He pinned her with his intense brown eyes. "Are you trying to provoke me into proving something we both may regret?"

She was surprised by the question—the probability of the theory. "Maybe," she conceded quietly. "Maybe I am."

His remark made her eyes sting with tears of disappointment. "You would regret it?"

Michael covered the side of her face with a gentle hand, erasing her frown with his thumb. "There is so much I would have done differently, if only I had known."

If only he had realized that love does not discriminate between race or social class, disparate backgrounds or personalities. That it is benevolent and forgiving—irrational and blind.

Six years of enforced silence, self-restraint, envy, heartache, and frustration—a bitter sacrifice—a lesson he still had not mastered.

"But I can't change the past. Your heart…your life…is unresolved. Until you face Moon and contend with your feelings for him, I can't… won't…do anything to confuse you."

Cara's expression became distant. Michael—always her leveler, her voice of reason, her conscience. She swallowed her misery and nodded, confirming her understanding. Wordlessly she got up from the bed, quickly walked to the door and silently closed it behind her.

Michael called after her in his thoughts. *Or allow my heart to be shattered in so many pieces it will never again be whole.*

He was pleased with neither himself nor his solution to this love triangle that ensnared them—in which all of them suffered bitterly.

♪ "Hold on Tight"
Boney James

THAT NIGHT, IN HIS DREAMS, Michael went to Cara.

He stood by her bed, watching her, the evening soft with the arrival of summer. Her room was awash with pale light from the full-faced and low-hung moon that peeked through the windowpanes of the French door.

She lay on her side, her back to him, body drawn into a despondent curl.

He threw off the coverlet that wound around her body, constrained her.

She turned toward him, cheeks tracked with tears—at first startled, and then pleasantly relieved. She reached for him without reservation—as a child would—seeking comfort.

He slipped beside her, protectively gathering her in his arms, remorseful that he had made her cry.

Unthinkingly, he crushed her body against his. He heard her soft whimper of pain.

"Forgive me, Cara," he murmured, penitent for so much more.

He kissed her face—comforting her in words rich with promise.

"Michael," she called his name, her voice husky with desire. "Michael."

He took his time unwrapping this much-anticipated and long-awaited gift. He savored with his eyes, stroked with his fingertips, brushed with his lips—every part of her that he laid bare.

He made surprising and pleasing discoveries of a woman he believed he had known all of his life. Her skin was supple velvet, sweet with a heady scent. Her hair was as fine as corn silk. Her breasts, full and ripe, were quick to respond to his caress. The pupils of her eyes enlarged, and she purred with pleasure deep in her throat, when aroused.

She was unashamed in her appreciation of him—her fingers combing through his hair, skimming over his full lips, his shoulders and back, his hips—worshiping him, making him burn—drawing his restraint to an end.

Her thighs opened to him, lush and inviting. He blissfully lost himself deep inside of her—wanting nothing more than to stay within her welcoming and enveloping warmth—a place from which he never could, never wish to, be free.

"Michael," Cara moaned with his even-paced rhythm, his provocatively slow and deliberate thrusts. "Michael."

Unwelcomed yet insistent—Michael heard the echo of disappointment and discontent in her voice—sensed her lack of fulfillment.

Michael...I need more! Give me more!

AWAKENING THE NEXT MORNING, MICHAEL attempted to lighten his heavy spirits.

It was just a dream. Only a dream.

Or was it, more truthfully, a realization that had plagued him for a very long time?

2
It's A Boy!

June 2006
Northern California – North Country

T HEY WERE IN THE KITCHEN preparing an early dinner, Cara laughing with Michael, his arms around her in a rare and playful hug. She glanced up, startled by a figure darkening the open French doors.

She inhaled a sharp breath.

Moon Hyo stood watching them, a firm set to his jaw.

Cara reflexively backed away, brushing against a salad bowl on the corner of the counter. It fell to the floor, glass shattering in jagged shards around her bare feet.

Moon rushed into the house. Before he could reach them, Michael had swept Cara in his arms and sat her on the kitchen counter. He wrapped a wet paper towel around a cut bleeding on her right foot.

"Don't step on any glass!" Michael cautioned Moon.

"Are you all right?" Moon asked Cara with anxiety.

She stared at him, a ghost from her past.

Michael used a broom and dustpan, carefully collecting the fragments of glass that had bloomed across the slate tile floor.

When he emptied the last dustpan into the kitchen trashcan, Cara distractedly cursed under her breath. "Damn it. That was my favorite bowl."

Michael disinfected and affixed an adhesive bandage to Cara's superficial cut, put her sandals on her feet, and stepped away to give Cara and Moon some privacy.

The two eyed each other warily.

"*Oraenmaniya,*" Moon murmured—the expression *long time no see* as common in South Korea as it was in the States.

Spine rigid with tension, Cara asked Moon in a stilted tone, "What can I do for you?"

He remained silent for a very long and uncomfortable moment, expression censorious. "You can take the hard edge from your eyes when you look at me."

Cara dropped her gaze—shaken by her feelings of contempt and anger, appalled that she was telegraphing them, reminded of how easily Moon could read her.

When she raised her chin, she wore the bland expression she had mastered during her career as an interpreter at the Chang Agency.

Moon did not like that any better. He let it pass. "I understand that we have a son."

Cara shot a bewildered glance at Michael. When his expression remained even and unapologetic, her features morphed into an incriminating scowl.

Betrayed by a man she trusted implicitly. A man who claimed he loved her.

Michael remained unruffled under her accusatory glare. "If you will excuse me," he said quietly, walking out on the deck.

Cara jumped down from the counter and winced in pain, reminded of the fresh gash on her foot.

Moon reached out and steadied her with a firm hold on her arm, a worried frown drawing his brows together. "Do you need to sit down?"

Cara stared up at him and nervously swallowed—very much aware of his unshakable appeal.

She lightly shrugged free from his hold. "No. I'm fine."

She walked down the hall toward the baby's room, casting a glance over her shoulder at Moon. He finally understood that she wanted him to follow her.

Cara soundlessly opened the door of the nursery and stepped inside, an eager Moon following closely behind.

Regalo was sitting up in his crib, entertaining himself as he often did, chewing on the stuffed gray bunny rabbit that was a gift from his Uncle Michael.

His expression brightened when he recognized his mother. He stared with unabashed curiosity at the man who stood at the side of his crib, smiling broadly.

His little face took on a serious aspect when he said, quite clearly, "*A...ppa.*"

Moon and Cara exchanged incredulous glances.

This was the first time, in all of Cara's patient prompting and Regalo's joyous gibberish, that he had repeated the informal Korean word for father.

Cara supposed there was no better time.

Moon carefully picked up his son and held him securely in his arms, kissing his chubby cheeks, overcome by pride and emotion.

His gaze questioned Cara.

She motioned to the framed photograph of him that sat on the end of a chest of drawers nearest the crib. "He should know his father," she explained briefly.

Moon's defenses melted, along with the tension in his face. His son still in his arms, he dropped to his knees before Cara in a Korean gesture that both extended respect and begged for forgiveness. He circled his arm around her hips and pressed his forehead against her belly. "Thank you, Cara. Thank you for our son."

He began to weep.

Overwhelmed, Cara squeezed her eyes shut and shook her head, unprepared for Moon's reaction.

Finally letting go of months of pent up anxiety and guilt, she also began to weep.

34

"Look what you do to me," she murmured breathlessly.

Moon tightened his grip.

"Look what you do to me," she repeated in anguish.

MICHAEL WATCHED THEM THROUGH THE window from the deck. Sorrowful and disheartened, he turned from the emotional reunion and woodenly walked down the steps to the pond.

Jezebel intuitively kept him close and solacing company.

If Not Now, When?

June 2006
Northern California – North Country

T HE NEXT MORNING, MICHAEL PACKED his bags under Cara's watchful and sullen scrutiny. After he had gathered the last of his belongings and stored them in the trunk of his leased car parked in the driveway, he stood before Cara who waited at the bottom of the stone pathway leading to the house.

There had been little opportunity to speak with him the night before. "Why did you do that, Michael?" she demanded. "Why did you contact Moon?"

"Because you wouldn't."

"I would have...eventually."

"Not soon enough for me."

Cara clamped her arms around him as he turned away from her, hugging him from behind, holding him tightly. "Don't go. Please, don't go."

She heard the echo, the desperation, of those exact words when Police Inspector Kang Dae Ho had pleaded with her not to leave him at the coffeehouse in Seoul. It was the last time they had been together.

Michael spared her a quick glance over his shoulder. "I'll always be a phone call away, Cara. You know that. I always have been."

"Yes, of course. I'm sorry, Michael," she apologized, properly chastised. "I know that." She released him—reluctantly, begrudgingly, angrily.

"Face your future, Cara. I will abide by whatever you decide."

"What do you want me to do, Michael?" she cried in frustration, turning him around to confront her. "What is it that *you* want? Tell me now, please."

"I want you to be happy," he said simply.

"Fight for me, Michael," she pleaded miserably. "If you want me, don't walk away. Fight for me."

"I don't want to fight, Cara. I want you to come to me willingly, because you love me. Not because I fought and won you...like a prize."

She wanted to scream at him, *Coward!* Until she grew weak with the realization that she was the coward—panicky and breathless with the betrayal of abandonment.

She collapsed in resignation on a stone step. "A prize worth fighting for," she grieved quietly.

Michael climbed into the SUV and started the engine. With one long, last soulful glance at Cara, he slowly cruised down the driveway to the adjoining artery that would take him to the Interstate 5 freeway.

Much Ado

September 2005
Northern California – North Country

WHAT MICHAEL COULD NOT HAVE known—did not witness—was Cara observing her peacefully napping son just days after his birth one late and bright September afternoon.

Guilt overwhelming her, she slipped from the nursery, quietly closing the door behind her, and made her way to the deck. The weather was pleasantly dry and warm—in the final phase of an Indian summer.

She had to tell Moon that he had a son. It was the right thing to do.

She quailed at the prospect of speaking with him—trembling at her core, hands shaking, cheeks flushed—as she gazed at the contacts on her cell phone. She scrolled to the personal cell phone number Moon had given her when they had parted at Shangri-La, her vacation home in the mountainous Gangwon Province of South Korea.

She had tucked away his business card in her Cherrywood keepsake box, along with the silk and bamboo fan he had purchased for her at the Sangju Farmers Market during a summer road trip they had taken together.

She procrastinated—deadheading spent chrysanthemum blooms from the copious plants in the flower boxes rimming the deck.

She paced—rehearsing what she was going to say to him, practicing just the right inflection.

She puffed calming breaths of air from her lungs—trying to steady the tremor in her voice.

It made her dizzy.

She staggered to a nearby lounge chair and put her head between her knees until the dizziness passed.

She began to play the self-defeating *what if* game. What if Moon refused to speak to her…did not want anything to do with her…or his son? She prepared herself for the possibility that he may be abrupt or accusing—even dismissive. Or, worse still, what if he demanded that she bring the baby back to Korea? Certainly, the prestige of his family name and the cadre of influential attorneys at their disposal could make that a reality.

Her insecurity exasperated her. After all, she had successfully dealt with this man before—withstood his disapproval, his stern rebukes, his...

She shook her head in self-derision. Look who had become Satan.

She freely admitted that, this time, she was wrong. She should have told Moon she was pregnant before leaving Korea. In retrospect, it may have been easier to tell him then.

Why hadn't she?

Because she had questioned whether Moon would allow her to leave. She worried that her sense of duty and responsibility would inescapably bind her to him. That she would become his captive.

He jokingly had said that to her once. *You are my captive.*

Then, alone with him at Shangri-La, she was pleased that he desired her.

Now, she steeled herself, activated the contact number and placed the call. Seconds ticked by, allowing her shoulders to tense with rising waves of anxiety.

Finally, it began to ring.

A familiar, lilting feminine voice apologetically announced in Korean that the owner of the phone could not take the call at this time. Kindly leave a message.

In a panicky reflexive action, Cara disconnected the call.

She came to her senses a second later. Damn. What was she thinking? She should have left Moon a message.

She settled down and then pressed the redial button. Once again, she waited for the announcement to conclude to begin recording her message. She heard the beep and drew in a deep breath.

Her mind went blank. She had entirely forgotten what she was going to say.

She stabbed the disconnect button with her index finger.

"Blessed Mother," she lamented, rocking back and forth over her knees. This was a simple task. "What is my major malfunction?" she wailed, quoting her former military husband.

Meanwhile, Moon attended an early morning meeting at the conference facilities of the Republic of Korea's Ministry of Foreign Affairs and Trade.

He frowned. This was the second time in minutes that his cellphone vibrated against his chest from the inside pocket of his tailored jacket.

The moderator of the multi-national meeting announced a short break and Moon purposefully headed toward his office, waving off the attempts of his persistent aide to engage him in conversation.

Sitting behind his desk, Moon pulled his hand phone from his jacket and accessed voicemail. Again, he was puzzled. No new messages.

He reviewed missed phone calls and found two, placed within minutes of each other, with an unfamiliar number.

He froze.

He recognized the country code for America, but the area code was unfamiliar. His research confirmed his suspicions. The telephone number was from Northern California—North Country.

His pulse became erratic. He felt his body flush with conflicting emotions—not all of them pleasant.

He debated, but only for a moment. He retrieved the second call and pressed Send.

He would satisfy his curiosity. He would confirm that all was well.

Cara was reclining on a lounge chair.

Jezebel ran a raspy, warm tongue over her cheek.

Cara smiled fondly at the concerned and conciliatory Golden Retriever. She ruffled the fur under her chin. "I'm okay, Girlfriend. I just need a minute to recoup my dignity, that's all. Who knew I could be such a dipshit?"

Jezebel suddenly sat and cocked her head, as if questioning this newly voiced word.

Cara gazed into Jezebel's expressive eyes. "Yes, I said dipshit. You know…moron, ninny."

Cara balefully shook her head. "When did my world become so narrow?" She sighed and smiled wanly at Jezebel. "I need to get out more."

Her cellphone rang. Thinking it was a family member, Cara flipped it open and declared, "Nitwit speaking."

An all-to-familiar, deep and velvet-toned voice inquired with some confusion, "Cara?"

Her eyes widened in astonishment. She bolted upright in the lounge and thrust away the phone as if it were a poisonous snake. It clattered noisily on the deck.

She could still hear Moon repeating her name, asking with anxiety if she was all right.

Just then, the baby awoke from his nap and began to cry from inside the house. Cara's attention swiveled from the house to her cellphone—attempting to reason, in her flustered state, which required her attention first.

She could not deal with Moon now—at least, that is what she convinced herself. She escaped from her quandary and hurried into the house to tend to her son.

CARA RHYTHMICALLY ROCKED WITH EACH pat to her son's back after he had finished his bottle—his tiny head on her cloth-covered shoulder—trying to lull him back to sleep.

When his beautiful almond-shaped eyes blinked sleepily then closed, and he breathed the unencumbered slumber of pristine souls, Cara nestled him back in his crib. She gently covered him with a lightweight flannel blanket decorated with cheerfully prancing blue elephants.

When she turned from the crib, Jezebel waited in the nursery doorway with Cara's cellphone softly transported in her mouth.

"Okay, Girlfriend…you're right," Cara granted, relieving Jezebel of the cellphone and wiping it dry on her jeans. "I am being a wuss. Let's see if Moon left us a message."

She went into the kitchen, fed Jezebel a homemade doggy biscuit, poured a glass of ice tea, and proceeded to the deck with Jezebel on her heels. Once again, Cara lowered herself on a lounge chair.

MOON TRIED TO MAKE SENSE of the two calls he had received with no messages—of Cara's reaction when he had attempted to speak with her. He leaned back in his executive chair and pensively gazed at the ceiling. Had he heard the cries of a baby, or was that his imagination?

He redialed. This time, getting no answer, he did indeed leave a message for Cara.

He wanted to scold her. *Why did you call twice and hang up without leaving a message?*

He resisted.

Instead, he was solicitous. "Cara, what...why did you call? Are you all right? I was...am surprised to hear from you. Is it about your family... are they well? Do you need anything?" He shielded his eyes with his hand, frustrated by this pointless one-sided conversation. "If you want to return my call, I will be here. I will answer...I promise."

CARA CLOSED HER EYES AND rested her head against the lounge cushion. Oh, that voice—so intoxicating, persuading, and reassuring. She listened to the message several times. Finally, after some deliberation and indecision—finger poised over the delete icon—she pressed it.

She would divulge this truth some other time. When she was focused and relaxed. When hormonal flare-ups did not dictate her behavior. When she was more rational. When....

Soon.

The Death Of Me

June 2006
Northern California

After an hour's travel south on California's Interstate 5, and the miles between him and North Country had created a safe buffer, Michael pulled the SUV off the freeway at a rest area, climbed out, and distractedly walked to the straw-strewn edge of tilled acres of farmland. The wind, unimpeded by trees in the wide-open expanse of earth, blew fine dust into his eyes. The heated rays of the sun high overhead penetrated his scalp and the tight skin over his prominent cheekbones.

He felt nothing.

Overwhelmed by a deepening sense of loss, and drowning in the worst despairing depression he had ever experienced, he felt physically ill.

Worse. He was alive—breathing, reasoning, functioning— manifested by skin, sinew, and bone. Yet, he felt as immaterial as a shadow—stripped of his essence—his purpose for living.

The precious months he had spent with Cara and Regalo were the happiest in his life.

He gazed into the black hole that was his future—that gave no hint of warmth or pleasure—and grieved over its anticipated loneliness, its hopelessness.

Once, he had feared that his broken heart might never recover—as fallow as the neat rows of dry, unsown topsoil that languished before him. Now, he questioned whether his soul would survive.

The ceaseless commotion of the living—the dull roar of freeway traffic, a commercial jet flying overhead, the comings and goings of travelers taking a break at the rest stop from the monotonous ribbon of roadbed that intersected the valley—prodded him to continue his journey.

At the rental car agency, after he had turned in his leased car. *Would you like a shuttle to the airport, sir?*

At an airline ticket counter in San Francisco International Airport. *Sir? Next. Yes, you. Next, please.*

Through a Homeland Security checkpoint. *Remove your shoes, and place all items from your pockets—including your wallet, belt, bulky jewelry, money, keys and cell phone—into the plastic bin and on the conveyor.*

In the airplane before takeoff. *Please put your tray tables and seats in an upright and locked position.* Once in the air. *Sir, would you care for a cocktail? What may I serve you for dinner?*

Food turned to sawdust in his mouth and lodged in his throat. He waved away his dinner and requested another scotch after an observant First Class flight attendant inquired if there was something wrong with his meal.

The heavy, dull pain in his chest—his consummate misery—kept him awake throughout the ten-hour flight to Seoul.

He berated himself for his foolishness. *You cannot lose what you never had, Michael.*

He became angry—so angry—with Cara. Recollecting how she had assured him it would be all right if he were gay. *I will always love you. We can still be best friends.*

So thoughtless as to be cruel.

She charmed him with her bright and easy smile, threw her arms around him, gratifying herself, without any idea of how much he cherished her—every facet of her character, the good with the bad.

He became angry with himself. *You held yourself back from her, thinking that one day she would turn and look at you—really see who you are. You waited too long to declare yourself.*

He shook his head, quashing that deceiving notion with its flawed optimism. No. The results would have been the same. He was only deluding himself.

He came to realize that his anger was destructive and unjustified— as pointless as his infatuation with this woman over the past six years.

He squeezed his eyes closed and rested his head against the plush leather cushion.

How to keep her lovely face from surfacing from the depths of the Delphic pool that reflected his every thought.

How to fill his hours—twenty-four of them a day—after completely immersing himself in her since the first day they had met.

Now what? Michael reflected in anguish. *Now what?*

3

Devotion

July 2006
Northern California – North Country

I<small>T WAS THE MUCH ANTICIPATED</small> annual Fourth of July bash at the lively Antonacci family home. Over a hundred family members, neighbors, and friends received invitations to eat barbeque and drink exotic summer cocktails at the famous all-day celebration.

Elder guests and married couples with babies laughed and chatted at the tables and chairs that filled the deck, while teens and youngsters spilled out over two acres of immaculately manicured lawns to throw Frisbees, play touch football or volleyball.

Late that afternoon, nearing evening, Cara got up from her lounge chair and called back to Moon, "I'm going to check on Regalo."

The immediate family exchanged like-minded glances when Moon followed her into the house.

"This is too weird," Gio announced with a woeful shake of his head.

Much to the family's consternation, Michael Lee had bid them all a fond goodbye when *Zia* Cara's ex-husband suddenly returned from Korea.

Over the past few weeks, the two had been living together in her house, acting—what did adults call it—civilized? It made Gio uncomfortable. What was this guy up to, anyway?

His grandmother smiled sadly. "It is a little weird, isn't it?" She turned to her first-born daughter. "Annabella, has she talked with you yet…about what's going on?"

Annabella shook her head, a worried expression on her plump but lovely face. "No. But he's here for a reason. And I don't think we're going to like it."

CARA HEARD THE ECHO OF footsteps in the hallway behind her and shot a curious glance over her shoulder.

Moon stopped short, appearing ill at ease. "I think I make your family feel awkward."

Cara felt it too. "Come with me."

Moon noticed a small arched cove set into the wall in the dimness of the hallway. In the nook stood a lovely painted statue of a tall, slender woman in long robes. Before the sculpture sat a clear glass bud vase holding a freshly cut long-stemmed white rose—its delicate fluted edges tipped in pink—and a lighted votive candle.

"What is this?"

Cara came back to stand at his side. "You were here before. You never saw the Madonna?"

"I didn't notice. Is it a shrine?"

"Of sorts. But really, it is more of a devotion." She nudged him with her shoulder. "You know, like Koreans lighting incense."

Cara admired the exquisite, hand-painted face of Mary of Nazareth. Her faithful, virtuous, and compassionate expression never failed to touch Cara's heart.

"Many devout Catholics display the Madonna in their homes."

Her parents had purchased the figurine in Florence when vacationing in Italy, carrying it with them to the Sunday Apostolic Blessing of the Pope in St. Peter's Square at the Vatican.

With grace and serenity, Cara recited a prayer taught to her by her mother, as was taught to her by her mother, and her mother before her. "Holy Mother, by the light of this candle, may you find your way to this house. May its flame warm you. May its light continue to burn bright from your purity and goodness, and may it protect those who tend it and bless your name. Keep us under your watchful guidance, Holy Mother, and in your prayers, until the hour of our death. Amen."

Moon swallowed the emotion that rose in his throat as Cara gazed at the Madonna. The clarity of her blue eyes burned bright with reverence, reflecting the flickering flame of the votive.

His heart brimmed with tenderness for her—for her unquestioning acceptance, her open heart, and loving spirit.

They quietly moved through the bedroom that had been Cara's until she had left home to attend Stanford University.

Baby paraphernalia had replaced the blue ribbons and trophies won at swimming competitions, art projects, childhood memorabilia, and posters of her favorite '80s bands that once devotedly papered the walls.

Now, stuffed toys overwhelmed every surface, and a musical merry-go-round nightlight on the chest of drawers softly illuminated the corners of the room.

Regalo was soundly sleeping in his crib, his breaths coming evenly and peacefully.

Cara checked his diaper.

Moon stood beside her and dotingly ran his hand over his son's little chest and belly, eminently satisfied with what he and Cara had conceived together.

His eyes turned toward her.

Cara pretended not to notice the feverish light in their depths. Heart fluttering in her breast, she backed away from the crib.

Moon knew exactly what she was doing. "Where are you going?" he teased with a smile, staying with her step for step.

Cara slowly shook her head. "No, no, no, Moon."

"Why? Because you grew up in this room or because it's your parents' house?"

"Yes." Her retreat was arrested when she backed into the closed bedroom door.

Moon flattened a hand against the panels on either side of her, provocatively leaning forward to kiss her.

She jerked back and cried out in pain when her head rapped smartly against the seasoned pine.

Moon laughed quietly, enjoying her skittishness. "Are you okay?"

Indignant, she pushed against his chest. He flew backwards. "No, Moon, I am not okay!" she hissed in a stage whisper. "*We* are not okay!"

She opened the door just wide enough to squeeze through.

When Moon followed her, he bumped into her father in the hallway.

Vincenzo Antonacci observed his daughter marching down the hall, straightening her shirt and smoothing her hair. He scrutinized Moon with suspicion and accusation.

Moon offered nothing in his defense. He merely bowed in respect and walked down the hallway as Cara had seconds ago, rejoining the family outside.

CARA WAS WORN OUT BY the heat of the day, the loud chatter, curious looks, and shared whispers about Moon and her—from the exhausting obligation to entertain her parents' guests.

She said to the family assembled on the deck, "I'm tired. I think I'll head home."

It was not even dark yet.

"But the fireworks haven't even started," Vincenzo Antonacci protested, glancing with acrimony at Moon. "You can't go home before the fireworks!"

"I can watch them at home too, Papa. I'll collect the baby and his things." She scanned the premises. "Where's Jezebel?"

"She walked with Franco to a friend's house," her mother reported. She grabbed her daughter's arm, sharp eyes searching Cara's to divine an answer to an unasked question. What she saw there made her immediately offer, "Leave the baby here. Come back for him tomorrow. Jezebel can go home with Franco."

Cara hesitated only for a moment, and then placed a grateful kiss on her mother's cheek. "Thanks, Ma."

She made a quick sweep through family, neighbors and friends with kisses and hugs all around. Moon followed her, politely making small talk and thanking the family for their hospitality.

Cara slipped into the driver's seat of her SUV, Moon in the passenger's seat, and they rode in silence the fifteen minutes it took to arrive home.

Cara ran up the stone steps ahead of Moon.

"Will you join me on the deck for a while?" he quietly called after her.

She turned around, her expression leery.

Moon was almost certain she would decline his invitation.

Cara scolded herself for being a coward. To avoid this man like a frightened child would be ridiculous.

"I'll get the wine," she relented.

Moon arranged the chaise lounges on the deck, and Cara joined him with a bottle of wine and two small stemmed glasses. She set a plate of chocolates on the narrow serving table between them.

Moon looked at her questioningly.

"This is a dessert wine. The chocolates will bring out its flavor."

She sat in the lounge next to Moon and together, in companionable silence, they watched darkness settle over the valley.

The sky was clear, splashed with stars of all sizes and brilliance. The clean, fresh air was sultry and mild. Bullfrogs croaked their gruff and persistent love songs down by the pond, stirred into life by a recent and quenching weeklong rain.

The first volley of fireworks climbed into the sky in the distance over Lake Siskiyou. The dazzling bursts of colors and shapes, followed by muted pops, fell like sparkling glitter toward the earth.

"Beautiful," Moon murmured.

"Mmm," Cara hummed in appreciation, for both the fireworks and the dark chocolate truffle she had just sampled.

It was just Moon's taste.

She tapped his shoulder. She held out the remainder of the truffle to him and placed it on his tongue, licking the softened chocolate residue from her fingers.

The gesture was so unaffected and natural. She had forgotten for a moment that they were no longer together—no longer a couple.

They both seemed to come to that realization at the same time, staring at each other, now a little strained by the implied intimacy of being alone.

The fireworks display ended twenty minutes later.

Cara lazily stretched, threw her legs over the side of the lounge and stood. She needed to put a little space between them. "I'm ready to get some sleep. Goodnight, Moon."

Moon delayed her departure with a gentle hold of her arm.

Her gaze was skeptical.

He slipped his hand in hers and gently drew her down to sit beside him on the chaise. Sensing little resistance from her, he grasped her shoulders and pulled her toward him, his expression receptive and inviting.

When she was within a breath of his lips, Cara murmured, "Did you call your fiancée to tell her you arrived safely?"

Moon pinned her with smoldering eyes, an indolent and slow-spreading smile on his face—although clearly, he was not amused. "Are you playing with me now?"

"Oh ho!" Cara exclaimed—voicing a common Korean expression to rebuke his audacity—peeved that he had the nerve to feel duped. "Perhaps I should be asking you the same question."

She attempted to pull away, but Moon would not release her.

"Let me go," she cautioned, the color of her cheeks rising high with temper.

"There...is...no...engagement." Moon said each word slowly and with emphasis, shaking her with each word to get her attention and stop her struggles.

He accomplished both.

"What?"

"We agreed to the engagement to please her parents and my mother. But she loves another man."

Cara squeezed her eyes shut and shook her head. Perfidy. A means to an end. But what end?

"And what did that accomplish, exactly?"

"It allowed us time…the time we needed to arrange our lives with the person we love."

Cara was bewildered. So, if not his fiancée, who was the person he loved?

Moon shook his head, perceptively resolving her confusion. "You, my sweet idiot."

Cara still did not comprehend the situation. "We're divorced," she reminded him.

"No. We are not."

She was at a loss. "But I signed the documents and returned them."

"And I received them. But I instructed my attorney to hold them… not to file them with the court."

Cara's eyes narrowed, looking at Moon with suspicion. "What's going on, Moon? Why? Why would you do that?"

"Because I want you back."

A strangled sound came from Cara's throat. Fuming, she pushed off Moon's chest and stormed into the house, leaving him sitting alone on the deck.

She should have known. The man was not frivolous. Everything he did—every move he made—had a purpose.

"Cara!" Moon called after her as she rushed down the hallway toward her bedroom. "Cara, wait!"

She slammed the bedroom door.

Moon heard the lock click from inside. He softly knocked on the door. "Cara, please, open the door. Talk with me."

"No!" she shouted from the bedroom. "Go away! I mean it! Go back to Korea! You can see your son anytime you want, I promise."

"This is not about our son, Cara. It is about you and me."

Nothing he could have said would have pleased her more. Still, she hesitated.

Moon put his hands on his hips, frustrated by his predicament and Cara's resistance. He paced back and forth, recalling another time when she had rudely locked him out of her bedroom, leaving him standing outside feeling mistreated and embarrassed.

He was not going to let her get away with it again.

He pounded his fist against the closed door.

Cara nearly jumped out of her skin.

"Cara, you have two choices. You can either have the door repaired tomorrow, or unlock it now. You decide!"

He checked his wristwatch and then scoffed at his foolishness. He was not timing an explosive—although that may well be the result.

Cara stood with her hand on the lock, debating. Moon's arrogant and authoritative manner never failed to irk her, yet she seemed incapable of ignoring him.

Moon felt her presence on the other side of the door.

He leaned his forehead against the wood panel and inquired gently, "Cara...why are you afraid?"

Cara closed her eyes and shook her head. Once a fool, always a fool. She unlocked the door and stepped away.

Moon tried the handle. The door latch released.

Cara stood in the center of the bedroom, arms folded.

He softly closed the door behind him.

"Leave the door open, please. You're not staying."

He cautiously approached her.

She huffed in aggravation. Of course. When did he ever listen to her?

"Cara, please...I just want to talk with you." He raised his hands to his sides, letting them drop in resignation. "I miss you."

"Miss what, Moon?" she demanded brusquely. She held her hands, palms out, on either side of her groin. She knew she was being crude and vulgar. She didn't care. "This? Do you miss this?"

Moon stared at her. Oh, this woman. This woman who so easily moved through a crowd and chatted with strangers—throwing her head back to laugh when genuinely tickled. This woman with her intelligent and frankly appraising eyes, her mesmerizing smile.

From the first moment he saw her she piqued his interest, aroused him—the only woman ever to prompt that immediate of a response from him.

He nodded, eyes lingering over the part of her body that had given him countless hours of pleasure. "Yes."

"Wow," Cara muttered, appalled by his effrontery. She looked away from him, willing him to disappear.

Moon stood before her. "Look at me, Cara," he coaxed softly.

She resisted.

He took the softness of her face between his hands and gently swiveled her head toward him. "Please. Look at me."

She lowered her eyes, refusing to comply.

Moon proceeded without her cooperation.

"Yes, I miss making love to you," he admitted gently. "But I have also missed this." He placed two fingers on her forehead. "And this." He put his hand over her heart. "And this." He lightly ran his thumb over her full lips.

She blinked, searching his face for a hint of deception.

"And the things I cannot touch," Moon said with a husky voice. "Your wit and stubbornness, your resilience and boldness...even your quick temper. I have missed all of them."

Tears sparkled behind her lashes. She squeezed her eyes shut. Not again, she prayed earnestly. Blessed Mother, please, do not let me make the same mistake again.

Moon placed tender and lingering kisses on her brows, her eyes, her cheeks, her full mouth.

Brimming with sorrow yet such longing for this man, she lamented breathlessly, "You make me crazy."

He sunk his hand in the silky curls of her hair, the other gripping the sturdy roundness of her ribs.

The last vestige of restraint shredded in Cara's consciousness when, in Moon's tight embrace, they fell across her bed.

It was as if they had never been apart.

A Dish Best Served Cold

July 2006
Northern California – North Country

EARLY THE NEXT MORNING, BOTH naked under a cool white sheet on her bed, Cara lay on her side with her back to Moon.

Moon propped himself up on one elbow and checked to see if she was awake. She appeared to be dozing. He skimmed his hand down her arm, leaned over and tenderly kissed her shoulder.

"Mmm," she murmured contentedly, burrowing deeper in her pillow. "Moon…is that you?"

She cried out in surprise when he rolled her over his body and pinned her underneath him on his side of the bed. "What do you mean…is that you?"

Cara squinted at him through one opened eye. "Yep," she said with a disarming grin. "It's you."

She dissolved into giggles when he buried his face in her neck and growled as if to devour her.

His playfulness took on a more serious aspect, with every kiss progressing toward her breasts.

"You taste good," he murmured, feeling her thighs part for him, making room for him as he eased down the length of her body.

Cara sunk her fingers in his thick and glossy hair, slowly tightening her grip until she made him hesitate—until, at last, she had his attention.

"Aaah," he cried softly. His glance was wary. "What?"

"You said you loved me."

"What?"

"You relentlessly pursued me. Gave me an ultimatum to marry you or leave you. Left me alone hours on end while you worked. Then, when your family needed you back in Korea, you let me go."

"Cara, I…"

"And now…now that I have returned to my family and am content… here you are. Wanting me back. Is that about it? Did I get it right?"

Moon grimaced and remained silent, confident that the question was rhetorical.

Cara unconsciously tightened her grip on the handfuls of his hair in her fists. "Do you have any idea how that made me feel?"

"Aaah!" Moon protested more vehemently. "Like pulling my hair?"

"It's a good start."

"I'm sorry, Cara," he offered contritely.

"And?"

"I was weak and thoughtless."

"And?"

His scalp was beginning to tingle at the roots from the tension. "And…I doubted your strength."

"And?"

"And I will never be so foolish again. I promise you."

He gasped in relief when she released him.

"Shit," he swore quietly, massaging his sore scalp.

Cara smiled in satisfaction. Moon rarely cursed. "Still love me?" she tested.

Moon had to admit he had that coming. "Yes."

"Really?" She expected him to be upset.

He laughed lightly, freeing her doubts. "Really."

"How much do you love me?"

Okay. Now Moon recognized that she was intentionally provoking him. He did not rise to the bait.

"Too much to measure," he responded softly.

"How long will you love me?"

Moon held her eyes with his. "Always."

She regarded him thoughtfully, seemingly mollified.

"Happy now?" he asked in Korean.

It had been a while since Cara heard the familiar expression laced with rare sarcasm. She smiled. "For now."

She gasped in surprise when Moon grabbed her hips and pulled her beneath him.

He set about his previous task in earnest, determined to torture this spiteful shrew with pleasure until she begged him to stop.

LATER THAT MORNING MOON KISSED the top of Cara's head as she lay in his arms. "Cara?"

"Hmm?"

"I want us to be together...you, me, and our son."

She involuntarily stiffened. Here it was, the subject she had been dreading. One she was not ready to discuss.

His voice was seductive and coaxing. "Come back to Seoul with me."

When she did not answer him, Moon impatiently pushed her aside and got up. He shrugged into his plush white terry cloth robe, jerking the ties into a knot. "Let's talk about this, please."

His indignant insistence annoyed Cara. "Not now."

"When?"

"I don't know."

"I love you, Cara. Do you love me?"

The lyrics of a song by Tina Turner rippled through her mind. Without thought, she repeated them aloud. "What's love got to do with it?"

Moon regarded her with a stony expression. He never did get her flippant humor.

"Sorry...joking. A hit song from the '80s."

"Stop it."

"There is a passage in the Bible...Corinthians I think...that says, 'Love bears all things, believes all things, hopes all things, endures all things.'" She propped a pillow under her head. "Love has never been our problem, Moon." As an afterthought she added, "Or sex."

"Then, if you love me, come back with me."

"Not if, Moon. I have loved you. I do love you."

His eyes expressed a warmth and softness—a relief—as he gazed at her.

"But love does not heal all wounds...time does."

He frowned and shook his head. "What are you trying to say?"

"I am not ready to talk about this."

"When will you be ready?"

She shrugged. "Later."

"Later?"

"Yes."

He blew out a breath of frustration. "I need a shower."

When he had closed the bathroom door behind him, Cara rolled over and drew the covers over her head.

Later.

After the seductive flare of passion that always ignited between them—that clouded her common sense and judgment—had extinguished itself. Until she could decide logically and unemotionally how she wanted to live from now on. When she could reason what would be best for their innocent and vulnerable son.

Later.

Cache of Memories

CARA STOOD ALONE, LEANING AGAINST the deck railing, lulled by the melancholy cooing of a mourning dove perched on a low branch of a nearby cedar tree.

She watched a mallard—with his brilliantly adorned emerald head and iridescent purple-blue wing feathers—comically paddle around the pond with his clownish, orange webbed feet. She smiled when he suddenly thrust his head under water to feed, gray and chestnut underbelly and tail feathers saying howdy the world.

When Moon quietly joined her, bringing with him his clean and masculine scent, Cara hoisted herself to sit on the balustrade, casually swinging her bare feet beneath her.

"Isn't it a beautiful morning?" she remarked contentedly.

Moon frowned. He disapproved of her carelessly perching on the edge of a ten-foot drop from the deck. He kept his apprehension to himself and leaned with his elbows on the railing within easy reach of her.

"It's cool," he observed neutrally, although he had much more pressing matters to discuss than the weather.

Cara noted his preoccupation. Her expression benign, she studied his strong profile.

"You are always with me," he said in a barely audible voice.

"What?"

He looked at her, almost in accusation. "You won't let me get over you."

Cara shook her head, perplexed.

"When you left Korea, I thought...I hoped...that with the passing of time, you would fade from my thoughts."

His eyes swept her face. "One day, the image of your hair shining in the sun would be gone. Then that little comma at the left corner of your mouth when you smile. And maybe, after that, the scented softness of your skin after you bathe."

His looked away from her, as if willing himself to push the memory of her from his mind, the muscles in his face taut with agitation. "When I meet new people, I wonder what you would think of them. If I read an article or listen to the news, I want to debate our points of view. If I voice an opinion, I visualize your expression—approving or flinching."

"Isn't that interesting?" she remarked dreamily.

Moon gawked at her in disbelief. "What?"

She leaned toward him and teasingly prompted, "What else?"

Moon shook his head and chastened her shameless vanity. "Tsk, tsk, tsk."

Cara laughed gaily. "Well, you have never shared these things with me," she offered in her defense. "Tell me more."

When Moon just stared at her, unsure of how to proceed, Cara grew serious. "If you want me with you, Moon, now is the time to convince me it is the right thing to do."

His mind went blank. He stood wordlessly—awkwardly.

Cara shrugged in resignation and nimbly hopped off the deck railing. "Okay. Let's just forget about it."

When she attempted to brush past him, Moon put his hands around her waist, swung her off her feet, and plopped her back on the deck balustrade with an emphatic thump.

It jarred her tailbone and made her backside sting.

He stood with his face inches from hers, a hand on either side of her, commanding her attention—demanding her respect. "I thought I made myself perfectly clear. I cannot forget about it. Or you."

Her eyes widened at his vehemence.

"I should have known," he mused. "The first time I held you in my arms as you slept. I should have known you were trouble."

He lamented, "What terrible crimes did I commit in a previous life to deserve you?"

Cara gaped at him in uncertainty.

A smile spread across his face, brightening his austere expression.

When Cara realized he was teasing—so unusual for him—she felt her body relax. She laughed sheepishly.

Moon gazed over her head in contemplation. "What else do I remember, you want to know…"

Cara attentively sat up and folded her hands in her lap, encouraging him with a grin.

His brows flicked in recollection. "I remember the day…soon after we were married….when you burst into my office at the Consulate during my first meeting with the Italian Ambassador to the U.S., and asked me to taste your new recipe for eggplant parmesana."

The grin faded from Cara's face.

Not exactly the most heartwarming memory with which to start.

"The Ambassador wanted a sample, too," she interjected softly.

Moon chuckled. "Fortunately, he found you charming."

"And you less stuffy," Cara reminded him.

Moon flashed her an indulgent glance, aware of her ruse to make him appear more approachable to the Ambassador. "Yes."

"He asked me for the recipe before he left the Consulate," Cara revealed with smug satisfaction.

Moon's expression relaxed as he reminisced, his voice husky. "And when we attended an event, surrounded by people, you would look at me from across the room with those eyes…as if you were making love to me."

Cara smiled, taking delight in his recollection.

"Then you would laugh, quite pleased with yourself, when I would lose my thought mid-sentence, and struggle to recover my composure."

How Cara celebrated those private moments—the gratifying glimpses, albeit brief, of Moon's feelings for her.

"I only did that once," she objected lightly.

"The Mayor's Inauguration Ball?" Moon reminded her with a raised brow.

"Okay, twice." She made a wry face. "But the man you were with was a talking head."

"He was an elected official."

"Exactly," Cara punctuated with a nod. "He was monopolizing you."

Moon recalled the elder statesman leaning toward him to whisper, "That young woman over there has her eye on you." He patted Moon's shoulder in good-natured acceptance and encouraged him to claim his prize. "Go. She's much prettier than I."

Moon shook his head, perplexed by the behavior of his wife but nonetheless amused. "Then there was the time you bought the entire supply of live baby octopus from that Koreatown fish market in Oakland and asked my driver, Tommy, to help you release them into the bay."

The Consulate of the Republic of South Korea employed Tommy, a poised and dignified Korean in his early sixties, to convey the resident Consul General and his family to and from his home, and anywhere in the Bay Area when on business of the Consulate.

Cara covered her eyes, suffering from guilt. "Aagh! Don't remind me!" Her reverie at rescuing the young octopus from being swallowed alive by adventurous diners was brief. After she and Tommy had released them, she discovered that many of the babies would feed the sea life that populated the ecosystem of the bay.

"How did you hear about that?" she exclaimed with a realization, staring at Moon. "Did Tommy confess?"

Moon chuckled and shook his head. "The octopus attached to his suit trousers gave him away."

The reserved and dignified Tommy was distressed that he had unintentionally exposed Cara's baby octopus rescue and relocation caper after she had sworn him to secrecy as her accomplice.

"Poor Tommy," Cara commiserated, remembering him fondly.

"But my most vivid memory of you involves a party chairman's wife," Moon reminded her with outright conceit.

"No doubt," Cara countered dryly. "The subtle art of seduction eluded the woman."

"She was merely courteous."

"Courteous?" Cara rolled her eyes, incredulous. "Men are so clueless."

Moon laughed quietly.

"The woman was enticing you with every smile…captivated by your every word…taking every opportunity to press her breasts against your arm."

Although Cara kept a pleasant smile pasted on her face throughout the evening, she resented the pampered Southern California woman with layers of highlighted blonde hair and newly minted triple D-sized breasts.

Cara gazed into Moon's eyes—shining pools of melted milk chocolate. How she reveled in and cherished his expression when there was just the two of them—open and engaging, attentive and caring.

Unlike his game face when performing his diplomatic duties for the Republic of Korea—jaw muscles taut and features tense, cool and guarded eyes—that made him appear so implacable and formal. That invited criticism.

"You enjoyed her flirtation," she chastised Moon. "Admit it."

He grinned. "I enjoyed your reaction."

With only a passing introduction to the green-eyed monster of jealousy prior to that occasion, Cara was just as confounded by her possessiveness as Moon was elated.

"I seem to recall making things right with you that evening," he reminded Cara.

Alone in their townhouse—emotions reaching their pinnacle—Moon had subdued her and made passionate love to her.

The rosy color of recollection that bloomed in Cara's cheeks gratified Moon. "Now you know how I feel when other men lavish their attentions on you."

"Lavish?" she questioned dubiously. "That's a bit effusive, isn't it?"

"These are my feelings, Cara, not one of my speeches," Moon retorted. "Please resist the urge to edit me."

The sting of his admonition was soothed by the affectionate tone in which it was spoken.

Disappointment creased Cara's brow.

"Do you realize," she whispered to Moon, "that most of the memories you recall are ones that relate to your work."

From the aggrieved expression on his face, it had not occurred to him.

"Why is that, Moon?" Cara mused.

"Cara, I…"

"I missed being with you…when you worked so many hours. There were times I felt so isolated…so invisible."

He hung his head. "I know."

"You know," Cara repeated flatly.

When Moon remained silent, she confessed, "I felt like I was in a waiting room, wondering when our life together would begin." As an afterthought, she murmured, "Catholics call it Purgatory."

He circled his arms around her hips and hung on to her tightly. "I will make things different for us this time, Cara. I promise."

Cara remembered another promise—from Youngblood—unfulfilled.

"You once convinced me that there was a solution to any problem," Moon prompted her.

Cara balked, questioning whether she had ever been that heedlessly optimistic. "I did?"

"Yes, you did," Moon insisted. "What should two people do who are passionate about each other, but cannot seem to survive together in the conventional world?"

"Whose convention? Whose world?"

"Point taken," Moon allowed with respect. "Let us say then…for the sake of argument…the world in which they find themselves."

"Are they certain it's nothing more than a physical attraction?" Cara asked, assuming an unbiased role.

"Yes. Strangely enough, he finds her intellect and temperament very much to his liking."

"And what of her?"

"I believe the feeling is reciprocal."

"Let us say then…for the sake of argument," Cara repeated slyly, "that is the case."

Moon's eyes reflected his smile. She was toying with him. A pastime that seemed to bring her perverse pleasure.

"What is their current situation?" Cara inquired, once again becoming impartial.

"They have been separated for over a year."

"And?"

"He wants them to be together again."

She questioned him with a slight lift of her shoulders. "What do you want of me?"

"Advice. What are our options?"

After a moment of serious contemplation, Cara offered, "You can each step away...living separate lives."

"Not an option I wish to consider."

"One of you can capitulate and agree to accept whatever the other asks, without question."

It took only a brief evaluation of their personalities for Moon to respond wryly, "Not likely."

"You can occasionally meet in a neutral location and love each other in the hours or days you carve out of your lives."

"Not interested. What else?"

Cara shook her head in amazement. "You expect so much from such a desperate situation."

"Can't you think of something?" he challenged.

"Why must I do the thinking?" she inquired evenly. "Isn't it you who initiated the separation?"

Masterful.

A perfectly executed straight thrust. Swift, though not without pain.

Yet, this is exactly what intrigued Moon about this woman, made him long for their next encounter. For the invigorating, friendly verbal combat that invariably ensued—the bold riposte or soft utterance of a truth laid bare.

He remorsefully reminded her, "I had obligations into which I was born...for which I had been educated and groomed."

"You had a wife and a yet-to-be-born son, and you pushed us away with both hands."

"Cara...can you find it in your heart to trust me once more?" Moon pleaded quietly.

Cara sadly shook her head. "I will not be another of your obligations. I can take care of myself...and our son."

She squirmed free of Moon's hold, jumped down from the balustrade and walked toward the house.

"I remember," Moon softly called after her, "one night when you were plagued by your dark dreams."

Cara halted in wonder. He spoke with such tenderness, as if he were caressing her with each word.

"You sat up in our bed, watching me as I lay beside you."

She recalled how his nearness and steadfastness had comforted her and soothed her fears.

"Finally, when you became sleepy, you curled your body around mine and pressed your cheek against my back."

Cara murmured, "And you reached for my hand and tightly held it against your heart until I fell asleep."

They stood silent, Moon's soft smile encouraging her confidence—Cara's eyes searching his for reassurance—until she dropped her gaze in confusion and disappeared inside the house.

Man To Man

August 2006
Northern California – North Country

MOON AND FRANCO SAT TOGETHER on a park bench skirting Cara's pond under the shaded canopy of a weeping willow tree, its feathered branches swaying sinuously in the soft summer breeze.

Moon had approached the solitary and daydreaming young man with Regalo in his arms, Jezebel on their heels.

"May we join you?" Moon inquired pleasantly.

Franco looked up in surprise, smiled shyly, and nodded. When Jezebel had settled at his feet, Moon sat the baby on the spongey grass next to his canine nanny. The baby tucked his two favorite fingers in his mouth and comfortably burrowed against Jezebel's side, eyelids shuttering drowsily.

After an agreeable silence, Franco keenly eyed Moon. "Mr. Moon, do you love my Aunt Cara?"

Moon's expression mellowed. His smile was warm and sincere. "Yes, Franco. I do. Very much."

Cara's nephew appeared genuinely puzzled. "Then, when you went back to Korea...why did you send her away?"

Moon hung his head, abashed by Franco's forthrightness—reminded again of his lapse of judgment. "That's a good question."

Franco was polite but persistent. "Are you going to answer it?"

Moon respected Franco's earnest and openhearted concern for his aunt.

In Korean culture, a member of Cara's family had every right to ask these questions of Moon. Moon had an obligation to honestly answer them, and with the seriousness in which they were intended.

Moon drew a thoughtful, deliberate breath into his lungs and slowly let it go. "After my father died, I doubted the responsibilities I had to fulfill...the life I had to assume...would make your aunt happy."

"You had to stay in Korea?"

"Yes."

"But Aunt Cara loves Korea."

"Yes, but…although she married me, she is also married to my family…as I am to her family."

"So?"

"My family is privileged and proud of their heritage. I did not meet their expectations."

"Because you married my Aunt Cara?"

"In part. But mostly because I am not, by nature, a diplomat. I prefer more academic pursuits."

"Like teaching?"

Moon rewarded Franco's insight with a smile. "I would find satisfaction in that, yes."

"So why don't you?"

Moon spread his hands, palms up, in a gesture of helplessness. "These things take time…reorganizing one's life, separating from your family, starting over in a new career and, perhaps, even in a new country."

After a significant pause, Franco declared with a faraway gaze, "I don't think I would be very good at love."

The gentle teenager's self-doubt surprised Moon. "Well, I don't believe it is a matter of being good or bad, but how it makes you feel." Moon grinned at the paradox. "Which can be good or bad."

"That's not very helpful."

"No, it isn't. I'm sorry." Moon shifted in his seat, crossed one leg over the other, and took on a thoughtful expression. "I'm not sure I should be the one advising you. I am still learning."

Moon privately reflected upon his dedication to his lessons in the art of love. It was amazing how far behind he had once been and how quickly he had caught up.

He fixed Franco with a questioning gaze. "Have you spoken with your father about the subject?"

Franco shook his head. "He's a good man, Mr. Moon, but not very worldly. I love him very much, but…" He hung his head, a bit embarrassed by his feelings.

Moon nodded and allowed a personal admission. "My father was certainly worldly, but I was not comfortable talking with him, or confiding in him."

He queried Franco, "Can you talk to your father?"

Franco nodded confidently.

"I envy you," Moon admitted sincerely.

"So what have you learned?" Franco backtracked with obvious eagerness.

When Moon frowned in bemusement, Franco clarified, "About love?"

Moon chuckled and then cleared his throat. "Well, personally speaking, it is an emotion that makes you feel at the same time euphoric with happiness and miserably inept. It makes you blurt out the most embarrassing things…makes you lose your common sense and what is left of your dignity."

Franco grinned from ear to ear, apparently appreciating or identifying with Moon's self-derisive interpretation.

"And yet…for me," Moon yielded with satisfaction, "it has been the most pleasurable experience of my life."

"Wow!"

Moon nodded in agreement, a gleam in his eye. "Wow, indeed."

Franco happily shrugged, seemingly encouraged. "Maybe I should give it a try."

Although not as handsome as his older brother, Franco was more engaged in the world and the people around him. As a result, Moon found him more interesting.

"Good man."

Franco grinned when he took notice of his little cousin and Jezebel. He took advantage of a photo opportunity and clicked several pictures with his cell phone of Regalo fast asleep, his two fingers in his mouth, comfortably pillowed against Jezebel's furry side. Jezebel dozed with her muzzle resting on her paws, content within her human pack.

Moon smiled in approval when Franco showed him the digital pictures. "Be sure to share them with your Aunt Cara."

Franco's fine brows knitted together in a pensive frown as he waded through his cumbersome thoughts. "Mr. Moon, are you going to take my Aunt Cara away?"

Moon replied honestly, "If she agrees to come with me…yes."

Moon marked the bleak expression that surfaced on Franco's young face. "You can come visit us in Korea, or wherever we live, any time you wish," he offered sincerely.

"My brother, Gio, remembered Aunt Cara from when he was a baby." Franco bowed his head. "A little anyway." He regarded Moon with regret. "I was born after she moved to Korea."

Moon gave Franco his undivided attention, encouraging him to continue.

"I'm happy that I finally got a chance to meet her…to get to know her. I like her…love her very much."

Franco studied Moon and spoke to him with candor, "I'm glad we had this talk. I didn't plan on liking you."

Moon smiled, pleased that he had made a friend.

Franco fixed him with a manly stare. "But, Mr. Moon…if you make my Aunt Cara cry again…" he punctuated his determination with a pregnant pause, "I'm going to kick your ass."

Moon did not doubt Franco in the least. He offered him his hand.

The young man firmly shook it.

"Yes, sir," Moon acknowledged respectfully.

The Three Bears

MOON LIGHTHEARTEDLY BOUNCED HIS SON on his knees as he sat on the rocking chair in the nursery. Regalo had awakened from his nap and cried for attention from his crib, and Moon promptly answered the distress call of his son.

Moon savored the sensation of Regalo's trusting little arms encircling his neck as he lifted him from his bed. The way his son cuddled against the expanse of his chest, taking comfort from the warmth and security of his arms.

Moon observed his son drool on his stuffed gray bunny—determinedly biting a slender pink ear made ragged by the long and uncomfortable process of teething.

Moon had shared his concern with Cara about the germs that must be breeding on the stuffed toy. She assured him that while their son slept through the night, she washed the bunny and sanitized it in the dryer for the following day.

Moon shook his head and murmured to his son in Korean, "That poor rabbit deserves to retire one day soon."

It was as if little Regalo understood his father's sentiment. He stopped chewing on the bunny's ear and stared at his father with big, soulful brown eyes.

"*Appa,*" he said seriously.

Perhaps it was just his guilty conscience, but Moon could have sworn his son's tone was reproachful.

He threw back his head and laughed. "All right, you can keep your *tokki* for as long as you like."

He pulled Regalo to his feet to stand upon his lap, the baby's little hands grasped in his, and began to sing the Korean nursery melody, *Gom Se Ma Ri,* "The Three Bears." The song was about three bears in one house—Daddy Bear who was fat, Mommy Bear who was thin, and Baby Bear who was so cute.

The toddler bounced on his plump little legs to the lively tune, grinning happily, until a movement captured his attention across the room. "Mama."

Moon followed his gaze to the doorway. Cara was leaning against the doorjamb, thoughtfully observing them.

Moon grew uneasy with her silence—her faraway expression.

"Cara? What is it?"

She focused her eyes and her thoughts. "You asked us to join you in Korea."

Anticipation and dread charged his tone. "Yes."

When Cara did not speak, Moon prodded, "What have you decided?"

She pushed away from her leaning position and announced before turning to leave, "We will join you."

Moon felt the tension drain from his body. He recollected with relief a remark Cara had made after she had introduced him to his son. *He should know his father.*

He grinned at the sweet little boy he and Cara would now love and care for together.

The Three Bears.

Goodbye, Girlfriend

August 2006
Northern California – North Country

CARA KNELT BEFORE JEZEBEL WHO patiently sat in the driveway at the bottom of the stone pathway waiting to begin her new life with a disabled little girl and her single mother.

Cara swallowed hard and took Jezebel's head between her hands. "Thank you, my sweet friend, for being with me during a difficult time in my life. For your immeasurable comfort, your cleverness and generous spirit…" Cara hung her head, overcome with sorrow, too tearful to continue speaking past the lump in her throat.

Jezebel lifted her large, fluffy right paw and placed it on Cara's forearm—as if to say, there, there.

Cara couldn't help but smile. "I will never forget you, Girlfriend."

Moon helped Cara to her feet and put a solicitous arm around her.

Franco stood apart from them, silent and sullen.

"Time to say goodbye, Franco," Cara prompted gently.

Hearing his name, Jezebel walked to sit before him. Franco fell to his knees and threw his arms around her. "I love you, Jezebel. I know you'll be a good girl for Molly."

When Jezebel licked his ear, he abruptly got to his feet, turned his back and walked a few steps away, self-consciously swiping away his tears with the palms of his hands.

"Thank you, Cara, for giving us Jezebel," Molly's mother praised her. "I know it must be terribly difficult for you to part with her."

Molly gaily laughed, squirming in her wheelchair, when Jezebel came up to her, tail wagging, and nuzzled her.

A spinal cord injury after a fall from her backyard swing set caused a lively and happy six-year-old to become wheelchair ridden, depressed, and temperamental. Paralysis and muscle atrophy, possible further neurological complications and organ failure were in her future—how far ahead, no one could predict.

Months before, Cara felt compelled to enroll Jezebel in service dog training—why, she was uncertain. Except to say that when she watched Jezebel so enjoyably undertaking the challenges presented to her and, once competently accomplished, accepting generous praise, her instincts were confirmed.

Jezebel met Molly and her mother on a training field trip to a hospital pediatric ward. When Jezebel rested her head on Molly's lap and gazed at her with compassionate and understanding eyes, the little girl smiled for the first time since her accident.

It was love at first sight.

Molly's mom shook her head and laughed. "Molly was so excited to come fetch Jezebel today she woke me before the sun was up…chattered the whole way here."

Cara hung a solicitous arm over Franco's slumped shoulders. She gripped a handful of his fine curly hair in her fist and gently coaxed his temple to her lips. "She'll be okay, *tesorino*," she soothed him, calling him the Italian name akin to sweetheart.

He nodded miserably, watching Jezebel jump into the van and assume her seated post next to little Molly's wheelchair.

"Moon and I couldn't take her with us to Korea," Cara assured Franco, tears blurring her vision.

"I know."

"They would have required her to be quarantined in a kennel for three months. That wouldn't have been fair to her."

Nor would it be fair to uproot and include her in an uncertain future, Cara had reasoned apprehensively.

Franco shot an accusatory scowl at Moon. "I know, *Zia*. But she could have stayed with me."

"In two years you go off to college. Then what would become of her?"

"I suppose you're right," he conceded grudgingly.

"Look at her," Cara said with a smile, pointing at Jezebel. "She is bright-eyed and watchful of little Molly, fully engaged in her new responsibility. She loves to work...loves her job. It's what makes her happy."

Jezebel watched them through the window as the van slowly proceeded down the driveway. She appeared to be smiling. As if assuring them that she, and they, would all be well.

"What do you say," Cara said hugging Franco's shoulders, voice thick with emotion, "I make us all some chocolate sundaes."

Franco hung his head and wrapped his arm around his aunt's waist. "No."

"No?" she verified lamentably.

Franco's weakness was ice cream.

"Strawberry," he murmured. "I want a strawberry sundae."

"With whip cream and a cherry on top?" Cara asked, trying to lighten their melancholy moods.

"Yes, please."

Cara kissed her nephew's cheek, hung an arm around his neck, and pulled him alongside as she headed for the house. "Two scoops."

"Three," Franco asserted firmly.

"Three," Cara confirmed earnestly. "You realize, of course, that you are making me fat. Moon might divorce me."

She cast her eyes over her shoulder. "Common, Moon," she prodded when he stood looking after them. "Ice cream sundaes!"

Moon smiled fondly at his wife and her nephew. Relieved and pleased to receive a full pardon, he followed them into the house.

Yet Another Parting

August 2006
Northern California – Seoul, South Korea

MOON HAD ARRANGED TO FLY his family back to South Korea on a private jet. He reasoned that, with the baby, it would be much more convenient and comfortable to travel the nine hours from San Francisco International Airport to Seoul.

Normally, when compelled to ride in a craft that maintained an altitude of 28,000-35,000 feet above the solid and familiar surface of the earth, and doing so without her sedative of choice—Vodka—Cara felt obliged to keep the plane aloft by her sheer force of will, knuckles blanched white as she gripped the arm rests of her seat.

However, the Learjet was a fine craft, designed to be luxurious, spacious, and relaxing. The quiet hum of the engines and the gentle vibration of the cabin as it cruised through the atmosphere at 533 miles per hour proved to soothe her.

She was grateful for the privacy—the time to sort through the thoughts that crowded her mind and jostled for precedence.

THE PARTING FROM HER FAMILY had been difficult—even more so than the last two occasions she had left them to live in South Korea.

"Each time it becomes harder and harder to say goodbye to you," Vincenzo Antonacci agonized, eyes shiny with tears.

Cara gave him a tight hug. He was growing older, feeling his age, his dark hair beginning to thin and turn silver. He wanted his family around him, needed the comfort of knowing that they were within his reach—his helping hands—if necessary.

"I feel the same way, Papa," Cara admitted sadly. "But we will visit you, I promise. At least twice a year."

"Are you sure you know what you are doing?" her mother asked, keeping her distance from her husband and daughter, arms tightly folded under her breasts.

Her body language spoke volumes to Cara. Her mother was anxious about the well-being of her daughter and grandson. Clearly, she was skeptical of Cara's decision to stay with Moon—regardless of whether he was still her husband. That was evident.

Among the family, Franco took her departure the hardest, tears streaking down his flushed cheeks. Gathering his slight build in her arms, Cara assured him, as did Moon, that he would be welcomed to visit them any time he wished.

That did little to comfort him.

As the chauffeur drove Moon, Regalo, and Cara down the driveway in a hired town car, Cara affectionately gazed back at her family clustered in front of her childhood home—her mother and father, sister and brother-in-law, and nephews.

They raised their hands in farewell. She blew them kisses, waving little Regalo's hand in return.

CARA STARED OUT OF THE port window at the fluffy, blindingly white clouds that slowly passed beneath them.

She was returning to the country she loved, with the man she loved—would always love. Would that be enough? Would things between them really be different this time, as Moon had promised?

Although it was only right that she should know, she was surprisingly reluctant to press Moon about his plans for them. Why? Her ignorance about her uncertain future caused her unnecessary anxiety.

Would they once again be subject to the capricious whims of his mother? Where would they live? Would Moon continue his career at the Ministry of Foreign Affairs and Trade? What was his strategy for a new life that gave him such confidence to make her promises?

Michael once suggested that Cara had been hiding away in her hometown, becoming a country mouse. Cara had to admit there was some truth to that, especially after the birth of Regalo. Yet, she knew that she could not stay indefinitely, remain in the backcountry she found so confining as a young woman, more so now since she had sampled the people and cultures of the world.

It was time for her to leave—time to begin a new life for herself and her son. She hoped for a community with energy and refinement, which would challenge her talents and engage her intellect. A place where Regalo could happily acquire the necessary skills to develop and survive in an ever-changing world.

Whether it would be in Korea was too soon to tell.

Sensing her troublesome thoughts, Moon sat beside her, solicitously taking her cool hand in both of his.

"Having doubts?" he inquired gently.

She looked into his eyes, recognized the tinge of apprehension in them, and felt compelled to reassure him with a soft smile. "More questions, than doubts," she admitted.

"Such as?"

She shook her head, grateful that he had asked, yet dubious about opening a discussion that may offend him or prove disappointing.

Moon offered intuitively, "Cara, I have set in motion events that will give us a fresh start."

Cara raised a questioning brow, hoping that he would expand upon his statement.

"Do you trust me?" he asked, squeezing her hand.

Cara remembered a time, not that long ago, when he had asked if she believed in him. *Do you trust me? Do you have faith in me?*

It had resulted in an exchange of marriage vows between them.

She wanted so much to trust Moon—to accept that he would be as good as his word. He was asking her to believe in him—have confidence that he would do whatever necessary to ensure their happiness. It was evident that he loved her—that he could not let her go.

For the sake of her heart, and their son, Cara was willing to give Moon the opportunity to deliver his promise.

She nodded solemnly. "Yes. I do."

He brought her hand to his lips and kissed it with tenderness. "I will make a new life for us, Cara. Be patient, I beg of you. Be patient."

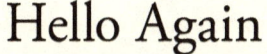

Hello Again

4
Déjà vu

August 2006
Seoul, South Korea

Their arrival in Seoul at the private aircraft terminal on the east side of Incheon International Airport, through customs and into an awaiting town car, was without incident or delay. So unlike the last time they had entered Korea together—a fiasco—with representatives of the media creating bedlam and splashing their personal business over daily newspapers, broadcast news, and the Internet.

It was late in the evening when the town car pulled up to their destination. Cara roused from a light doze to look with startled foreboding at the Moon family estate.

Moon whispered in her ear, "My mother just left on a world cruise. We will be gone by the time she returns."

Moon's sister, Sang Hee, threw open the front door and ran down the steps to greet them.

Cara was thrilled to see her former ally and friend. "Sang Hee!" she exclaimed with a lighthearted laugh. "It's been awhile."

The two women embraced.

Her sister-in-law held her tightly. "*Unni!*" Older sister. "I am so happy to see you! Welcome home."

Manager Park barked orders to the uniformed household staff who spilled over the steps to collect the luggage from the trunk of the town car. He hustled his staff inside and up the curved stairway to the second floor, encouraging stragglers.

Once in the foyer and out of the cool night air, Moon introduced his sister to a sleepy Regalo.

Sang Hee visibly melted from pure pleasure. "Look, look, my sweet nephew," she cooed. She carefully pried Regalo from Moon's arms, and held him tenderly against her breast, her hand supporting his head. "*Gomo* is so happy to meet you," she breathed, kissing the soft, silky hair at his temple.

Etiquette would require Regalo to address Sang Hee, his paternal aunt, as *gomo*. In Korean, he would call Annabella, his maternal aunt, *imo*.

Sang Hee cheerfully relayed that she had personally prepared a nursery for Regalo between the two bedroom suites for Cara and Moon.

Cara shot an amused glance at Moon.

Since Sang Hee's father and mother had maintained separate bedrooms and, by her mother's design, Sang Hee and her husband each had their own rooms—it was only natural for her to separate Moon and Cara.

Moon answered Cara with a conspiratorial smile. All he required was an unlocked door—they would not be sleeping apart.

"You both must be tired," Sang Hee observed graciously. She looked down at Regalo, sleeping soundly against her shoulder. "I know this little boy is." She looked between Moon and Cara and ventured hopefully, "I can take care of the baby if you would like to retire for the evening."

Cara sighed, weary from the trip, always grateful to her kind and generous sister-in-law. "Thank you, Sang Hee."

She scanned the familiar surroundings—the foyer, the adjoining study and sitting room, the beautifully curved balustrade of the stairway leading to the second story bedroom suites.

Try as she might, she could not shake her uneasiness—recalling the brief but unhappy time she had spent here. A debacle that culminated in a distrustful confrontation between she and Moon and a mutual agreement to separate—he living on one continent, she on another.

There was one bright light of hope shining upon Cara at present. The incessant irritant, and instigator of their separation—Moon's mother—was thankfully absent.

Sensing her thoughts and acknowledging her anxiety, Moon reassuringly took Cara's hand in his. "Trust me," he murmured soothingly.

Together, they ascended the stairway to settle in their assigned rooms.

A Matter of Time

September 2006
Seoul, South Korea

L IFE ASSUMED A RELAXED AND even cadence on the Moon family estate. Moon left for work at the Ministry each morning after breakfast. Cara and Sang Hee enjoyed each other's company and the freedom to come and go as they pleased. Sang Hee doted on her nephew, voluntarily undertaking more and more responsibility for his care.

On Cara's birthday, Moon commanded her to close her eyes and keep them closed as he led her by the arm outside and down the front steps. Cara joyfully laughed at Moon's unusual whimsy. When he gave her the all clear to open her eyes, a shiny red sports car convertible awaited her under the driveway portico.

Cara cried out in delight, threw her arms around Moon, and enticed him with a whisper in his ear, "Take a ride with me."

He checked his watch and regretfully shook his head. "I'm sorry, Cara. Some other time. I've got to get back to work."

The mysterious "work" that occupied his time was a cruel and demanding master. It became voracious for his waking hours, robbing him of leisure time with his family, with Cara.

Eventually, Moon ceased coming to her bedroom at night.

Curious, one evening Cara quietly made her way downstairs and saw the light from his desk lamp shining under the door of his study. She stood at the door—imagining Moon at his desk, head wearily propped up by his fist—debating whether to coax him to her bed to rest beside her.

She determined that her entreaty would be futile—envisioning the impatience and disappointment in Moon's eyes at her indifference to his endeavors, whatever they were—anticipating that her well-meaning gesture would create derision and divisiveness between them.

She climbed the stairway, footsteps and heart leaden, aggrieved by a situation over which she had little control and even less understanding.

MOON SAT BEHIND HIS DESK in his study and looked up from his books when he recognized Cara's light tread approach his door. He waited for her soft knock or request for permission to enter. His tensed shoulders fell when neither came.

He gazed soulfully at the door, crestfallen and sorrowful, picturing his wife standing indecisively on the other side. How he wished he could invite her in and explain what he had been doing these past months—that he anticipated several more taxing months and a trip to America to achieve his objective.

Although he attended the University of California at Berkeley, studied and earned his Bachelor's Degree in the English language, he had been young and eager, and that was many years ago. Now, with the books written in English spread before him, at times he struggled with the unfamiliarity, the contradiction of the vocabulary—a word, a turn of phrase, an important concept that was essential he master.

When the print of his studies grew blurry and indistinct, he liberally applied eye drops to his strained eyes and resolutely refocused on the paperwork before him.

He felt so isolated in the silence of slumbering souls. Alone, night after night.

How he longed to knock on Cara's bedroom door and, upon hearing her hushed and surprised invitation to enter, slip on the bed beside her to feel the solacing warmth and comfort of her arms around him. If only he could sleep for more than three hours a night, abandon the alarm that jolted him from a deep and dreamless oblivion—relentlessly prodding him to begin another day. A day just like the day before, and the day before that.

When Cara no longer stood outside his door, Moon collapsed against the back of his chair. His exhaustion flooded him with feelings of hopelessness.

He mentally shook himself, sitting straight in his chair, and irritably brushed aside his crippling pessimism. Although his hands trembled from too much caffeine, he forced down another cup of strong, tepid black coffee.

He had to succeed in this undertaking. For the sake of Cara and his son. For the sake of their lives together. He must succeed. Failure was not an option.

MOON BEGAN TO LOOK HAGGARD, became impatient and clipped in his response to questions from Cara and his sister. He kept a grueling schedule—working all day at the Ministry, eventually skipping dinner with the family to cloister himself in his study until the early hours of the next morning. On weekends, special occasions, or holidays, the family rarely saw him.

His arcane endeavor was taking a heavy toll on his physical stamina and mental health—on the people who could do nothing more than helplessly watch him struggle. The people who loved him.

Return Of The She-Devil

October 2006
Seoul, South Korea

T HE MOTHER OF MOON HYO entered the front door of the family estate—expression pinched in suspicion—a woman on a tireless and righteous mission. She heard voices in the study and walked with an unwavering purpose across the foyer.

"Mother!" Sang-Hee called after her in astonishment, standing on the stairway with Regalo in her arms. Her mother had returned from her world cruise ten months early.

Mrs. Moon dismissed her daughter—and the little bastard whom she had just learned was born in America—with a grim set to her mouth and a stone-cold glitter in her eyes.

Sang Hee glanced with horror at the closed study door, attempting to descend the stairs to halt her mother or at best warn Cara and Moon Hyo of her unexpected arrival.

Mrs. Moon held up an imperious hand to stay her daughter, viewing her as an unredeemable traitor.

Sang Hee froze on the spot.

Cara and Moon were embroiled in a frank discussion when Mrs. Moon opened the door and stood her ground, brazenly eavesdropping.

Cara had followed Moon into his study after he had breakfasted with the family and stood before his desk. "I would like to take advantage of your rare availability, Moon."

Moon straightened his paperwork and quickly closed the opened books spread across his desk.

Cara cocked her head, amused. "You hide your work from me? Are you doing something I shouldn't know about?"

He looked weary. "Of course not."

"Should I have made an appointment, Consul General?"

He fixed her with a stern stare, too exhausted to go a few rounds with his lovely and contentious adversary. "Don't be absurd. You are my wife."

"No," a strident feminine voice behind them insisted. "She is not!"

Moon and Cara turned in unison to stare at the well-dressed and haughty woman glaring at them from the doorway, chin triumphantly held high.

"Mother." Moon greeted her without enthusiasm. Her words finally struck a chord in his consciousness. "What did you just say?"

She entered the room, a smirk on her face. "I said she is not your wife!"

Cara looked to Moon for guidance. He could offer her none.

Instead, he gazed at his mother without comprehension.

"You are divorced," she claimed with certainty.

"We are not divorced, Mother," Moon insisted. "I ordered my attorney to hold the divorce papers."

"But I ordered your attorney to file them," Mrs. Moon divulged with defiance. "If you didn't have the courage to do so, I certainly did!"

MOON HAD REQUESTED THAT HIS attorney draw up and deliver divorce papers to Cara for the sole purpose of curtailing the ceaseless haranguing of his mother, who simultaneously pressured him into a marriage contract with the young daughter of an industrialist who lived in a palatial residence not far from the Moon estate outside of Seoul.

Months later, visiting the law firm on another matter, Mrs. Moon casually inquired about her son's divorce proceedings. With some surprise, the attorney handling the case haltingly advised Mrs. Moon that he was holding the documents until he received further instructions from her son.

"File them," she commanded tersely, aggravated by her son's reticence to rid himself of this foreign woman.

Astounded by Mrs. Moon's suggestion that he supersede the instructions of his client, the attorney stuttered, "But...madam."

"I am certain he has been too busy to call," Mrs. Moon assured him offhandedly.

"I will call the Consul General..."

"Unnecessary," Mrs. Moon interrupted coolly. "Do you like your position here?" She blatantly threatened, "I am sure I could drop a word to your superior about my dissatisfaction with your services."

The attorney bowed his head to avoid her intimidating glare. "Mrs. Moon, I..." He had been with the firm for thirteen years and was now middle aged. An inopportune time in life to seek other employment.

She turned before exiting his office and demanded, "I will expect to see a stamped copy of the documents filed with the court."

The attorney winced. So much for that strategy.

He exhaled a helpless gust of air from his lungs. What to do? What to do? Either way, he was sure to lose his position with the firm.

FURIOUS, MOON DIALED A NUMBER using the phone on his desk. He spoke rapidly, earnestly, to his attorney. A look of incredulity crossed his features. "Without my authorization?"

The coerced and hapless attorney sputtered on the other end of the line.

"Fix it," Moon commanded. "And if you cannot, your firm will no longer function as legal counsel to the Moon family. Do you understand, Attorney Chen?" He slammed the receiver on the cradle.

Mrs. Moon indignantly turned on Cara. "You bring this woman into my house?"

"This is my house, Mother," Moon reminded her. "Cara will remain here with me."

His mother challenged Moon with a poorly timed and ill-conceived ultimatum. "I will not remain in the same house with her."

"That is your choice," Moon countered crisply.

His mother fell a step back, as if Moon had slapped her. She gathered her fur scarf and the tattered remnants of her dignity about her, spun on her heel and marched from the room. They heard the front door slam behind her.

Sang Hee sorrowfully closed the door of the study, providing Cara and her brother with privacy to work through this unwelcomed complication.

Her sweet soul suffered immeasurably from her mother's shameless treachery, the narrow confines of her tolerance, and her bitter jealousy of Moon Hyo's love for Cara.

Sang Hee seriously doubted whether she could forgive her mother for this transgression, and whether Cara and Moon Hyo could survive yet another, more critical, obstruction to their foundering relationship.

Ties That Bind

October 2006
Seoul, South Korea

MOON STEPPED AROUND HIS DESK to stand before Cara. "We will resolve this, Cara," he assured her.

Cara gazed at him with vacant eyes, overcome with confusion and doubt. When Moon steadied her by taking her shoulders in his hands, she blinked as if coming out of a trance.

"Can I just say…" she stopped to moisten her lips with the tip of her tongue, "what I had planned on saying earlier…before we were interrupted."

She declared to Moon, "The inability of men and women to communicate with one another aside, I don't understand the way you think.

"I once reasoned that it wasn't important if we sang different childhood songs growing up—I would teach you mine and I would learn yours. It didn't matter that I came from a simple, working-class family on another continent. That we didn't share the same religion or have the same native tongue. I still believe that to be true.

"I'm not so sure that cultural differences are the problem here. I think it's even more fundamental than that—it's about human nature."

Moon cocked his head, attempting to follow her logic.

Cara made herself perfectly clear. "I give and you take."

He dropped his hands from her shoulders, clenching his jaw in agitation.

"I don't know if you have given this much thought, Moon, but do you realize…since we met…we have spent more time apart than together?" She eyed him sadly. "What does that suggest to you?"

"That we have been unlucky."

"Unlucky?"

She mocked herself with a joyless laugh. "How easy I must have seemed to you, Moon. You wanted me...I came to you. You tired of me...I left."

Moon allowed himself a mirthless smile. "You have been many things to me since knowing you, Cara. Easy has never been one of them."

He reminded her, "When we returned to Korea, after my father's death, I saw the life that was ahead of me. I did not want you to suffer it with me. I wanted to protect you. I had no other choice than to send you away."

"You coward." It hung on the air, like a nasty smell in the room that no one wanted to acknowledge much less claim.

"Do you remember asking me the weekend we spent together at Shangri-La, 'why can't we just live the way we want?'

"I warned you then that we could...but there would be a cost. The sad truth is, Moon, you didn't want to pay it. You wanted it all. You wanted to be happy but didn't want to make the changes necessary to make that a reality. You sacrificed our life together because it was the path of least resistance...because it was easier.

"And now we have a son...a tie that binds us together...whether we like it or not."

Moon remained stolid, his expression guarded, throughout Cara's narrative. Now, he admitted with reluctance, "I was trying to get you pregnant."

Cara's mouth fell open. "Whaa?"

"I wanted you tied to me."

Moon was not proud of his diffidence when it came to his relationship with Cara but, finally, he had unburdened himself with the truth.

Cara was stunned. The words tumbled out of her mouth. "You selfish bastard."

He glanced down at her hands, drawn up into fists. "Would you like to strike me?"

Cara pierced him with her eyes. "Yeah. I would. I really, really would."

"Do it."

Cara thought back to the only time she had lashed out in fury at another human being. She was living in Seoul and working at the Chang Agency. Michael had asked her to represent the agency at the police precinct following the arrest of employee Danilo Mercado for the near-death drug overdose of pop star Myrissa Taylor. When Mercado deliberately provoked Cara with a comment both egregiously misogynistic and cold-blooded, she had slapped him across the face with such force that her hand ached into the following day.

She could not fathom deriving the same satisfaction from deliberately hurting Moon.

She shook her head in frustration. "I don't think that would make me feel any better."

Moon gazed at her, his expression mournful. "What is it you want, Cara?"

"I want a man who views me as more than a social accessory."

His jaw took on a firm set, words clipped. "And what, by your definition, is a social accessory?"

"A necessity for anyone who seeks validation in your culture…a spouse and a family."

Moon was deeply offended. "You're talking nonsense."

"I want a lover and a friend. That is what I want, Moon."

Cara was offended, too. In their time together, she thought Moon's insatiable appetite for her was because he desired her. Apparently, all he desired was to get her pregnant.

Moon read her thoughts. "Don't misunderstand, Cara. I always want to make love to you."

She summarily dismissed his sentiment. Too little too late.

"Do you know why I didn't want to get married when I was young?" It just dawned on her that she was free to decline further participation in the institution. "I'm still not sure about it, truthfully."

The irony was Moon had thought their marriage almost perfect. "Why?"

"Two people meet, fall in love, and get married. They go about the happy process of getting to know each other and having lots of sex.

Then the children are born, and the couple begin to call each other mommy and daddy. Then when the grandchildren come, they become grandma and grandpa. They live their lives through their children and their children's children, talking about nothing but them, their lives no longer their own. They lose touch with each other…become strangers… forget the love, passion, and intimacy they once shared."

"It's only natural," Moon reasoned softly.

"Maybe for some," Cara replied with conviction. "But not for me."

Moon barked out a contemptuous laugh. "You amaze me. You still believe, like a simple schoolgirl, that you can do as you please. That you have no responsibilities other than to yourself."

"And you believe that you can make your son and me happy when you yourself are not. How simple is that?"

She was provoking him. She could see it in his eyes.

"I told you things would be different this time," Moon said with exaggerated patience, "and I will honor that promise."

"How?" She looked around her and held out her hands at her sides in disbelief. "How is this different?"

"Cara…"

"You may come home every evening, but then you seclude yourself in your study until the early morning hours. What are you doing in here, Moon? You keep your thoughts to yourself, and make plans for us without giving me the benefit of knowing what they are. Do you still not understand that your decisions affect me? And Regalo?"

"You are my…" Moon had begun to remind Cara that, as his wife, he expected her to do as he commanded. The sudden realization that she was no longer his wife—at least in the eyes of the Korean courts—shook him to his core.

Cara smiled, deriving some gratification from the stricken look on his face. "That's right, Moon."

She smoothly assured him, "I will fulfill my responsibilities, but I refuse to be chained by them. If you think you can use our son to hold me hostage, you'd better think again."

"Where are you going?" Moon called after her.

She threw open the door. "Right now, about as far away from you as I can get."

"Cara!" Moon pursued her out of his study.

"I am so stupid!" she rebuked herself as she crossed the massive marble-tiled foyer.

She whirled around, eyes feverish and a little wild with a fresh realization. "Do you know how Einstein defined insanity? Doing the same thing over and over again and expecting different results."

She shook her head and murmured, "I'm not stupid." She raised her face to the high coved ceiling and shouted, "I am insane!"

Her anguished voice echoed back to taunt her.

Moon grimaced.

She opened the front door and ran down the steps. Her car. The car Moon had given her on her birthday was parked on the side of the house. She jumped in, found the keys in the ignition, started the engine, and revved it to get it warm.

Moon ran out from under the portico toward her when she put the car in gear and spun out into the driveway.

If he hadn't jumped out of the way, she would have clipped him with the car.

"Cara!" Moon shouted after her in frustration.

Cara threw a worried glance over her shoulder. She could have injured Moon. Badly. A sharp pang of fear and guilt made her nearly breathless.

Moon stood with his hands on his hips, grimly staring after her.

Wild And Reckless

October 2006
Seoul, South Korea

CARA PULLED THE CONVERTIBLE OVER to the curb outside the high-rise building where Michael conducted his security business. There was a moving van parked in the plaza directly outside the front doors with three men loading a conference table, an executive desk, and chairs.

Cara had her hand on the handle of the car door when she saw Michael emerge from the building lobby.

He spoke with a representative of the moving company and reviewed the paperwork on a clipboard the man handed to him. He nodded briskly, signed at the bottom, and returned the clipboard.

"You're leaving?" Cara whispered the accusation with a strangled breath. "Are you leaving, Michael?" she demanded, almost yelling.

Michael watched the moving company employees stow the last item, roll down and lock the rear door, and climb aboard the van.

Devastated by Michael's deliberate omission, Cara started the engine, shifted gears, and stepped on the gas pedal.

If the driver of the passing taxicab had not spontaneously swerved, he would have sideswiped her car. The startled and angry driver called attention to her negligence by laying on the horn.

Michael's head swiveled in her direction. Their eyes met.

Aggravated that he had seen her, Cara cursed under her breath.

This time, she checked over her shoulder for oncoming cars, waiting for traffic to clear, and then accelerated out of the parking space.

She stomped on the brakes, her body thrown forward, restrained by her seatbelt.

Michael stood on the street, directly in her path, blocking her exit.

"Damn it, Michael!" she screamed at him, her heart thumping wildly against her ribcage. "I just about ran you down!"

She gripped the steering wheel, knuckles blanched white, to steady her shaking hands.

What in heaven and on earth possessed her? In the same day, she had nearly caused injury to the two men she loved.

Michael calmly walked around to the passenger side of the car, opened the door, and slid on the seat. He buckled his seatbelt and waited expectantly.

Cara glared at him with acrimony.

Michael refused to engage her, focusing straight ahead.

Fine.

Cara shifted the transmission into second gear and, leaving two patches of tire tread on the pavement, shot out from the curb and into the flow of traffic.

♪ "Woke Up This Morning" - Instrumental
The Brothas and Sistas

Using all four lanes, she artfully dodged her way through traffic, expertly threading her way through the city that had been her home for nearly half of her life—past the landmarks and the places that were achingly familiar and reminiscent of fond memories—the city she had come to love and was once grievously compelled to leave.

Today, it was closing in on her. Too many people. Too much traffic. All she wanted was out—unnerved and spurred on by a fanciful notion that, like a monstrous python, it was about to suffocate and swallow her.

Her head swiveled from side to side when she merged from one busy boulevard to another, eyes darting between the two mirrors on either side of the car and confirming her bearings in the rear view mirror.

An emergency or police vehicle siren wailed, lost on the wind and left behind as Cara shifted into high gear and increased her speed to reach the much less traveled straightaway leading west out of the city.

Once there, she released the horsepower of the engine. Zipping around law-abiding vehicles—nothing more than indistinct blurs—she challenged the handling, steering, and braking of the high-performance sports car.

At one point, Michael cooly peered at the speedometer. They were approaching ninety-five miles per hour.

Cara was smiling—reveling in the speed, the rush of wind tangling her hair, her escape to freedom.

Michael observed that she was in control, handling the car and the speed just fine. If she became dangerous to them or others, he was prepared to intervene.

Cara sped the sports car into a parking lot adjacent to a long and wide stretch of beach—taking the turn from the two lane coastal highway on outside wheel rims. She swung into a parking space at the far end and hit the brakes. They screeched to a stop.

She jumped out of the car, slammed the door, and headed for the beach.

Michael released the tense lungful of air he had been hoarding since marking the expression on Cara's face as she watched him from her car parked at the curb. He leisurely climbed out of the sports car and caught up with Cara when she paused at the tide line to look out over the breaking waves. He stood at her side.

"I've sold my business," he announced mildly. "I'm leaving Korea."

Cara's heart sank. She covered her disappointment and anxiety with a smirk. "So I noticed. Were you planning on dropping me a postcard?"

Michael fixed her with a disapproving frown. "You know better than that."

"When are you leaving?"

"In a few days."

"Where are you going?"

"I have a six-month renewable contract with the FBI starting in a couple of weeks—teaching at the Academy in Quantico."

His decision to leave Seoul was dispassionate and logically executed, prompted by a recent chance meeting with a former classmate from Columbia University, now working at the FBI Academy in Quantico, Virginia.

Jack Costello seemed galvanized by the serendipity of their encounter and, after inquiring about Michael's current situation, had asked him to come teach at the Academy—actually begged him. A pet project of his required Michael's expertise, or so he claimed.

Cara's eyes filled with bitter tears. "You said you loved me. You said that hadn't changed."

She despised the words the instant they left her mouth. "I can't believe I just said that," she muttered in self-mockery.

"My love hasn't changed, Cara. The situation has."

Michael grasped her shoulders and turned her to look into his eyes. "The first time I saw you in Seoul, while I was waiting for an elevator in the Chang Building..."

Intent on matrimony, a Hmong florist had chased Cara, in the company of her friend, Philippe, into the lobby of the building where they scrabbled to a halt next to Michael.

Marriage me, the little guy had pronounced with gusto and a toothy grin, thrusting a bouquet of red roses at her. Cara's frustration at her inability to communicate with the man to kindly dissuade his amorous intentions was evident.

Michael suavely intervened—speaking with the Hmong in his own language—mysteriously, and finally, discouraging any further attempt to court Cara.

Michael smiled. "You have never asked, but do you know what I said to your persistent admirer?"

Cara smiled wanly and shook her head, soothed by the memory. "What did you say?"

"That you were my woman. That I was going to marry you."

Cara squeezed her eyes shut. How did everything go so wrong?

"I didn't make you aware of my feelings because I was on a long-term assignment in Seoul, and Philippe conveniently provided me with the perfect cover."

Philippe was gay and had wrongly assumed that Michael was as well. As a result—and without a denial from Michael—so did everyone else.

"Then you met Moon Hyo." Michael lowered his head, suffering as he always did, retrospectively, from his lack of clarity. "I didn't think it would last. I was wrong. You love each other. More than you both realize."

Cara huffed in frustration and turned her face away from Michael, unwilling to hear him voice defeat.

Michael forced her to look at him. "I lack his passion, Cara...his boldness. I realized that, ultimately, I would not...could not satisfy you. Not really."

Cara thought back to Michael's unilateral decision to call Moon and summon him to America to meet Regalo. He had already given up on their relationship.

Her bark of laughter was dry and humorless. "Why is it when I put my happiness in someone else's hands, I suffer?"

Michael looked remorseful, but stated firmly, "Don't assume that I know what I want."

Cara frowned, at a momentary loss.

"Isn't that what you said to me once?"

"Moon and I..." She regarded Michael dolefully. "And now we have brought an innocent child into this world, making our problems his. Bravo. Good job, kids."

"Thank you for Regalo, Cara," Michael said with affection. "For making me a part of his life." He gazed out over the horizon. "A childhood disease prevents me from having sons or daughters of my own."

Cara was at once astonished and shamefaced. How insensitive she was—always so concerned about her own happiness—giving little thought to Michael or what he endured. "Is that why you have been hiding your heart all these years?"

Her question seemed to surprise then unsettle Michael.

Cara took the edge from her voice. "Do you believe that all women want or need to experience motherhood?"

She wrapped comforting arms around him. "Don't you see...you love Regalo and he loves you, regardless of whether he came from your body."

Michael could not allow Cara's embrace to seduce him—tempt him to stay. "Give me the keys to the car," he ordered, pushing her away. "I'll drive back."

Cara smarted from Michael's rebuff—from his curt and cool dismissal. She felt the fuel of anger, frustration, and grief ignite her heart and inflame her cheeks.

First, her nemesis, Moon's mother, smugly validating the reality of their divorce.

Then, the confrontation with Moon and his staggering admission that he had intended to get her pregnant—to bind her to him.

Now, Michael, the one constant in her life, admitted that he was leaving Korea, essentially giving up on her—on them.

Cara gazed at the car keys on the palm of her hand. Without another word, she drew back her arm and gave the keys a long, furious toss— worthy of any major league baseball outfielder—into the ocean surf.

She was satisfied. That was the closest to a *fuck you*, aimed at Moon and Michael, she could comfortably manage.

She eyed Michael, challenging his objection.

Michael glanced out to sea, not even considering recovering the keys. He promptly retrieved his cell phone from inside his suit jacket and made a call, watching Cara slowly work her way down the beach, head and spirits low.

MICHAEL SAT WITH THE DRIVER high in the cab of the tow truck idling in the parking lot, waiting for Cara to join them. She stood at the tide line, seemingly entranced by the tidal surge that danced and foamed over her bare feet.

The driver kept looking at his watch and then at Michael, taking his cue from him as to when they were going to pick up this stubborn woman and get back to the city before the peak of rush hour.

He secretly denounced Michael for his inability to control his woman. If this pretty American were his, he would drag her back to the truck and hoist her ass into the cab.

Michael was aware of the driver's anxiety and impatience, but ignored him. He would wait until Cara was ready.

Although he did not understand her reluctance to return to Moon, he was clear on her disappointment and unhappiness with him.

But he needed to distance himself from Cara and Moon—forcing them to settle their differences, if they could, without Cara's reliance upon him.

After the months he had spent in California with Cara and Regalo, he was no longer willing to stand by and watch—to wait indefinitely. His self-respect and diminished spirit needed healing—something only detachment and time would allow.

At the very least, Michael hoped they could all remain friends.

Disgrazia

October 2006
Seoul, South Korea

Moon heard the roar of the tow truck as it pulled up the driveway and stopped under the front portico. He threw open the front door and stepped out to investigate.

Cara jumped down from the cab, walked past a stiffly composed Moon without a glance, and disappeared through the wide-open door of the house.

Mouth agape, the tow truck driver stared with unabashed curiosity, baffled by the presence of this elegant, distinctly possessive, and royally pissed-off man standing on the steps.

He glanced at his passenger. He remained serene and assured.

The driver privately speculated. *Whose woman was she?*

"Where do you want it?" he shouted at Moon over the roar of the motor.

Moon pointed to the side of the house.

The driver watched Michael slide out of the vehicle. *Was this man her lover?*

He put the truck in gear and pulled around the circular drive to unload the luxury sports car.

"*Aigoo,*" he bemoaned, peering in his driver's side mirror at the two men now facing off. He was going to miss a good brawl.

"I'm sorry," Michael said to Moon. "The keys are lost. They will have to be replaced."

Moon nodded.

That was the lesser offense of Cara's joyride to the ocean. Moon's lawyer had to pacify the police who had captured her on camera traveling over ninety miles an hour on the straightaway outside Seoul.

His attorney promised to pay the fines and donate to a charity in the name of the district police if the incident did not appear in their reports or on the evening news.

A settlement was agreed upon that was satisfactory to both parties. Moon was livid.

Before today, his family name had never been linked with, or disgraced by, such a flagrant disregard of the law.

He looked to Michael for answers.

Michael offered none. "I'm leaving in the next few days to live in America. If I can do anything for you before then…"

The hard set of Moon's jaw indicated otherwise.

Michael wanted to catch a ride back to his apartment with the tow truck driver. He held out his hand. "Take care of each other."

Moon looked at Michael's hand and, for a moment, Michael thought he was not going to take it.

He did finally, giving Michael a firm handshake. He expelled a deep breath of anxiety and said with resignation, "Thank you, Michael. Good luck in America."

When Moon turned to come back into the house, he glanced up and saw Cara watching them from her bedroom window.

MOON SUMMONED THE HOUSEHOLD MANAGER.

Silently, with dignity and grace, both men climbed the stairs to stand before Cara's bedroom door.

Moon held out his hand. "I need the key to this door."

Manager Park, a trusted and loyal retainer of the Moon family for over thirty years, looked bewildered. Under the flinty gaze of his employer, he quickly replaced his expression with one more neutral and unoffending.

He identified the key and handed it, still on the ring, to Moon.

Moon securely locked the door from the outside.

Cara heard the lock click in place and could have cared less. She sat in a chair by the window and watched the tow truck disappear down the driveway, taking Michael with it.

She thoroughly regretted her behavior toward Michael. She had not offered to let him say goodbye to Regalo, nor told him she would miss him, nor wished him well.

Moon handed the household manager the keys. "Do not give the key back to me. Regardless of what I say. Regardless of what I threaten. Understand?"

The manager observed the fire that blazed in Master Moon's eyes. Yes, now he did. He bowed. "I understand, sir."

Moon stalked to his study. Closing the door behind him, he leaned against it, shamed and devastated by the thoughtless actions of the woman he prized more than life itself.

Even so, he was certain that if he got his hands on her, he could do her harm.

A Sad Affair

October 2006
Seoul, South Korea

Early evening three days later, Cara lay on the cushioned chaise in her bedroom, head thrown back on the rounded armrest, eyes closed.

She had remained sequestered in her bedroom suite. Sang Hee visited her often, providing her consistent visits with Regalo and her daily meals—the latter of which Cara did not touch. Although Sang Hee encouraged, even begged her to eat, Cara had no appetite.

Moon's sister was too timid, too polite, to ask what had happened to cause her brother to behave in this way toward Cara. She was saddened and distressed for both of them whom she adored—knowing the way Moon Hyo felt about Cara, and believing that *Unni* felt the same about him. Yet, these two people could not stop hurting or disappointing each other.

Cara heard the soft tread of Moon's footsteps after he unlocked her bedroom door and walked to stand behind her—detected the tang of scotch on his breath.

She had not seen or spoken with him since that day Michael had brought her back to the family estate. Michael—probably now in America—was going on with his life, leaving her to make peace with hers.

Moon stood silently, his thighs pressed against the armrest of the chaise, observing Cara. He marveled at her composed expression.

"Sang Hee said you are not eating," he stated with quiet concern.

Her eyes opened. She gazed unblinking at Moon as he stood over her. "I'm not hungry."

"Are you planning to die of starvation?"

Her chuckle was mirthless. "I'm no martyr. Or saint."

"That much is true," Moon responded sardonically.

He was surprised when Cara laughed quietly.

"Took you three days to calm down?" she inquired, now quite serious.

Moon allowed himself a wry smile and shook his head slightly.

"I see," Cara murmured when he made no comment. "Maybe you could use a couple more."

Moon's expression hardened.

He shocked Cara with the speed in which he stepped around the chaise, roughly grabbed her by her shoulders and drew her to her knees.

He thrust his face in hers.

"Do you have no feelings for me at all?" he agonized. "Do you think I enjoy seeing you with another man…happy and laughing in his company? Watching you suffer when he has decided to leave?"

His remark puzzled Cara. Was he referring to the day he had unexpectedly arrived at her home in North Country—watching from the doorway as she and Michael laughed together, Michael's arms around her? Had he witnessed her impassioned and woeful goodbye to a voluntarily departing Michael the following morning?

Cara discerned the uncertainty clouding Moon's eyes, felt his hands clench on her shoulders with an emotion rubbed to its rawest state.

Moon shook her. "Do you think my heart is made of stone?" he asked in anguish. "That it doesn't ache with jealousy and sorrow?"

A tidal wave of remorse washed over Cara, nearly drowning her. "I'm sorry, Moon," she murmured, her voice catching in her throat.

Feeling lonely and hollow inside—she craved the reassurance and comfort that lovemaking with Moon always yielded.

She skimmed her hands over his thick hair, and grasped the back of his neck, encouraging his closeness.

He peered at her through suspicious eyes—neither believing nor trusting her motives. "Am I your fool?"

The brittle menace of his tone unnerved Cara.

His mouth and hands became cruel and insistent—reflecting the bruised aspect of his heart.

Cara resisted. If he had wanted to make love, that was one thing. But this—this was an attempt to assert himself over her, dominate, and reclaim her.

Her pride would have none of it.

"Moon, stop," she begged with a feigned calm, the blush of anger rising in her cheeks. "Stop!"

Moon grabbed a handful of her hair in his fist and kissed her deeply, fiercely.

Coming to the realization that he was not about to listen, that he was not prepared to stop, she put her hands against his shoulders and pushed with all her strength.

Now infuriated by her resistance, Moon picked her up in his arms, carried her the short distance to her bed, and threw her upon it.

His coordination was sluggish from the four tumblers of scotch he had consumed within a space of thirty minutes—attempting to numb his sorrows. But he managed to catch Cara by her foot as she tried to roll away and escape from him on the far side of the bed.

She shrieked in surprise when he grabbed the other foot and yanked her across the bed. He quickly subdued her beneath his body and pinned her wrists to the bed within his strong and painful grip.

"I asked you...am I your fool?" Moon growled.

"No!"

"Is that what you think of me?" he persisted furiously.

Stung by his accusation and alarmed by his wrath, Cara began to weep. "No!" she cried in frustration.

Moon felt her ribcage convulse with sobs, saw the tears squeeze from the corners of her eyes and dampen the fine hair at her temples.

He blinked, feeling his body release its tension—as if shaken awake from a violent dream.

His head dropped beside hers. He soothingly whispered in her ear, "Don't cry, Cara. Please...don't cry."

He rolled away from her, threw his arm across his eyes, and passed out.

IN THE DUSKY LIGHT OF early morning, Moon stirred beside Cara. He took a moment to gather his wits about him—surprised to find himself in Cara's bedroom, lying beside her. He slowly drew himself to a sitting position on the side of the bed.

Cara could feel his eyes on her—trying to recall the events of last evening—confused and speculating.

He raked his fingers through his hair. A dull, heavy ache at the base of his skull muddled his thinking.

"Did I hurt you?" he asked with a raspy voice, his heart in the grip of a cruel fist.

Cara didn't respond. She had surveyed the deepening bruises on her shoulders, wrists, and ankles when she had bathed earlier that morning.

"Cara?" He gently picked up her hand and turned it over—observed the blooming bruises on her wrists, her upper arms.

What had he done? Clearly, he had lost control of himself and the situation. Everything was unraveling.

When he brought Cara back to Seoul, he had been so sure that their love for each other would sustain them—that they could begin to rebuild a future together.

He hung his head in disillusionment and despair.

Cara had never seen Moon like this—could not bear to see him like this. She silently slipped behind him on the bed and wrapped her arms around him, resting her cheek against his shoulder.

"The last thing I wanted was to hurt you," Moon confessed, voice fogged with self-loathing. He broke away from her arms.

Cara watched him in silent misery as he walked from her bedroom and quietly closed the door behind him.

Michael

5

Costello's Pet Project

Late October 2006
FBI Academy – Quantico, Virginia

JACK COSTELLO STOOD TO WELCOME his former classmate from Columbia University, Michael Lee, to his office at the FBI Academy. Michael confidently gripped the broad hand Costello, a former NFL all-pro defensive end, extended across his desk.

"Good to see you, Michael," Costello grinned. "Did you get settled okay?"

"Yes, thank you."

Unsure of his tenure with the Academy, Michael had not secured private living quarters in the area. Consequently, he was a guest of the Academy in utilitarian quarters used expressly for that purpose.

Costello gestured to a comfortable armchair, unbuttoned his suit jacket and loosened his tie as he came around his desk to sit in the chair opposite Michael.

"Thank you for doing this favor for me, Michael. I owe you one."

"Probably," Michael acknowledged, relaxing against the back of the armchair.

He still had no inkling about his assignment. His friend was playing his cards close to the vest.

Costello reached for a file on the edge of his credenza and passed it to Michael. "This is why I asked for you."

Michael read the name on the jacket. *Mairet McCarron.* "How do you pronounce the first name?"

Costello's pronunciation sounded like *mare-et.* "New Agent Trainee Mairet McCarron," he emphasized unnecessarily.

Michael was affronted. "*This* is your pet project?"

Costello raised his hand to stay his friend's impatience. "I found her at some think tank funded under the auspices of MIT…wasting her considerable talents."

He earnestly leaned forward in his chair. "The girl is a phenom, Michael. I've never seen the likes of it…whiz at mathematics, breaking codes, research and analysis."

Costello motioned with his head to her file and highlighted its contents. "Mother killed by a bomb blast in a department store in Belfast. She was a clerk. Father was IRA. When they sentenced him to twenty years in prison, he arranged to send his daughter to the U.S. to live with his only surviving brother. She came from a violent and impoverished background…underweight and malnourished when she arrived in the States."

"How old was she?"

"Seven years old."

"Where is her father now?"

"Died in prison."

Michael stared at his former classmate. Not a great way to begin life.

"The brother, also former IRA, fled Ireland a number of years earlier before he was apprehended and imprisoned. He served in the U.S. Army and did two tours in Viet Nam. He was badly wounded and spent over a year recuperating in a veterans hospital in Hawaii. That was where he met his wife, his nurse in the hospital, an American-born Irish woman from Boston."

"So McCarron was reared in Boston by her uncle and his wife?" Michael confirmed.

Costello nodded. "She attended all-girl parochial schools and kept getting pushed forward…until the uncle was convinced to send her to a private school for gifted scholars."

Costello tugged thoughtfully on his ear. "It makes sense that she is emotionally immature…growing up in the company of kids much older in age, all of them kept like lab rats within the confines of their studies."

"So what do you expect of me?"

"She struggles with the physical training. We're hoping you can help us with that."

While attending Columbia University, Michael had earned with honors a master's degree in Kinesiology with disciplines in biomechanics, physical and strength training, and orthopedics. His second master's degree was in a totally unrelated field—unquestionably more relevant to the academic disciplines of the FBI Academy—Strategic Intelligence.

"How did she pass the initial physical fitness tests?" Michael inquired with interest.

The first order of business at the Academy was running new agent trainees through a physical fitness grinder—beginning day one of their class cycle. Standards were rigorous enough to cull ten to twenty percent of the trainees from the program within the first few weeks.

Costello dropped his gaze, ill at ease with his admission. "I convinced the Assistant Director to test her after you have whipped her in shape."

Michael's eyebrows rose. An exception to procedure.

Apparently, Costello was optimistic about the considerable contribution his protégé would make to the Bureau. Enough to convince his superiors to make an allowance for her. Enough to stick his neck out a country mile.

Except now, Michael recognized the burden to produce results was on his shoulders. "Priority in addition to my curriculum load?"

"High." Costello looked a bit apologetic. "This training cycle is scheduled for twenty three weeks. She's got to make it in that time."

Michael tilted his head, perplexed. The cycles were normally twenty-one weeks.

Costello nodded, reading Michael's mind. "In December there is going to be a nationwide joint forces Homeland Security exercise that will effectively lock down the Marine Base here in Quantico. No civilian traffic. We're sending our trainees home the week before Christmas until the New Year."

Michael allowed his skepticism to surface in his expression.

"I know it's unprecedented, Michael. But when our Assistant Director mentioned that to a three-star general of the Joint Chiefs of Staff, he acerbically remarked that if our trainees could forget two months of training in fourteen days, they weren't worth their salt."

Michael returned his focus to McCarron's file.

Costello quirked his bushy brows. "Also, I don't know what you can do about this, but McCarron can't seem to put a filter on her mouth. The other day, she told one of her instructors, in front of his class, that his lectures were useless, pointless, and endless."

Unperturbed, Michael thumbed through McCarron's file. "Are they?"

His friend chuckled, reminded of Michael's astuteness. "Well, we won't be renewing his contract come spring."

Michael closed the file.

Costello eyed his friend with a troubled frown. "You seem a bit... preoccupied. You okay?"

"I'm fine," Michael stoically assured him, perhaps a bit too quickly.

Costello let it pass. None of his business.

"I'm counting on you, Michael." Costello shook his head, dismayed. "You know the system. It's unforgiving. If we send her on a field assignment, she has to be fit."

He eyed Michael with pointed keenness. "Please, Michael. Do your magic for us. Along with all of our puzzle-solvers, linguists, and code geeks, she'd be a significant addition to our intelligence community."

New Agent Trainee
Mairet McCarron

November 2006
FBI Academy – Quantico, Virginia

MAIRET MCCARRON WAS ILL PREPARED for the self-defense class in which she now found herself enrolled. The class of approximately twenty trainees formed a straight line shoulder to shoulder along one wall, instinctively aware of how to prepare for the class. She followed their lead and pushed her way into a space in line.

She curiously peered at her classmates in each direction from where she stood. The class was mostly comprised of men, with a sprinkling of a few women—fit specimens, nearly every one.

The instructor entered the room, dressed in a crisp white jacket secured with a black belt, and wide legged floor-length pajama-like pants. There were some interesting designs or insignias on the uniform. He wore no shoes.

McCarron noted with satisfaction that he was Asian. Somehow, in her mind, that gave legitimacy to his credentials—to the course study.

He looked physically fit. The serious type. Unsmiling, he began to walk slowly down the line, scrutinizing each of his students.

An inspection?

McCarron had read somewhere if you stood straight it would make you look five pounds thinner. She stood tall, threw back her shoulders, and sucked in her stomach.

The classmate next to her respectfully bowed and greeted their instructor as he walked past. "Master Lee."

McCarron sniggered after the instructor moved on. "Master?" She nudged the bantamweight who so shamelessly kissed the arse of their instructor. "Who is this guy? God?"

Instantly, the instructor retraced his steps and thrust his face in hers.

Startled, McCarron jerked back.

"In this *Dojang*, Ms. McCarron," Michael assured her, "I am."

He knew her name. McCarron swallowed nervously, fully experiencing the intimidating glare of Master Lee.

Although unsure about his reference to a *Dojang*—a Taekwondo training hall—she muttered, "Okay."

"Okay, what?"

"Okay, Master Lee."

He continued his walk down the line of students, all of whom bowed as he passed.

Mairet McCarron leaned out to watch him. Tall, broad shoulders—terribly lean, though. Nice hair. Lovely and exotic eyes—killer eyes.

Ah, well, she gaily acceded with a shrug—even if this class was useless in her training—at least the scenery was interesting.

AT THE END OF THE first introductory course, Master Lee dismissed the class.

It was all very formal. His students—feet together and hands placed tightly at their sides—ceremoniously bowed to their instructor and boisterously shouted a phrase McCarron could not distinguish.

Surprisingly, it impressed her.

She hurried after the person who had been standing next to her at the beginning of class. He did well during the exercises. She was hoping he would impart some useful tips to keep her off Master Lee's shit list.

"Ms. McCarron," Michael called after her. "A word."

She halted, hesitantly threading her way through the departing students. Master Lee no doubt believed she could benefit from a lecture on martial arts etiquette.

Instead, he beckoned her using all four fingers and took a wide stance on an exercise mat.

She humbly stood before him, a bit self-conscious now that she found herself alone in his presence.

"Okay," he said quietly. "Show me what you've got."

She appeared baffled.

Michael backtracked and patiently expanded upon his request. "Show me what moves you have learned from your previous courses."

McCarron enjoyed a private little moment with herself. Oh, her moves!

She assumed a position—all wrong—and advanced against him.

Michael easily blocked her.

She exclaimed in pain and massaged her stinging wrist.

Michael walked around her. She sucked in a surprised breath when he ran his hands over her shoulders, upper arms, forearms, and thighs.

"You have no muscle mass. You are ignorant of the basics and undisciplined."

She grumbled, "Nobody told me I had to be Jet Li when they recruited me."

More like Jackie Chan, Michael thought, entertained by her comical antics.

"You must know how to protect yourself, Ms. McCarron," he insisted. "To give chase to your suspects." He cocked his head, giving her serious consideration. "Or outrun them."

She heaved a breath of exasperation. "So, now what?"

"Now we get to work. I will have a nutrition and fitness plan designed for you by the end of the day. Come by my office first thing in the morning and we will review it."

"I don't think I'm going to like this," she muttered.

Michael allowed himself a smile. He knew she wasn't going to like this.

COSTELLO ENTERED THE *DOJANG* AND walked to where Michael was stowing equipment. "How goes it Professor Higgins?"

Costello's reference to the George Bernard Shaw play about a scholar who vowed to make a lady of a guttersnipe flower girl did not amuse Michael. His expression conveyed that sentiment.

Costello laughed anyway, enjoying his own humor. "I heard some of the chatter and laughter from your students as they were leaving." He took a seat on a nearby bench. "Had our first encounter with Trainee McCarron, did we?"

"We did."

"Asking how things went would be a bit smug, I suppose."

Michael shot him a discouraging glance. "Your pet project, Jack, not mine."

"Point taken," Costello grinned, hoisting himself with some effort off the bench. "Keep the faith, my friend."

"You could use a good workout yourself," Michael ridiculed him, staring at the belly overhanging his belt. "You still play racquetball?"

"Been awhile," Costello admitted diffidently. The blowout of his right knee that ended his football career plagued him if he overstressed it during cardio workouts. He admitted as much to Michael.

Michael offered to wrap his knee. "I'll make sure it's well supported."

Costello's head bobbed reflectively. That might work.

"Four o'clock?" Michael challenged.

"Four it is," Costello grudgingly agreed, now regretting that he had come to his friend's *Dojang*. "We'll go to my club."

Kill Joy

November 2006
FBI Academy – Quantico, Virginia

MAIRET McCARRON SAT ALONE AT a table in the academy cafeteria during her lunch break, her food tray placed before her and a folded *Washington Post* to her right.

She had met with Instructor Lee earlier that morning and, as he had promised, he presented her with a "new program" of nutrition and exercise that he had expressly designed for her. He gave her a journal with which to record her daily food intake and physical activity.

As he briefed her on the regimen—her eyes wide in disbelief—she struggled to appear attentive to what he was saying.

Was he kidding? He had limited her daily intake of calories to so few she would surely starve to death in a week. Cheeks sunken, dark circles rimming her hollow eyes, hair falling out from the abnormal stress on her body, she would shuffle off this mortal coil.

Not yet twenty-eight years old. Still a virgin.

She hung her head. Oh, the festering injustice of it.

She glanced up in time to see Instructor Lee enter the cafeteria, accept a food tray from the attendant behind the counter, and turn in her direction.

She snatched up her newspaper and fanned out the pages, using them to camouflage her presence.

Michael stopped at her table. He waited a beat for her to acknowledge him. When that did not appear imminent, he remarked dryly, "I can see you."

McCarron lowered the newspaper and let it hover over her lunch tray, attempting to conceal its contents. "Oh…Instructor Lee."

Michael slid her tray out of her reach.

Her face crumpled in disappointment when she surveyed the tray he exchanged for her meat loaf, mashed potatoes and gravy, rolls and butter, and apple pie. It contained raw vegetables, fresh spinach with no dressing, and a lean ground turkey patty with not a condiment or slice of bread on or about it.

She looked up, squinting at him in dissatisfaction. "You feed this stuff to an Iguana."

"You have an Iguana?" Michael inquired with interest.

"No," she muttered, returning her unhappy gaze to the meal before her. "But I think it's time I get one."

She amused Michael. "From this point forward, we will work together to reduce your fat intake and build muscle."

She eyed him with something akin to desperation. "I used to suck my thumb. I replaced that with nail biting. Then I tried to smoke and drink…I threw up. And now you're asking me to give up food?" She leaned forward, earnestly emphasizing each word. "I…love…food!"

Michael recollected that when she arrived in the U.S. as a child she was underweight and malnourished. He understood that she identified food with safe harbor, and sympathized with her compulsion never again to experience hunger. Yet he would not enable her—allow her—to continue this unhealthy and destructive behavior.

"I encourage you to pursue a pastime with more cardiopulmonary benefits," Michael advised her.

"I'm working on it," she assured him with an impish sparkle in her eye. "But the pastime I am pursuing doesn't think of me as an exercise partner."

Michael briefly questioned whether he was the object of her disconcerting bluntness. He remained composed, more curious than offended.

He motioned to her tray. "Remember, I may not always see what you eat, but you can be sure I will notice the results."

McCarron stared at him with a slack jaw, confounded. He must have been reading her mind. As soon as he left the cafeteria, she had intended to go back through the line and duplicate her confiscated meal.

As for the many varied snacks and soft drinks she had stashed in her dorm room, locker, and women's bathrooms around campus, she was in a quandary. She could happily stuff her face in private, but once it showed up on her butt, Instructor Lee would be the wiser. He might just as well catch her with greasy potato chip crumbs on her lips.

Michael watched her perform her mental machinations and smiled knowingly. "We have a training session at the gym in two hours." He motioned to her tray. "Eat slowly. You will feel full more quickly and consume less."

"No problem there," she muttered to his back as he carried off her high-calorie lunch. She watched him deposit her meal tray next to Neddie Fritz. He spoke with him briefly, leaving Neddie looking after him with a perplexed expression.

The kid was brainy but needed to bulk up. He was a flyweight—though not easily subdued in physical training—and nearly always the butt of his classmates' jokes and pranks.

Mairet and Neddie gravitated toward each other—the two class misfits. They confided in and encouraged each other, alternating in fortifying their flagging spirits.

When Michael exited through the open doors of the cafeteria and disappeared down the hallway, Mairet McCarron's eyes filled with tears of wretched misery.

Her sweet and salty life, as she knew it, was about to come to a screeching halt.

She was consummately depressed.

The Surveillance

December 2006
Stafford, Virginia

IT WAS ONE O'CLOCK IN the morning. The surveillance team restlessly shifted in the tight quarters of the van parked outside their subject's apartment building.

Instructor Lee had appointed Trainee Brian Dietrich—all-star defensive lineman from Dartmouth with a master's degree in criminal justice—leader of the team comprised of McCarron, Alcosta, Fritz, and Blevins. Their assignment—to monitor the movements of a suspected terrorist. At least, that was the intelligence report Michael provided Dietrich.

Little did the trainee team suspect that this assignment was more of an exercise to observe whether they would adhere to procedure, remain alert and focused, and cope with the boredom factor of a long and uneventful six-hour surveillance.

After the rigors of a full day—classwork, firearms training, and running PT drills—the energy and attention of the group was conspicuously flagging midway through the exercise.

At the moment, they were loudly arguing a tactics problem posed to them in a course that was reputed to wash out more FBI Special Agent wannabes than any other compulsory subject in the academy curriculum.

"But that would be impossible!" Dietrich shouted, red faced with the conviction of his own theory. "That guy couldn't have escaped through the ventilation system!"

"Never discount the ingenuity of the human mind when it comes right down to it," McCarron cautioned mildly. "Where there is a will, there is a way."

"True, true," Neddie Fritz chimed in sagely.

Dietrich shot a distasteful glance at the pair of them.

McCarron wearily leaned her head back against the wall of the van and laughed quietly. "It puts me in mind of a joke I heard some years back."

"Jesus, the Irish and their stories," Dietrich groused. "Keep it to yourself, McCarron."

"No, no," Alcosta, the good-looking Cuban-born cop from Miami, protested. He liked listening to the soft and lilting Irish of her voice. "We could use a little humor right about now. Go ahead, Mairet."

Her laugh lines deepened as she began to relay the story. "A farmer stopped by the local mechanic shop to have his truck fixed. They couldn't finish it while he waited, so he said he didn't live far and would just walk home.

"On the way he stopped at the hardware store and bought a five-gallon plastic bucket and a gallon of paint. Then he stopped by the feed store and picked up a couple of chickens and a goose. But now, struggling to get outside the store, he had a problem—how to carry all his purchases home.

"While he was scratching his head and pondering the dilemma, he was approached by a little old lady who was lost. She asked him how to get to Mockingbird Lane.

"The farmer said, 'Well, my farm is very close to Mockingbird Lane. I would walk you there but I don't think I can carry all of this.'

"The old lady looked at his purchases and said, 'Why don't you put the can of paint in the bucket. Carry the bucket in one hand, put a chicken under each arm and carry the goose in your other hand?'

"The grateful farmer did just that and proceeded to walk the old girl to Mockingbird Lane.

"On the way, he suggested taking a short-cut through an alley that would get them there in less time.

"The little old lady looked him over cautiously. 'I am a lonely widow without a husband to defend me. How do I know that when we get in the alley you won't hold me up against the wall, pull up my skirt, and have your way with me?' "

Fritz and Alcosta guffawed. Blevins, the law student from St. Louis, shuddered—the thought of doing a little old lady too much for him. Dietrich just squeezed his eyes shut and shook his head.

"So what happens next, Mairet," the handsome Cuban encouraged her, white teeth flashing.

"So, the farmer says, 'Holy smokes, lady! I'm carrying a bucket, a gallon of paint, two chickens, and a goose. How in the world could I possibly hold you up against the wall and do that?'

"The old lady replied, 'Set the goose down, cover him with the bucket, put the paint on top of the bucket, and I'll hold the chickens.' "

The van rocked with laughter. Even Dietrich wore a grudging grin.

He suddenly grew serious, thinking back to the tactics problem they had attempted to reason earlier. "Hold on a minute. You made me think."

McCarron derisively eyed him. "I'm sorry. Did it hurt?"

Dietrich sat back in his seat, thrust his beefy hands in his jacket pockets, and sneered. "I know why Neddie, The Geek, is here...for comic relief. But what's your deal?"

"My 'deal' as you so finely put it, is to make you look good."

"Funny, McCarron. I don't believe you should be doing field work."

"Just me or women in general?"

"Take your pick."

"What is it you think I should be doing then?"

"What all women should be doing. Staying at home."

"Ah, I see. Your wife will prettily greet you when you come home every evening, have your meal waiting on the table, your slippers and pipe by your favorite chair. And at night, a little, 'Oh, baby, yeah...oh, baby,' and it's off to sleep. Another perfect day."

Dietrich kind of got off on her throaty dirty talk. How creepy was that? "Sounds pretty good to me."

"It would. Can I give you a little advice?"

"What's that?"

"When you're employed, if you're ever employed, sign up for the health plan with the best drug benefits. Your wife will need to be sedated daily."

"And what about you?" he scoffed over the howling laughter of his teammates. "Making cow eyes at Instructor Lee. What is wrong with you? What are you thinking? Like he'd be attracted to a rude, fat potato farmer like you."

He farted.

Dietrich's teammates complained loudly. Although the outside temperature was close to freezing, Alcosta scrambled to roll down the window on the driver's door.

"Jesus, Dietrich," Blevins protested, pulling his sweater over his nose.

Mairet could have sworn the air was tinted a bright yellow from sulfur fumes. She pulled a pint-sized emergency oxygen tank and breathing mask from her duffel and attached it to her nose. "Your parents must be so proud."

Neddie admired Mairet's preparedness. "She must have gotten wind of your previous close-quarter assignments, Dietrich." He cracked up, enjoying his own pun.

Dietrich rubbed his belly after giving Neddie a painful punch on the shoulder. "I can't help it. Fast food and sitting around in cramped quarters tears up my guts."

"Where did you get that?" Alcosta blurted, pointing at the oxygen mask in McCarron's possession, trying to hold his breath and claw the apparatus from her hand.

"Ladies and gentlemen." Michael's smooth voice came over their communicators. "I don't suppose you have taken notice, but your subject just left the building and is getting in his vehicle to leave the surveillance area."

All of them froze, staring at one another in disbelief. They piled out of the surveillance van and watched the suspected terrorist, a fellow academy trainee, jauntily wave to them in his rear view mirror as he retired to the academy and, after a long night, a soft warm bed.

Michael's raised voice interrupted the surveillance team's resultant finger pointing and rousing rendition of the blame game. "You have exactly thirty minutes to return to the academy and muster in my classroom. Do you copy?"

"Yes, sir," they responded unanimously, understandably without much enthusiasm.

THE TEAM WAITED WITH TREPIDATION in Instructor Lee's classroom, restlessly anticipating his appearance. They expected that he would grade their performance, pick apart their weaknesses, make suggestions on their efficiency and—well, basically—rip them a new one.

"This is your fault," Dietrich accused McCarron.

"Mine? Who was in charge of F Troop this evening?"

Neddie put his head down and giggled. He was a latchkey kid growing up and had watched rerun after rerun of the classic television show from the '60s. "I loved those guys!"

"Who?" Dietrich demanded.

"Sorry." McCarron made quotes with her fingers. "The Surveillance Team."

"Look you, I've had just about enough…"

"Stiffen the sinews, man…summon up the blood," McCarron heckled him, loosely quoting Shakespeare's *Henry V.*

His mouth dropped open and he shook his head in confusion, pretty much appearing like the philistine he was. "What?"

McCarron saw Instructor Lee approach the classroom door from the hallway. She leaned over to Dietrich and said plainly, in words he could understand, "Grow a set."

Michael walked into the room and looked sternly at each of them. Without exception, every member of the team sat at attention, feet together and flat on the floor, eyes focused straight ahead.

He threw the manila folder he carried on his desktop and waited to speak until he had everyone's undivided attention. "You have failed this assignment."

Shifting in seats, followed by groans and clearing of throats.

"Failed miserably."

Dietrich opened his mouth to speak, but promptly snapped it shut when chilled by the cold displeasure in Instructor Lee's eyes.

"Mr. Fritz."

"Yes, Instructor Lee?"

"Define the word *team*."

Neddie cleared his throat and called out with authority, "A group of people with complementary skills required to complete a task, job, or project."

"And what are the four common attributes of a team's members, Mr. Fritz?"

"Sir! Team members (1) operate with a high degree of interdependence, (2) share authority and responsibility for self-management, (3) are accountable for the collective performance, and (4) work toward a common goal and shared reward or rewards."

Verbatim. You had to give it to him.

"Thank you Mr. Fritz," Michael commented quietly.

Neddie proudly threw back his shoulders, head held high. "Yes, sir!"

"Team." Michael emphasized the word again as he shared his glance among his recalcitrant students. "That means that some of you on the team might have been tending to business while other members were exchanging barbs and personal insults with each other. You disgraced not only yourselves, but you disgraced me as your instructor."

Every head of the surveillance team bowed in shame.

"We will be reviewing, in depth, the audio from your surveillance."

"You mean you surveilled our surveillance?" Dietrich exclaimed, clearly offended.

"This was a field test, Mr. Dietrich, not a class excursion to the National Zoo."

"So…" McCarron ventured. "You heard…"

"Everything," Michael confirmed.

She ducked her head, mortified now that Dietrich had outed her.

Michael moved in front of his desk and crossed his arms over his chest. "I can assure you, ladies and gentlemen, that failure of another class assignment given to you by this instructor will not be tolerated. Should it occur again, I will personally sign each of your dismissal letters from this academy and, if necessary, help you pack. Do I make myself clear?"

"Yes, sir," the class responded half-heartedly.

"Do I make myself clear?" Michael reiterated.

"Yes sir!"

"Mr. Dietrich."

"Sir?"

"The Nineteenth Amendment to the Constitution of the United States, giving women the right to vote, was ratified in 1920. Get over it."

McCarron snorted loudly.

"Ms. McCarron?"

She snapped to attention. "Sir?"

"Please stay behind." He swept his gaze over the rest of her classmates. "We meet back here tomorrow at oh eight hundred. Dismissed."

Before leaving the room, Dietrich gave McCarron a pleased smile behind Instructor Lee's back and ran his thumb across his throat. He jabbed his finger at her and waved goodbye.

When they were alone, Michael took a stance in front of McCarron's seat.

She couldn't bring herself to look at him.

"Ms. McCarron."

She didn't respond.

He rapped his knuckles on her desktop. "Look at me."

"Do I have to?"

"You do."

She gave him a brilliant smile. "Yes, Instructor Lee?"

When she smiled, her face lit up and appeared almost beautiful. And she knew it.

Michael stared at her until the smile faded.

She lost a little of her confidence. Oh, those eyes—those intense, stern, unforgiving—exotic, intoxicating, shining pools of brown.

Michael witnessed the expression on her face transform from cowed to dreamy.

He sighed. "Ms. McCarron, we have a fourteen-day Christmas break beginning next week. I encourage you to consider whether you really want to be a member of this organization."

At last, he had her full attention.

She sat up in her seat, hurt and dismay in her eyes. "Are you dismissing me from the academy?"

He did not have that authority. But she didn't know that.

"When you return, prove to me that you are taking your nutritional and physical training seriously. Show me that you can curb your restless mind and runaway tongue." He moved to his desk and picked up his file folder. "In short, convince me that you are serious about being a part of this program."

Michael left the room before the tears building up behind her eyelids spilled over her lower lashes and tracked down her flushed cheeks.

He walked down the hallway to his office, berating himself for making her cry.

The last thing he wanted to do was to break her spirit. She could never give in—buckle under—to the Dietrichs of this world. However, her survival within the Bureau depended upon shedding her adolescent daydreams and casual disregard of its rules.

Once again, he saw her open and shining face crumble under his icy stare and feigned indifference. The only thing that made him feel worse was the prospect of going home for Christmas to visit his parents.

He unlocked his office door.

McCarron did have a flair for telling a joke. He shook his head, laughing quietly. *I'll hold the chickens.*

여섯

6
Merry, Merry Christmas

December 2006
South Boston, Massachusetts

"MAIRET, HONEY, ARE YOU FEELING all right?" Aunt Coleen asked her with concern.

All eyes of the close-knit McCarron family gathered around the Christmas Day dining table—including daughters-in-law, sons-in-law, and seven grandchildren—swiveled toward Mairet. To her everlasting discomfort.

"You haven't touched the mashed potatoes or stuffing. No gravy or rolls." Coleen's graying auburn brows puckered in a worried frown. "Are you ill?"

Mairet piped up before Aunt Coleen dashed off to retrieve a thermometer to take her temperature. "No, Aunt Coleen. I'm fine."

Truthfully, she was miserable. All of her cherished holiday foods, which over the years had provided such comfort and joy, were within her reach. However, this Christmas—perhaps forevermore—they would remain untouched, untasted, and enjoyed.

Her favorite time of the year had become pure torment.

"Ah, leave the lass be, Coleen," her uncle chimed in with a wink in Mairet's direction. "The FBI has strict rules on fitness, you know. It'll do her good."

When it was time for dessert—pies, cakes, puddings, brownies, and ice cream—Mairet excused herself from the table and escaped to her bedroom.

SHE TOOK ADVANTAGE OF THE rare quiet moment in the McCarron household and penned with precision in her daily journal what foods she had consumed at her Christmas feast, and in what proportions. It was not going to take long.

"Yo!"

Mairet looked up to find her first cousin, Ashling, slouched against the doorjamb with arms folded across her budding chest.

The family referred to Ashling as "the mid-life crisis baby." At least, it became a crisis when Coleen, at the age of forty-three, discovered she was pregnant.

Ashling was seven years' junior to the fourth of the McCarron's five children, the only offspring still living at home—the least ambitious and, without doubt, the most precocious.

"What's his name?" she probed bluntly, a smirk on her pale and freckled face.

Mairet spared her a moment. "Who?"

"The guy...the reason you are losing weight."

"I would say J. Edgar Hoover, but he's deceased," Mairet shot back, dodging the question.

Ashling plopped on the bed next to her. "Mairet, you're adorkable."

Like generations before them, the kids today spoke their own language. They created new words by merging two. That Ashling called her both a dork and adorable was not lost on Mairet.

"Please," Mairet muttered.

Her young cousin announced with authority, "A woman doesn't give up something she loves unless it's for something she loves more."

Mairet arched a brow at her cousin's impressive and unexpected revelation. "And this you have deduced at the tender age of thirteen?"

"I read it somewhere," Ashling admitted loftily.

"Better you tend to your schoolbooks, my girl."

"One genius in the family is enough," Ashling countered with a sweet and contented smile. She playfully nudged her cousin. "Common. Give it up. I promise I won't tell a soul."

She took notice of the three-ring binder opened on Mairet's bed. It contained segmented sections entitled Fitness, Exercise, Nutrition, and Mind-Body-Spirit. She flipped it over to inspect the cover, impressively emblazoned with the FBI Academy logo.

"Prepared for Mairet McCarron by Instructor Michael Lee," Ashling murmured with interest.

Mairet's head snapped up. She snatched the binder from her cousin's grasp.

"An instructor?" Ashling needled laughingly. "You want to hook up with your instructor?"

"Sssh!" Mairet dashed to her door and closed it.

"Is he Irish?"

"He is not," Mairet replied crisply.

"Ah-ite." Ashling bounced off the bed and skipped to the door, casting a teasing glance over her shoulder. "I'm going to Google him!"

Mairet had already thought of that. He was impressive—a Renaissance man. There was little shame in admiring a person of his accomplishments.

"Google him then, you little pest." She snapped her journal closed. "Just leave me in peace."

Ashling laughed gaily. Swinging her long red hair over her shoulder, she closed the door behind her.

"Saints in Heaven," Mairet bemoaned with a sorrowful shake of her head. "Will I ever be allowed any dignity?"

MAIRET'S UNCLE, AUNT, AND COUSIN Ashling stood with her on the Amtrak South Station platform, waiting for the arrival of the train that would take her back to Quantico before the New Year. It was just before 8:00 a.m., snowing steadily, miserably slushy, and bone chilling.

Mairet fondly smiled at her family. "You don't have to wait with me. It's freezing out here. Go home and enjoy a warm fire."

"Nonsense," her uncle shouted vehemently, vapor puffing from his mouth. He briskly rubbed his gloved hands together. "It shouldn't be much longer now."

Ashling sidled up to Mairet and produced a paperback novel she extracted from the deep pocket of her coat. "Here," she whispered, surreptitiously thrusting the book into Mairet's hand. "A little something to read on the train. Time will fly."

Mairet examined the paperback. Her literature teacher in parochial school, Sister Mary Elizabeth, would say the book had the well-worn appearance of a woman of easy virtue—passed around and enjoyed by many.

A skillfully designed torso of a naked and splendidly muscled young man filled the cover, a barbed wire tattoo adorning his well-developed upper arm.

Mairet shot a startled glance at her wickedly grinning cousin who just recently graduated from tween to teen. "Do your parents know you read this stuff?"

Ashling cocked a hip and placed her hand upon it, feigning insult at her cousin's presumption. "It's a mystery!"

Puzzled, Mairet again inspected the cover. "A mystery?"

"It will be to you," Ashling wisecracked under her breath.

The McCarrons observed their daughter conspiratorially whispering with her gullible cousin. They exchanged suspicious glances, curiously pondering what mischief she was hatching.

Ashling felt her parent's eyes upon them and ground out between clenched teeth, "On the down low." She shoved the book clutched in Mairet's gloved hand into the depths of her carry-on tote.

"Here we are now!" Mairet's uncle cried jovially, heralding the arrival of the train.

The approaching Amtrak locomotive announced its mighty presence by shaking the platform beneath their feet as the engine powered down and the train rumbled into the station.

No. 99 - Destination Quantico

December 2006
Amtrak Northeast Regional Route

MICHAEL STOOD ON THE PLATFORM at Penn Station beneath Madison Square Garden in Manhattan a little past one-thirty in the afternoon, waiting to board the Amtrak train that ran the Northeast Regional Route. The train was about fifteen minutes behind schedule.

He had spent the last two days reconnecting with old friends in New York City, taking advantage of the extra time available to him after concluding his visit with his mother and father in Washington D.C.

Michael checked his wristwatch. With no additional delays, he should reach Quantico in another four and a half hours—about six o'clock that evening.

The Marine Base was no longer under restrictions, and he was returning to Quantico several days early hoping to settle into a routine, tweak some lesson plans, and take advantage of the peace and quiet before trainees returned from their holiday break.

At least, that is how he justified his premature departure to his parents.

Truthfully, he was relieved to take his leave of them. His relationship with his parents was, at best, distantly polite. At worst, wordlessly strained.

MICHAEL'S PARENTS WERE BUSY PROFESSIONALS. His father served as a top-security analyst for the federal government in the Pentagon, and his mother was a graduate school educator with a doctoral degree.

Seeking to assimilate their son into the culture of his birth country, they enrolled him in well-respected public schools in their affluent Georgetown neighborhood.

When Michael was thirteen, an outbreak of mumps occurred in his secondary school, galvanizing distressed parents to keep their children at home until the incubation period of seven to eighteen days had passed without another reported case.

Ten days after being exposed, Michael suffered all the classic symptoms—neck swelling, fever, headache, joint aches and, unfortunately, inflammation known as orchitis.

Clinical studies reported that only thirteen percent of postpubescent boys or men who suffered from the viral condition experienced reduced sperm counts. Permanent infertility in mumps-related orchitis was extremely rare.

Michael was one of the hapless exceptions.

His traditional Korean parents agonized without end. Whenever they received a wedding invitation or baby announcement from their family and friends, they steeped in their misery. Riddled with guilt and grief, they believed their irresponsibility had cursed their handsome, intelligent, and talented only child to live a lonely life—unable to find a Korean bride willing to remain childless. He would never have a family. They would never know the joys of grandchildren.

Regardless of how many times Michael assured them that all would be well—that he was content—they would lower their eyes, too ashamed to respond.

WHEN THE TRAIN STRETCHED ITS shiny silver length before the station and stopped to board passengers, the conductor directed Michael to the passenger car on his left. Michael found his reserved seat next to the aisle, stored his carry-on luggage overhead, sat, and stretched out his long legs. The extra legroom, wide and comfortable seats were enticing incentives for riding Business Class.

After a short wait, the train pulled out of the station.

Michael was pleased. So far, he was not sharing his seating with anyone—the advantage of traveling before the end of the holidays. Passing a curious glance around the coach, he noticed that it was not even half-full.

His eyes stopped on a young woman who sat by herself, facing him, two seats up and to the right. He frowned. She looked vaguely familiar.

She turned from observing the wind-driven sleet outside her window to look straight ahead, her normally lively brown eyes glazed with boredom.

It was McCarron.

Michael cocked his head. Her chestnut hair, subdued into a regulation ponytail at the Academy, was loose about her shoulders. He had not realized it was so thick and shiny.

He observed her absently tuck a curl that brushed her jawline behind her right ear, revealing a rosy, freckled cheek. Was it his imagination, or was her face thinner? She still had the prominent rounded cheekbones, but the fullness—pudginess—appeared to be missing.

He turned on the overhead light, lowered the fold-down tray in front of him, and placed his laptop on it. With one last glance at McCarron, he opened his lesson plan program and began to type.

Two hours later, Michael rubbed his eyes and stretched his long arms over his head. He was satisfied with his progress and put aside the laptop.

He checked on McCarron. She seemed restless.

If she was traveling from Boston—that Michael reasoned was logical—she had boarded the train about five hours ahead of him.

She rummaged through her travel tote and extracted a paperback novel. Inspecting the title, she dubiously shook her head and flipped to the opening page.

Michael kept her in his sights as he reclined his seat, lulled by the rhythmic click-clack of the wheels and rocking motion of the rail car.

McCarron was a fast reader, thumbing with rapt interest through the beginning chapters of the book.

Michael smiled his thanks and accepted a cup of hot coffee from an attendant sporting a neatly trimmed gray beard and an immaculately pressed uniform.

Another amenity of Business Class—complimentary beverages and newspapers to read while traveling.

The attendant stopped by McCarron's seat and voiced a brief comment. She dragged her attention from the book, grinned at his remark, and requested a bottled water.

Good choice. Michael was impressed that she had shunned the array of high-calorie carbonated and artificially sweetened beverages on the serving cart.

She immersed herself once again in her reading, now moving on to the right-hand page of the paperback. Her eyes suddenly widened in shock, immediately followed by a strangled cry.

She leaned toward the print as if disbelieving what she had just read. Nonsensically, she rechecked the book title then flipped back to the text where she had left off.

Clearly agitated, she decisively abandoned the book, flattening it on her lap. Reclining her seat, she squeezed her eyes shut and shook her head, muttering to herself.

This was too tempting for Michael to ignore.

When she appeared to be dozing, he righted his tray table and made his way down the aisle. He nonchalantly leaned against the seat directly beside McCarron, and canted his head to read the book title.

It seemed innocuous enough, although there was a shirtless hunk of manhood on the cover with a barbed wire tattoo circling his muscular bicep.

Interesting. He had not pegged McCarron for a fan of erotic romance.

He eased the book off her lap and skimmed the paragraphs where she appeared to have lost it.

Michael's eyebrows rose. Oh, yeah. Erotic romance.

The obligatory sinuous golden-skinned woman—who may or may not have been wearing panties—her stilettoed heel placed on the masculine chest of a dark-haired Gypsy, forcing him to lie on the ground, sitting on his face….

McCarron turned her head toward Michael. She opened her eyes, blinking sleepily, and smiled as though he were appearing to her in a dream.

Eyes focused. Thoughts crystalized. Realization dawned.

She glanced at the book in his hand, then her lap. She sucked in a horrified gasp, snatched the paperback from Michael's hand and clumsily stuffed it back in her travel bag.

Michael could not resist teasing her, deepening the rosy tint of her cheeks. "Provocative reading."

She turned away in an attempt to hide her face from him. "It's not mine."

He did not sound convinced. "On loan?"

She looked up at him in annoyance. "Where did you come from?"

He motioned with his head to his seat. "Over there."

He caught bits and pieces of her indignant mumbling that sounded like, "…get my hands on that juvenile delinquent."

"Why are you embarrassed?"

"I'm not."

He chuckled, not bothering to disguise his amusement. "You're not?"

She slid down, put her elbow on the armrest and her hand up to screen her face. "Go away."

He sighed and unfolded from his casual leaning stance. "Okay. But if you want somebody to read to…"

She burrowed deeper in the cushions of her seat, attempting to shrink to as small a target as humanly possible.

Michael grinned when she quietly scolded him. "Villain!"

He took his seat and settled back. Admittedly, it was not his usual style, but Michael got a kick out of ribbing McCarron. It surprised him that he had made his presence known to her. Pleased him, actually. He was feeling more lighthearted than he had in a long while.

He glanced in McCarron's direction to find her peeking at him over the headrest of the facing seat.

She promptly dropped below his line of sight.

Michael smiled, closing his eyes to take a short nap.

Quantico Marine Base

December 2006
FBI Academy - Quantico, Virginia

T HE TRAIN SCREECHED TO A halt in front of the little station that offered no services at the Marine Base in Quantico, Virginia. It was 6:32 p.m.

Michael got up from his seat and stretched the hours of inactivity from his cramped muscles. He opened the overhead and collected his carry-on bag.

He glimpsed a petite McCarron struggling with the latch of her overhead. When she finally got it open, she strained to reach her bag, jostled out of her reach during the trip by the vibration of the coach. The hem of her sweater hitched with her upward stretches, exposing her bare midriff. Her ribs were visible.

Michael came to her aid and retrieved her bag.

"Oh," she murmured, avoiding eye contact, and accepted the bag from his hand. "Thank you." She started down the aisle.

"McCarron."

Muddled, she swiveled around. "Yes?"

"The exit is that way." Michael pointed in the opposite direction.

She hesitated a painfully awkward few seconds, and then squeezed past an entertained Michael.

"Wait," Michael called after her, picking up a knee length down parka from her seat. "You forgot your coat."

She stopped short, shoulders falling, and shook her head in disbelief. She walked back to Michael, forced a smile, accepted the coat, and left the train.

IT WAS DARK AND LIGHTLY snowing when Michael disembarked.

McCarron was standing by her luggage under a warm pool of light in front of the small station, shivering.

"Put that on," Michael ordered, taking the coat from her arms and slipping her into it. "It's cold."

She mumbled something about being bossy as Michael efficiently encased her in the jacket and zipped it closed. He wrapped his warm muffler around her neck and tucked the ends into the neckline of the coat.

She looked up at him in surprise, bright eyes searching his.

Michael removed his hands from her collar, now aware of the familiarity of the gesture. "I'll call for a shuttle," he offered. "We can share one back to campus."

She nodded, dubiously eyeing him. Had his attitude changed toward her, or was he just more relaxed away from the regimen of the academy?

They rode in silence to the training facility. Michael felt her gaze on him, but when he turned in her direction, she glanced away and stared out of the window.

The shuttle dropped them off on the rim of the academy campus. The two walked toward the dormitories in light and fluffy snow flurries that aimlessly swirled about them.

"Why did you come back early?" Michael asked McCarron.

She shrugged. "I thought it would be easier to limit my food intake here. And I could use the gym when it's not so...crowded."

More than likely, full of classmates who would heckle and make fun of her, Michael concluded.

He was pleased with her discipline. It must have been difficult staying on her diet during the holidays. He said as much.

Mairet was delighted by his observation—his praise. "My family thought I was sick and kept trying to feed me."

"Have you tracked your weight loss?"

She nodded. "Eleven and a half pounds."

Michael frowned. "In less than two weeks?"

Again, she nodded.

"Let's slow that down a little."

White steam billowed from her mouth in a huff of disappointment.

"Don't misunderstand, McCarron," Michael soothed her. "I'm pleased with your progress. But it's difficult to maintain quick weight loss. I would be happy with two pounds a week."

"You said we would start building muscle once I lost some weight," she reminded him.

Michael nodded. "Correct."

"Can we start tomorrow?"

Michael had asked for her commitment and he received it. Now it was up to him to support her and sustain the momentum. "Meet me at the gym tomorrow morning at oh nine hundred."

She wiggled with excitement then suddenly grew serious. "What time is that?"

Michael telegraphed his disapproval with a frown.

She grinned. "Joking." She looked around, marking their progress as they walked across campus. They had almost reached the dormitories.

"Are we officially back?"

"Not until we check in."

"Right!" She threw a fully packed and perfectly round snowball she had been hiding behind her back. It exploded on his shoulder.

She doubled over with gales of laughter.

Once again, Michael was at Shangri-La with Cara, her head thrown back in laughter, egging him on for a snowball fight.

McCarron observed his faraway look. "You're reminiscing," she said, pulling him from his reverie.

"You reminded me of someone just then."

"Who?"

She prompted Michael after he failed to reply. "A woman?" A lover?"

"A friend."

"Friend," McCarron repeated flatly. She cocked her head, not in the least deceived. "So...you loved her then."

He turned away.

"Ah," she said softly, coming to a realization. "Still love her." She was hurt, certainly, but very much more envious. "How grand that would be, to have someone love you and never forget you."

"For whom?" Michael responded with a sharp edge.

"Tsk, tsk!" she scolded him. "Tis the heart that decides, Michealeen, and that's the truth of it."

Michael's gaze swiveled toward her, surprised at hearing his name in the Gaelic.

McCarron sighed wistfully. "And how sad and lonely it is, as you well know, to love someone who will not, or cannot, love you back."

She left Michael looking after her with a thoughtful frown as she crossed the campus toward the coed dormitory.

일곱

7
The Workout

Last Week In December 2006
FBI Academy – Quantico, Virginia

T HE NEXT MORNING MICHAEL AND Mairet arrived at the same
time in front of the darkened and deserted gymnasium. Mairet
followed Michael inside where he accessed the bank of switches for the
overhead lights. The place blazed with white-hot light, making the silver
metal of the equipment gleam and twinkle.

"Where do we start?" Mairet asked, eager to begin her physical
training.

"Slowly," Michael cautioned her. "We start slowly."

While Michael was adjusting the correct weights for McCarron on
a Nautilus machine, she wandered over to a piece of equipment, trying
to figure out its purpose and workings.

She slipped on the seat, wrapped her forearms around the padded
wings, and attempted to draw them together. She huffed and puffed,
legs threshing the air, but could not budge them.

However, she did feel the tension it created in the muscles across her
chest. "Hey," she called out to Michael with a grin. "Will this…thingy
make my boobs bigger?"

Michael threw her a reproving glance. "Filter."

"What?"

"Filter what you are thinking before it comes out of your mouth."

"I beg your pardon, your lordship," she wisecracked, missing the
point. "Will this make my *breasts* bigger?"

Michael approached her, shaking his head in mild frustration.

When he leaned toward her, breeching the boundaries of her personal space, she shrank down in her seat.

He reached behind her to remove the round weights, one by one, that were stacked like donuts on a metal spindle on each side of the mechanism.

"Try it now," he offered.

Feeling foolish for being such a faint heart, Mairet pulled herself straight in the seat, and used her forearms to draw the padded wings together directly in front of her.

"Oh!" she cried with delight. "This is much better."

"What you are feeling is the pull on the pectoral muscles...the muscles underlying the breast. The breast is made of connective and fatty tissue. You will not increase the size of the breast with this exercise, but build the muscle beneath it, which will make the breast appear larger and firmer."

She gaped at him, impressed by his articulate discourse and knowledge of the physiology of the female body. "Well, that's something, isn't it?" she replied happily.

A little over an hour later, Michael called a halt for the day.

"So soon?" Mairet questioned, sounding disappointed. "I feel great."

"Let's keep it that way," Michael insisted. "If your muscles become too taxed, your workout tomorrow won't be as effective."

He threw her a towel. "Soak in the whirlpool. Eat a modest meal for lunch and be sure to add a protein for dinner. I'll see you here tomorrow morning, same time."

When she made no effort to leave, Michael regarded her with a curious tilt of his head.

"Thank you, Instructor Lee," she intoned blissfully.

Before she pushed through the women's locker room door, she glanced over her shoulder. She hid a grin of pleasure behind her gym towel.

Instructor Lee was standing where she had left him, speculatively gazing after her.

The Bright Berry From
The Naked Thorn

December 31, 2006
FBI Academy – Quantico, Virginia

New-Year's Day

"At such a time, the merry year is born,
Like the bright berry from the naked thorn."
–Hartley Coleridge

MAIRET SAT CROSS-LEGGED ON HER bunk in her dorm room on New Year's Eve, listening to the persistent and boisterous sounds of distant reveling. She absently fingered the soft folds of the scarf Michael Lee had wrapped around her neck when they arrived at Quantico.

She dreaded New Year's Eve. It was melancholy—looking back at the previous year—reviewing its unfulfilled longings and regrets. It was burdensome—anticipating the bright promise of the New Year—contriving overly optimistic resolutions made in haste and, invariably, repented at leisure.

More's the pity, she had never celebrated the occasion with anyone but her family. Never attended a New Year's party. Never shared a New Year's kiss with a boy—a man.

Her thoughts turned, as they frequently did, to Michael Lee. She wondered what he might be doing at this hour. If he suffered the aloneness as keenly as she did. If he would be annoyed if she sought out his company.

She restlessly walked to her window. The night sky was clear. Moonless. She gazed down at the well-lit quad below the dormitory building. It was deserted.

She glanced at the digital alarm clock on the nightstand next to her bed. It was 11:46 p.m.

She had to do something to repress her powerful and persistent craving for food—seducing her like a cruel lover with hollow promises of gratification and contentment.

She pulled on a knitted cap, her coat and gloves, determined not to let another New Year find her alone in her room. When she reached the front door, she hesitated. She impulsively retraced her steps, grabbed Instructor Lee's scarf from her bed and coiled it around her neck.

She took the stairs double time—huffing and puffing after she had descended five flights—and burst through the outside doorway into the frigid night air.

Michael halted under a light in the quad, hands thrust in his overcoat pockets, startled by McCarron's explosive exit from the dormitory emergency stairs.

She caught sight of him and grinned, flustered. "Hi. How are you?"

Amusement sparkled in Michael's eyes. "Where's the fire?"

Mairet privately celebrated this chance encounter, seeking to detain Michael for as long as possible—to be in his company. "What are you doing?"

"Going for a walk. You?"

"The same."

"Let's walk together then," he suggested mildly.

She shrugged happily. "Okay."

They walked side by side down the broad sidewalk lined with shrubbery mantled in the frozen lace of uniquely patterned snowflakes.

She glanced askance at Michael, admiring his poise, enjoying his calming presence.

She was smitten. She accepted it. There was no relief or known remedy for it.

"Classes begin again on Monday," she ventured, filling the extended silence.

"They do," Michael affirmed.

"So," she began timidly, "I just wanted to say…before everyone returned…that I…"

Pop. Pop. Pop.

A brilliant array of fireworks exploded in the distant sky from the direction of the Potomac River.

"It must be the New Year," Mairet murmured.

Michael checked his wristwatch. "Just." He smiled down on her. "Happy New Year."

She nodded, feeling ambivalent. "You, too."

"Finish what you were about to say," Michael encouraged her.

"Oh…well," she stuttered, encouraged by his interest in her thoughts. Or, at the very least, impressed by his fine manners. "I just wanted to tell you…how much I appreciate the hours you have spent with me over the past few days. I know you won't have time after…after classes begin." She concluded sheepishly, "So, thank you."

"Why won't I have time?" Michael queried with interest.

"What?"

"We will continue what we have begun, you and I," he stated with conviction.

"We will?"

Oh, how her eyes brightly reflected the stars.

"We both have responsibilities," Michael reminded her. "Yours is to graduate the academy. Mine is to make sure you do."

That jarred her back to reality. "Responsibilities." Her eyes became vague. "Responsibilities. Of course." She pulled away from him.

"Where are you going?" Michael inquired with a frown.

"Well, I…I'm a little tired. More than I realized."

"Take tomorrow off from your training," Michael recommended. "You've been working hard. Enjoy your holiday."

Mairet lowered her eyes to hide her disappointment. "Sure," she agreed without much enthusiasm. Another free day. Another twenty-four hours of inactivity and solitude. Just what she needed.

Abashed, she realized that she was wearing Instructor Lee's personal property. Wordlessly, she pulled his scarf from her neck and thrust it at him.

"Well, then, I'll…good night." She turned on her heel and purposefully headed toward her dormitory.

Michael looked after her, fully aware of what he had just done, and not particularly pleased with himself. He gazed at the scarf, the heat from her body warming his hand.

He, too, decided to return to his quarters.

Trial and Tribulations

January 1, 2007
FBI Academy – Quantico, Virginia

Michael walked through drifting snow to his office on New Year's Day with the intention of completing his preparations for the remaining two months of this training cycle.

The weather service predicted that the storm front moving through the area would prove insignificant. As testimony, snowflakes fell on the ground all around him and melted on impact.

He frowned when he passed the gym. The lights were on.

The campus deserted, it was no doubt McCarron.

Michael gave a mental shrug. If she wanted to work out on her holiday, that was her prerogative. He checked his watch. Ten after ten.

After she had used every piece of fitness equipment with which Michael Lee had made her familiar, Mairet was running on the treadmill.

Responsibilities. That is what he had said. *We both have responsibilities.*

She agonized over the words that ran in a merciless and continuous loop in her mind.

What a fool she was. What a simpleton.

He was not intentionally cruel, but cruel nonetheless. Emotionally remote, he had no appreciation of her feelings for him.

She angrily stabbed the mph button on the digital console, making it shrilly beep twice. She began to sweat in earnest, burning calories—burning Michael Lee from her consciousness.

Just before three o'clock that afternoon, Michael was satisfied that he was prepared for the classwork to commence the following Monday. He shrugged into his coat, turned off the desk lamp, and secured his office door.

Again, when he passed in front of the gym, the lights were on. He stopped, questioning how McCarron could sustain a workout for this length of time.

Annoyed that she had ignored his advice to skip a training day, Michael climbed the three flights of stairs to check on her and, if necessary, physically remove her from the premises.

His displeasure gave way to alarm when he found McCarron in the gym, dressed in her street clothes, eyes closed, sitting on a bench, slumped against the wall.

Michael lightly shook her to rouse her. "Ms. McCarron."

She groaned and opened her eyes. "Instructor Lee."

He hunkered down before her. "Are you ill?"

"I worked out until I was exhausted. So I showered and dressed, intending to go back to my room. But this is as far as I got."

Michael checked her pulse.

He retrieved a sports drink from the men's locker room, thoroughly shaking it before he popped the top and handed it to McCarron.

"Drink this. It will replace the carbohydrates and sodium your body lost during your workout."

She sipped it. "Mmm, it tastes good."

"Drink it all," Michael encouraged her when she attempted to put it aside. "You need to rehydrate."

Mairet sipped the salty drink, trying to get it down her throat without choking. She fretted about the loss of her credibility now that Instructor Lee had witnessed her absence of common sense.

Michael patiently waited until she had finished the contents of the bottle. He rechecked her pulse. Her heart rate was almost normal.

He gravely scrutinized her. "When are you going to do what I ask?"

"I don't know," she replied in a small voice.

Michael leaned toward her. "What?"

"I don't know," she repeated, too depleted to put up much of a defense.

Michael chuckled. Well, that was honest if nothing else.

"Have you eaten anything today?" he probed.

"No," she admitted reluctantly.

He shook his head. "Are you still dizzy?"

"I'm fine now."

"Can you stand on your own?"

"Yes."

He helped her to her feet. She was a little shaky, but appeared capable of walking.

After they had reached the first floor, they exited the elevator and stood outside under the building overhang.

Michael ordered McCarron to stay put. "I'm going to get my car."

"Why?" she asked, a little disoriented.

"We are going to get something to eat."

Mairet gaped at him. This was not how she imagined their first date. And she had imagined it quite a bit.

She should be wearing artfully applied makeup and lipstick—hair twined into a sophisticated French braid—a slinky black dress with stiletto heels and silk stockings with little pink bows on the garters.

"I'm really not hungry," she declared regretfully.

"I really don't care," Michael countered sardonically. "You are going to eat something, even if it is a bite of poached fish and some steamed rice."

Mairet anticipated swallowing mouthfuls of sawdust, and inwardly shuddered.

Wait a minute.

If this meant she could be with Michael Lee for even a brief time, who was she to spurn this divinely inspired gift.

"Okay," she acquiesced, convincingly sounding meek and resigned.

Winelight

January 1, 2007
Occoquan, Virginia

F OR THEIR DINNER VENUE, MICHAEL chose a cozy, unpretentious
bistro tucked in the center of a historic community located on
the south bank of the Occoquan River. The cuisine was country French.
The chef—whom Mairet presumed was also the owner—called out a
greeting in his native language to Michael from the open kitchen, clearly
pleased to see him. He gestured for Michael and Mairet to sit at a private
corner table, the only one available, and directed his waiter to remove
the reserved sign from the tabletop.

Not five minutes later, the slight, stubble-chinned chef—crop of
curly dark hair in wild disarray—arrived at their table with a bottle of
Cabernet Sauvignon and two glasses. He efficiently popped the cork
and poured an opulent Tyrian purple wine for Michael to taste. Michael
swirled the wine in the globed glass, lifted it to his nose, and took a sip.
He smiled, conveying his approval with a nod.

The chef cast a martyred glance heavenwards and huffed, "*Voila!*"

After pouring wine into each glass, he briskly relieved his guests
of their menus and spoke rapidly to Michael, his eyes bright with the
elucidation of his culinary expertise and the sumptuous recipe—with
its exotic textures and enticing flavors—that he intended to prepare
especially for them.

The chef's head swiveled toward Mairet in irritation when Michael
responded that while he would be delighted to partake of the special
dish, his dinner companion would require something less rich.

Michael chuckled when Mairet squirmed in discomfort under the
culinary master's inquisitive and annoyed stare. He introduced her to
the restauranteur, who rebounded with a gallant bow. "*Mademoiselle.*"

To her relief, Michael worked out a suitable meal for her and the temperamental Frenchman retired to the kitchen—shouting orders to his sous chef—to begin preparing their feast.

With all the savory aromas wafting from the kitchen, Mairet's stomach began to clench in hunger. "Am I really getting fish?" she inquired of Michael.

"Yes," he confirmed inflexibly.

Crestfallen, her smile wilted.

Surely, all the martyrs and saints in the Kingdom of Heaven knew she had her share of fish growing up. Every Friday and Holy Day. As a result, she was not terribly fond of fish.

"Francois is a culinary genius," Michael assured her. "You won't be disappointed with your dinner, I promise."

Satisfied, she nodded trustingly and glanced at the wine glass to the right of her place setting.

"Are you going to try the wine?" Michael prompted.

"Should I?" she answered brightly, essentially asking for his permission.

The hopeful sparkle in her eyes swayed Michael.

It would probably make her drunk. However, he conceded, it was a holiday. She deserved a reprieve from her rigorous self-imposed training regime. "Sip it. See if you like it."

Mairet emulated Michael, swirling the wine in her glass. It coated the inside of the globe, making leggy trails as it settled back into the bowl.

"Why am I doing this?" she inquired of Michael, fascinated by the ritual and the reflection of candlelight in the richly cast purple wine.

He laughed quietly, entertained by her ingenuous nature. "It opens up the aromas in the wine, softens the acid in the tannins...helps the wine to breathe."

Again, she imitated Michael and held the glass to her nose. "Smells nice." She took a sip.

Michael waited for her reaction.

She looked up at him and smiled contentedly, placing the glass back on the table. "It's delicious."

"Can you describe the flavors?"

Reflectively gazing over Michael's right shoulder, she ventured, "At first, it tastes like wild berries. Then...a bit of vanilla and...smooth... like expensive chocolate."

Michael nodded in agreement, impressed with her perception of this Loire Valley, French countryside Cabernet Sauvignon.

"I'm glad we came here," she ventured shyly. "It's wonderful."

Michael seriously observed her for a long and silent moment. "Promise me that you will not repeat what you did today."

She dropped her eyes, subdued by his earnestness, embarrassed by her recklessness. "Mr. Costello will not be very pleased when you report my behavior, will he?"

Michael leaned back in his chair, taken aback by her realization, uncertain of the consequences.

He waited until their server, who brought them a basket of crusty French bread, bustled away from their table. "You know about that?"

"That you were assigned by Mr. Costello to help me graduate the academy?" She laughed shortly. "I will admit my ignorance about many things, but I am not an idiot."

Her statement held no rancor, but still managed to sting Michael. He was not quite sure how to respond to his implied betrayal.

Finally, he asked McCarron, "Would you prefer to work with another instructor?"

"Is that what you want?" she probed bluntly, placing the onus on him.

He held her steady and inquisitive gaze. His admission amazed him as much as it did McCarron. "No."

Her expression glowed with gratitude and pleasure. "Thank you, Instructor Lee."

"The truth is," Michael generously stated, "your talent is respected and prized in the intelligence community."

"It's a curse," she revealed sadly.

Michael was mystified. "Do you really believe that?"

"Assigning mathematical formulas to everything within one's sphere is an esoteric skill," she replied, apparently under no illusions. "Not something you can chat about over dinner."

Intrigued, Michael inquired, "Did you recognize your gift as a child?"

She spoke softly, her eyes losing their focus. "I don't remember much of my early life…my childhood…in Ireland. All I have are impressions, mostly. Secret meetings around our kitchen table, loud and angry voices, suspicion, fear, grief…hunger.

"My Da would say that people of the world mistook The Troubles in Northern Ireland as one of religious differences. But, really, it was about sovereignty.

"Protestants loyal to Great Britain wanted to remain under its rule. But minority Catholics wanted Ireland to rule itself, to once again unite North and South." She shook her head. "After three decades of sorrow, it sorted itself out."

Michael reflected on the child who had lost both parents…one to violence, the other to an unforgiving system.

Time passed pleasantly, unheeded by either of them, until the chef arrived in the company of his server with their gourmet meal. With a flourish, he placed their plates before them, once again addressing Michael in French.

Mairet deeply inhaled the luscious aroma rising from her succulent grilled white fish. It made her mouth water. She cried happily, "This smells heavenly!"

The chef ceased his diatribe with Michael to look upon Mairet with fresh favor. *"Bon appetit, mon ami."*

When they were once again alone, Michael raised his wine glass to McCarron. He held it steady until she realized he was waiting for her to lift her glass to his.

When she had done so, he reminded her of her foolhardy workout and his previous request. "Promise me."

She complied with an awkward twitch of her shoulders and a rosy blush on her cheeks. "I promise."

The evening passed in a soft haze of winelight—without awareness of time or shared space—in quiet conversation and candid revelations about each other's life experiences and observations.

It was illuminating.

It was stimulating.

It was the most enjoyable evening Mairet could ever remember in her lifetime.

8
Silence Is Golden

January 2007
FBI Academy – Quantico, Virginia

MAIRET'S REVERIE WAS SHORT-LIVED, HOWEVER, when coursework commenced in earnest after the holidays and she faced off with Michael during a mock interrogation.

It was not only compulsory that New Agent Trainees be skilled in interrogation but that they professionally comport themselves should they undergo questioning from hostile factions.

Michael's dissatisfaction with Mairet's performance was evident.

Drilling her with questions, contradictions, and psychological ploys, Mairet became flustered, chattering nonsensically.

Michael was uncertain if she reacted this way because he was doing the interrogating or if she actually would be this useless in the field.

At one point, he abandoned his role-play persona and suggested that it would be in her best interest to remain silent.

She shook her head, clearly beyond advice. "Excuse me?"

"I want you to be quiet."

'Okay. Sorry.'

His eyes narrowed.

"I know," she muttered, lowering her head, acknowledging his frustration. "I do try to be quiet, but it's the silence in the conversation. It makes me nervous. When I get nervous, I rabbit on."

She saw the confusion in his expression. "Talk too much," she clarified the Irish slang.

Michael waited.

"All right. I'll be quiet."

Michael raised his eyes to the ceiling in ill-concealed impatience.

She opened her mouth to speak again, and Michael raised his hand to silence her.

"Sorry," she murmured.

Michael placed his hands on his hips. "Obviously, this isn't working."

He addressed the observers behind the two-way mirror. "Everyone clear the room." He directed his next remark to the technician operating the surveillance camera. "Stop the video camera, please."

He waited an interminable minute before grabbing the arms of McCarron's armchair and jerking her to face him.

"The more you chatter, Ms. McCarron, in an attempt to fill the silence, the more you give away. The more secrets you divulge. The more lives you place in jeopardy, including your own. Is that your intent?"

"No, sir."

"Then be silent."

She twisted her hands together. "For how long?"

Michael didn't answer her. Instead, his eyes bored into hers, almost daring her to speak.

To her credit, she didn't. For nearly one hour and fifteen minutes.

Finally, a masculine voice came over an intercom from behind the mirror, "Instructor Lee. Sorry, sir, but the next class is waiting. We need the room."

Michael was satisfied that he had made his point. "That will be all, Ms. McCarron."

She visibly seemed to deflate, releasing the tension from her muscles. "Yes, sir."

She let herself out of the interrogation room, quietly closing the door behind her.

Michael released a lungful of air, spent from the retained accumulation of her stress and his own.

Was he the right person for this assignment? Was anyone?

THEREAFTER, McCARRON WORKED OUT ALONE and at odd times of the day and night, avoiding Michael whenever possible. She reported to him once a week at the gym, weighing in and turning in her weekly journal. With very little chitchat and business concluded, she would excuse herself to put some space between them.

Michael's contact with McCarron at the *Dojang* was professional and perfunctory. Her interaction with him was now minimal, having completed his required two courses and receiving passing grades.

Michael let her work through her hurt and disillusionment, realizing that their last encounter had pushed her over some emotional edge. She kept to herself, sustaining her studies and her physical training. There was little more that he could expect or demand of her.

Still.

He missed her reliance upon him.

He missed her quirky bluntness and untethered enthusiasm to try things she had not yet experienced.

He missed her company.

He missed her.

Exercise In Futility

February 2007
FBI Academy – Quantico, Virginia

MAIRET WAS WORKING HER WAY through the compulsory tactical weapons training course, forcing herself to suppress the urge to fire her weapon at anything that moved. The more targets thrown in her path and the longer the exercise continued, the less focus she seemed to retain. She started to feel panicky and overwhelmed.

She cast a recriminating glance at the controller in the observation tower. Couldn't he see that she was floundering?

Michael Lee stood next to the granite-faced former Marine, exchanging a few words with him as he watched her move through the exercise.

Nonplussed, Mairet lowered her weapon.

Immediately, she felt the force of several paint cartridges hitting her body. Thump! Thump, thump!

She gazed with dismay at the blood-red splatters that attested to her momentary lapse in concentration and failure to pass this training sequence.

Michael descended the stairs of the tower, swung open the metal gate of the chain link fence, and entered the training course. He took his time to reach McCarron. She was rooted to the spot, head hung dejectedly.

When he stopped in front of her, Michael emphasized his every word with a vehement poke of his finger at the dried red splotches on her padded chest and torso. "You…are…dead!"

Wide-eyed and slack jawed, Mairet protectively crossed her arms over her body and shrank back, startled by Michael's uncharacteristic outburst.

"Do you get it?" he persisted in agitation. "You are dead!"

He turned on his heel and angrily stalked across the training field, not trusting himself to stay without further demoralizing her.

"What do you care, anyway?" Mairet muttered bitterly, turning her back on him in abject humiliation and disgrace.

Michael wheeled around. "What did you say?"

Her shoulders stiffened, but she remained silent.

He strode back to her, grabbed her arm and spun her around. "Say it again!"

"What do you care?" she screamed in his face. She yanked her arm from his grip. "I am weary of feeling the sharp edge of your disappointment in me!" She flung her weapon to the ground. "I'm done!"

"What does that mean?" Michael demanded as she stormed away.

She swung around, fists clenched at her sides, and shrieked, "It means I'm quitting. I'm leaving! I don't need this shite!"

"You are not going anywhere," Michael assured her, dialing down the rage and frustration with a soothing, reasonable tone.

She was incredulous but followed suit, saying more calmly, "Watch me."

"One month, Mairet. You only have one more month before graduating. You are going to stick it out. Do you understand me?"

Tears brimmed in her eyes. He had called her by her given name. She swallowed hard and said with a shaky voice, "Why? Why should I?"

Michael slowly approached her, gazing down on her bowed head. "If you don't, you will never forgive yourself."

He placed a consoling and steadying hand on her shoulder. "I understand that you're struggling. This is a new discipline for you. It's probably the only course work that hasn't come easily to you."

She raised her chin, her eyes wounded and sorrowful. "It's more than that."

"I know," Michael admitted gently, and for the first time. "You can do this. But what is important is that you do it for yourself...not for me."

She barked out a short laugh. "Of course I'm doing it for you! Why would I care about shooting people?"

"Do you care about staying alive?" Michael attempted to reason. "If you are sent into the field, you may be called upon to defend yourself... to survive."

His query did not resonate with her.

"All right, then," he conceded, tamping down his impatience. "Do it for me."

She was skeptical of his quick turnabout. "Really?"

"Yes." He motioned to the course controller to reset the test for another round. "Try it again. And this time, concentrate."

She nodded numbly. "Okay."

Michael walked toward the exit, hesitated, then turned back to her. "And, just for the record…I have never been disappointed in you."

Her face filled with sweet light. "No?"

He slowly shook his head.

The way he was looking at her caused butterflies to lift off and flutter in the pit of her stomach.

"Concentrate," Michael reminded her solemnly.

She reclaimed her fully loaded weapon from the field supervisor, pulled on her protective goggles, and made her way to the start of the course.

She briefly glanced up at the observer's tower and glimpsed Michael, arms folded across his chest, watching with expectation.

"Okay, McCarron," she murmured. "They call us the Fighting Irish."

She bolstered herself with freshly infused determination and spirit. "*Faugh a Ballagh!*" Clear the Way!

Just Two People

March 2007
FBI Academy – Quantico, Virginia

T HE TRAINING CYCLE FOR NEW Agent Class (NAC) '06-03 had concluded. Trainees who survived the grueling 850 hours of instruction proudly stood together—comrades amalgamated by a baptism of fire and their significant accomplishment—and participated in the austere graduation ceremony of the Federal Bureau of Investigation Academy.

Michael attended, watching an FBI-approved physically fit Mairet McCarron cross the stage and accept her credentials and badge, family members proudly cheering when the Director announced her name.

A wide smile brightened her face when she glimpsed Michael in the crowd. The corners of his mouth involuntarily lifted when she shared an expressive glance with him.

TWO DAYS LATER, MICHAEL SAT behind his desk in his office, wrapping up the required paperwork prior to the arrival of the next training class.

A knock at the office door.

"Come in," Michael called out distractedly.

McCarron stuck her head around the opened door. "Am I disturbing you?"

Michael was pleasantly surprised to see her. "Not at all. Come in."

She softly closed the door behind her, expectantly standing across the room from him.

"Did you receive your assignment?" Michael prompted.

She smiled. "I will be shuttling between Washington and the Pentagon."

"Top secret clearance," Michael posited.

She shrugged self-consciously. "What about you? Are you staying?"

Michael nodded. "I have been assigned another project."

"Another woman?"

Michael shook his head.

He smiled when she contentedly sighed and said under her breath, "Good."

Mairet eyed him shrewdly. "Now that I have graduated, we are just two people who work for the FBI, aren't we?"

"We are," Michael affirmed, serenely anticipating her point.

"Were you thinking about asking me out?"

"We have already been out," Michael reminded her, shamelessly trifling with her.

"And I enjoyed myself very much."

He matched her candor. "So did I."

"Are you planning on asking me again?" she persisted.

Michael tilted his head and paused contemplatively. "I am considering it."

She made an impatient face. "While we're both young?"

Michael stood, walked around his desk and perched on the front, long fingers cupped under the edge. "Would you like to join me for dinner tonight at my new place?"

He had leased a condominium that suited his tastes in Woodbridge, a high-end community located fourteen miles from Quantico.

"We'll celebrate your graduation."

"And your renewed contract," Mairet appended, thrilled that he was going to stay.

When she fidgeted by the office door, Michael goaded, "Why are you standing over there?"

She grinned sheepishly and walked to stand before him.

"I am no knight in shining armor, Mairet," Michael cautioned kindly, attempting to dispel any remaining adolescent notions she may be harboring.

Mairet accepted that Michael was more often than not emotionally remote—guarded. However, there were, on rare occasions, sparks of sensuous light in his eyes—convincing her to risk her heart and faithfully tend the embers that may someday flare between them.

"You are to me," she admitted delicately.

"Mairet, if you want a family..." Michael began regrettably, determined to be honest with her from the beginning.

"What I want is a love affair," she interrupted confidently. "I want you to see me in a little black dress with high heel shoes...and some indecent lacey underthings."

Look out.

The more worldly women of the graduating class had generously gathered Mairet under their wings, and promptly divested her of any vestigial innocence. They had insisted on a shopping excursion that she purchase feminine trappings designed to not only disarm but also vanquish unsuspecting members of the male species.

Michael conceded with warmth, "That would be something to see."

Mairet took his square jaws between her hands. "Thanks to you." She kissed his full lips with tender regard and great care.

Michael could not remember receiving a sweeter kiss.

Mairet heard the hum of approval deep in his throat.

She parted from him and held out her hand, now all business. "Your cell phone."

Michael frowned, leaning forward slightly. "What?"

"I need your cell phone."

Bemused, Michael took it from his inside jacket pocket and handed it to her. She pressed a series of buttons and then saved her cell number under Contacts. She disconnected and returned his phone. "Text me with the time and the directions to your place."

"I will pick you up."

She shook her head, following the instructions of her wily classmates to the letter. Far better if he opened his front door and first beheld her framed within it—like a dazzling full-length portrait. Much bigger impact.

"I will see you there," she demurred mysteriously.

She had almost reached the door when, unable to resist, Michael intuitively called after her, "Did you practice that?"

All artifice fell away from her as she grinned, eyes bright and telling. "I did! What do you think?"

Michael laughed quietly, disarmed by her admission. "Excellent. Very effective."

She shrugged happily. "Thanks."

When she had closed the door behind her, Michael shook his head and laughed again.

He got up with a revived sense of purpose and a lighthearted mood. If he was going to cook a traditional Korean meal for Mairet, he had better finish his reports and do some grocery shopping.

A Continent Conquered

March 2007
Woodbridge, Virginia

MICHAEL FINISHED DINNER PREPARATIONS IN the spacious gourmet kitchen of his recently leased condominium, satisfied their meal would keep until he and Mairet were ready to dine.

He hesitated and frowned. Was that a knock at the door? Another set of raps, this time a bit louder—more confident.

He opened the front door to Mairet McCarron.

Speechless, he stepped back to admire the sight of her—tailored coat and gloves, sheer black hosiery and stiletto heels, and shiny chestnut hair curling over the tops of her shoulders.

Mairet derived great satisfaction from the appreciation evident in Michael's eyes. Her all-knowing mentors had brilliantly schooled her, and she would kiss each one of them—whether they liked it or not—when she saw them again.

"Good evening," she chirped, breaking the spell.

As always, Michael maintained his poise, handsome in a teal long-sleeve knit shirt and rich beige tailored slacks.

"Good evening," he responded, widening the door in an invitation to enter.

Mairet's bright brown eyes surveyed the fine furnishings and amenities in the newly built 1,700 square foot condominium. "Well now...this is something, isn't it?"

"May I take your coat and gloves?" Michael inquired, holding out the smooth, finely veined hands that never failed to draw Mairet's admiring gaze.

More accustomed to the roughened and calloused hands of the working class, she often mused that Michael's might be those of an artist, or a scholar. Or, more probable, a young man blessed with a gentle upbringing.

"Mairet?" Michael prodded her from her reverie. "Your coat?"

Mairet glanced down, as if the thought of taking off her coat had not occurred to her. She removed her gloves and placed them along with her petite, delicately beaded handbag on Michael's upturned palms. Unhurried, she worked top to bottom to release the broad and shiny black buttons.

"Yes," she finally thought to say with a shy smile, and thanked him.

Michael chuckled. Her Irish was showing—perhaps more pronounced when she was nervous. She had said *tanks* instead of *thanks.*

He placed the bag and gloves on the foyer table and hung her coat in a nearby closet.

"Would you care for a glass of wine?"

She hummed and nodded. "Lovely."

He poured a Chardonnay while her eyes took in the elegant table setting for dinner and the many small, colorful, and varied side dishes arrayed on the kitchen island counter.

"You prepared all of this yourself?" she asked with wide eyes and a hint of reverence.

"I did," Michael affirmed, handing her a long-stemmed glass beginning to frost on the outside from the chill of the wine.

"I can't cook," she admitted shamefaced. "I never learnt how."

Michael nodded his understanding. He was not surprised given her childhood and her ensuing concentration on academics.

He gestured to the living area where a fire burned brightly. "Let's enjoy the fire."

Mairet stood to one side of the fireplace, toasting her backside, while Michael eased onto the mustard-colored couch, masculine with its richly textured fabric, clean and functional lines.

He enjoyed a peaceful moment in which to drink Mairet in—pairing her pleasing appearance with the buttery Chardonnay on his palate.

The red-orange glow of the fire burnished her hair to a coppery chestnut. Her full figure nearly burst the sleek confines of her little black dress, the hem hugging high on her smooth thighs. Nicely shaped legs and ankles.

Michael thought back to her earlier mention of some indecent lacey underthings. He was intrigued.

Mairet suffered the sharp twinges of nerves, an accelerating heartbeat, and a flush of heat in her cheeks as Michael leisurely appraised her from head to toe and back again.

She cautioned herself to refrain from fidgeting and remain focused. "Michael?" she ventured.

He inclined his head slightly. "Yes?" His voice was low and mellow.

"You made mention of something this afternoon..."

"Which was?" he prompted when she hesitated.

"You said something about...if I wanted a family."

She observed his shoulders stiffened and his expression assume a serious aspect.

Michael did not hesitate—did not spare either her or himself. "I cannot father a child," he stated bluntly, holding her eyes steady with his own.

She shook her head, bemused. "Do you mean to say that you could not accept, care for, or love a child?"

Regalo immediately leaped into Michael's mind. "No. I mean that my body is incapable of creating a child with a woman."

Michael's heart sank when she lowered her gaze and fell silent.

At last, in a quietly thoughtful voice, she offered, "I was only a child myself when I was tasked with watching over the younger children in my tenement." She reengaged Michael's gaze. "Caring for children is a solemn and worrisome responsibility."

He nodded. "Yes, it is."

"It is a full-time and lifelong responsibility."

Once again, he nodded in agreement.

"I respect those who are willing to make that sacrifice."

Michael gave her his full attention when she took a deep breath—as if screwing up her courage to say what was to come next.

"My Aunt and Uncle McCarron had a houseful of children, yet they took me in...fed and clothed me, educated me, protected me, and nourished my soul. More importantly, they loved me as if I was one of their own."

Michael's eyes shined with respect for her while he listened, the muscles across his back and shoulders releasing some of their tension.

Mairet charmed him with a wistful smile. "I love them no less because they are not my Mam and Da. You might say...because of that very reason...I love them more."

"So, tell me," Michael raised the subject, "what is it that you want for yourself?"

Mairet was pleased that he cared enough to ask, warming to the subject. "For now, I simply want a man."

Michael reflexively laughed before he could quell the impulse. Her artless candor nearly always caught him off guard.

"Not just any man, Michael," she lightly scolded him. "A bold and steadfast man. One who will allow himself to touch and be touched, who will freely take his pleasure in me and with me."

Michael admired her conviction—her realization of who she was and what she wanted. This was no dreamy-eyed schoolgirl who stood before him, but a determined and sensual woman.

Mairet noticed with gratification the aspect of arousal now softening Michael's features.

"So, Michael," she ventured, a bit breathless, "what is it that you want?"

He hesitated.

Why?

In good conscience, he could not cite Cara. They had not spoken since he left South Korea. Perhaps because she was reciprocating the same time, space, and freedom he was granting her. Or, perhaps, her silence was testimony to her resentment of his perceived abandonment of her.

In any case, Michael recognized that there was more distance between them than mere geography.

So, what was holding him back?

He contemplated the woman standing before him—watching him run through his thoughts—her smile patient and encouraging.

Nothing. Nothing was holding him back. It was time for him to move on with his life, to end his loneliness and heal his heart.

He placed his wine glass on the end table adjoining the couch.

Mairet's watchful and curious gaze never left him as he rose and walked to stand before her. He took her wine glass from her grip and slid it on the wide mantelpiece.

Firelight flickered in the depths of his eyes as he gripped her shoulders in his hands. When he bent to kiss Mairet, her lips parted—desirous and willing.

Softly, eagerly, sweetly, she leaned into his body. Michael felt her hands caressing his back, their heat permeating his shirt and warming the skin beneath it.

When he withdrew, she sighed—savoring the kiss.

Her eyes popped open and she slyly gazed at Michael. "Well then, Michael Lee," she murmured teasingly, "is it your intention to claim this continent?"

An appreciative chuckle vibrated deep in Michael's chest.

"Plant your flag?" she incited whimsically.

This last audacious inducement pushed Michael well beyond his point of resistance.

Mairet gasped in delight when he took her face between his hands and vowed, "I claim thee, Mairet McCarron, for the good, peace, and happiness of my kingdom."

Without further word, he gripped her hand in his and led her up the stairs to the master bedroom suite that was his private haven from the demands of life and discontent of the world.

Tonight, it promised even greater contentment.

OH, HOW GENTLE, HOW TENDER he was.

Michael.

Mairet was enthralled by his even, gold-tan skin tones; his muscled chest and washboard stomach; his beautiful, smooth hands caressing her face, skimming over her shoulders, breasts, waist, and thighs; his sentient, admiring and respectful almond-shaped eyes; his encouraging smile when, at times, she became awkward or shy.

The man who had gained her esteem and respect over the past four months made certain—in his special instinctive and unselfconscious way—that she was ready to relinquish her virginity.

When she inspired him to continue, he whispered endearments in her ear, his breath warm and sweet. He protected her dignity—allowed an unhurried and mindful access to a part of her body not yet explored— time to adjust to this foreign and profoundly primal, yet inevitable, initiation of life.

Mairet studied with fascination his facial expressions when he was inside of her, the expressive and desirous tension of his features, the riveted and luminous shine in his eyes, his deeply intense and seemingly pleasurable climax when he could no longer hold back.

In the afterglow, Mairet gazed at a serenely sleeping Michael through a sultry and tranquilizing haze of sexual intoxication—her body throbbing with the enduring sensation of their encounter. Mind and spirit reeling with conflicting yet uplifting emotions, she realized how blessed she was that he had been her first.

She affectionately brushed her cheek against the smoothness of his chest. When he murmured in his sleep and reflexively drew her tighter within the circle of his arm, Mairet relinquished her heart to him with a sense of enlightened satisfaction and a soft sigh of contentment.

Michael.

Madame Chang

아홉

9

Confession

April 2007
Seoul, South Korea

CARA WAS ALWAYS DELIGHTED TO dine with Madame Chang in her tastefully appointed penthouse. Madame was an extraordinary host, an engaging conversationalist, and an interested and supportive friend.

This evening, Cara had accepted Madame's invitation in a rare opportunity to be on her own and entertained away from the Moon family estate.

A local and world-acclaimed culinary chef prepared the gourmet cuisine. Madame's houseman of twenty years perfectly executed the table service. The wine poured throughout the meal was from prized vintages.

After dinner, the two women relaxed in the expansive living area with a decanter of very aged and mellow Courvoisier.

Cara stood before the floor to ceiling windows of the penthouse, unusually preoccupied and introspective, blinded to the spectacular nightscape of Seoul.

After some perceptive prompting from Madame, Cara confided her frustration with her uncertain and quiescent existence since returning to South Korea.

Cara admitted, in all fairness, that Moon had attempted to keep her from languishing from boredom. He arranged a trip to Jeju Island for her, Regalo, his sister and her husband. He encouraged Sang Hee to include her in her many and varied social and philanthropic activities.

Yet, the one thing that Cara craved most—the one thing he seemed incapable of giving her—was himself.

"Would you consider coming back to the Agency?" Madame offered, skeptical that Cara would accept.

"I don't think Moon would approve of me spending that much time away from Regalo."

Madame fearlessly dived into troubled waters. "What about the divorce? Any news from Moon Hyo's attorney?"

Cara recounted Moon coming to her late one evening in her bedroom suite, softly knocking on her door and asking her permission to enter.

Stiffly, he conveyed the inability of his attorney to file a petition to abrogate the finalized divorce decree. The court denied it, referring the matter of alleged malpractice to civil court.

"I see," Cara had responded, equally rigid.

His eyes searched hers, begged her understanding and patience. "Another promise from me would only seem hollow. Know that I love you and want to spend the rest of my life with you...as my wife."

Cara stood silent, tears of frustration building behind her lashes.

Moon gently stroked her cheek with the knuckles of his fingers. "Stay with me, Cara," he beseeched her quietly. "Please."

Madame shook her head in wonder, aware that there was only one finespun thread connecting Cara to Korea—her love for Moon Hyo.

Cara's thoughts traversed the same path, wondering how long blind faith and love could endure. Love—such a fragile emotion—as easy to break, in a careless gesture, as a favorite glass bowl against a slate floor.

Madame ventured, "So, he spends his evenings with you and your son, and his family?"

After their argument, in deference to Cara's objections to his absences, Moon began to make a concerted effort to spend the early evenings with Cara and his son.

"We act like polite strangers," Cara brooded aloud. "Then he excuses himself to work in his study until the following morning."

"How exhausting."

Cara sadly studied Moon's appearance over the breakfast table most mornings before he reported to work at the Ministry. "You should see him, Madame…the way fatigue lines his eyes."

"Apart from your concern about his health, what else troubles you?"

Cara felt like a schoolgirl standing before the Headmistress, being encouraged to reflect upon a misdeed.

She was not about to allow her feelings to be trivialized. Her voice became ardent with her conviction. "This is not just his life, Madame, but our life. It has been seven months. Why must I be kept ignorant about his plans?"

Madame remained unruffled. "What if he is attempting to accomplish something that may result in his failure?"

Cara had not even considered that likelihood.

"He may prefer to fail privately," Madame proposed gently, familiar with the sense of pride instilled and so evident in the Korean male.

She sat back in her armchair, satisfied with the results of her investigation. "I am having difficulty finding fault with your Moon Hyo."

"I am no longer in control of my life…of anything," Cara quietly objected in dismay.

"Have you spoken with Moon Hyo about your feelings?"

Cara winced. "I tried…once." She recalled the disastrous results— her high-speed escape from Seoul and Moon drowning his sorrows in scotch. "He begged me to trust him…" Cara shook her head and squeezed her eyes closed, ashamed of her disloyalty. "How can I admit to him that I am…"

"Impatient."

"Having doubts," Cara corrected mildly.

Madame pursed her lips, eyeing Cara with doubts of her own.

Once before, Cara had been in a similar state of mind—her strength ebbing, overcome with misgivings about herself and the direction of her future. On that occasion, as well, it was largely due to her turbulent and inconstant relationship with Moon Hyo.

Cara dreamily gazed at the lights of the city. "How I envy your situation, Madame...relying on no one but yourself."

Madame confessed without hesitation, "I have a man." Warmed by the thought of him, she admitted, "One I have depended upon and loved since I was a young woman."

Cara swiveled from the scenic window to gape in shock at the woman she had admired and respected for nearly twenty years.

A woman, as it turns out, she did not know at all.

Humble Beginnings

1952
South Korea

IT WAS THE AFTERMATH OF World War II and the end of Japanese occupation when the Soviet Union supported Democratic People's Republic of Korea—North Korea—pushed south into the American supported Republic of Korea, engulfing almost the entire peninsula and cornering ROK forces in a small area surrounding Pusan.

To stop the advance of communism in South Korea, the United Nations sent military forces from fifteen member nations to the peninsula, with the United States dedicating the greatest number of troops.

Eleven months after the invasion, a squalling infant girl, just days old, was left on the doorstep of a Catholic convent in the less populated and mountainous northeastern region of South Korea.

Her mother, barely in her teens, could not bear the disgrace of her rape by an invading soldier, or her resultant pregnancy.

Bringing shame upon her family and shunned by her village, she gave birth to the baby in an ignorant, agonizing, and protracted labor in a cave where she used to play as a child with her brothers and sisters.

She limped seven miles to the convent—her traditional white skirt, *chima,* stained with the umbilical cord blood that had dried on her legs—and bid a tearful goodbye to her newborn daughter.

In a nearby mountain stream, the young woman waded into the icy-cold depths of a still, deep-water pool. She became hypothermic in a matter of minutes. Her frail and exhausted body peacefully drifted downward—like a withered leaf caste off from the branch of a tree—to rest on the sandy bottom. There, her spirit broke free, gratefully released from the heartache of her short and ill-fated life.

UNAWARE OF THE HISTORY LEADING to her birth, and the tragic suicide of her mother, the child came to assume that her illegitimacy was dishonorable, resenting it for its commonness.

The name the nuns had given her was perfunctory and utilitarian. When she was old enough to resent this, too, she would only answer to the name of Hyun-Ae—one she had chosen herself—in part, meaning smart and clever.

Many, though not all, of the children who lived at the convent shared her circumstances. Yet, she remained separate from them, content in her own company, taking comfort in her faith by attending Mass every day.

She excelled in her studies, particularly in mathematics, and garnered the attention of a scholarly teacher born in mainland China. Recognizing her intelligence and potential for distinction, the young nun accelerated Hyun-Ae's studies, pushing her faster and further than her parochial school classmates.

The young nun surreptitiously taught Hyun-Ae the Mandarin dialect so that she may once again have the pleasure of speaking in her mother tongue. The latter was an admittedly frivolous and self-serving endeavor, for which the young nun begged forgiveness in her daily vespers.

When Hyun-Ae had attained the age of twenty, the sisters of the convent sought to keep her among them, to apply her keen mind and spiritual conviction to their young and impressionable flock.

One soft and early summer day, Mother Superior—a reserved yet compassionate woman—interviewed Hyun-Ae for just that purpose.

Hyun-Ae bowed deeply and expressed her profound gratitude to Mother Superior for providing her food, shelter, and an education over the past twenty years—but respectfully declined.

Mother Superior was dismayed though not surprised. This young woman had a wanderlust in her eyes and the intelligence and confidence to go out in the world—to succeed.

"What will you do?" Mother Superior asked with sincere interest. "Where will you go?"

Hyun-Ae smiled. "Whatever I must. Wherever I wish." She turned back to Mother Superior when she had reached the door. "When I am prosperous, I will not forget you. You will have whatever you need for your convent and your school."

Mother Superior nodded and graced her with a knowing smile. This was not a baseless boast but an honorable vow. Of this, she had no doubt. "Thank you, Hyun-Ae."

Hyun-Ae left the convent with a letter of introduction from her Chinese instructor and enough money to board a ship bound for Taiwan where she could live modestly for two weeks—three weeks if she were very careful. There, she would meet her teacher's younger brother, an accountant in the country's capitol, the City of Taipei.

"You are leaving a sheltered life in the mountains for a much different kind of life in a metropolitan city," her teacher cautioned her, tears in her eyes. She was going to miss the orphan, her protégé, whom she had come to love. "You will need all of your faith to stay strong. All of your common sense not to be swindled. Do you understand?"

Hyun-Ae nodded.

"Are you ready to begin your life?"

Hyun-Ae threw her arms around her beloved teacher and held her tightly. "Yes, dear Sister. I am ready."

So much noise, so much traffic on crowded streets, so much haste to get from place to place. Taipei overwhelmed Hyun-Ae at first. She took time to sit on a street bench, to put things in perspective, and watch the world sweep by her.

People rushed past, some sophisticated and well dressed—others clearly of meaner status and class. They were people, just like her, whose prospects may be better or worse. She became calmer, determined.

Hyun-Ae stood, checked her appearance in a mirrored vending machine on the street, and entered the front door of a three-story office building whose address her teacher had provided. She was ready to present herself to her potential employer, Lin Hong—to live the life of an independent and self-sufficient woman.

Mr. Chang

1949-1980
Taipei, Taiwan

CHANG. A NAME HE HAD ASSUMED. Born a lowly peasant in a farming village in the Hubei Province in central China, known as the Land of a Thousand Lakes, he grew into a strong and ambitious young man with little conscience—a weakness he could not afford.

He escaped from mainland China within months of its fall to communism in 1949 and Mao Zedong's announcement of the birth of the Communist People's Republic of China. He swam ashore in choppy seas from a refuge boat, nearly drowning, under the radar of the newly ensconced and empowered Taiwan Garrison Command—two months before the declaration of martial law by the vanquished forces of the Republic of China now residing in, and in control of, Taiwan.

It would become the longest imposition of martial law by a regime anywhere in the world at that time—thirty-eight years. The Kuomintang, or KMT, the Chinese Nationalist Party led by Chang Kai-shek, suppressed communism and independent political activities in Taiwan by censoring media, prohibiting unlawful assembly and punishing rebellion or opposition—real or perceived. This period of history, referred to as "White Terror," wreaked havoc on the intellectually and socially elite of Taiwan, with thousands of them disappearing, thrown in prison, or executed.

Yet, Chang prospered.

A brilliant strategist, Chang aligned himself with powerful and lawless factions in Taipei, seducing or corrupting the ranks of the regime within his sphere of influence. As he amassed his fortune and his syndicate rose in power, he was consistent in his expedience to kill his enemies—or his allies.

Deprived as a child, he reveled in every form of debauchery and excess—women, liquor, food, tobacco, occasionally opium and heroin—

sometimes driving him to temporary madness. He was corpulent and seemingly jovial, often underestimated—but only once.

Dreaded for his eerie knowledge of the activities of his rivals, and his precognition to events about to unfold, his adversaries little suspected that Chang's loyal and well-compensated eyes on the street watched them wherever they traveled—from boardrooms to cardrooms, from the swankest private gambling clubs in Taipei to the most sordid and repulsive joy houses.

He was known by many names—Old Wizard, The Shark, Yellow Death. But in his presence, you lowered your eyes, bowed in respect, and called him Mr. Chang.

Daan

1971
Taipei, Taiwan

O LD CHANG. NOW IN HIS early sixties, weakened by ill health and threats against his empire from competitors and politically ambitious detractors within the regime, Chang retained an attorney who had come highly recommended and practiced out of an elegant law office in the more affluent district of Taipei.

The lawyer was a soft-spoken aristocrat whose family was well connected and clever enough to survive the purge by the KMT of the moneyed and intellectual in Taiwan.

His confidence-inspiring presence reminded Chang of an older brother who had died of consumption when they lived like urchins on the streets of Peking.

The young attorney had a remarkable foresight, recall of acquired facts, sang-froid and grace that soothed Chang's volatile nature. The old gangster came to rely upon him, calling him Daan. In Mandarin, it meant *the answer—the key—the solution.*

Daan became Chang's eyes, ears, and voice—his trusted advisor. He was known for his accommodating smile, reasonable and conciliatory words during negotiations—feared for his promise that, once given, he would not recant by either bargaining or pleading.

As A YOUNG MAN, DAAN had yielded to the accepted convention of his culture and conceded to an arranged marriage.

Two families of great affluence and social prominence—determined to keep their wealth intact and their bloodlines pure—matched their enchanting daughter with their handsome son, which they felt sure would bring beautiful grandchildren and good fortune to their respective houses.

Not altogether indifferent to his chosen bride, Daan married Xiu. She was, without question, as fine and beautiful as her namesake. Unfortunately, she was irreversibly spoiled and unabashedly haughty.

Early in their marriage—pouting, throwing temper tantrums, cursing Daan with every abusive name she could call to mind—Xiu displayed an exponential insecurity and jealousy over his attention to other women, no matter how innocent, and whether at a family, social, or business occasion.

Capitulating to family expectations and pressure, they brought into their joyless world two children in five years—a boy and a girl.

A second trimester into her third pregnancy, and convinced that Daan was having an affair with a longtime family friend, Xiu taunted Daan by teetering over the edge of the sweeping staircase in their home.

Recognizing too late her malicious intent, Daan shouted a warning to Xiu and sprinted down the hallway to restrain her. Almost within his grasp, she allowed herself to fall, a glint of satisfying revenge in her beautiful and disturbed eyes.

Miraculously, both she and the baby survived the headlong fall that deposited them in a twisted bundle at the base of the stairway. However, the infant girl was born five weeks premature and suffered cognitive impairment from her pre-natal trauma.

Given the name Chen Chae—meaning tenderhearted—she was destined to live her life as a simple, loving, sweet being. The apple of her father's eye.

There would be no more children—no longer a shared marital bed. Only a grinding daily routine, a frail civility between the couple when in the presence of their children and respective families.

Believing that his heart had died—bludgeoned by unrestrained privilege, jealousy, and madness—Daan concentrated on his legal practice and his most profitable client, Old Chang.

However, Daan was destined to meet someone, atypical of his tastes and entirely unanticipated, who would prove him wrong—who would restore both his heart and his spirit.

Opportunity Knocks

1975
Taipei, Taiwan

Who made these suggestions?" Old Chang demanded of his accountant who fidgeted nervously before the warlord's ivory-inlaid desk. For emphasis, Chang used his pudgy finger to stab at the columns of numbers before him.

Lin Hong, the owner of the professional accountancy firm who had overseen Chang's financial affairs for the past twelve years, felt beads of sweat break out on his forehead.

He had given the firm's most substantial and lucrative account to his sister's protégé, the Korean woman, Hyun-Ae, after she had shared her ideas—impressed him—with ways in which to increase return on investment and legally hide more of Mr. Chang's assets.

Since the death of Chang Kai-shek in early April of that year, Hyun-Ae had monitored the loosening of the martial law noose around Taiwan's neck. Relaxation of certain restrictions presented favorable possibilities to a nimble and innovative mind.

Mr. Lin was the boss and, having given Hyun-Ae permission to proceed with her strategies, was prepared to direct Chang's presumed dissatisfaction and anger toward himself.

"I...I did sir," he stuttered.

Chang sat back in his chair, glittering eyes narrowed and appraising. He bared his yellow and snaggled teeth in a cynical sneer. "No, you did not."

Chang trusted this man never to steal from him—he did not have the balls. However, Chang was also clear on the concept that Lin Hong's lack of ingenuity was a double-edged sword—he possessed little vision or real skill in his chosen profession.

"Bring him to me," Chang tersely commanded with a dismissive wave of his hand.

"Her," Lin Hong ventured timidly.

"What did you say?" Chang snapped.

"*Her*, sir," Lin Hong repeated with increased confidence. "Her name is Hyun-Ae. She was my sister's pupil at a convent in South Korea…her protégé. She has been employed with my firm for three years."

"Then bring *her* to me," Chang said with a lecherous smile.

"Yes, Mr. Chang," Lin Hong complied, bowing his head—now questioning his wisdom in bringing the reserved and bookish Hyun-Ae to the old devil's attention.

HYUN-AE STOOD BEFORE THE DESK of Old Chang, returning his stare without blinking.

"A mere woman…and an ugly one at that," Chang spit out in contempt. "And you have the audacity to change my accounts?"

She bowed deeply from the waist and responded quietly, "Yes, sir."

"Look at me, girl," he growled.

Composed, Hyun-Ae did as he commanded.

"You are not frightened of me?" he inquired with obvious amusement.

"Yes, sir. You frighten me."

"You and I will get along much better if you do not lie," he warned.

"Yes, sir."

"Well?"

"Your displeasure frightens me."

"Who said I was displeased?"

"You called me ugly."

"You are!" he said with an astounded bark of laughter.

"You do not approve of what I have done to your accounts."

"Who said so?"

She was abashed. "But…I…"

"Don't stand there stammering, girl. Come here." He motioned for her to join him behind his desk.

When she had done so, he pointed to a ledger of accounts. "Look at this. Tell me if I should invest in this project."

Hyun-Ae smelled the sour decay of his body, the putrid stench of rotting teeth on his breath. Surely, the repugnant stench of evil personified. She pushed aside these unpleasant realizations as she stood by the old gangster's side.

Fortunately, she did not have to study the account ledger for long. She was familiar with this construction company. One of her peers at the accountancy firm had sought her help to reconcile the books. A careless and talentless hand had manipulated them.

To confirm her suspicions, Hyun-Ae had gone to the construction site of the newly designed and rising five-story building, lingering around the worksite to overhear conversations, observe delivery of substandard supplies at overblown prices, and the exchange of graft money between hands. The project was over budget and the infrastructure underbuilt with inferior products. The building would be unlikely to withstand the frequent typhoons and earthquakes that occurred in Taiwan.

"I cannot recommend it, sir," she reported respectfully.

Old Chang frowned up at her. "You have not even given it serious consideration. How can you say this?"

"I have given it serious consideration, sir. Before I came to be in your office."

"It was brought to your attention previously?"

"Yes, Mr. Chang."

"How? Why? By whom?"

"Within the realm of my responsibilities at the firm, sir. That is all I can say."

"The hell it is!" Old Chang exclaimed.

"Yes, sir," she affirmed with a quiet and steady conviction. "The hell it is."

Her reply brought forth a belly laugh from Old Chang. He laughed, and laughed, and laughed, until he was swiping at tears running down his cheeks.

"Sit down," he gestured to a chair before his desk.

Again, she did as he commanded.

He seemed to be looking at her with different eyes. "I shall have need of you, miss…"

"Hyun-Ae, sir."

"Hmmm," he said, regarding her speculatively. "I like your mind. The way it works. Your powers of observation, your creative vision… and discretion."

She bowed her head.

"How is it that you are not as ugly to me now?" Old Chang ruminated in amazement.

Mud Face

1975
Taipei, Taiwan

O LD CHANG'S MEN SNIGGERED BEHIND his back. Among themselves, they referred to his new wife as "Mud Face."

An imprudent and dangerous undertaking.

When he overheard them, Daan discouraged their foolishness with a withering glance.

"Wait," they forewarned him with sly whispers. "Wait until you meet her. You will see."

Old Chang had stunned his brethren in crime when he had married a Korean woman in her twenties, a bookkeeper employed by his accountancy firm, in a private ceremony attended only by the officiant, he, and his bride.

Old Chang offered no professions of love or explanations for his puzzling—and seemingly sudden—decision. He proclaimed that Madame Chang would be at his side and consulted on important financial matters of the organization.

In Old Chang's estimation, this was all that anyone needed to know. He expected, and received, their cooperation. Everyone beholden to, or within the influence of, the old gangster's syndicate paid their respects to Madame Chang and kept their opinions to themselves.

Shortly after the marriage, Old Chang summoned Daan to his office and, in his haste to get right down to business, off-handedly introduced his Korean bride, Hyun-Ae.

Instead of her wide-set, small dark brown eyes, Daan saw intelligence and humor sparkling in their depths. Instead of the plain way she braided her hair and coiled it at the nape of her neck, he saw its luster and thickness, imagining it loose about her shoulders. Instead of her placid expression, he discerned a fierce pride and clarity on the caprice of providence.

She was present but unnoticed, sturdy yet graceful, humble yet confident, unremarkable in every way save one—she accepted herself as she was and made neither excuses nor apologies.

Soon after meeting Madame Chang and spending time in her presence, Daan realized that she was a freshwater pearl—perhaps not as prized as the cultured pearls of the sea, but just as lustrous and luminous.

10
Ching Shih

1980
Taipei, Taiwan

O LD CHANG WAS DEAD.
Hundreds attended his funeral. Former allies and adversaries alike paid their respects. All eyes, sparkling with venomous speculation, focused on a composed and regal Madame Chang—taking her measure.

Now, the real test of her affiliation with Old Chang was at hand—and the empire he had crafted with the black arts of treachery, ruthlessness, and bloodshed in the balance.

THE EMISSARY OF ONE OF Old Chang's contentious allies stood before the desk of Madame Chang, squirming under her direct and unblinking gaze.

He had come at the bidding of his master, Benjamin Wong, to arrange a meeting between the two factions—to propose a redistribution of territories allegedly promised to him by Old Chang before his death— to collect on a promise.

Daan leaned over and spoke quietly, firmly, into Madame Chang's ear. "They are testing you."

Madame Chang glanced up, startled by his boldness—discomposed by his nearness.

"It is time to show strength," Daan advised.

Madame discreetly turned her face away from Wong's emissary and murmured, "I do not wish to engage these men."

"Respectfully, Madame," Daan persisted patiently, "whether you wish it or not, it must be done."

Madame abruptly waved away the emissary and her private secretary. "A moment, please."

Her secretary's eyes widened in surprise, hesitant to brush aside propriety and leave Madame alone in a room with a man—even if he was her attorney—absolutely forbidden when Old Chang was alive.

Secretary Lau noted the expression of outright authority on the countenance of Madame Chang and, with it, the expectation of his obedience. He quickly altered his attitude and shooed Wong's emissary from the office, softly closing the door behind them.

Madame swiveled in her chair and looked with sternness upon her deceased husband's advisor. "Speak your mind."

Daan casually extracted a slim gold cigarette case from the inside pocket of his impeccably tailored suit coat. Madame nodded when he asked for her permission to smoke, waving away his offer of a cigarette.

He lit the cigarette, politely blowing the smoke toward the ceiling. "Have you ever heard the true story of Ching Shih?"

Madame Chang shook her head.

"She was thought to be one of the most successful pirates in history."

Madame Chang expelled a bemused breath of air. "Pirate?"

Daan grinned, enjoying her reaction, relishing the parallel he was about to draw.

"Her birth name was Shi Xiang Gu. Unlucky in her early life, she was born into a poor family in the Guangdong Province of China. As a young girl, she worked as a prostitute on a floating brothel in Canton to support herself. Her luck changed for the better, however, when pirates captured her and, in the early 1800s, she married a pirate by the name of Zheng Yi, a descendent of notorious thieves. He commanded the Red Flag Fleet, with hundreds of ships and thousands of men.

"When her husband died six years later, Gu became known as Ching Shih, widow of Zheng.

"Everything Yi built was at risk of falling apart. However, Ching Shih was quick to seek help in assuming the leadership of the Red Fleet. She enlisted the aid of her in-laws and Chang Pao, a fisherman's son who had been adopted by Yi, to help her with the day-to-day operations of the legion pirate army."

Madame's nod was barely discernable. So, this is where he was leading her.

Daan remained poised under Madame's pointed and perceptive stare.

"The two proved to be a formidable team. Three years later, the Red Fleet had grown to thousands of sailing vessels with over eighty thousand crewmembers. Ching Shih set up her own government, established laws, and even taxes. Disobeying her laws resulted in beheading. She came to be feared and respected from as far away as Great Britain.

"Some nine years later, Ching Shih and her fleet were offered amnesty if they promised to quit the piracy business.

"To be granted amnesty, however, a pirate must bend a knee." Here, Daan paused to smile, marking the stubborn pride of Madame Chang. "Which was considered a sign of shameful surrender.

"So Ching Shih employed a shrewd scheme in compromise. With Pao, and a retinue of women and children in tow, she marched into the office of official Zhang Bai Ling and requested that he marry her and Pao.

"He did, and the newlyweds knelt to thank him."

Madame Chang chuckled, appreciating the ingenuity of Ching Shih—and Old Chang's attorney.

"It is said that Ching Shih retired with her new husband, her dignity, and all of her unlawful gains from piracy," Daan summarized in conclusion. "She lived to be nearly seventy."

"I will see Wong's emissary now," Madame Chang abruptly announced, turning back to her desk.

Daan bowed, unperturbed by her dismissal. "Yes, Madame."

A Profession of Faith

1980
Taipei, Taiwan

Two weeks later, Madame Chang was preparing for a joint meeting that she had proposed—with the assistance of Daan—among Old Chang's acquaintances, friends, allies, competing crime lords, and their legal representatives. All were standing by, waiting for the call that would announce the location and commencement of the gathering.

There were strict rules of attendance. Invitees would have only one hour to respond. Arriving late would exclude the tardy individual from the meeting room. Security would be tight. Participants would be subject to an electronic sweep for weapons and promptly relieved of those in their possession.

Madame gracefully rose from her executive chair and walked with purpose around her massive desk. "It is time," she said to Daan. "Place the calls."

Daan nodded to an assistant who swiftly retired to a command center filled with a dozen men and telephones. Each man in the room received a slip of paper with an address of a venue in Taipei and instructed to call their assigned telephone numbers.

Madame Chang exited her office, shadowed by her flighty secretary, Lau.

Daan held his ground, bowing deeply as she left the room, eyes respectfully cast down.

There had been no indication from Madame whether she wished him to attend the meeting. He made no assumptions.

Of course, he would serve at her pleasure—accompany her or stay behind. The latter was not his preference. He believed he could provide guidance and moral support to the circumspect and tenacious woman—if she but asked.

Madame Chang and her retinue proceeded down the hallway. Daan heard the hollow echo of their footsteps against the intricately designed parquet flooring stall and then halt. Evidently, Madame had just realized he was not among them. There was a brief hesitation. A light feminine tread retraced the path to the office.

Daan resumed his bow—eyeing the tips of his highly polished hand-made shoes—just as Madame Chang's presence filled the doorway.

His pride prevented him from making this easier for her—allowing her expectation that he would dance on attendance.

He felt her piercing gaze, heard her draw an inward breath as if she were about to speak.

Without uttering a word, she rejoined her group. A muted conversation ensued, followed by the purposeful stride of another pair of shoes approaching the office.

A delicate cough.

Daan raised his bowed head to look upon Secretary Lau standing in the doorway.

"Sir, Madame Chang requests that you accompany her to the meeting," Lau announced respectfully.

Daan smiled. Apparently, Madame found it less ignoble to task her secretary with the invitation. "As she wishes."

MADAME CHANG TOOK HER PLACE at the head of the oblong conference table in a private meeting room of a centrally located and respected international hotel.

Madame greeted the meeting attendees with a regal bow of her head. "Thank you for taking time from your businesses and personal lives to be here today. My participation in our meeting will not be long."

The thirteen men seated around the table shifted uncomfortably in their cushioned armchairs. Their legal representatives standing behind them surveyed the exits of the room in dread and suspicion. Should this be a trap to eliminate them, they would be helpless to defend themselves. They would all be dead.

If Madame Chang was aware of the uneasiness and tension in the room, she did not acknowledge it. "I am here today to assure you that the Chang organization will continue its operation. Any promises given by my deceased husband, once verified, will be honored."

Benjamin Wong, seemingly uncomfortable and not particularly pleased by Madame's announcement, dropped his gaze to the table when she cast a glance his way.

She beckoned Daan, standing to the left and behind her chair.

"As you are aware, Daan handled the day-to-day operations of the organization on behalf of my husband. Particularly after he was unable to do so himself."

The men around the table nodded knowingly—uncertainly.

"It is my wish that Daan continue in that capacity."

All eyes were riveted on Daan.

"He earned my husband's trust, and he has mine," Madame Chang stated unequivocally.

With that, she rose and smiled at the assembled group. "If you will excuse me gentlemen, I will leave you to your business."

She gestured to the chair she had just vacated at the head of the table for Daan to take his rightful place. She passed her even gaze around the meeting room.

"Understand this, gentleman." She glanced at a still-standing and composed Daan. "You will continue to give Daan your utmost respect and cooperation."

She inclined her head to no one in particular—to them all. "Good evening."

Secretary Lau hustled to open the door, and Madame Chang left the conference room and the group assembled there in a deafening silence.

Arguing Absolution

1980
Taipei, Taiwan

ALONE IN HER NEWLY RENOVATED apartment, Madame Chang luxuriated in a hot bath, powdered and perfumed her body, applied makeup to her face, attractively styled her hair, adorned herself with silky, feminine undergarments and finely woven gold jewelry.

It was a rare occasion when she thought of nothing but herself, celebrating the freedom to do as she wished, now that Chang was dead.

She was not so cruel as to be happy that he was dead, she was merely relieved. She had faithfully performed her duties to Old Chang. No one—not even her critics—could fault her for that.

OLD CHANG. HIS WHEEZING, STINKING breath. The teeth that required extraction, one by one, because they were rotting in his mouth.

His parchment-like skin, thin and pale—blue diseased veins bulging beneath.

His glittering dark eyes that so accurately detected deceit and fear—discerned weakness.

His swift and brutal retaliation for treachery and disloyalty—actual or imagined.

As he lay dying, quavering in terror, he begged the deities to spare him from the mythical ten courts and eighteen levels of Hell that promised an arduous and agonizing journey for criminals.

Specific and painful tortures awaited him. Boiling in a cauldron of oil, being sawn in half by demons, thrown into the flames of a volcano, crushed and pulverized in a stone mill—retribution for murderers and thieves, those who abused their power and subdued the weak, the corrupt who exploited loopholes in the law and engaged in nefarious business practices.

Withstanding the relentless and ruthless rigors of this gauntlet, Chang could perhaps atone for the crimes he had perpetrated in his life. Unless, because of the magnitude of his sins, he suffered banishment to the 18th level—from which there was no prospect of escape, redemption or reincarnation.

At the end, his mind hallucinated—plagued by shadowed and shrouded beings who circled his deathbed and whispered his birth name, rattling the chains they would coil around his body to paralyze and usher him to his torment.

Trusting no one, Old Chang demanded the execution of all who kept vigil over him—of those who had already died by his hand or command.

His death was a blessing.

DREAMY AND RELAXED, MADAME CAME from her bedroom and leisurely crossed the living area toward the bar.

She started in surprise, her breath catching in her throat.

Daan relaxed in a plush tan suede armchair—confident and quietly expectant.

Taipei City and the freshwater Danshui River—whose journey ended just beyond in the Taiwan Strait—shimmered as a brilliant backdrop to his handsome silhouette.

Madame fleetingly allowed that her heart pounding so fiercely against her breast was not entirely due to his bold and unexpected appearance.

Over the past months, she had become increasingly aware of Daan. His close proximity when he leaned over her shoulder—finely sculpted nose, strong jaw and unlined face next to hers—explaining a legal clause or requiring her signature on a document. The tone in which he spoke to her—as if it were an endearment. The way he looked at her—eyes expressive and approving.

Unaccustomed to evoking the awareness of the opposite sex, Madame found Daan's attentiveness unnerving—so pleasantly unsettling.

He said quietly, "I have a wife and a family."

"I am envious of neither your wife nor your life with your family," Madame admitted candidly. "I prefer my independence."

She laughed lightly at the foolish contradiction. "I just don't want to hear about them."

"Speak with me about your Christian God. I would like to know…"

"To know what?"

"I am a married man."

"Yes." She nodded soberly. "You are a married man."

He ventured mildly, "To know the pleasures of another woman other than my wife would, in your God's eyes, be a sin."

"For which you would burn in Hell for all eternity," she affirmed with certainty.

"And the woman with whom I shared pleasure? She, too, would burn for eternity?"

"Yes."

"Does your God not know my heart?"

"That does not matter."

"To whom?"

"To his Commandments."

"As prescribed by man?"

"As prescribed by Him."

"I see," Daan murmured, although his expression and the tenor of his voice disputed his words.

"And this God recognizes that I am just a man—of flesh and blood, fears and desires, sin and redemption?"

"Yes."

"As a married man, would it also be forbidden to lust for you in my thoughts?"

"Yes."

He stood and walked toward her.

She braced herself, wary of this dangerous game.

Circling her slowly, his brown eyes—liquid and shining—began to break down her barriers.

"How much more eternal damnation would there be, if any, to kiss your lips?" He lightly ran his thumb over her full lower lip. "To look at you with eyes filled with love and imagine the scent of your smooth skin?" He placed his hand over her vigorously beating heart. "To run my palms over your breasts, and feel them peak with pleasure?"

She blinked, as if coming out of a trance, willing herself to back away from him.

He captured her by the small of the back and enticed her forward, to stand between his knees as he perched on the high curved armrest of the tasteful sofa.

His eyes lowered to the belt that held together her silk robe. He slid it free of its light knot, exposing her bare midriff, her breasts, to his gaze.

"To dare placing my hand where your hips would thrust against it, taking no pleasure of my own but yours, until you called out my name with abandon and reverence...as if I were your God."

"You blaspheme," she objected in confusion, avoiding the seductive pools of his eyes.

"If I am damned by mere thought, and you as well, then let us seek the pleasure of each other, and damn us both...for surely in the judgment of your God, we will burn for the sin of one just as easily as the other."

He swept her in his arms, supporting the small of her back with his thigh. He freed her hair from its restraining and decorative fasteners, letting it cascade in a silken and shimmering waterfall over his monogrammed shirt cuffs embellished with 24K gold studs.

Cradling her head in his hand, his pleasant breath caressing her upturned face, he vowed, "In your office...in the Board Room...while engaged in your business...you are my Queen. I will always revere you as such."

He placed a soft and gentle kiss upon her breast, slid his warm, searching fingers over her flat belly and under her modest silk undergarment. "Here...when we are alone...I am Master."

This man persuaded her—with his tranquil assurance and steadfast allegiance—to leap, unafraid, over the precipice.

"Yes," she responded breathlessly, seeking his lips.

He withheld them. "Say it."

Caring nothing about her damnation or his, she responded to the man who had won her—heart and soul—who she knew would be her only love in this lifetime. She felt no shame or remorse for wanting Daan, believing that she would die with his name on her lips.

She granted what he demanded. "Here...you are Master."

As though confirming her instincts—validating her desires—Daan's warm, expressive gaze caressed her every feature, appreciating more than what his eyes beheld. Matching her accelerating heartbeat with his own, he thrilled her with the intimacy of his touch.

Her gasp was smothered by the ardent kiss of her devoted consort. Her forever love. Her Master.

Wake Up Call

April 1987
Taipei, Taiwan

Madame Chang and Daan, accompanied by his sweet and simple daughter, Chen Chae, relaxed in their favorite dining room in the quiet of late evening, relishing the rare occasion they could put business aside to speak of art, music, literature and philosophy. Envisioning traveling the world in the pleasure of each other's company. Anticipating a time when they could be together each day, every day, for as long as they lived.

"I know where I would like to visit, Papa," Chen Chae grinned happily.

Daan affectionately smiled at his daughter and teased, "I bet I can guess."

"Can you guess, Auntie?" Chen Chae gaily challenged Madame Chang.

Madame Chang brushed the tips of her beautifully manicured fingers against Chen Chae's smooth cheek. "I think I can, yes." The twelve-year old girl chattered about nothing else. "But do you want me or your Papa to answer?"

"Papa!" Chen Chae shouted excitedly. The genteel couple at the next table glanced their way in annoyance.

Daan ignored them. He knew, with Chen Chae fast approaching womanhood, that her childlike behavior was certain to draw ridicule and scorn from those who were unaware of her affliction. He was fiercely determined to protect his blithely unaware daughter—the innocent casualty of her parent's marital discord and her mother's vindictiveness—from these insensitive and intolerant people. The world if necessary.

He leaned toward his daughter and whispered, "Disneyland!"

She giggled and, following his lead, whispered, "You guessed, Papa!"

Daan glanced at his watch and shook his head. "It is late. It is time for you to be in bed."

Chen Chae skipped ahead of them out on the sidewalk, Daan guiding Madame Chang from the establishment with a protective and lingering hand against her lower back.

Their dispassionately efficient bodyguard, Hong, formerly Taiwan Garrison Command, awaited them outside. Now that Madame Chang had assumed leadership of the powerful Chang organization, Daan had insisted he hire a bodyguard for her protection.

Hong waved forward the driver who sat behind the steering wheel of the car parked a block away.

The car did not move.

Hong frowned. The driver was looking straight ahead. Surely, he had seen Hong beckon him.

Hong held up a staying hand to his charges. "Wait here, please."

Hong cautiously approached the car from the front passenger side. Still the driver stared straight ahead. Hong backed away, tilting his head to peer inside the vehicle.

The driver, an eager and trustworthy young disciple of the Chang organization, seemed unaware of Hong's presence. Hong circled around back, scrutinizing the body of the car as he mindfully walked around to the open driver's window. Closer inspection revealed blood seeping from under the driver's cap, running down his sideburn and blooming like a red rose on his left shoulder.

Hong shook his head in disgust and quickly made his way back to the trio waiting on the sidewalk in front of the restaurant.

Daan exchanged a look of comprehension with Hong. "Dead?"

"Yes, sir."

The muscles of Daan's jaw rippled with anger.

Hong hustled them toward the street where he flagged down passing taxis. He waved away the first three that pulled over and stopped at the curb. His excess of caution and due diligence made him the target of innovative curses from the brusquely dismissed drivers.

When the next taxicab he hailed pulled over, Hong leaned down to scrutinize the driver, making sure that the license photo on the dash matched the face behind the wheel.

Hong opened the back door of the cab. "I'll take care of things here."

In response to Madame's bewildered and apprehensive gaze, Daan nodded his reassurance and allowed her and Chen Chae to enter first.

Over his shoulder, he quietly ordered Hong, "I want to see you at my office first thing tomorrow morning."

Hong briskly bowed his head. "Yes, sir."

DAAN GAZED AT THE EXPLOSIVE device Hong had placed on his desk and unwrapped for his inspection.

Hong explained, "The bomb was magnetically attached to the undercarriage. The detonator was set to trigger when the doors were opened."

"My daughter was with us. My daughter!" Daan emphasized with righteous indignation.

He leaned back in his chair, fist clenched, knuckles blanched. "They expected us to walk to the car."

"Yes."

Hong further corroborated the scheme of the attempted assassination. "As a rule, nobody pays attention to the driver."

Daan knew exactly who had masterminded this power play—this attempt to displace Madame Chang and him from the Chang organization and appoint himself emperor.

Daan glanced up in fury at Hong. He wanted to hear it from him. "Who approached you?"

"Wong's man," Hong replied unflinchingly.

Benjamin Wong.

Daan nodded perceptively. He had anticipated that a mouthpiece of Wong's crew would attempt to bribe a close and trusted member of the Chang organization to look the other way. Fortune had smiled on him, Madame Chang, and his beloved Chen Chae, that they had approached Hong.

Daan hesitated and flashed an inquiring glance at Hong. "What did you just say?"

"Sir?"

"About the driver. Did you just say that nobody pays attention to the driver?"

Benjamin Wong.

He and Chang, both young and vigorous emigres from Mainland China, came up the ranks together in the chaotic and loosely organized street gangs of Taipei.

There is a common dogma—a shared attribute among those who are successful. What makes one person succeed when others do not is their willingness to do what others cannot or will not.

Old Chang was an adherent of Chinese military strategist Sun Tzu's treatise, *The Art of War*, written in the 6th Century B.C. In Chapter III, *Strategic Attack*, the general theorized, "It is said that if you know your enemies and know yourself, you will not be imperiled in a hundred battles...."

Old Chang knew Wong. He did not fear him. For Wong did not dirty his own hands to advance his empire. He was cunning but cowardly; rapacious but indolent; covetous of riches but gambled away his ill-gotten gains.

Wong did not know himself.

After Madame Chang relinquished the day-to-day operations of the organization to Daan, Wong wisely did not call attention to himself. He did not press his claim for the territory allegedly promised to him by Old Chang.

Instead, he plotted murder.

Zai Jian – Goodbye

April 1987
Taipei, Taiwan

CHEN CHAE CHATTERED GAILY, DANCING with excitement in Taipei International Airport while they waited to board their flight to South Korea. Madame had difficulty keeping her in bed the evening before, trying to coax her to sleep, to rest before their emigration to South Korea.

Immediately following their assassination attempt, Daan implored Madame Chang to return to the safety of her homeland and, tears glistening in his eyes, take Chen Chae with her—to love her and keep her safe from harm.

Madame agreed.

Chen Chae's doting father quieted her for a moment with a hug and a goodbye kiss. "You be a good girl for your Auntie," Daan fondly encouraged his daughter.

Madame smiled at the sweet spirited child and asserted with affection, "She is always a good girl."

"*Baba*, kiss Auntie goodbye, too!" Chen Chae entreatied.

Her father lightheartedly teased his treasured daughter. "Should I?"

"Yes!" Eyes wide and innocent, Chen Chae looked with reverence upon Madame Chang. "I love Auntie," she professed with pure adoration.

"I am very glad," Daan responded with mock seriousness. "Because I do, too."

He embraced Madame and, sharing with her an expressive and soulful gaze, kissed her lips with tenderness and longing.

As always, he made her breathless.

It aggrieved Daan to say goodbye—to see his regret and misery mirrored on the face of the woman he cherished.

"When things are more settled here, I will come to you."

"This obligation you have undertaken on my behalf," Madame began solemnly, "can easily be passed on to an administrator of your choosing. I trust your judgment."

"You realize as well as I that the end of martial law in the coming months will create new challenges as well as opportunities."

"Do you trust the rumors?" Madame inquired skeptically.

"I have it on good faith," Daan replied, privy to the decisions being made within the currently purposeless and crumbling regime.

He noted the disappointment that surfaced in Madame's expression. "You have entrusted me to legitimize the organization and restore honor to the name of Chang," he gently reminded her. "I will not abandon that assignment."

He caressed Madame's smooth cheek. "I will not abandon you. I will look after your interests to the best of my abilities."

"Then I am confident I am in good hands," Madame conceded, although with little enthusiasm. She would have preferred that Daan accompany her and Chen Chae to South Korea.

It was as if he read her mind. "I shall never be far from you. I shall always seek every opportunity to be with you. I shall always love you."

Madame nodded, yet strangely ill comforted. "Promise me you will be careful."

He smiled encouragingly at his Queen and promised, "I will be careful."

Retribution

May 1987
Taipei, Taiwan

H E STEPPED FROM HIS OFFICE, on his way to his favorite gaming club. The Fates were forecast to be generous, and Benjamin Wong was not one to turn his back on the Fates.

He rode the elevator to the lobby with his secretary, wordlessly waving him off as he left the building.

It was raining.

The door attendant bowed, offering to shelter Wong with an umbrella to his car waiting down the street.

Preoccupied, Wong impatiently waved him away as well, purposefully striding the short distance to the luxury automobile idling at the curb. He entered the vehicle from the left rear side and slid in on the fine tooled leather bench seat behind the driver.

A gaily wrapped and ribboned package awaited him. He smiled. His wife remembered their wedding anniversary.

He frowned. Wasn't that next month?

Curious, he tore away the bow and wrapping and lifted the lid. A heavy linen notepaper, folded in half, lay on top. The contents beneath were obscured by tissue paper.

The elegantly penned note read *I believe this is yours.*

Wong pushed back the tissue paper and gasped. An explosive device filled the box.

Wong had just seconds to comprehend that the bomb on his lap was the same one he had ordered planted under Daan's automobile. But more importantly, and perhaps fatally, he had underestimated Daan's capacity to be ruthless and vindictive.

The driver behind the wheel smoothly swiveled in his seat—arm fully extended. In his grip was a pistol fastened with a silencer, steadily and reliably aimed at the head of Benjamin Wong.

One shot. A small, tidy round hole in the middle of the forehead.

The .22 caliber bullet ricocheted off the confines of Wong's skull, damaging everything it passed through, until the dense mass of his brain slowed, and finally halted, the velocity of the slug.

When the light of life left the astonished eyes of Benjamin Wong, a small trickle of blood seeped from his right nostril. His head tipped forward, chin to his chest, as if he were sleeping.

Hong smiled. Nice and neat, just like the boss ordered. No messy blood or brain splatters. No noisy blast. No destruction of property or innocent civilian casualties.

The retaliation was swift and decisive. It solved potential conflict within the organization and discouraged others from tempting the same fate.

Hong slid the pistol into the inside pocket of his silk lined suit jacket. He exited the car, quietly closed the driver's door, and walked unhurriedly to a car parked nearby.

When he slid in on the front passenger side, the car eased down the street, its driver meticulously observing traffic laws, cruising well within the acceptable speed limit.

Kang

11
The Demise of Boss Jeun

March 2007
Seoul, South Korea

BOSS JEUN WAS DYING.
It started with labored breathing. Then a cough. A bloody handkerchief.

Kang sat next to Jeun in the back seat of his chauffeured town car as they drove to the Port of Incheon, the main seaport in South Korea, forty kilometers southwest from Seoul, to keep an appointment with a notorious black market importer/exporter.

A long-time acquaintance of Kang's, Alexei Kosovskaia, had theorized that putting the two organizations together would benefit not only them, but also himself. He had arranged the time and place of the meeting, and would provide introductions. His disciplined and coldly competent crew would be on hand to provide security.

"Do you trust him?" Boss Jeun had inquired of Kang when he had relayed Kosovskaia's proposal to him. Whether Kang considered him a friend or not, the old man exercised caution.

Kang bowed. "Yes, sir. I do."

Now, on their way to keep that meeting, Kang observed the old man cough and cover his mouth with a clean white handkerchief. The sputum was bloody.

Kang stared out of his window and remained silent.

The old man quickly wiped his mouth, neatly folded the handkerchief, and stashed it in his inside pocket of his suit jacket.

This had been going on for weeks.

"Have you seen your doctor?" Kang asked quietly.

Boss Jeun said nothing for a moment. "No."

"Perhaps it is time," Kang observed respectfully.

The old man nodded thoughtfully. "I have never considered myself a coward...until now." He glanced at Kang and smiled sadly. "Make the appointment. I will go."

The introductory meeting with Kosovskaia's associate went well. Kosovskaia's business proposal intrigued Boss Jeun.

Grateful to Kang for suggesting the introduction, the Old Boss gifted him with a sculpture of a respected Korean artist whose work Kang admired. He was pleased with his gift choice when he observed the look of awe and appreciation on Kang's face.

Kang bowed deeply and sincerely thanked him—overwhelmed by his generosity and the value of the gift.

"It shall be your first piece of fine art to start your collection," Jeun proudly affirmed with a smile, recalling the occasion when Kang had mentioned his desire to collect.

THE APPOINTMENT WITH THE DOCTOR for the Old Boss did not go nearly as well.

The initial examination, and a battery of subsequent tests, revealed a large mass in his right lung, with a grape-cluster of smaller tumors the size of a man's fist in his left. The consequence of a lifetime of smoking—five packs a day for over sixty years.

Doctors were not encouraging. They asserted that, because of his age and state of diminished health, Jeun was not a good candidate for surgery. More than likely, he would not survive the operation.

What they did recommend, however, was a regimen of radiation and chemotherapy to slow the growth of the tumors and prolong his life—for how long, exactly, they could not promise.

The Old Boss shunned the suggested treatment, deciding to make the best of the time he had left without the incapacitating, painful, and disfiguring burning and poisoning of his body.

An Inspector for the Seoul Metropolitan Police Agency, Kang was assigned to infiltrate Juen's crime syndicate a number of years ago. Over time, with patience and diligence, Kang had gained the trust of the gentleman gangster. But troubling to both his conscience and sense of duty, Kang had come to respect Jeun—more than he ever had his own father.

Hearing the bleak prognosis for the Old Boss, Kang was devastated.

Glasnost

March 2007
Seoul, South Korea
Russian [glahs-nuh-st] - noun
Meaning, literally, "openness"

ALEXEI KOSOVSKAIA CAUGHT THE EYE of his friend, Kang Dae Ho, and enthusiastically waved him over to join him and his companions in a secluded corner of the premiere dance club in Seoul's trendy Gangnam District.

Techno music blared from speakers that circled the club. Lights flashed and multicolored laser beams sliced over the roiling sea of humanity—fashionably dressed twenty somethings that swarmed the dance floor and enticed one another with provocative glances and moves.

It was not Kang's preference for a meeting place. But the boisterous, hard-drinking Russian who had been his long-time acquaintance—sometime adversary, sometime brother—had asked Kang to join him here.

Kosovskaia made room for Kang to slide on the seat next to him in the wide plush booth that filled the back corner.

"*Preevyet*," he greeted Kang. Hi.

Kosovskaia introduced Kang to the Ukrainian-born manager of the club—broadly smiling with satisfaction and pride when the manager ordered their table filled with complimentary bottles of liquor and champagne.

Kosovskaia poured Kang a generous glass of premium Russian vodka. "Drink my friend," he shouted in English. "I am glad you are here."

When Kang tipped the rim of his glass against Kosovskaia's, the Russian grinned and issued a familiar Korean drinking challenge. "One shot!"

When their empty glasses were back on the tabletop, he laughingly clapped Kang on the shoulder.

Kang smiled at his friend and settled against the backrest of the booth.

"So?" Kosovskaia inquired, getting down to business. "How did it go?"

"Well," Kang responded evenly. "Boss Jeun was satisfied with the delivery and the merchandise."

The Russian nodded, pleased by Kang's succinct report. "Excellent! Perhaps we do business again one day," he initiated confidently.

"That may be possible," Kang admitted. Boss Jeun had indicated an interest in other contacts the innovative and widely connected Kosovskaia could provide him.

Kang's friend regarded him through expressive ice-blue eyes, his pupil's dark with concern. "You did not take delivery yourself, did you?"

When Kang shook his head, Kosovskaia visibly relaxed.

"You worried about me?" Kang inquired, amused.

"Yes," Kosovskaia replied without hesitation.

"Why?"

"I never claimed to understand your dedication to policing, my friend. Or your ambition to infiltrate Jeun's organization. But now…for you…both of them trouble me."

Kang made no comment.

Over the years, Kosovskaia had witnessed his friend's growing admiration—silent allegiance—to the crime lord of the small but powerful syndicate that operated efficiently and lucratively under the radar of law enforcement in Seoul.

"Jeun is a charismatic man, is he not?" Kosovskaia persisted.

Something on the other side of the club diverted Kang's attention.

Kosovskaia gripped his forearm to reclaim his focus. "I know where I belong. I am not confused about that."

"Am I confused, Alexei?" Kang inquired quietly, an edge to his voice.

"*Prasteete*," Kosovskaia murmured, excusing himself. "But you are the good guy," he trumpeted with gusto, replacing his uneasiness with a quick grin. "You are my rock."

Kosovskaia reminded Kang of when his younger sister, Anessia, was murdered by her pimp, Danilo Mercado. "I once cried in your arms like a baby, do you remember?"

Kang mellowed with the memory. How could he remain annoyed with such an affable and protective friend?

"You will do the right thing," Kosovskaia said with trusting bravado, followed by a confident nod of his head. "This I know."

Kosovskaia's troubled mind at ease for the moment, Kang's eyes followed a woman, thick braid of ash blonde hair hanging down her back, who was standing at a table at the far side of the bar.

"What are you looking at?" Kosovskaia finally demanded with impatience.

He recognized the voluptuous, buxom young woman who had captured Kang's attention. The manager of the club liked to hire sexy Russian girls to serve as hostesses to his clientele.

"Ahhh." He grinned, pleased by his friend's interest in a woman of his country. "Do you wish me to call her over?"

The young woman turned so that Kang could see her clearly. She was pretty but bland. Unlike the enigmatic and sensuous woman he had known so long ago who had performed his rite of passage into manhood.

"No," Kang politely but firmly demurred, conceding—with a surprising twinge of melancholy—the statistical improbability of ever encountering her again.

Irina.

Coming of Age

August 1986
Pusan, South Korea

TYPHOON WAYNE—WHICH WOULD GO ON record as one of the longest lasting tropical cyclones in the northwestern Pacific Ocean—was creating chaos in southern China, the Philippines, Hong Kong, Taiwan, and Vietnam, battering everything in its wake with torrential rains and gusts of wind up to nearly 98 miles per hour.

Kang Dae Ho had been land locked for over a week. The fleet of fishing boats on which he had labored for nearly three years crazily bobbed side by side, choking the harbor of Pusan—the largest port city of South Korea on the southeastern most tip of the Korean peninsula.

When he had graduated from secondary school in Seoul and turned the legal age of eighteen, Kang served his mandatory twenty-one months' active duty in the Army of the Republic of Korea.

He found his way to Pusan by a stroke of fate. A fellow soldier who had befriended him, the son of a captain who berthed his fishing boats in Pusan, approached Kang with a job offer when they received their discharges in the same week. With no plans of his own, and no objections to the work, Kang accepted.

While Typhoon Wayne disrupted trade and travel in the Pacific, Kang spent his time at a local harbor café he had found when he first arrived in Pusan. Its proprietor, and therefore the cuisine, was Russian. Kang did not care for the menu, although portions were generous and the prices cheap. He was not there for the food.

There was a woman—big boned, ruddy-cheeked, coffee and cream-colored eyes, a thick hank of braided blonde hair that hung down the nape of her neck—who served the café's customers. Her male admirers camped out day after day, boasting to one another and laughing as they ogled her enormous breasts and apple-shaped bottom.

Kang kept himself apart from these men, sat alone. He shunned their offers to speculate on the mystery surrounding this care-worn woman who defied an assignment of age.

She was from the Ukraine—they conceived.

She was a well-educated and vocal dissident against the brutality and social injustices of the Communist regime—they whispered among themselves.

She had escaped from a Soviet forced labor camp in Siberia and, in gratitude, married the man who rescued her, who had risked his own life to free her—they romanticized.

She was unmarried, sister to a drunk and seafaring older brother, who was a brute and beat her, who extorted the pitiful wages she earned as a server—they sympathized.

Kang cared nothing about these rumors. In his innocent and impressionable youth, he was content just to sit and look at her as she moved around the café—sensual yet remote, eyes direct and piercing— as if she was aware that she had captured his imagination, but was impervious to either admiration or insult.

Her name was Irina.

Late one evening Kang emerged from the café after the proprietor churlishly put out the lights and prompted him to leave, hearing the door slammed and locked behind him.

It was raining. More of a mist than a rain. The wind was calm—at least for the moment.

Kang thrust his hands in his pockets, restless from his idleness and discouraged over lost wages. He hung his head, watching his step as he started down the wharf.

He felt a presence hugging the darkness under the eaves of the old building, smelled the acrid smoke of the cheap and roughly cut tobacco of a filterless *papirosa*, or Russian cigarette.

The end of the cigarette sparked and flared from a deep draw, briefly illuminating the sharply defined features of the face behind it.

Irina.

She threw the cigarette aside. It extinguished with a hiss in a shallow puddle of rainwater. She stepped out of the shadows and gazed unblinking at Kang—eyes shrewd and assessing.

Drawing her scarf snugly around her neck against the damp, she began to make her way over the uneven planks of the pier.

Kang noted a slight limp—that her left calf bowed outward. There had been some speculation about a broken leg being improperly set after her escape from the Gulag.

When Irina failed to hear the fall of footsteps behind her, she stopped and cast a questioning glance over her shoulder—waiting.

Kang's eyes widened in surprise when he realized she expected him to follow her. He lurched toward her, his movements jerky and unsure.

A mocking smile curled the corners of her mouth.

Kang's inexperience embarrassed him, made him feel callow and miserably inept. Still, he stayed with her, hesitating when she did, stopping when she did—never too close yet never too far behind.

The strangely silent woman led him to a squalid, two-story building at the end of the wharf and up a flight of stairs. She unlocked the door and entered her living quarters, throwing the door wide for Kang to follow.

The interior was gloomy. A blood red floral wallpaper, stained with years of careless living, subdued the cramped rooms of the apartment. Dark, heavy pieces of furniture crowded the space—stifling and rigid in their mass. The airless interior smelled richly of garlic and dill, cabbage and fish.

Kang closed the door.

Irina shucked the worn coat that brushed the top of her knees, the knitted scarf around her neck, the woolen gloves, and threw them on a chair by her bed—unmade and redolent with her feminine scent.

She lit several candles around the room and retrieved a bottle of vodka and two shot glasses from the lower cupboard of a nearby sideboard. The nearly full bottle of vodka sloshed and glasses noisily clinked together as she roughly set them on top of the buffet.

Kang watched in fascination as she unselfconsciously unbuttoned the top of her dress and pushed the fabric from her shoulders, unclasped her brassiere and tossed it, too, on the chair by the bed.

Her breasts were pendulous, nipples and areolas large and brown. They were perfect for wet nursing—or inciting foolish young men into mindless acts of lust.

Kang willed himself to look away, to hide his arousal from her, but could not resist watching her as she drew water into a basin, soaped a cloth, and began to scrub herself—first her arms and armpits, her neck, torso, and breasts. Then she shed her dress, drew down her rude undergarments and washed between her legs. When she had rinsed and toweled herself dry, she beckoned Kang.

Ignoring his painful awkwardness, she undressed and washed him in the same perfunctory manner—as if he were a child—as if she needed him to be clean and new.

When she had finished, she poured a generous glass of vodka for him and one for herself.

Kang emptied his glass as he had observed Irina do—in one quick shot. The fiery bite of the cheap vodka scorched his throat and forced him to inhale a sharp lungful of air.

Irina took his hand and wordlessly led him to her bed, pulling him down to lie beside her. She began to teach him the pleasures of the body, taking his hand and placing it over the thick blonde thatch at the base of her thighs—that heretofore mysterious and forbidden place.

She enjoyed Kang without reserve or conscience.

He was aware that this woman had lured him, that she was flagrantly using him—as the puppet master with the puppet—but did not allow his tender ego to discourage this newly discovered, and profoundly pleasurable, pastime.

When at last he fell back, breathing hard, slick with her sweat and his, thinking he could do no more, she hummed deep in her throat, nuzzled him, enticed and roused him with murmured Russian endearments, bringing him into an exhausted but swelling heat.

Imaginative and experimental, she was very nearly insatiable. She made him believe that he was invincible—omnipotent.

EARLY THE NEXT MORNING, SENSING Irina's restlessness and readiness for him to leave, Kang quickly dressed and stood with her at the apartment door. He politely and tentatively offered to pay her.

Irina impatiently pushed away his hand and jerked open the door.

Kang slinked by her, wretched in spirit and certain she would never want to see him again.

"Come again tomorrow." she growled in Korean.

Kang made his way down the stairs with relief and renewed confidence.

Irina.

His heart sang her name—thrummed with the remembered energy of her willing body, the earthy scent of her feverish skin, her soft cries of release when he explored ways to satiate her sensual gluttony.

She was the carnal fantasy of every eager and inexperienced young man. Truthfully, the carnal fantasy of any man.

Paying the Piper

August 1986
Pusan, South Korea

T HE FLUSH OF SEXUAL EXCITEMENT waning, Kang dragged himself back to his rented room, every previously unfamiliar muscle in his body throbbing in agony.

The *ajumma,* elderly woman, from whom he rented his room—a widow driven to eccentricity by the loss of her husband at sea thirty-four years earlier—cackled when she took one look at Kang.

"You! You punk! You think you have that Siberian tiger-bitch by the tail, do you? Eh?" She cupped her bony hand into a claw. "No, no! She has you by the balls!"

She howled like a demented spirit—her teeth yellow from her pipe always burning in the bowl—appreciating her own humor.

Already edgy from fatigue, *ajumma* raised the hair on the back of Kang's neck. He needed a hot soak and some sleep. Lots of sleep.

A WEEK LATER AND STILL Typhoon Wayne raged on. Kang bided his time at the café during the day and with Irina in her apartment at night.

He was convinced that he was in love with her—erring, as tender and innocent hearts do, in confusing sex with love. When he attempted to learn more about her and ask about her childhood, family, and current circumstances, she shrugged and evaded his questions in a heavy Slavic accent. "Not interesting."

AFTER THIRTY DAYS, TYPHOON WAYNE had finally spent itself. Hundreds were dead and tens of thousands left homeless, requiring world aid to dig out from the destruction and rebuild.

Kang had received notice to report to the fishing fleet in two days' time.

He had reveled in Irina's company every evening over the past two weeks. In his naiveté, he did not question his good fortune, thinking it would last forever.

Recently, however, he noticed that she had begun to act differently—troubled, agitated, and wary. Kang knew better than to query her yet felt uneasy, unconsciously sharing her watchfulness.

It was nearly midnight. They were lying side by side, breath labored from their last bout of sexual acrobatics, when a man's robust and drunken voice bellowed in Russian from the street below.

"Irina, you whore! I am back!"

She raised up on one elbow and looked at Kang with a palpable fear, panic in her voice. "You must leave."

Respecting her sense of urgency, Kang sprang from the bed and scrabbled to sort through the pile of clothes on the floor. All very good and well, he thought in fear and confusion—stung by her gruff eviction—but there was only one way out.

When Irina leaned out of the window, the Russian observed her with fiercely burning dark eyes. "*Myshka,*" he crooned. Little mouse.

"Well, well," Irina sneered. "Look what the storm washed ashore."

"You have been busy, so I hear. You have a man...a boy...you have been keeping in your bed!"

"He's more of a man than you will ever be, imbecile!"

"Imbecile?" He threw his head back to glare at her and stumbled backwards into the arms of his equally inebriated comrade. "Imbecile, is it?"

"You let her talk to you like that?" his companion smirked, inciting him.

Furious, the brute clumsily hauled his bulky two hundred and eighty-five pound frame up the narrow, steep stairway—drunk enough to challenge the steps to the second story apartment—sober enough to worry if he would make it to the top without breaking his ridiculous neck.

He pounded on the apartment door, determined to have it opened or break it down.

Kang was appalled when Irina wrapped herself in her robe and fearlessly threw open the door. The bull of a man standing on the other side pushed his way into the apartment, roughly knocking Irina to one side.

He focused his anger on Kang.

Still not quite dressed, Kang stood his ground and watched the man charge him like an enraged rhino. Irina attempted to block his way, shoving against his chest, hurled to the floor for her efforts.

Kang ran to help her, trying to assuage the hulking and darkly hairy beast with words of reason—apologizing for his mistake if he had unknowingly slept with his woman.

Kang's lean body valiantly planted in front of Irina, his audacity and composure infuriated the man.

"She is my wife!" the oaf roared, lifting Kang under his arms and shaking him like a rag doll.

When her husband's drunken companion decided to wade into the fracas, Irina viciously pounded him with her fists, pulling his hair, shrieking and cursing him in Russian.

The small man tried his best to fend her off, arms protecting his head. "Crazy bitch!" he screamed, running from the apartment. "Let me be!"

She chased the little coward down the stairs and from the building.

She burst back into the apartment in time to see her loutish husband bashing Kang against the walls of the small room, picking him up, and launching him again.

"Marat!" she screamed at her husband from the door. "Stop!"

Sneering at her, Marat picked up Kang by his shirtfront, pulled back his ham-sized fist and smashed him in the face.

Kang felt the skin over his right cheek explode in agony, saw a brilliant white light behind his eye, and fell heavily to the floor.

He heard Irina scream.

Marat picked him up, shoved him through the front door, and lofted him over the stairway landing.

Kang's stomach lurched in momentary weightlessness. His body slammed against the filthy wall of the stairway. Helplessly rolling down the steps, he agonizingly cracked his ribs and spine on the edges of the stair treads.

He arrived at the bottom of the landing in a breathless, bloody, and broken heap.

A fine rain pelted him—nudging him toward consciousness—mingling with the seeping wounds over his brow and cheek. Watery blood dripped from his jaw onto his shirtfront.

Kang slumped there, unaware of how long, until he was recognized by a crewmember from the fishing fleet passing by on his way home. Drunk himself—and assuming Kang was in the same condition—he clumsily hauled Kang to his feet, dragged him to his boarding house, and rudely deposited him on the front stoop.

Ajumma heard the loud thump against her door and promptly investigated the source. She cried Kang's name and cursed the Russian slut who had brought him to this sorry end. She shouted for the old man who had been a friend of her husband and her renter for nearly thirty-three years. Together, they hauled a semi-conscious Kang to his room and laid him on his *yo*—mattress on the floor.

Kang was conscious enough, however, to push away the old woman's trembling hand, poised with a needle and thread over his cheek, as she squinted under the dim light of the naked bulb overhead. Her eyesight was no better than her unsteady hands.

Kang preferred to bear a crescent-shaped scar on his cheekbone—the edge of the signet ring Irina's husband wore on his left hand—rather than a jagged and unevenly sewn gash.

"Don't worry," his landlady murmured comfortingly, lighting her pipe and shaking her head as she settled nearby to watch over him. "You will still be pretty. And now, with that scar, you may also be interesting."

OVER TIME, KANG RECOVERED FROM his injuries, but felt bereft of heart and soul. He was miserable without Irina, crushed over her deception and cold-hearted exploitation of his callow devotion.

A friend reported that Irina was still serving at the cafe, while much more subdued and sullen these days. Although her black eyes had healed, she still displayed a broken nose as testament to her husband's rage.

Kang returned in earnest to the backbreaking and dangerous labor aboard the fishing fleet. Four months later, during the harsh winter months, his mother contacted him. She reported that his father was dead—brutally stabbed to death in the alleyway adjacent to their apartment—and begged her son to return to Seoul for his funeral.

Despite Kang spending several miserable hours watching Irina through the café windows from a concealed vantage point on the pier, he left Pusan without speaking with her.

Little did he suspect that he would never return to the fishing port—that he would never see her again.

열둘

12
The Finger Of Suspicion

April 2007
Seoul, South Korea

O N A CHILLY EARLY SPRING morning, after receiving no answers to repeated missives and numerous voice mail messages, Superintendent Ryu, Kang's undercover handler at Seoul Metro, confronted Kang as he stepped outside of his luxury apartment building.

Ryu's neck was out as far as it would stretch before he was in jeopardy of losing his rank and his pension to excuse his protégé's lengthy silence. After their brief encounter, Kang understood that he could no longer ignore his superior.

They met at their usual spot, a less traveled and obscure location along the Han River.

"Where have you been?" Ryu demanded as they stood together in the deepening night.

Kang remained silent, staring at his old friend.

"Kang Dae Ho?" Ryu's voice lowered with concern. "What are you doing?"

Kang hung his head, unable or unwilling to hold his mentor's disappointed gaze.

"*Aigoo!*" Ryu sighed heavily and paced in front of Kang. "I am bringing you in."

Kang's head snapped up. He was incredulous. "Are you serious?"

"You haven't contacted me in over two months. I had no idea whether were dead or alive."

Kang's apparent indifference to his sleepless nights of worry wounded Ryu. "Or, more importantly, why you did not report the recent shipment of arms Jeun received from Russia."

Kang's eyes narrowed. There could be no way Ryu would have known about that, unless he had another source of information inside the organization. Another cop?

"Where does your allegiance lie, Kang Dae Ho?" Ryu pressed. "Do you even know anymore?"

"These meetings compromise my cover," Kang protested stonily. "The closer I get to Jeun, the less freedom I am going to have."

"I understand that you are nearly always at his side. Overseeing his gambling operations, his clubs…"

Kang clenched his jaw. He refused to accept the Agency's surveillance, as if he were incompetent—or worse—untrustworthy. Not now. Not after all he had sacrificed to do his job.

Jeun watched Ryu and Kang from the back seat of his chauffeured town car, hidden under the recesses of a highway overpass. He noted Kang's rigid and resentful body language, his remote expression. He nodded and smiled—both relieved and pleased.

"Everything is as it should be," he assured the young man, Kang's accuser, sitting in the passenger seat in the front. "There is no need to stay any longer."

The driver eased the car from its hiding place, lights off, until they were well away from the rendezvous spot of Superintendent Ryu and Inspector Kang Dae Ho of the Organized Crime Division of the Seoul Metropolitan Police Agency.

Benevolent Spy

May 2007
Seoul, South Korea

KANG BECAME VIGILANT—SUBTLY OBSERVING THE comings and goings of everyone surrounding him. No one was exempt from his scrutiny.

She had come into the crew almost three months ago through Cheong, muscle for the organization and self-professed playboy. He was more brawn than brain and, as a result, was not trusted with assignments requiring a modicum of finesse. He would most likely remain a lower echelon soldier until his foolish weakness for pretty women, or his lack of focus, got him cornered by law enforcement or eliminated by a rival crew.

Cheong called her Nari—lily flower.

She was pretty—with a narrow pale face, thick shiny hair, and long straight legs. Always in Cheong's company, she sat in the background, unobtrusive and respectful, her watchful brown eyes deceptively vacant.

This evening, about a dozen members of the young crew and their girlfriends, or girl for the night, were hanging out in a private room at one of their favorite clubs owned by Boss Jeun. The music was loud, the liquor flowing, and the women predisposed and eager to be lavishly entertained.

Cheong was dancing with Nari—clearly infatuated with her.

He was not aware of Kang's arrival until he stepped between them.

Nari suffered an uneasy moment under Kang's intense stare.

"What do we have here?" Kang murmured, eyes burning with resentment.

He roughly pulled her into his arms and hung a kiss on her that dropped jaws and popped eyes.

Not one person in the room moved, as motionless as a freeze-frame effect in the cinema.

The unexpected and unusual behavior of his *sunbae* shocked Cheong. The longer the kiss lasted, the more confused and angry the young kid became.

Kang released Nari and locked his gaze on her. "Do you want to come with me?" he inquired softly.

Wide-eyed and breathless, she glanced uneasily at Cheong. A game smile surfaced on her face, revealing a deep dimple in her right cheek. "Yes."

Kang looked at Cheong with a perceptive smile and made a wry observation about love. "So fickle."

He stalked to the exit of the room, turned to the startled group, and impatiently motioned for Cheong to follow him.

The kid, clearly stymied, remained rooted to the spot. "Sir?"

A friend in the crew pushed him forward to obey Kang's order.

When Cheong started across the floor alone, Kang shook his head. "Bring your friend."

A shiny black luxury town car idled outside on the street. Kang waved the girl through the open door to sit in the back seat. While Cheong boarded behind her, Kang slipped in from the other side of the car, effectively boxing the girl between them.

The girl's expression became tense with apprehension.

Cheong uneasily gazed at the rigid back of Kang's lieutenant, Yi—a fiercely loyal and feared enforcer—who sat in the front passenger seat.

Kang made Cheong aware of the duct tape and coils of rope on the floorboard under his feet. "Wrap our package."

Cheong stared at Kang in distress and confusion. "What?"

Yi turned in his seat and flashed a warning glare at Cheong. "Do it."

"*Oppa,* what is this man going to do to me?" The frightened innocent, Nari clung to Cheong and pleaded with him, "Please, help me!"

Kang smirked. Well done.

He had to give the girl credit—she had identified the weak member of the organization, culled him from the pack, successfully attracted his attention and captured his affections. She had the free run of the organization for three months without drawing Kang's notice.

She had played her part well. But the time for playing was over.

Kang grabbed the duct tape, tore off a strip, and clapped it over her mouth. He looked at Cheong expectantly.

The young wiseguy broke out in a sweat, but obediently tied his girlfriend's hands behind her back, her ankles together.

The girl breathed panicked huffs of air through her nose, fearful mewling coming from deep in her throat.

NARI—POLICE OFFICER KO YOUNG IL—was a clever and ambitious twenty-six year old with two years' experience in Seoul Metro, and recently engaged to be married to a handsome brute employed by the National Police Agency.

She had faithfully attended the undercover assignment entrusted to her by her superiors. Over the past months, she had watched Kang move confidently and at will within the hierarchy of the Jeun organization—acting as Jeun's right-hand man, relaying orders to the managers of his holdings, given the prerogative to make requisite policy and personnel decisions.

Police Officer Ko noted that Kang was regarded by those under his purview with respect and, in some cases, outright veneration. His manner and method of communication was calmly commanding. No one questioned his authority.

Ko found herself drawn to Kang, watching him interact with the young and impressionable men in his crew. His self-assurance and soft-spoken manner were inspiring—his charismatic yet understated authority potently alluring.

Although she refrained from putting her personal opinions or thoughts in her reports, what concerned Ko—played in a troubling and continuous loop in her mind—was where Kang's loyalty currently resided. Either he was flawlessly playing the part of a rogue cop, or he had been seduced by, and crossed over to, the dark side of the law.

KANG FELT NARI'S BODY TREMBLE as she sat next to him on the backseat of the town car.

He stared out of the window.

Ryu had forced him to do this.

Kang did not enjoy frightening Nari. He would have preferred another solution to rid himself of this excess baggage. Yet, he was willing to do whatever was required to protect the fragile trust it had taken him years to earn within the Jeun syndicate.

He was going to deliver a message.

When they had reached their destination, Yi, and a flummoxed Cheong, removed the bundle from the back seat. On Kang's orders, they laid Nari at the top of the steps of the Itaewon District police station, currently in between shifts and relatively quiet at this odd hour of the morning.

Kang dismissed his men and hunkered down beside his fellow police officer.

Ko relaxed, now that she realized she was being spared a one-way boat ride off the coast of the Yellow Sea to a deep-water grave.

Kang quietly encouraged her, "Tell Superintendent Ryu that I do not need any supervision on this assignment."

He stood. From her perspective, Kang seemed to gaze down on her from a great height. He promised, quite earnestly, "The next time, I will not be as generous."

Once Kang had settled inside the town car, his lieutenant secured his door and resumed his position on the front passenger seat. A door slammed and tires squealed as the driver accelerated the luxury car down the street.

Police Officer Ko squeezed her eyes closed, remembering her shameful arrogance when she assured her superiors that she was capable of handling the surveillance of Inspector Kang Dae Ho. She would observe his movements, assess his loyalty, and report her progress.

She could still feel the fear that had gripped her belly under the icy gaze of Inspector Kang, hear his words of warning—his promise—to the next cop who attempted to infiltrate the Jeun organization.

Ko had truly believed that her young life—her bright future—was going to end this evening.

The girl began to shake violently from the cold concrete upon which she laid, and the shock of her near-death experience. Sobbing in relief, she wet herself.

CHEONG DROPPED TO HIS KNEES before Kang after they climbed out of the town car in front of the club where they had found him. Cheong bowed and cried with fear and remorse, "Please forgive me, *Sunbae*. I had no idea...I didn't know that she was a..." He was about to pronounce with a filthy mouth that she was a cop.

Everyone knew Kang was a cop. They accepted it because Jeun had drawn him into the day-to-day business of the organization—relied upon him.

"What?" Kang pressed with a deceptive smile on his lips. "That she was a what?"

Cheong glanced up at Kang, mortified by the situation he had brought upon himself. The danger to which he had exposed the organization. The compromise of their privacy and security.

He employed a rarely used gesture in modern day Korea and briskly rubbed his hands together, begging for forgiveness under this most dire and shameful circumstance. "I promise to work hard in the future, *Sunbae*! I am a fool! Please forgive me!"

Kang walked into the club, leaving Cheong kneeling on the sidewalk, forehead against the pavement, blubbering like a baby.

Yi warned Cheong to stay put until Kang decided what to do with him. Then he, too, left him alone on the sidewalk to review and repent his sins.

A Serving of Humble Pie

May 2007
Seoul, South Korea

RYU UNEASILY SHIFTED IN HIS chair as he sat with his peers and superiors in a conference room at Seoul Metropolitan Police Agency headquarters in a clandestine debriefing of Police Officer Ko Young Il.

Each panel member had a copy of her report before them on the conference table and was thumbing through it, seeking the damning information they would require to indict Inspector Kang Dae Ho of malfeasance and formally relieve him of duty.

Police Officer Ko nervously sat across the table from her tense and solemn superiors, all eyes and hopes pinned on her.

Superintendent General Shin, senior ranking officer present, commenced the proceedings by inquiring, "Did he threaten you in any way?"

Ko remembered Kang's solemn promise to the next undercover cop who attempted to spy on him. Yet, he did not verbally threaten her personally.

"No, sir."

"Did he take you or transport you against your will?"

Ko flinched. She had been painfully honest in her report. As they could read for themselves, Kang had asked her if she wanted to go with him. She willingly agreed.

"No, sir."

"Did he assault you?"

Ko recognized the direction in which her superiors were trying to drive her, and neither appreciated their efforts nor respected their motives.

She glanced at an uncomfortably silent Ryu. He smiled weakly, encouraging her to continue.

"He put tape over my mouth to shut me up," she replied honestly, "but that was all."

A few members of the panel cleared their throats, suppressing their amusement.

"Did you at any time feel that your life may be in danger?"

"Yes, sir, I did," Ko replied candidly. Her superiors exchanged triumphant smiles. "But," she interjected quickly, "my inexperience and flawed perception of the man I was assigned to surveil caused me to overreact and panic."

One panel member castigated her, glaring at her through narrowed eyes. "You are not as confident about your abilities now, are you Police Officer Ko?"

Graduating at the top of her class from the police academy, articulate and self-assured, Ko had convinced her superiors that she had the right stuff to undertake this task.

Ko hung her head in shame. "I am sorry, sir."

Ryu spoke up in her defense. He reminded those members present who had sanctioned her assignment and signed her orders, "It was our judgment that was at fault when we cast Officer Ko into these deep waters."

An apropos metaphor.

Ko revisited her terror when she believed Kang was going to dump her body offshore in the Yellow Sea. She shivered involuntarily.

An uneasy silence ensued.

"What, in your opinion, is the character of Inspector Kang Da Ho?" one Senior Superintendent pointedly inquired of Officer Ko.

She raised her head and stuck out her chin, speaking with authority about her observations of Kang. "His men look to him for leadership since the Old Boss has become a recluse. He honors Jeun by continuing the precepts that made both him and his organization successful. He discourages conflict, wading in only if necessary, and then distances himself by relying on his enforcers. He is respected by both the crew and the managers of Jeun's properties that he oversees."

"Do you admire him?" Ryu asked with a kindly tone.

Ko was ashamed to admit, even to herself, that she had been attracted to Kang.

When he entered a room and circulated among his men making genial conversation—the young wiseguys pouring his drinks and hanging on his every word—she couldn't take her eyes from him.

If he distractedly glanced her way, Ko became flustered and immediately dropped her gaze.

"Yes, sir. I do," Ko admitted cautiously, aware of the displeasure on the faces of her superiors. "But I hope that I never have to face him again."

The End of Days

June 2007
Seoul, South Korea

THREE MONTHS AFTER BOSS JEUN received a diagnosis of lung cancer, he became bedridden twenty-four hours a day and dependent upon an oxygen machine to breathe.

Although it was difficult for Kang to see the old man's vigor dissipate in the debilitating and terminal stages of cancer, he came every day to his estate to visit him and receive orders to continue the daily operations of the organization.

Over the years, Boss Jeun had given him more and more responsibility, using him as a sounding board—sometimes confidant.

Kang respected Jeun's intelligence, his honor and wisdom, and his extraordinary ability to interpret the character of people and encourage them to do his bidding.

The success of Jeun's organization depended upon a well thought-out strategy, and an understanding of the limitations imposed upon it by the capricious tolerance of a civilized society.

Kang understood the path that Jeun had chosen for himself. A fatherless punk who once lived on the streets, Jeun had not only survived by his own wits, but also prospered.

Although Kang lived with both parents while growing up, was educated, and never went hungry, he just as easily could have pledged himself to a gang to fulfill a sense of belonging that was absent in his turbulent home life.

KANG STOOD OUTSIDE JEUN'S SICKROOM, confided in by a trusted physician that someone had come to visit the terminally ill boss.

Kang focused on the door when it opened, observed a young man with his face pinched in anger emerge, felt the solid strength of his shoulder as he rudely pushed past him and stalked down the hallway.

"It is his son," the physician whispered in disapproval. "Jeun Ji-tae."

"Kang Dae Ho," Boss Jeun called out weakly from his bed. "Come in."

His eyes mirrored his pain as Kang stood at his bedside. "Prepare yourself."

He struggled to take a breath. Kang placed the oxygen mask over his mouth and nose to allow him to acquire painful and desperate gulps of air.

Finally more comfortable, Jeun pushed aside the mask. "When I have drawn my last breath on this earth, my son will return from Japan to claim what he thinks is owed to him."

Regretably, Jeun acknowledged the unspoken and tenuous relationship between fathers and sons—the father's high expectations and critical eye—the sons jealousy, resentment, and insecurity. "What has taken me forty-five years to build will be rent apart like cheap silk."

Jeun's progeny—sullen and secretive even as a child—had never allowed his father close enough to come to know or understand him. Their rapport had deteriorated to the point where Jeun had sent Ji-tae to Japan under the guise of looking after his interests there.

Jeun regarded Kang fondly, squeezing his hand. "I don't know why you stayed by my side, why you did not report to your superiors the activities of the organization but...I thank you."

"Sssh," Kang soothed, placing the oxygen mask over Jeun's face.

Once again, Jeun pushed the mask away. He murmured with great effort, "When I die, go immediately to the club where we first met. In my office, look under the floor of my desk. Ji-tae must never possess the documents you will find there. Never!"

"What do you wish me to do with them?" Kang inquired with a solicitous frown.

Jeun smiled warmly, the lines on his face deepened with suffering. "Do what you will with them. You have worked hard. You have earned whatever reward and recognition they will bring you."

Jeun closed his eyes, satisfied that he had completed his Last Will and Testament and placed it in trusted hands.

He required rest from the exhausting struggle of living—and dying.

Declaration of War

July 2007
Seoul, South Korea

JEUN WAS RIGHT. HE WAS not even dead thirty-two hours and the foundation of his organization was beginning to fracture.

Reports verified that his son, Jeun Ji-tae, was on his way back from his forced exile in Japan with a sole purpose—to claim what was rightfully his. It was clear he intended to make a clean sweep of the outfit and eliminate those who were loyal to his father—to become the undisputed monarch of his own malignant empire.

Jeun Ji-tae was an acknowledged sociopath—deriving pleasure and satisfaction from inflicting pain—seeing the reflection of fear and suffering in another man's eyes. The hoodlums he attracted to serve under his dark rule were just as barbaric, indulgent, and immoral.

It was the end of cooperation and prosperity among the syndicates in northeast Asia. It was the end of an era. For Jeun's crew—it was the end of times.

KANG PAID HIS FINAL RESPECTS to the Old Boss and his family. The crew parted for him as he entered the mortuary, formed a protective circle around him and stood close to him for reassurance and guidance.

He knelt and touched his forehead to the floor before a framed portrait of Jeun, draped in black ribbon and surrounded by spicy scented white chrysanthemums.

Then, heart heavy with grief, he set about the business of fulfilling the last request the Old Boss had made of him.

In the company of his trusted lieutenant, Yi, Kang drove to the club on Hooker Hill where he had first met Boss Jeun.

Yi helped Kang move the heavy mahogany desk from which Jeun had once directed the most influential and profitable syndicate in South Korea, and roll up the immense Oriental rug upon which it stood.

Kang ran his hand over the exposed bamboo floorboards, gritty from the fine silt that had sifted through the carpet. A slight ridge caused him to pause. He accepted the *Bi Su* fighting knife Yi offered him and carefully inserted the sharply honed blade between the narrow gap in the flooring. He removed the length of board that popped up and set it aside.

They meticulously displaced board after board to reveal a four-by-four foot concrete lined alcove. It contained one item—a long and shallow rectangular silver metal box. Yi lifted it from its concealment and placed it next to Kang.

Kang tried the latch. He glanced up in wonder at Yi when he found it unlocked. He wiped the dust from the top, flipped the latch, and cautiously opened it.

He discovered three oversized, two-inch thick accounting ledgers that smelled musty with damp and age. Kang lifted the topmost ledger— the most current from the dates inscribed on it—opened it, and thumbed through its contents.

All the illicit and unlawful business of the Jeun organization was captured on these pages—presumably in all three journals—investments and offshore bank account information, owned real estate, business partnerships, human assets and contacts the world over, lists of paid politicians and officials, legally binding contracts, and much more. Far too much to audit here and now.

Kang expelled a gust of air he had been holding in his lungs.

Do what you will with them, the Old Boss had invited him. *You deserve whatever reward or recognition they will bring you.*

Kang promptly put the book back in the box and secured the latch. "Hurry," he encouraged Yi, pushing the box aside. "We must put everything back as it was."

"Does that matter?" Yi asked with an incredulous laugh. "If those are what I think they are, we have nothing to fear. The organization is yours."

Kang met Yi's even gaze and slowly shook his head.

"That is what Boss Jeun wanted," Yi pressed. "Why else would he tell you where the books were?"

"Are you ready for a bloody war?"

Yi lowered his eyes in frustration.

"It will begin the minute Boss Jeun's son steps on Korean soil."

Yi proclaimed with sincere conviction and a proud tilt to his chin, "I am ready to fight for what is ours."

Kang smiled at his loyal and brave lieutenant. "Is it ours?"

"As much as anyone's," Yi replied feebly.

Kang picked up the box and offered it to Yi.

The strongly built man blanched and recoiled, as if it were poisonous. "Sir, I am no leader," he protested. "The men will look to you!"

"Right now, they will look to you," Kang stated firmly. "Spread the word. Tell them to do what they must to be safe."

"Hide?" Yi demanded in astonishment.

"Live to fight another day," Kang reasoned calmly.

Yi became shamefaced. "Sir."

"Right now, I have to find a safe place for this," Kang determined, gesturing with his head to the metal box.

"I will come with you."

"No," Kang insisted, putting a reassuring hand on Yi's shoulder. "Better if you don't know."

Yi bowed in acquiescence. He would never voluntarily divulge its whereabouts or betray Kang but, under duress, only the strongest will could withstand the persuasion of torture.

"I will meet you afterwards," Kang assured him. "Then we will visit each of Jeun's businesses and warn them about what is coming."

He grimly eyed the silver box. "That's the least we can do."

Cara

열 셋

13
Boiling Point

July 2007
Seoul, South Korea

IT WAS EARLY MORNING. PUFFY silver-gray clouds crowded the sky and threatened a downpour in the wettest month of the monsoon season.

Cara heard a car pull up under the portico. She peered out of the window to see Moon's uniformed driver rise from the family's black town car, open the trunk, and walk toward the house. He returned carrying two modest-sized pieces of luggage. He stored them in the trunk, slammed the lid closed, and hustled to open the rear passenger door.

Before Moon eased into the town car, he glanced up at Cara's bedroom window.

Cara stared back at him, eyes wide with astonishment. She scrabbled with the latch on the window, trying to open it.

"Moon! Moon Hyo!" she shouted as he slipped over the leather seat and disappeared behind the door the driver secured.

"Wait!" Cara pounded her palm in frustration against the unyielding window. "Where are you going? Wait!"

She threw open her bedroom door and sprinted the length of the hallway, past a startled Sang Hee, down the curved staircase and out of the front door. When she ran under the front portico, all she could see were taillights flashing as the driver paused the car before pulling out on the highway.

Sang Hee fretfully hovered in the opened doorway.

Cara swung around and demanded breathlessly, "Where has he gone?"

"To the airport."

"Whaa…what? Why?" Cara stuttered.

"He said that he had to complete several important tasks."

Even though Sang Hee was her closest ally and friend, Cara was too proud to inquire why Moon had not spoken a word to her about these tasks.

"How long will he be gone?"

Sang Hee's shoulders visibly tensed. "Several days…maybe more."

Cara blew a breath of exasperation from her lungs. "Well, this just won't do," she stated, her tone eerily devoid of inflection. Bearing the oppressive weight of fury pressing on her chest, she brushed past Moon's fretful younger sister—on a mission.

Sang Hee knew her friend and former sister-in-law well. She recognized the firm set to her jaw, the stiff and adamant posture. "*Unni,* please. Do not do anything rash."

"My ass," Cara muttered running up the stairway. "Goes off without a word…no discussion, no explanation, no consideration."

"He said he is doing this for you and the baby!" Sang Hee called after her, beginning to panic—dreading the consequences of her brother's secrecy.

"I've had enough!" Cara shouted. She turned back to Sang Hee, suddenly serene. "I am going back to America with the baby."

"Please, no!" Sang Hee cried in distress, beginning to tremble.

Her brother had not shared with her the purpose for his absence— gave her nothing with which to reassure Cara. "Don't leave again, *Unni*! Please!"

AFTER CARA HAD PACKED HER and the baby's belongings and taken a taxi to Incheon International Airport, Sang Hee sat in her father's study and sobbed, tears of desolation tracking down her flushed cheeks.

What would she say to her brother when he returned to discover Cara and his son gone? How could she explain to him that she understood Cara's impatience and resentment—her need to return to her homeland—to her family and the people who would support and love her?

What would she say?

The house phone rang. Sang Hee picked up without thought and, upon hearing the brittle voice on the other end, grimaced. It was her mother.

"You sound like you have been crying," her mother observed shortly. "Is it that woman? Did she make you cry?"

"She has left the house," Sang Hee replied vaguely. "She is going back to America."

"With the boy?" Mrs. Moon demanded incredulously.

Too late, Sang Hee realized her blunder. Her silence lit the short fuse of her mother.

"I demand to speak to Moon Hyo immediately."

"He is out of the country."

"Sang Hee, you never fail to disappoint me," her mother accused in a tone corrupted with resentment.

"*Eomeoni*," Sang Hee weakly protested her mother's deliberate cruelty.

"If you cannot handle this matter properly, then I will!" Her mother disconnected the call.

Sang Hee stared at the phone receiver clutched in her hand, a fresh wave of apprehension overwhelming her fragile soul. "What have I done?"

Butterfly Net

July 2007
Seoul, South Korea

WHEN HER FLIGHT NUMBER TO the States was finally announced for boarding, an emotionally frayed Cara gathered her peacefully sleeping son in her arms and her carry-on bag and took her place in the queue—behind the elderly and infirmed, and families with young children who were allowed to embark the airplane before its other passengers.

She numbly rocked Regalo from side to side—more so to soothe a nagging precognition that screamed of urgency. An ominous forewarning that she needed to leave the country—and quickly.

Forward, forward. They moved slowly, but at a respectable pace. She was within an arm's length of the attendant who was taking boarding passes, when she felt a detaining hand on her shoulder.

She turned to find several male police officers, accompanied by a female officer, representing the airport police.

"Ms. Young," a twenty-something police officer pleasantly addressed her in English. He bowed, ill at ease when she pinned him with inquiring eyes. "Would you come with us, please?"

When he referred to her by name, Cara's stomach cartwheeled. "What is the matter, Officer?" she inquired politely.

He was surprised when Cara spoke with him in Korean. Promptly regaining his composure, he gestured with his arm, away from the line of people boarding the plane. He reverted to speaking Korean. "May we speak with you privately?"

Cara realized that the young officer was being courteous to a fault, even by Korean standards. He certainly was not required to treat her as deferentially as he was, as evidenced by the stares of wonder from his fellow officers.

Cara noted the name badge pinned on his uniform and bowed respectfully.

How ironic that his surname was identical to the stern, middle-aged police officer who had interrogated her years ago at a hospital in the Itaewon District of Seoul. This young law enforcement officer, at least, deferred to her citizenship and social rank.

"Of course, Officer Choi," she agreed pleasantly, casting an envious backward glance at passengers boarding the aircraft.

Travelers moved aside and curiously watched as airport police escorted Cara to the security office at the hub of the airport.

It reminded Cara of another life altering event in her past, when she had walked surrounded by guards to board an airplane bound for the States after living in South Korea for fifteen years—her second, and she believed last, separation from Moon.

Cara realized with a knot in the pit of her stomach that she was going to miss their flight to America—that someone was preventing her from leaving the country. Why? Whom?

An officious little man wearing an expensive suit and a self-satisfied smile awaited their arrival in the security office. In an unconscious gesture, he smugly adjusted the knot of his tie when he observed Cara safely in the custody of airport police.

A lawyer, Cara quickly surmised.

When everyone took a seat, the attorney cleared his throat. "My influential client," he began by indulging his vanity, "is the grandmother of this child." Here he gestured to a sleeping Regalo. "Mrs. Moon asserts that her grandson is being kidnapped by his mother and illegally removed from South Korea without the consent of his father."

Cara—and everyone else uncomfortably wedged in the tight quarters—stared in disbelief at him. Then all eyes questioningly turned toward Cara.

She mentally cursed. The bitch who had shown very little interest in her grandson, who most probably could have cared less, never ceased to interfere.

Cara nodded in agreement. In this situation, honesty was the best policy. "It is true that his father and I are estranged, and that he is currently out of the country."

There was an uncomfortable shift of bodies in the room.

What Cara could not have known was that Korean family law was a slippery slope, granting the grandparents of a child certain custody rights in the absence of the biological father and proper registration of the child's birth.

Cara knew enough, however, to play the citizenship card. "My son is an American citizen...as I am." She shot a disdainful glance at Mrs. Moon's attorney. "We have valid passports."

She made a polite request of the young officer, apparently the senior officer in charge—at least for the interim. "I would like to speak with a representative of the American Embassy."

The officer promptly ordered a subordinate to contact the American Embassy in Seoul. He was more than willing to let a higher authority assume responsibility for this convoluted case of citizenship and rightful child custody.

"That's all very well, Ms. Young," Mrs. Moon's attorney said with a malicious glint in his eyes, "but in the meantime, my client wants the child put under protective custody."

The female officer advanced toward Cara, intending to take Regalo from her arms.

Cara heard her father's voice. *Do you love your son?*

She tightened her grip on Regalo, her lungs so tense with anxiety she could barely draw a breath. She was not about to allow Regalo to be taken from her or entrust his care to strangers.

If her dread about Regalo's welfare, and fury at being forcibly separated from him was love, then—yes, by God—she loved her son.

Cara's eyes glittered like a feral cat. She spoke each word emphatically, her voice a menacing growl. "You will not take my son from me."

The female police officer's expression filled with apprehension as she warily backed away from Cara.

"Come, come, Ms. Young," the attorney huffed, getting to his feet.

It would not due to disappoint Mrs. Moon. One did not disappoint Mrs. Moon and maintain one's employment. "When Consul General Moon Hyo returns, we will revisit this situation."

A sharp and determined feminine voice inquired from the doorway, "And what situation is that?"

Madame Chang cast a withering glare at Mrs. Moon's legal representative. Sang Hee stood behind and to her right, and a poised, silver-haired man with a briefcase stood on her left.

Cara let out an audible sigh of relief.

Officer Choi got to his feet, clearly confused. "May I inquire who you are, madam?"

Madame Chang presented her attorney. "My legal representative, Attorney Park."

He answered the inquiry of the young police officer on Madame's behalf, voice deep and confidence inspiring. "Ms. Young was employed by my client, Madame Chang, for a number of years and is a close personal friend. We are here to support Ms. Young, and offer a resolution to the alleged kidnapping of this child until his father returns from abroad."

The young officer in charge, indeed his entire force, appeared to relax. "And your resolution, sir?"

"Sang Hee, the father's sister and the child's aunt, will care for him in an apartment that Consul General Moon maintains in Seoul, where child protective authorities can visit daily, until the Consul General is present for an interview."

When their eyes met, Sang Hee offered Cara a wan smile. Cara reciprocated and mouthed a grateful *thank you* as Sang Hee gently eased the baby from her arms. Regalo settled comfortably, sleepily, against his aunt's shoulder.

"Now just a moment," Mrs. Moon's lawyer objected weakly, aware that he had been outmaneuvered by Attorney Park.

Madame Chang interrupted him with quiet determination, almost daring anyone to dispute her wishes. "Ms. Young will accompany me this evening and will remain with me for as long as it takes to settle this matter."

She glanced at her attorney, cuing him to resume.

"I will be filing additional paperwork in the courts first thing tomorrow morning." Attorney Park glanced at Mrs. Moon's attorney. "Attorney Noh, you can be sure that I will be working closely with the American Embassy. I will also verify that you have filed the necessary documents for your actions today and not overstepped your legal bounds."

Noh telegraphed his anxiety by unconsciously adjusting his tie. Charges of wrongful detainment and malpractice insistently rang in his ears. "I would expect nothing less."

Madame Chang concluded the proceedings. "Are we finished here?"

Her attorney passed a thick set of documents to Officer Choi. One month on the job, the young man swallowed hard, overwhelmed by the sheer volume of legally filed court forms. He nodded numbly.

"We are finished here," Attorney Park announced briskly, efficiently ushering the three women from the airport security office.

Woe Is Me

July 2007
Seoul, South Korea

CARA LAY WITH HER HEAD upon Madame Chang's lap in the back seat of her limousine, tears of remorse and grief streaming from her eyes.

Madame soothingly stroked her hair. Notwithstanding, her tone when speaking to Cara was anything but soothing. "Did I teach you nothing in our years together? Never…never, let the opposition know what you are thinking or planning. Never let them drive you to anger or carelessness. Never make a decision based on desperation."

Cara drew in a ragged breath. "I am at such odd ends, Madame… Moon left Seoul for God knows where and how long."

She admitted with anguish, "And now, after trying to leave Korea and reclaim my life, I'll be lucky if I get my son back." She hid her face behind her hand, exhausted by the length and events of the day. "It seems so hopeless."

"My lawyers will handle that," Madame reassured her confidently. "Meanwhile, your son will be safe and well cared for by your sister-in-law."

"Thank God," Cara murmured with immense relief. She trusted Sang Hee implicitly—her constant ally and consolation—especially now.

After a long silence, Cara shared with Madame Chang another fact that clawed mercilessly at her heart. "And Michael left me."

Madame did not sympathize. "About time," she said under her breath.

"Why, Madame?" Cara begged her revered mentor. "Why did he go to America and leave me when I needed him the most?"

"Stupid girl. Did you not see how he suffered? All those years with no one but you in his eyes. Nothing but his own longing and misery to keep him company."

Madame's observation made Cara feel cruel and self-indulgent. "I thought…"

"You thought, you thought," Madame interrupted impatiently. "You don't think. That is your problem. You follow your wildly irresponsible heart like a lovesick fool. You are blind to those around you…those who suffer the misfortune of caring for you…of loving you."

Cara sustained a shocked silence. Finally, she admitted in a small voice, "Michael once called me a fool when it came to love."

"No truer words were ever spoken," Madame pronounced flatly.

"Madame, I have made such a miserable mess of things," Cara lamented woefully.

"Self-pity does not become you," Madame scolded her mildly. "Use this time for some much needed introspection. It will serve you better."

Cara pulled herself together and sat up, swiping away the shiny tears that tracked over her cheeks. As always, there was much wisdom in Madame Chang's words.

"Yes, of course, Madame," she agreed sheepishly. "Thank you."

Madame affectionately gazed upon her accomplished yet surprisingly vulnerable protégé. "My girl, you are nothing if not consistent," she granted kindly. "Strong and fiercely independent when you rely on no one but yourself…weak and off-balance when you surrender your spirit to your passions."

Cara smiled wanly, unable to deny Madame's astute assessment of her character flaws.

"Still, you are true to your nature and have a generous and kind heart," Madame noted with tenderness. She placed a soft, warm hand upon Cara's cheek. "And I shall always love you."

Cara's breath hitched in her throat as she marked the significance of the moment—the first time Madame had ever shared her feelings toward her.

Cara covered Madame's hand with her own, leaning into the comfort of her touch. "Thank you, Madame," she murmured. "And I will always love and be grateful to you."

Hold, Please

July 2007
Seoul, South Korea

Madame Chang had eagerly anticipated a long awaited vacation in the temperate South Pacific Islands to sit on the beach in the all-too-rare company of her lover, Daan, and his daughter, Chen Chae.

When Madame announced she was going to cancel her trip and remain in Seoul until they had satisfactorily concluded the matter of Cara's detainment in Korea, Cara would not hear of it.

"You will go, Madame," Cara asserted firmly. "There is nothing more you can do here."

After Cara had worn her down with protracted protests, Madame agreed to keep her travel plans. However, she insisted, "I will call you every day."

Cara smiled at her affectionately. "If that will make you feel better, but it isn't necessary. Your attorney keeps me advised."

After Madame's reluctant departure, Cara moped around her penthouse—aimlessly wandering from room to room to room. After three days, she finally decided it was time to quit feeling sorry for herself—stop behaving like a victim—bathe, shampoo her hair, brush her teeth, and get dressed. She needed to be among people—preferably people she loved.

She called Philippe.

Although they had spoken often on the phone after her return to Korea, they had not been together in a while. He seemed excited to hear from her, but distracted.

His fashion designer partner was premiering his fall line of clothing at a luxurious Seoul venue the following afternoon. There was much to do and little time in which to do it.

Philippe invited, in fact begged, Cara to come backstage as his guest and observe the insanity. Having never before witnessed such a spectacle, Cara agreed, relieved to have some interesting plans for the following day.

She filled her remaining hours, in part, with a daily call from Sang Hee. Sang Hee regaled Cara with a bulletin that Mrs. Moon had, just that day, presented herself at the door of Moon Hyo's apartment and demanded admittance.

Madame Chang's attorney had persuaded the court that it was in Regalo's best interest not to expose him to other family members, save Sang Hee and her husband, until his father had returned to Korea and they could address the matter of child custody.

Sang Hee reported with pride that her husband had called building security to remove her mother—furious and stubbornly immovable—from the premises.

Cara unmistakably heard the satisfaction in Sang Hee's voice when she recounted how her mother railed against her mistreatment, swinging her handbag at the security guards, threatening them to release her as they unceremoniously dragged her down the hallway to the elevator.

At the conclusion of their entertaining conversation, Sang Hee put the phone to Regalo's ear so that he could hear his mother's voice.

He jabbered happily, cherished and content in the center of his aunt and uncle's world.

Cara embarrassed Sang Hee with profuse praise and thanks to both her and her husband for taking such good care of their nephew.

"I don't worry about him knowing he is in your safekeeping," Cara murmured tearfully.

News from Madame Chang's attorney—more of a reassurance and courtesy call than anything else—was upbeat but unchanged.

Attorney Park gently advised Cara that before he could successfully petition the court to release Regalo into her custody—and he believed he would be successful—Moon must return to Korea.

Cara could do nothing more than strive to master one of seven heavenly virtues—that of patience.

More waiting.

Philippe

July 2007
Seoul, South Korea

The next afternoon, Cara timed her arrival at the fashion show venue when the bulk of preparations for the showcase had been accomplished. She preferred not to be a distraction or impede Philippe's completion of his assigned duties.

His face visibly brightened, punctuated by dimples, when Cara cleared the security check at the rear door. He fussed over her and settled her in an advantageous spot he had arranged for her comfort and visibility, and encouraged her to help herself at the catered refreshment table.

"We'll drink some champagne together later."

"Toast your success," Cara inspired him with a smile.

Before sprinting away, he kissed her cheek and announced breathlessly, "I am so happy you are here."

Cara looked on as Philippe abided his lord and master's incessant whining and satisfied his capricious whims, dashing from model to model—solving an accessory crisis here, a fitting emergency there—running himself ragged. This, in addition to overseeing the intricate hair designs of twelve models.

Cara did not like it. She did not like it at all.

She squinted in disapproval at the diminutive designer, his expression pinched in cranky and chronic discontent, his attitude bloated with self-importance.

The little pisher.

He was younger than Philippe by about four years—a spoiled and gifted child who had been sent abroad to study in America. In public, he spoke to Philippe informally, without the polite Korean observance of honorifics—a grammatical form of speech used when conferring honor and respect upon a superior or elder.

If only his stature was as monumental as his ego, Cara mused uncharitably.

After months of protracted planning, weeks of preparation, days of harrowing timelines, and final hours of chaotic crises, the designer showcase began.

In just an hour and a half, it was over—the finale, the curtain call, the speech, the irritating strobe effects of the photo shoot, the promotional seduction of the media.

Philippe stood by Cara, watching his partner bask in the limelight and the accolades of his admirers.

Cara slid a comforting arm around Philippe's waist. "Thank you for inviting me today, *Dongsaeng*." Little brother. "I am reminded of how talented you are." She looked up at him with unabashed admiration. "Your confidence under pressure and creative contribution behind the scenes made the show a success."

His smile was wistful as he gazed at Cara, eyes glistening from her praise.

Cara would not be surprised if a generous investment from Philippe's inheritance had capitalized the designer showcase. Although none of her business, it rankled nevertheless.

The show officially concluded. There was a backstage toast with champagne, a hollow expression of thanks from the designer, a final cheer among the participants for their accomplishment.

Emotionally drained after five months of preparation, everyone haphazardly scrambled to gather their personal belongings and vacate the premises.

Cara and Philippe followed suit, following his partner and his retinue to a stretch limousine waiting at the curb.

Philippe mentioned that they were on their way to a lavish club in Gangnam-gu to host a party for about 250 of their closest friends.

"Come with us please, *Noona*," Philippe begged, pulling her behind him.

Cara was not in the right frame of mind for the pandemonium, crush, and superficial chatter these events invariably warranted.

She begged off, shaking her head. "This is your night, Philippe. Your celebration."

With uncommon solemnity, Philippe murmured intuitively, "You haven't seen him at his best. The show almost drove him crazy."

Cara was saddened that Philippe felt the need to make excuses. "Be good to yourself, *Dongsaeng*."

Philippe hugged her tightly, deflecting her concern. "I love you, *Noona*."

Cara affectionately squeezed him. "I love you more."

"Philippe!" his lover impatiently summoned from inside the limousine.

"I'll call you!" Philippe promised as he scrambled aboard.

It began to rain.

Cara stood on the sidewalk, watching the limousine pull away from the curb and disappear in traffic on the boulevard, heartsick for her much beloved friend—and herself—for their dubious fortunes of love.

14
A Coincidence. Nothing More

July 2007
Seoul, South Korea

CARA AIMLESSLY DROVE THE STREETS of Seoul, repeating a previous occasion in her young life when she had felt similarly rudderless, powerless, and alone. Only this time, she was not walking the unfamiliar streets of Seoul as a newly arrived foreigner. She was driving a Mercedes-Benz sedan that Madame Chang had offered for her use—in a city she knew like the back of her hand.

An emergency medical transport—siren wailing and lights flashing—blasted past her, rocking her sedan from side to side with a rush of wind and speed.

Unconsciously, the EMT crew triggered thoughts of Kim Jae Sun—the young boy she had rescued after a beating by gang members in the Itaewon District of Seoul nearly twenty years ago. The boy who had grown into an accomplished young man and continued to impress her with his courage, selflessness, and honor—who would always hold a special place in her heart.

Jae Sun initiated the last communication between them. He happily reported in a text, with modest pride, that he received a promotion within the EMT ranks at the hospital and given his own unit to command.

Cara teasingly attempted to finagle an admission from him regarding a love interest. Although he denied an existing romantic relationship, by all indications, his cousin, Dalisay—who had been in love with him since childhood—was playing an increasingly prominent role in his life.

CARA IMPULSIVELY STOPPED BEFORE A noraebang in Gangnam-gu—a very upscale, plush Korean karaoke drinking club.

Before she could change her mind and drive on, the valet opened her car door and gave her a ticket. The door attendant smiled a greeting and swung the front door wide for her to enter.

Once inside, the manager of the club escorted her with deference to a private room and inquired if she expected more people in her party. When she numbly shook her head, he suavely offered her the companionship of a young man for the evening. When she once again shook her head and dismissed him with a quiet thank you, he bowed respectfully and, on his way out, briskly reminded his serving staff to be attentive to their guest's comfort.

Cara's attendants directed her to a plush and comfortable bench seat in an intimate corner of the room, and placed an artistically arranged plate of sliced fresh fruit with serving skewers on the table to accompany a full array of liquor bottles. They adjusted the lighting to a softly illuminated, meditative setting and closed the door behind them, leaving her alone.

For those patrons wishing to sing along with the hottest Korean boy and girl bands, management provided a wide video screen, microphones, and powerful speakers. The eclectic song menu on the table also touted Japanese, Taiwanese, French, Italian, and classic American music of the '80s and '90s, as well as contemporary musical artists.

Cara did not wish to sing—she wanted to drink. Actually, she wanted to get drunk. She chose a selection of American Pop videos from the '80s, turned down the volume, and hesitantly eyed the bottles of liquor.

She recalled, with a fanciful wave of nausea, the last time she had too much to drink. Was it wine? Yes, at the hotel suite in New York City where she had accompanied Moon for a weeklong conference at the Korean Consulate.

Moon had thoughtlessly stood her up for a romantic dinner she had planned in their hotel suite. Out of frustration and spite, she had nearly finished a three-hundred-dollar bottle of California Napa Valley Cabernet Sauvignon.

She felt lousy the next day.

Moon was amused but unsympathetic.

She expelled a frustrated breath of air. What was it about the man that drove her to drink?

She grabbed the bottle of select vodka and poured three fingers into a cocktail glass liberally stacked with ice.

The first gulp tasted like poison on her tongue. The second swig was not as bad. The third was better still.

CARA OPENED HER EYES.

Kang. Handsome in an expensive black designer suit and brilliant white dress shirt, shiny black hair artfully styled. He looked down at her as she lay on the bench seat—his earnest gaze skimming over her features as if attempting to recall them, or commit them to memory. The expressions of bewilderment and concern were equally evident on his face.

Am I dreaming? Cara asked herself.

THIS NORAEBANG WAS ONE OF Boss Jeun's most lucrative clubs. Kang came every week to meet with the manager, go over the accounts, and collect the profits.

The manager—who had held the position for over seventeen years—was honest, competent, and eager to please Jeun. As usual, everything was in order.

Kang gravely praised him. "You have worked hard."

The middle-aged club manager smiled broadly and bowed respectfully. "Thank you, sir."

"Changes are coming," Kang forewarned.

The manager became flustered. "Sir?"

"Take whatever precautions necessary to protect yourself and your family...and your employees."

"But..."

"I encourage you to find another position."

"Am I being fired?" the manager breathed, quailing at the unfairness, at the ultimate futility of his years of dedicated service and loyalty.

"If you stay, you will become a slave...or worse," Kang cautioned him.

"What could be worse?" the manager inquired in confusion.

"Death," Kang abruptly guaranteed him. "You could be dead."

He handed the manager the week's profits for the club. "Take this and distribute it among the staff—it should provide a month's severance for all of you."

The manager had been attentive to the rumors—the speculation—that had run rife in the organization since the recent death of Boss Jeun.

He bowed deeply, finally absorbing the direness of Kang's message. "Thank you, sir. I will do as you ask." He gestured for Kang to proceed him. "Allow me to escort you out."

Kang found several of his men loitering in the hallway outside the door of a private guest room. They were gawking through the narrow window, whispering and laughing among themselves.

"What's this?" Kang asked, startling them.

They stepped away from the door, bowing self-consciously, murmuring their apologies.

Kang glanced through the window. A foreign woman was reclined on the bench seat, arm thrown over her eyes, shoes off, and skirt hiked up her shapely thighs.

The muscles in Kang's belly clenched.

He would know her anytime, anywhere, anyplace. "Cara," he murmured breathlessly. "What are you doing here?"

Kang looked to the club manager for an explanation.

The manager blanched under the fierceness of Kang's glare. "I believe she is an American woman, sir."

"How long has she been here?" Kang demanded.

"Several hours."

Kang shot a look at his men that commanded them to disperse. They did so promptly, hurrying down the hallway toward the front entrance.

"I need Yi," Kang called after them.

"Yes, sir!" they cried in unison.

He waved away the club manager and quietly entered the room. The table was full of liquor bottles, but the seal had been broken on only one—the vodka. It was about a quarter-empty. The fruit plate remained untouched.

He stood looking down at her—observed her quiet breathing, the flush of liquor in her cheeks, the smooth white skin of her inner arm. Her copper hair was in wild disarray—as though she had been thoughtlessly dragging her fingers through it.

CARA GROANED AND STRETCHED TO ease the painful kink in her left hip. She blinked several times. The illusion of Kang remained—silent and watchful.

"Am I dreaming?" she questioned again, this time aloud.

She started when Kang hunkered down next to her and responded quietly, "No."

She frowned, hesitantly reaching out to touch his chest with her index finger.

He smiled at her wide-eyed amazement when she confirmed he was flesh and blood.

Gasping with the realization, Cara struggled to pull herself together—to sit up. "Ooh," she whimpered, clutching her head. "Dizzy."

Kang supported her as he swung her legs off the cushioned bench and planted her feet firmly on the floor.

She pushed away his hands. "What are you doing here?" she asked in agitation, attempting to mask her embarrassment.

"I could ask you the same thing."

"You could, but I wouldn't expect an answer."

She seemed stymied by her inability to fit her left shoe on her right foot.

Kang took the shoe from her grasp and smoothly slipped it on her left foot, following suit with the remaining high heel on her right foot.

"I would think you could make better use of your time," he chastened her wryly, confounded by the atypical behavior of this uncommonly resilient woman.

His connections to the police department still intact, Kang was aware of the latest hurdles placed in her way. Was she weakening under seemingly overwhelming odds? Buckling under pressure when her marriage and the custody of her son were in such precarious balance. Or had she finally concluded that she had enough?

She cocked her head and focused on Kang, one eye squeezed shut. "Didn't you and I agree never to meet again?"

His chuckle was mirthless. "You may have mentioned it."

"And so?"

"Our meeting is a coincidence. Nothing more."

"Coincidence." Cara chortled, threw her head back on the cushion and looked up at the ceiling, quoting '50s American Beat Generation author William S. Burroughs. "In the magical universe there are no coincidences and there are no accidents..."

She needed a nap.

Kang caught her as she attempted to lie back down. "No, no." He brought her back to an upright position, sat beside her, and circled a stabilizing arm around her shoulders.

He beckoned his lieutenant, Yi, who patiently waited in the doorway. "Call a driver for Ms. Moon." He found the laminated valet ticket in her handbag and tossed it across the room. Yi deftly caught it. "Her car is parked outside."

Yi bowed and briskly ordered the club manager to call a designated driver.

Widely prevalent in South Korea—reputedly the hardest drinking country in the world—the designated driver served those who had imbibed too much and needed to be chauffeured home in their own vehicles.

Replacement drivers, as they were also known—unappreciated, underpaid, and sleep-deprived—were dispatched through central call centers 24 hours a day and well worth the $16-$18 fee to reach home safely.

The young driver arrived in less than twenty minutes.

Kang walked Cara through the heavy monsoon rain to her car. Yi held an umbrella over both of them and opened the rear passenger door. Kang got Cara settled and buckled her seatbelt.

"Thank you," she managed to mumble, more emotionally deplete than intoxicated.

It reminded Kang of the early morning they first met—Cara thanking him after he had buckled her seatbelt in the police cruiser.

It rubbed a sore spot on his heart. He should be the one to drive her.

But with events now in play, accelerating exponentially, he could not risk putting her in harm's way. He was a hunted man.

"Take her wherever she asks to go," Kang commanded the young driver.

Yi gave the kid two hundred dollars. The young man's face brightened and he bowed several times in appreciation. "Thank you, sir!"

"It's time to go," Yi reminded Kang.

Kang nodded, watching the Mercedes drive away. He turned to accompany Yi and saw from the corner of his eye the brake lights flash, the car stop. He frowned. It was no longer moving.

Yi grasped his arm when he started toward the car. "Kang Dae Ho, we must go!" he whispered urgently.

Kang raised a staying hand. "Wait a minute."

When he knocked on the driver's side window of the Mercedes, the young kid lowered it. Eyeglasses speckled with rain, he did not bother to hide the frustration written on his broad face. "Sir, she said she doesn't know where to go!"

Kang peered through the window, getting soaked by the rain.

Cara sat with her head thrown back against the seat, eyes closed.

The rookie driver objected to the illogical situation in which he found himself. "Sir! How can I take her home if she doesn't know where that is?"

Kang gave Yi a meaningful look when he joined him. "Go. Find a place that will be safe."

"Kang Dae Ho!" Yi protested over the steady drum beat of rain against the car roof. "What is this woman to you? Let the driver take her to a hotel."

Kang shrugged off Yi's grip and gave him an encouraging push. "Go now!"

Kang beckoned the perplexed driver. "Get out. I'll take over from here."

Relieved, the young man sprang from the car. Regretfully—respectfully using both hands—he offered Kang the return of his two-hundred-dollar fee.

Kang waved it away. "Keep it."

The young man grinned widely, ecstatic with his good fortune. He energetically bowed several times. "Thank you, sir! Thank you very much!"

He would go home, two hundred dollars richer, and gratefully climb into bed beside his pregnant wife—but not before eating a steaming bowl of hot soup. He was soaked to the skin.

Kang slipped into the driver's seat, closed the door, and buckled his seat belt. He adjusted the rear view mirror and exchanged a soulful and long-suffering stare with Cara.

In a numbed state of disbelief, Yi watched Kang put the Mercedes in gear, smoothly accelerate away from the club, and drive down the street.

Twice Upon A Dream

July 2007
Seoul, South Korea

IT WAS A LITTLE BEFORE three o'clock in the morning when Kang pulled up and stopped the sedan in the predominately Korean neighborhood where he had lived as a modestly compensated police officer before his undercover assignment to infiltrate the Jeun syndicate.

He maintained the apartment anticipating occasions when he may need to disappear. Where he would not have to look over his shoulder or pretend. A retreat where he could put some distance between him and his new friends—to clear his head.

Kang turned off the headlights and the engine. He slipped out of the driver's seat and softly closed his door, attempting to keep a low profile so as not to alert the neighbors of his presence.

He walked with purpose to Cara's side of the car and opened her door. She looked up at him with apprehension, the moisture in her eyes reflecting the muted glimmer of the streetlight in the rain. She anxiously looked past him, trying to reason their whereabouts.

Kang could not indulge her hesitance. He unbuckled her seatbelt, pulled her from the backseat and, with a firm hold on her arm, guided her up the steps to his apartment.

Inserting the key he extracted from his inside jacket pocket, he opened the door and prompted Cara ahead of him. A bright light automatically came on in the foyer when they crossed over the threshold.

Kang secured the two deadbolts on the door.

When Cara turned to face him, Kang half-expected her to berate him for bringing her here without her permission. Instead, her expression was inquisitive.

"Is this your place?" she asked.

He nodded. "I was living here when we first met."

When she walked into the combined living and kitchen area, Kang switched on a table lamp.

Cara looked around with polite interest, appreciating the efficient floor plan and cleanliness of the apartment.

"It's very nice," she commented graciously, sincerely.

Kang could not help staring at her. She was just as he had pictured her so many years ago, standing in the middle of his apartment—filling it with pleasurable possibilities. He was finding it difficult to believe she was here with him now.

She blinked drowsily at this familiar stranger—some of the same thoughts going through her mind. She smiled shyly.

"I'm sorry," Kang apologized in a rush, becoming galvanized to attend to the comfort of his guest.

He eased her out of her damp coat and hung it with her handbag on the hook by the door. "Are you cold? Would you like a hot shower and some tea?"

"Hmmm," she purred deep in her throat, closing her eyes at the soothing prospect. "That would be wonderful."

He ushered her into the bedroom, grabbed clean towels and a set of his Seoul Metro workout gear from the cupboard. He turned on the light in the bathroom and moved aside to let Cara enter. "You can hang your damp clothes over there." He motioned to a rack with hangers at the far side of the bathroom straddling a heating vent in the floor.

Cara looked at the bundle Kang thrust in her arms, and then up at him. "Thank you, Kang Dae Ho." Her hypnotic blue eyes were warm with gratitude.

Kang fleetingly got lost in their depths. He backed away.

It was gratitude, he cautioned his lonely heart. That was all.

He closed the door behind him and went to the compact kitchen to make tea. He filled the teapot with water from a carafe in the refrigerator and placed it on one of two burners on the small stove.

His hands were trembling.

When Cara emerged from the bathroom, her hair was towel dried and curly, her skin a rosy pink and scented with his shower gel.

Kang admired the way she filled out the androgynous bagginess of his workout gear with new and interesting curves.

"Feel better?" he inquired.

"Much better," she confirmed with a contented smile, eagerly accepting the cup of tea he offered her. "Thank you." She sipped the tea and questioningly looked at him. "What about you?"

"What?"

"You are wet, too."

He looked down at his damp and wrinkled shirt and trousers and laughed quietly. He had not even been aware. "So it appears."

He grabbed some towels from the cupboard. "I'll be right out. Make yourself comfortable."

He closed the bathroom door and looked around in amazement.

Her used bath towel was neatly folded in half and hanging on the towel bar. She had wiped dry the sink, vanity, and mirror. Her clothing fastidiously hung over her perfectly aligned shoes.

He smiled. The woman of his dreams seamlessly fit into his reality.

The Face Of Fear

July 2007
Seoul, South Korea

Kang stepped from his bedroom handsomely dressed in a tailored bright white dress shirt and dark slacks.

Cara perched on his couch, seated forward as if in anticipation. She greeted him with a spontaneous and appreciative smile.

His heart skipped in an irregular beat.

He addressed her tentatively. "Cara…"

Eyes wide, she prompted, "Yes?"

"I would like to ask you about something…that may be very personal."

She seemed confused.

He held out his hand to her. "Come with me."

She stood and walked toward him, eyeing his hand before delicately laying hers on his.

He led her into his bedroom and invited her to sit on his bed.

Still wary, she did as he asked.

She watched him walk to his closet, push aside precisely organized clothing hanging from wooden hangers, and press a spot on the back wall. A wide panel swung opened revealing a private cove lined with shelves and a three-foot-by-three-foot safe. He spun the dial on the safe several times, opened it, and extracted something from its interior.

He hunkered down in front of her, his expression solemn, and handed her two photos.

Curious, Cara accepted and inspected them.

They were pictures of her—much younger—head bowed and eyes covered with a blue silk scarf. She was half-sitting and subdued with her hands tied over her head to what appeared to be the slats of a futon bed. The poses were identical, as if they had been captured one right after the other.

Cara's face blanched of color and she gasped, flinging away the snapshots.

She was breathing irregularly—rapid and shallow—as if she were in shock.

Kang placed steadying hands on her knees.

AFTER MERCADO'S HOMICIDE, THE POLICE had thoroughly searched his residence and nightclub on Hooker Hill.

Kang had come across the photographs of Cara in a locked desk drawer in Mercado's office. Although risking a reprimand or outright dismissal from the force for impeding an ongoing investigation, he had surreptitiously slipped them into the inside pocket of his suit jacket, withholding them from the evidence locker and keeping them well hidden until he had the opportunity, if ever, to speak with Cara.

KANG RETRIEVED THE PHOTOS FROM the floor and studied the misery on Cara's face.

"Where did you find them?" she murmured, trembling.

"Mercado had them locked in his desk at his nightclub."

"Mother of God," she lamented, her breath hitching in her throat. She grew weak with the realization. "Mercado. All this time…it was Mercado."

"What went on here, Cara?" Kang kindly but firmly questioned.

Cara had never shared this incident with anyone—hiding the memory away like dirty laundry from the eyes of unexpected houseguests. Yet, it festered deep within her, plagued her when she was feeling particularly vulnerable, stressed, or insecure. On these occasions, she resisted sleep—leaving on a light or playing music—until she could no longer keep her eyes open. Then, succumbing to the dreaded realm, disjointed and menacing images chased her dreams.

Now, hesitantly, she began to shed light on what had so very long remained in the dark and fearful depths of her mind.

However, neither she nor Kang—from her telling of it—were privy to the full story.

Only one demon knew that—and he was dead.

Mercado

열 다섯

15
Crucible

April 1991
Seoul, South Korea
cru•ci•ble - noun
A place or occasion of severe test or trial

IT WAS THE WEEKEND. CARA decided to go to the cinema to watch a Saturday afternoon matinee to avoid the anticipated 100,000 people celebrating the Lotus Lantern Festival.

As was sometimes her misfortune when she attended the movies alone, three high-strung teenaged boys, sitting one aisle behind and five seats to her right, heckled her—whistling, wolf calling, and speaking to her in an inappropriate manner.

Danilo Mercado watched it all from his seat four rows back on the other side of the theater—read the discomposure in the American woman's body language, noticed the uneasy tension in the muscles of her jaw.

He crouched down and crossed the aisle to sit directly behind the teens. He kicked the back of the seat of the wiseass ringleader.

The kid glanced over his shoulder, reasoning that it was an accidental brush.

Mercado kicked the seat once again, making his intention clear.

The kid exploded with a curse, and he and his two sidekicks turned to confront Mercado.

Mercado's eyes shined wickedly, his white teeth flashing in a matching grin. He gripped the hilt of his eight-inch Italian stiletto knife in his right fist—the finely honed steel blade flashing from the glare of the cinema screen as he pivoted the point into the palm of his left hand.

Appearing almost black—a shiny, thick, and slow running rivulet of blood leaked from the tip of the knife, down his palm, and continued its gradual descent on his sinewy forearm.

The teens exchanged panicky glances. In unified and unspoken agreement, they jumped out of their seats and, prodding one another to move faster, exited the theater.

Mercado saw the confusion on the American woman's face as the trio beat an abrupt and hasty retreat. He slouched down in his seat when she flashed a curious glance around her.

He felt a surge of satisfaction as he watched her settle back in her seat and smile in relief, returning her full attention to the action on the screen.

Mercado wiped the blood from his switchblade and his skin, and settled back as well—waiting for the movie to end and the house lights to go up.

THE LOTUS LANTERN FESTIVAL—THE CAPITOL city's annual celebration of Buddha's birth and blessings of health, long life, and abundance—was in its final phase.

A parade concluded the two-week festival, closing off adjacent boulevards. It was a spectacular event of vivid sights and sounds— beautifully illuminated fire- and steam-breathing dragons and animal-shaped floats, and brilliant splashes of watercolors in the ancestral and magnificently attired dancing troupes and musicians that marched through the heart of Seoul.

Colorful lanterns in the shapes of animals, fruits, and flowers hung for miles along both sides of the Han River and all around the city, symbolizing the light of wisdom.

Cara was blissfully distracted by the exquisitely designed lanterns constructed of silk or traditional paper, called *hanji*, displayed in a false ceiling overhead. She smiled as she made her way through the maze of detours and throngs of people—unaware that she was being stalked.

Mercado stayed right with her, keeping her in his line of sight, watching her being jostled away from the parade by spectators, bumping her back, back, back near the mouth of an alley.

He made his move. Approaching her from behind, her captured her with a restraining arm around her waist.

She gasped, trying to see who was behind her, to see the face of the man who had her pinned against his body. Mercado swung her around and forced her into the shadows of the nearly deserted alley.

She began to comprehend her situation and started to struggle, opening her mouth to scream. Mercado silenced her by pressing a cloth dampened with chloroform against her nose and mouth.

She shook her head from side to side, trying to avoid breathing the sweet-smelling vapor, bucking against Mercado's body, kicking, reaching up behind her to claw at his face. She managed to grab a handful of his long hair and give it a vicious yank.

He shouted an oath in pain.

At last, she dizzily weaved and slumped in his arms, unconscious.

Mercado chuckled. She was no coward. She put up a good fight.

He was going to enjoy this.

MERCADO CARRIED HER PIGGYBACK STYLE—like a child—or a woman who had too much to drink during the day's celebration.

They drew scant attention from the people they passed. Those who were curious quickly averted their eyes when Mercado threatened them with an intimidating scowl.

He wasted no time in reaching his destination, a working-class neighborhood where food carts choked the narrow street, and grocers and merchants went about earning their daily living.

Chloroform was tricky to use—too much could cause cardiac arrest, too little would induce a temporary and unpredictably timed unconsciousness.

He silently slipped the key he had duplicated into the lock of a second-story studio apartment, carefully eased Cara across the futon bed, and secured the three locks on the inside of the door.

He stood there for a moment, allowing his eyes to adjust to the darkness he had created. To obscure his identity and the passage of time—whether day or night—he had draped a heavy cloth over the expansive window that overlooked the busy neighborhood.

Cara stirred and opened her eyes, trying to get her bearings. An acrid chemical taste filled her mouth and tainted her sense of smell.

Dread filled her heart when she saw a figure moving around the darkened room, saw him reach for what looked to be a length of rope, and walk toward her.

She closed her eyes and remained absolutely still. She felt the calf of his leg brush against hers as he stood by the bed. When he grabbed her wrist, she sprang up and pushed him with every ounce of strength she possessed. He flew backwards and hit the floor hard, landing on his back.

She ran past him, frantically kicking him when he attempted to grab her leg. Brain muddled, she felt her way to the door and scrabbled with the locks.

She had managed to unlock all but one when her abductor cursed in Korean and put his hands on her. He roughly grabbed her by her arm and swung her away from the door.

"Help!" Cara shouted at the top of her lungs. "Help! Call the police!"

Mercado clamped his hand over her mouth.

She shook her head and managed to get the web of flesh between his thumb and index finger between her teeth. She bit down hard.

She had no time to revel in his sharp intake of breath or the metallic taste of his blood on her tongue. He growled deep in his throat, spun her around, and furiously slapped her across the face.

The momentum of the blow knocked her off balance, her body slamming with full force against the floor. Her right hip and shoulder absorbed the bone jarring shock of impact. She lay immobilized—the side of her face on fire, a shrill ringing in her ear—shattered and stunned.

Mercado took that opportunity to drag her to the futon mattress, supported by a base no more than a foot off the floor, and heave her on it. He grabbed the rope, quickly bound her wrists, and threaded and knotted the ends of the rope together through the slats of the headboard.

"If you don't want me to hurt you," Mercado warned fiercely, "don't cry out again."

She was breathing heavily from exertion and fright, angrily testing—jerking on—her restraints.

Still fuming from her attempted escape, Mercado climbed on the bed, perched on his knees, grasped her hips and yanked her body towards him—creating a taut and painful stretch on her shoulder joints and wrists.

She cried out in shock and pain.

He reached under her gauzy skirt, tore her pink lace panties from her hips, over her legs, and threw them aside. His breathing rapid and ragged, he raised and then pillowed her hips level with his. He impatiently unzipped his jeans.

He sensed, more than saw, her cat-like eyes on him—accusatory, defiant. Her body was rigid, but she did not resist.

Mercado grudgingly admired her courage, her pride.

She had asked no stupid questions of him. Who are you? What do you want?

She was not going to give him the satisfaction of struggling, crying, or pleading.

It took the wind from his sails.

He debated while battling to curb his eagerness. This would be over too quickly. It would not satisfy his lust for this woman. It would do little to feed his enormous ego.

She made him want to seduce her, persuade her to willingly spread her legs for him—to coax her to climax and hear her cries of pleasure.

Reluctantly, he decided to wait. He grabbed her under her arms and hoisted her back to the top of the bed, loosening the tension of her ropes.

A diaphanous blue scarf hung next to the closet. He snapped it from the hook and roughly tied it around her head, covering her eyes.

He would not tolerate their condemnation another minute—not until she looked at him with different eyes—until she looked at him with love and respect.

Mercado sat in an armchair before the shielded windows, his dark silhouette absorbing what light managed to leak through the edges of the window, quietly watching Cara.

He took a deep, agitated draw on his cigarette, the red-orange tip illuminating the glittering obsidian slivers of his eyes.

Oh, man, what was he doing? Why hadn't he just pulled her into the alleyway where he captured her, rape her, and be done with it?

Because, he grudgingly admitted, that had never been his intent.

Since the first time he had seen the American woman—when she rescued his cousin from an assault by gang members after Mercado had deserted him. Since keeping vigil with her as she stood for hours outside Jae Sun's ward at the hospital. Since watching her dole out cash to help his mother pay for part of his young cousin's medical bill.

Why he followed her day in and day out after discovering several years later that she had returned to Seoul.

Why he had kept an eye on the neighborhood adjoining hers, watched the comings and goings of its residents—witnessed the professor with his bags hail a taxi and heard him, through the open window of the cab, ask to go to the airport. Why he passed himself off as a student and learned from the manager of the apartments that Professor Jhang would be on sabbatical to Thailand for three months.

Since then, since now. He had watched and waited. He had made plans. That is why. That is why.

A Torch In The Darkness

December 1988
Seoul, South Korea

THAT DECEMBER IN 1988, MERCADO hovered in the shadows at the end of the hallway with a clear view of the door to Kim Jae Sun's hospital room. He was hanging around hoping to overhear a conversation about his cousin's condition.

Fuck. When he ran out of the alley, he thought the little shit was right behind him. When his conscience had gotten the better of him, he had double backed to find the little punk. He found him where he had left him, now laying on the ground with a young foreign woman kneeling beside him.

An ambulance was slowly weaving its way through the littered alley toward the two—swirling lights splashing a rainbow of colors against the dingy brick walls of the adjacent apartment buildings. When the ambulance had picked up the pair, Mercado ran behind them the three miles to the hospital.

He took in every detail of the lovely white skinned young woman as she leaned against the wall outside his cousin's room, apparently waiting, as he was, to hear about his condition.

When the physician emerged from Kim Jae Sun's ward, Mercado craned his neck around the corner to eavesdrop on their conversation.

She was an American.

The doctor assured her that the little punk was going to be okay.

Mercado's dark eyes glittered lecherously. "Well, well. How did you come to be here?" he whispered to her as she entered his cousin's hospital room.

He shrank back when his mother, half-sister, and neighbors straggled down the hallway and crowded into Kim Jae Sun's room. The last thing he needed was his mother creating a scene, berating him yet again for dealing drugs and associating with the hoodlums that swarmed in the lawless underbelly of the district.

MERCADO WAS BORN IN THE Philippines.

His father, a petty thief barely able to feed, clothe, and keep a roof over the heads of his wife and son, was discovered outside of a Red Cross warehouse with stolen food supplies on his truck, the load so heavy it nearly flattened the tires. In a period of famine and homelessness brought on by one of the worst typhoon seasons in history, an enraged mob pulled him from the cab of his pickup truck and beat him to death.

His mother, a devoutly religious Christian woman, was taken into the merciful fold of her well-meaning brethren who urged her to accept a proposal of marriage by mail from an equally devout but lonely widower in South Korea.

Newly arrived in Seoul from Manila, a bitter and resentful eleven-year-old Mercado met his mother's new Korean husband. He became sullen and determined not to be reliant upon, or beholden to, a man who at his best treated him with indifference.

Life on the streets was predatory and brutal, but Mercado fearlessly battled his way to the top of the heap, made good alliances, and even better money. He had earned recognition and respect in his barbarous world. If not respect—fear.

Exchanging once set of tragic circumstances for another, Mercado's mother bent her back in hard labor each day to help support her newlywed husband's household, which included an elderly and chronically ill mother. It so happened that the widower was more in need of a housekeeper, cook, and caregiver than a loving companion for life.

As is often the case with the luckless and beleaguered, her Korean husband died of a heart attack not long after his mother had preceded him into the next life. Once again, Mercado's mother had to support herself. But now, that also included a young daughter born to the couple a year after they married.

She did her best, and without complaint.

MERCADO SHADOWED THE AMERICAN WOMAN when she emerged from his cousin's room and completed a cash transaction with the clerk at the hospital service counter. He hung back when a district police officer hailed her and proceeded to question her in the lobby.

Mercado recognized the old bastard and his rookie partner. They had rousted him on a drug-related death in the neighborhood. When he had attempted to evade and outrun them, the overzealous probationary police officer had wrestled him to the ground, painfully wrenched his arms behind his back and cuffed him.

Mercado recalled the pointed and agonizing force of the young cop's knee in the middle of his back, his hand grinding his face into the filthy concrete—his outrage at being treated so disrespectfully.

It was not because he was innocent—he did sell the uncut dope to the junkie that caused his overdose. Mercado pragmatically viewed his first experience selling drugs as would any bottom-line entrepreneur. Cutting the base to dilute its potency would go make it go farther on the street and increase his profit margin.

The two cops had hauled him to the district police station for questioning. Narcotics officers hammered away at him, letting him cool his heels in a dimly lit interrogation room for hours. Ultimately, they were obligated to release him when they could not produce enough hard evidence to satisfy the prosecutor.

The policeman assistant who had busted Mercado knowingly eyed him, not fooled for a minute. Mercado flashed him a cocky grin as he threw open the door and skipped down the stairs of the station house, a free man.

Mercado committed to memory the rookie's identification badge—Kang Dae Ho. He would not underestimate Kang in the future. He would not forget him, either.

MERCADO HAD PATIENTLY WAITED OUTSIDE the hospital while the American woman was briefly questioned, intending to follow her and discover where she was staying.

Jaw tightly clenched, he watched Kang take her arm and escort her to his patrol car parked nearby. Mercado caught himself, suppressing a foolish temptation to intervene.

He fumed as the two of them talked in the squad car for several minutes before Kang started the engine and cruised out of the parking lot.

No. He would never forget Kang. Or, more pleasantly, the American woman.

IMAGINE HIS SURPRISE THREE YEARS later when he and two of his enforcers—after cleaning up some business with a low-life dog who had reported him to the cops—dropped into an unassuming little diner under an elevated highway in the central district and discovered the American woman clearing tables and serving customers.

Chingu – Friends

1991
Seoul, South Korea

CARA HAD FOUND HER WAY to the Kim's *hanshik jum* serving traditional Korean food in the company of acquaintances from the language class she attended every Tuesday evening.

When the group boisterously volleyed their newly assigned Korean words and phrases back and forth over the table, Mrs. Kim chimed in with a wide grin, gently correcting their pronunciation.

Cara liked Mrs. Kim's kind and open broad face, the gap between her large square white teeth, her friendly personality, and lively delivery of the language. She dressed in the typical *ajumma* or older married woman attire—long skirts and short-sleeve tops, wildly printed and mismatched.

Mr. Kim was a serious man, as reserved as his wife was outgoing. He smiled shyly when Cara bowed to him during his wife's introduction.

Cara began coming regularly, eating her one substantial meal a day at the Kim's, doing her homework from language class, soaking up the chatter among the patrons.

Mrs. Kim would sit with her when she wasn't busy, helping Cara with syntax and proper tense of verbs, encouraging her, praising the painstaking and incremental progress of her reading and writing skills.

One evening, a group of teens and their parents, coming from an event at a nearby school, flooded into the little dining room, overwhelming Mrs. Kim with orders.

Cara tentatively got to her feet and answered a patron's call for more *soju*, and then another patron's request for more dumplings. She saw tables that needed to be cleared, and did so quickly and efficiently. At Mr. Kim's direction, she began to deliver food to the tables.

So began Cara's as-needed and personally satisfying pastime of helping Mr. and Mrs. Kim.

Understandably, Cara's blue eyes and white face attracted attention. Some of it unwanted. When the male patrons became a bit too bold, loud, or unruly, Mr. Kim would fly out from the kitchen and protectively post himself in a wide stance near Cara. Arms folded over his chest, a butcher knife grasped in his fist, he conveyed his displeasure with a firm set to his jaw and a menacing glare.

The miscreant would invariably beat a hasty retreat from the premises, obligingly fall silent, or humbly reclaim his chair at his table.

Young Korean women who dined at the Kim's eyed Cara with bald animosity and, for the most part, treated her dismissively. Competition for future husbands was intensely fierce and unforgiving—driven by the culture's conviction that a young woman who was not married by the time she was twenty-five was past her prime, her existence as a miserable and unfulfilled spinster to be pitied.

Cara stoically shrugged off her ostracism among the marriageable-aged women of Seoul. They were not necessarily kinder to one another, so she expected little better for herself.

She had witnessed young women mercilessly browbeat and belittle a weaker or lower caste member of their sex, shamelessly embroil in shouting matches, mean-spirited name calling and, in one embarrassing display, pulling each other's hair while rolling on the ground. To add insult to injury, the cause of the disagreement just stood back and watched, laughing at the girls battling to win his favor.

Feigned indifference to the opposite sex as a teaser must have been an American—or French—affectation. The young women of Korea would coo, openly admire, and praise a man they found attractive. They chattered among themselves, loudly enough for everyone to hear, about his physical attributes or handsome features.

Cara was too proud in nature, too embarrassed by the practice, to subscribe to it herself.

CARA'S FAVORITE TIME WITH THE Kims was when they would lock the doors of the restaurant and close for the evening. They would sit together and share a meal and some *soju*, and learn more about one another and their cultures.

The Kims were childless, an unfortunate circumstance for such a loving and generous couple. They talked with Cara about the continents they dreamed of visiting—America and Europe—and the islands of Hawaii and the Caribbean. They showed her pictures, exactingly trimmed from travel magazines and the *National Geographic,* of landmarks and wonders of the world that captured their awe and imagination.

"One day," Mr. Kim pronounced with confidence and a broad grin, "we will travel, my bride and I." He lovingly gazed at his wife. "We will see the world."

MERCADO'S CUNNING EYES NEVER LEFT the American woman as she moved from table to table in the crowded and noisy place—smiling, nodding, and tilting her head to one side when she did not understand the words spoken to her.

Mercado noticed that the middle-aged cook—perhaps also the owner of the restaurant—watched him with suspicion. Apparently, he was protective of this young foreign woman.

Fine with me, hal-abeoji, Mercado generously allowed, referring to him as grandpa. *You keep the rabble away from my woman.*

When she served a couple at the next table, Mercado willed her to look at him. *Look at me. Look at me!*

Then she did—with those eyes. Though not long enough. Or with any association or discernable emotion.

He glanced under the table and shook his head in amusement. She had aroused him.

Mercado was convinced that evening—after losing track of her over the past several years—that finding her again meant they were destined to be together.

He wanted this woman. He would have this woman.

SHORTLY AFTER CARA HAD BEEN hired by the Chang Agency, Mercado sat before Madame Chang with a smug smile.

Madame had not seen him since her husband's death. Yet here he was, presenting himself to her and assuming that she would put him on the Chang Agency payroll.

Madame was under no illusions that she could refuse him—it was he and other cutthroats that helped her husband amass his fortune. And because she had taken the Chang Conglomerate to legitimacy over the years, she was not about to lose her company, reputation, or social standing because of a whisper to a police investigator, or an inflammatory statement given to some unscrupulous tabloid reporter.

"Why here? Why now?" Madame had probed with curiosity.

"Why not?" Mercado replied with a smirk, arrogantly denying her an explanation.

"You'll have to work for it," Madame assured him. "We must be discreet."

Mercado was determined to have unimpeded access to the American woman, whenever and wherever he pleased.

He shrugged, unperturbed. "Do what you have to do."

Cruel Persuasion

April 1991
Seoul, South Korea

Cara shook Mercado from his musings when she declared in a weak voice, "I have to use the toilet."

Mercado cursed himself. He had given no thought to this part of her captivity. Naturally, she would have to use the toilet. She would have to drink. She would have to eat.

She would be his responsibility until—again a scenario he had not predetermined.

Mercado pulled himself out of the armchair, untied her restraints, and led her into the bathroom. He moved her body in place.

She could feel the cold porcelain of the toilet bowl against the calf of her leg. It made her squeamish.

"Sit down."

"I can't."

"You said you had to go."

"I can't sit on something I can't see."

"What?"

"I hate dirty toilets."

"Sit."

"No."

"I said sit!" He shoved her backwards.

She grasped fistfuls of his shirt, almost pulling him down on top of her. He sprang backwards, righting himself, and her.

She heard him laugh—incredulous.

He wavered, fiercely gripping her arms to punctuate his promise. "You see my face...I will have to kill you."

Cara was relieved. Whatever his plans were for her—according to him—it did not include murder.

"So?" She waited. "Are you leaving?"

"Jesus," he cursed under his breath.

Cara heard the door close behind him. She waited a beat to make sure he was not lurking inside the bathroom.

"Make it quick in there," he cautioned from outside of the door.

Cara pulled the scarf down around her neck, blinking her light sensitive eyes in the ambient brightness of the bathroom. It was old but neat and clean.

She quietly slipped to the window and looked outside. It faced a blank wall of the building next door. She strained to open the window until she felt the blood rise in her face. Hindered by the throbbing pain in her shoulder, and layered with years of paint, she could not get the window to budge.

"If you're not done in thirty seconds," Mercado snarled, "I'm coming in."

Cara sighed in resignation, determined not to lose hope. She would have to wait until another opportunity presented itself.

She quickly concluded her business and washed her hands.

"Cover your eyes," Mercado warned before entering the bathroom.

After he secured her on the bed, testing her ropes, he asked in a hushed voice, "Are you hungry?"

Cara cocked her head, confounded by his accommodation to her comfort. She marked that he never spoke in a normal tone of voice, perhaps trying to disguise it. He spoke to her in Korean, sometimes in English—speaking both well.

Cara pictured him to be about four inches taller than she, hair to his shoulders, and medium but strong build. She was uncertain about his ethnicity.

She nodded in answer to his question. All she had eaten was breakfast that morning.

"I won't be long," he promised, closing and locking the door behind him.

Mercado heard her tugging against her restraints, futilely sawing them against the wooden slats, softly crying out with the effort and the agony of the friction of the ropes abrading the flesh of her wrists.

When he quietly stepped back into the apartment, she had painfully torqued her body to kick the slats of futon with her heels, trying to free her ropes.

He shook his head. He had been too trusting.

She cried out in surprise when, in a matter of seconds, he gagged her and roughly repositioned her body to tie her hands behind her back, attaching them with a length of rope to her ankles.

"*Hangal na babae*," he muttered in Tagalog. Silly girl.

Although he would have preferred otherwise, Mercado decided when he returned and after she had eaten, he would sedate her. He needed to reduce her combativeness and stress.

His, too.

MERCADO RETURNED WITH SEVERAL CONTAINERS of hot food. When he opened the cartons, Cara's stomach growled and her mouth watered from the familiar aromas.

After Mercado had removed her gag and once again secured her hands to the headboard, he prompted her to open her mouth. "Here."

He offered her a *tteokbokki*, a rice cake in a spicy red sauce, a popular snack sold by street vendors, and a favorite of hers.

"I can feed myself," she protested softly.

"No, you can't," Mercado assured her, visualizing the damage she might attempt to inflict on him with a pair of chopsticks. "Go ahead. Take it. There's no meat in it."

Cara's breath caught in her throat. He knew her—at least knew she was a vegetarian.

She shivered with a chill of reality. She ignorantly and quite happily had gone about her daily routine without realizing her vulnerability.

Who was her captor?

An employee of the law firm? Someone who worked in her building? A student in her language class? A customer at the Kim's restaurant? A neighbor? A man she may have passed—perhaps innocently smiled at—on the street?

Cara realized that she dared not allow him—whoever he was—time to register his blunder. She obediently opened her mouth.

Mercado placed the small, tube shaped rice cake on her tongue, watched her roll it around her mouth to cool it before chewing, and heard her hum of appreciation. He smiled.

As well as the *tteokbokki,* he fed her deep fried dumplings and vegetables, Korean fast-food snacks she often purchased from her favorite street vendors' carts.

"I'm full," she admitted when he offered another mouthful. "Thank you," she added politely.

She could feel him pause to stare at her, taken aback by her civility.

Maybe she could sway this man—earn his trust with kindness and respect—lull him into believing she would cooperate and be submissive to him. Then, perhaps, she could catch him off guard and somehow incapacitate him.

She would have to get him to untie her first. She could do nothing while trussed like a turkey.

She heard him open other cartons of food and feed himself—hastily—ravenously.

When he had finished, she pulled herself up to sit in a more comfortable position. "Could you could loosen these ties?" she asked experimentally. "My hands are going numb."

Mercado paused, staring at her suspiciously. The nice manners, the enticing tenor of her voice when requesting this favor. What was running through her mind?

He felt her involuntarily stiffen at his touch when he checked the ropes. He loosened them a bit, and then stepped back.

No, she was not ready yet. Not by a long stretch.

He poured a glassful of water from the filtered water container in the refrigerator and briskly stirred in some white powder. He frowned, estimating—questioning—its strength.

The red pepper flakes in the *tteokbokki* sauce made Cara crave water. Although she normally only drank bottled water, she gratefully accepted the glass offered to her and drank thirstily, aware of the odd taste, but accustomed to the unpredictable water quality of the districts around the city.

At this point, she thought with a peculiar irony, she was less concerned about the risk of parasitic diarrhea than her current circumstances. Who knows? It might even revolt him enough to set her free.

CARA SLUMPED DOWN ON THE bed, suddenly sleepy, limbs heavy and muscles non-responsive.

After a while, she became vaguely aware of her abductor's body stretched out on the futon mattress beside her.

Mercado leaned over to whisper in her ear, his breath warm, "Let's play a game."

A game?

A hazy, yet continuous, cadence of lascivious words assailed her consciousness, fueling vivid images of the ways he would seduce her—the mastery of his touch on every sensitive and private part of her body, the positions he would enjoy with her, his observations about how she would look, feel, and smell—his anticipation of her response. He left nothing to her imagination. Nothing to spare her dignity.

Verbally assaulted. Violated.

Then he got up from the bed and left her alone for a while, closing himself in the bathroom.

TIME BECAME IRRELEVANT, INDISTINGUISHABLE. HAD she been here two hours or two days?

Human voices, traffic noises from the street, quieted. Was it night?

Water. He kept giving her water.

What was that bright flash of light? Was it her imagination? Another flash.

Dizzy. She was so dizzy. Any movement of her head in the cloaking darkness brought with it a sickening wave of nausea.

Her stomach lurched at the sweet stench of rotting fruit from the street below, the putrid stink of garbage that had stewed in the sun all day. The stifling and airless room smelled as though it had been undisturbed for some time.

She moaned. She was sick. So sick. Miserable.

She roused, unaware that she had drifted out of consciousness.

He was lying next to her again. This time, he changed his strategy. Instead of entertaining himself with obscene sexual details, he romanced her by whispering soft and sweet endearments in her ear, and a voluptuous, and seemingly endless, narrative of how he would worship her—undress her, fondle and caress her, use his tongue to arouse and bring her to climax.

Finally, he whispered hoarsely, "I'll make you a deal. If you're not wet, I will let you go."

He skimmed his hand under her skirt and confirmed his suspicions.

Cara choked out a protest and shrank from his probing fingers, burying her head under her arm in repulsion and humiliation.

He laughed coarsely—triumphantly—and rolled off the bed.

"Why don't you just get this over with and kill me," Cara begged, her words clumsy and slow.

His laugh was brittle. "Oh, you're going to die alright...but with me...it will be from pure pleasure."

Her brain was feverish.

Youngblood appeared to her with his wide, easy smile—a look that once melted the most frustrated and discouraged heart.

"Kidnapped," she rasped indistinctly.

His soft-spoken voice surfaced from the delirious depths of her awareness. *You're not being kidnapped. You're being abducted.*

"Youngblood," she mumbled, somehow hopeful.

I don't want to keep you or ransom you.

"Youngblood...why are you here? You went away," she muttered, accusatory—confused.

HIS ASSIGNMENT FULFILLED AT OSAN Air Base a year after his arrival, Tay was leaving South Korea. He had called Cara to say goodbye.

"I'm out of here next week."

Cara felt a despairing dip in her belly, even though they had not seen each other since he had driven away from their apartment four months earlier. "Where are you going?"

"Special Tactics Squadron. Kadena Air Base in Okinawa."

"Be safe."

"Always," he affirmed affably. "You doing okay? Need any money?"

Cara smiled. He was a wonder. Always generous with his money. But her salary from her job with an American company in Osan adequately provided for her needs. "I'm good, thanks."

"Some of the guys told me they saw you in the Vill."

"Oh?"

"Said you are one hundred percent."

"Oh," she murmured modestly.

"Why not come with me to Okinawa?" he tested mildly.

He shook Cara to her foundation. She finally managed to say, "Not this time, Tay."

"It was worth a try."

She could almost see him shrug good-naturedly.

"I'm surprised you would even consider it," Cara breathed. "I thought taking responsibility for me made you miserable."

He did not deny it. Instead, he admitted quietly, "I will always love you, *Hinha'n*."

His familiar endearment in the Sioux dialect, calling her White Owl, struck a melancholy chord in her heart. "That's the first time you said you loved me," she whispered in astonishment.

His laugh was uneasy. "Really?"

"Really."

He reluctantly signed off. "Take care of yourself."

Cara felt bereft, wanting somehow, unreasonably, to hold on to the moment—to him. "You, too. Give my love to Winona when you speak with her."

"I will."

After he had hung up, Cara murmured despondently, "I will always love you, too."

Mercado listened to her hallucinatory murmurings and frowned, resentment oozing from every pore. Was she talking to another man?

He felt her forehead and cursed himself. He had given her too high a dose of barbiturates. She was burning up. Her lightweight blouse seeped with the sweat that dampened the sheet beneath her.

He brought a rubber basin filled with cool water and a fresh washcloth to her bedside. Immersing the cloth, he wrung it out and patiently, gently, respectfully, ran it over her skin.

She moaned restlessly.

He removed the blindfold over her eyes and blotted her fair face, letting the cool cloth remain on her skin before refreshing it again, and again. After a time, she calmed down. So did the heat radiating from her body.

She seemed to be resting comfortably when Mercado noticed the time of night. He had an appointment—a new customer from the United States Army garrison in Youngsan. He could not be late.

He stopped at the doorway and looked back at Cara. She should remain sedated until morning. Still, meeting with a first-time customer was always risky. He did not anticipate any delays but, if that should be the case, he untied her hands as a safety precaution.

Putting his lips to her ear, he whispered like a lover, "I'll be back."

Mercado met with the army slick sleeve outside the gates of the garrison at Youngsan. They had just concluded the exchange of drugs for American dollars when the snot-nosed private wrestled Mercado to the ground. At that point, U.S. Military Police besieged them and took Mercado into custody.

His captors exchanged bewildered glances when Mercado threw back his head and mocked himself—and them—with hearty laughter.

How could such a primitive sting snare him? He was Mercado—Jack of Spades—the Knave.

Sitting in his cell, awaiting his right to due process and the administration of justice, Mercado cursed himself for an asshole. His obsession and dalliance with the American woman had distracted him—made him too trusting and foolhardy.

His hearing before a judge was swift, the proceedings brief and his sentence unremarkable—six months for a first-time offense dealing drugs.

During his incarceration, Mercado was quick to learn prison hierarchy and establish his place within it. He made contacts while confined that, once he gained his freedom, would be invaluable.

One day, to dispel the debilitating boredom of prison life, he sought out a talented tattoo artist who was doing a stretch of one to three years. Mercado told him exactly what design he wanted implanted under his skin on the right bicep of his upper arm.

He had proudly worn the tattoo years afterward to remind him of his foolishness—of the woman he had yet to make his.

Deliverance

July 2007
Seoul, South Korea

"I was drugged and dozing," Cara confided in Kang. "He whispered in my ear, 'I'll be back.'

"When I woke up, I didn't feel his presence in the room." Cara inspected her hands, as if reliving the realization. "He had untied me."

She said nervously, "I cautiously removed the mask from my eyes. I was alone. I called out to him. When I was sure he was gone, I stumbled to the door, dizzy and weak. The hallway was clear. I left by the outside stairway...blinded by the brightness of the day."

"Why didn't you go to the police?" Kang inquired neutrally, without recrimination.

"And tell them what?" Cara protested. "The way he described how and where he was going to touch me, but didn't touch me. How he threatened to hurt me, but didn't. How he humiliated me, and then tried to seduce me?"

Kang was skeptical. "He never touched you?" This was not the game sexual predators liked to play.

She cringed, once again shamed by the memory of Mercado's crude and probing fingers. "Only once."

Kang placed a reassuring hand over hers and waited for her to continue.

She hung her head. "I never saw his face," she reported to Kang. "When he spoke to me, he always whispered...sometimes in Korean, sometimes in English."

She swallowed hard, her eyes wide with remembered fear. "For months I stayed in my apartment, only going to and from work...always making sure I was in a crowd or with a friend. If I had to go out at night, I would never go alone.

302

"Every man I knew, whether an acquaintance, co-worker, neighbor, or a server in a coffee shop or a food cart, I viewed with dread and suspicion. Was it you? Or you?

"Until I changed jobs and started living in the security of the Chang Building, I was always looking over my shoulder.

"'I'll be back,' he promised. I kept wondering…would that be in a week, a month, a year? Would it be the one day I was not watchful, when my guard was down…that he would come for me again? And, maybe… this time…never let me go?"

Kang lowered his eyes, his face a mask.

Cara was grateful for Kang's understanding silence, his controlled expression. "All these years," she whispered miserably, "I was still his captive."

The truth was Kang felt anything but controlled. If he had any lingering doubts or regrets about his part in Mercado's death, he was shed of them now, convinced he had done the right thing.

She hung her head, drained. "I am so tired."

Kang took a quilt from a nearby cupboard, gently settled Cara on his bed and wrapped the comforter securely around her. "Rest now. I'll wake you in a few hours."

MERCADO STOOD OVER HER, STARING at her with that cocky grin she despised.

"*Michinnom*," Cara quietly cursed him in Korean for the crazy bastard he was.

He laughed, almost boyishly.

"Why Kang?" Cara demanded. "Why did you use Kang to hurt me…try to kill me?"

A darkness surfaced in Mercado's eyes, stripping them of light.

Cara visualized herself at the police station the night Mercado was held and questioned in a drug bust Kang had orchestrated.

Through Mercado's eyes, she witnessed Kang incline his head toward hers, their enamored expressions as they gazed into each other's eyes—

experienced the sting of betrayal and hatred toward them, a murderous jealousy of the mutual attraction they so obviously shared.

"*Demonyo*," Cara cursed him, petrified by what she felt—the malevolence that distorted his rational thought and poisoned the core of his being.

She returned to her dream. Mercado glanced at his right shoulder. He placed two fingers against the dove tattooed there and brought his fingers to his lips.

He smiled then, and looked at Cara with the soft, warm eyes he possessed as a child. Speaking to her in Filipino and English, he murmured, "*Paalam*, White Dove...*mahal ko*." Goodbye, White Dove... my love."

He vanished in a swirling wisp of blue vapor.

Cara gasped and started awake.

Put a face to your demon, and be at peace, echoed the consoling words of the mysterious fortuneteller at Sinsa-dong. *He can harm you no more.*

Cara filled her lungs with cleansing air and pulled the coverlet around her, suddenly chilled. She cursed Mercado once again. "*Michinnom.*"

Kang eased his hand on her shoulder. "Cara?"

She rolled over, relieved and happy to see his face. "I'm awake."

He perched on the side of the bed and eyed her with concern. "Are you okay?"

She sat up and slipped her arms around his neck. "Yes. Thank you."

She unhinged Kang. "For what?" he asked softly.

She rested her cheek against his chest. "For setting me free."

Kang eased his arms around Cara and tightly embraced her, eyes closed, holding his breath—feeling the soft roundness of her breasts against his chest, the sweet scent of her hair.

How many years he had waited for this moment—for her to come to him—to hold her in his arms.

"I've got to leave here...Seoul...for a while," he said, resisting the need to release her. "I'll take you home."

She frowned. "To America?"

He sounded amused but regretful. "That would be nice, but I was thinking of someplace closer. Someplace where you will be safe."

She threw off the blanket and reached for her shoes. "I'm coming with you."

He wanted nothing more, but he shook his head. "No."

"We can take my car," she offered.

His eyes followed her every movement as she neatly smoothed the bed and folded his blanket. "I hurt you once. I don't want to put you in harm's way again."

While Cara had been resting, Kang paced his apartment, planning his strategy to manage the arrival of Jeun's pernicious son, Jeun Ji-tae.

He had gotten an anxious call from his friend, Alexei Kosovskaia, who had eyes and ears monitoring the quicksilver changes of fortune within Northeast Asia's viciously competitive underworld.

"He is coming," Alexei warned Kang with a glacial tone. "And his first order of business is you."

Cara had changed her clothes and collected the rest of her belongings. When she came out of the bathroom, she asked, "Where are we headed?"

"No, Cara," Kang said more firmly. At least it sounded that way. Privately, he was beginning to waiver—considering leaving behind his common sense and taking her with him, instead of the other way around.

The last thing Cara wanted was to return to the empty gilded cage of Madame Chang's penthouse. She urged him with sorrowful eyes, "I have nowhere to go, and all the time in the world to get there."

Kang needed to disappear. Cara sought temporary relief from Seoul. Knowing this, accepting this, what better company could they keep than each other's?

Kang grasped her hand and squeezed it. "Then, let's go. Now."

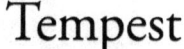

Tempest

열다섯

16
Escape from Seoul

July 2007
Seoul to Hwacheon District – Gangwon Province

CARA RODE ALONG WITH KANG in the passenger seat of the Mercedes. She silently observed what seemed to be a dire rush on Kang's part to leave Seoul, overheard his cellphone conversation with someone she assumed was a friend about a place to stay and where Kang could find an extra key stashed in a secret spot.

On the way out of the city, Kang explained to Cara that they were traveling to Hwacheon—three-hours northeast of Seoul in the Gangwon Province—to a fishing cabin owned by his superintendent at the Seoul Metropolitan Policy Agency.

The province was mountainous and wild with thick forests and pristine valleys. In close proximity to the DMZ, Korean De-Militarized Zone, the region flourished with rivers and lakes known for first-class fishing and water sports.

Cara relayed to Kang that she was familiar with the area. Gangwon-do was where she had built a vacation home she had christened Shangri-La, a refuge from her busy career with the Chang Agency. Before Moon had come back into her life, and upon Cara's request, Madame Chang had sold Shangri-La for a tidy profit. The windfall was earmarked for Regalo's education.

Cara experienced a sharp pang from a sudden twist of her heart—for one of many treasured things in her past that were now lost to her.

Kang told her that Ryu also enjoyed getting away from the demands of his job although, by Kang's account, all too rarely. Ryu was an avid angler and fished the abundant freshwater trout, known as "Queen of the Valley," that swam in cold and unpolluted local waters.

They stopped along the way three times. Twice to allow Kang to pace outside of the car in frustration and make cellphone calls that, in both instances, yielded no response—much to his evident consternation. Once to fill the gas tank and stock up on provisions.

Even in Kang's haste, they arrived at the cabin mid-afternoon— nearly missing the turnoff from the main road. Kang drove slowly down the narrow and winding dirt road. Without human intervention, indigenous plants and evergreen seedlings strained toward the clearing of unfiltered sunlight, narrowing the road from either side.

Kang found the key where Ryu had promised, and they began the process of settling in—airing out the stuffy, closed up quarters by opening all the screened windows, clearing out the cobwebs and sweeping the floor. Cara scrubbed clean the tiny kitchen and refrigerator. Actually, given the fact that Superintendent Ryu had not visited the cabin for a long time, everything was neat and orderly.

They unloaded the provisions they had purchased along the way— drinking water, food, paper goods, personal care and hygiene products and some extra clothing.

The overcast sky threatened rain. The temperature was hot, and the humidity high.

Kang raked his hair back from his face with his fingers, caught site of Cara wrestling the padded futon mattress out of the cupboard in the bedroom, and ran to help.

"Let's take a break," he encouraged Cara with a smile after they unrolled the *yo* on the varnished floor.

She huffed and drew her sleeve across her damp brow. "Sounds good."

"The lake is just down the rise," Kang reported with satisfaction. He found a picnic blanket in the cupboard, Cara grabbed two bottles of water, and they started for the lake.

"Beautiful," Cara breathed, observing a lush stretch of wooded shoreline and the magnificent backdrop of purple-hued mountains against the deep blue of the water.

Kang spread the blanket on a level clearing near the lake. "Swim?" he challenged Cara with a smile.

She removed her sandals and tested the water temperature with her toes. The water was ice cold. "Ooo, no," she balked with a shiver. "Too cold."

She did, however, roll up her pants and bathe her legs, arms, neck and face, trying to cleanse and cool her moist and heated skin.

They sat together in silence on the blanket, enjoying the serenity, evergreen scented mountain air, and the soothing pulse of gentle waves lapping against the pebbled shore.

When Cara inquired about the curious absence of tourists, Kang informed her that few sports boaters ventured to this more rocky and secluded area of the lake.

Cara sat with arms circling her knees, Kang reclining at her feet and propped up by an elbow, facing her. He noticed the scar on the shin of her left leg.

"The scar on your shin...the wound looks like it went to the bone," he observed in English. He brushed his hand over her leg. "How did that happen?"

Cara smiled with the memory. "In my childhood home, we lived about a mile from the railroad tracks. If you ventured deep in the woods, sometimes you would stumble across an old hobo camp, some from as far back as the Depression in the 1930s, and after World War II in the '40s. They gave me the creeps." She shuddered just thinking about them.

"But one day my older sister, Annabella, and I were out riding our bikes and she dragged me with her to explore an old shed she had found far back off the road by the tracks. Inside were filthy leaf-littered mattresses and blankets, ropey strands of cobwebs, tins of opened and long-dried out food, a couple of dead rats. I was terrified that a tramp may be lurking outside, peering at us through a window.

"Then Annabella cried out that she saw something move in the trees, something big and hairy. 'It's Big Foot!' she screamed."

Kang cocked his head questioningly.

Cara paused her dramatics to explain to Kang, "A legend in the Pacific Northwest—half man, half animal, standing eight feet tall and walking upright." No recognition in Kang's expression.

She bent her fingers like claws, bared her teeth and snarled, making wet, sloppy drooling sounds.

Kang laughed, highly entertained. "So what happened then?"

"I took off on a dead run, and when I got to my bicycle I pedaled for all I was worth to the highway. But when I got to the highway, dirt to asphalt, I didn't have control of my bike and I flopped face-first on the pavement. Loosened a tooth," she said, touching her front tooth. "Fortunately, it was a baby tooth."

She lightly skimmed her fingers over the scar. "The pedal from my bike ripped open this gash on my leg."

Kang sympathetically surveyed the scar.

Her eyes sparkled wickedly. "When we got home and Papa found out what had happened, he smacked Annabella around good!"

Kang laughed outright when she made a delighted face, lips parted in a triumphant silent laugh.

She became serious as her eyes went to the deep crescent-shaped scar that marred his right cheek. She leaned forward and gently touched his face with the tips of her fingers. "What happened here?"

"Jealous husband," he replied honestly.

Cara tipped her head and pensively observed him. "Really?"

"Unfortunately," he confessed wryly, "I was not aware the woman was married."

"Ah," Cara commented, nodding sagely. That made more sense.

"To be truthful," Kang offered with a sheepish grin, "I was not aware of anything but my own pleasure in her bed."

"Was she your first?" Cara inquired lightly.

His gaze was warm—marking her intuition and absence of condemnation. "Does that excuse it?"

Cara shrugged, her mood too relaxed to moralize. "Depends upon the woman."

Kang shook his head, bemused. Without question, Cara was distinctive among her sex. "What about you?"

"What?" Cara asked, unsure about the point of the question.

"As a married woman, would you have sex with another man?"

Cara held his steady and inquisitive stare, surprised that it was taking her this long to answer him. She took the quickest and safest route that came to mind. "When I was married, I did not have sex with anyone but my husband."

Kang's body tensed and he sat up. "What are you telling me?"

Her response was purposefully ambiguous, avoiding the answer Kang sought. "That I was faithful to my husband."

Kang patiently indulged her deflection. "Not that. You said, 'When I was married...' "

She self-consciously dropped her eyes to her knees clasped before her, embarrassed that Kang was all too familiar with their tempestuous history, their seeming inability to make their relationship work. "Moon and I are divorced," she confessed.

Kang stared at her—speechless. He wanted to ask so many questions.

If she and her husband were divorced, why did she come back to Korea? Did they intend to live together for the well-being of their son? Or, was it her intention to return to her home in America?

Is that why the police detained her at the airport? Was she was trying to escape with her son from her ex-husband and his family?

Cara raised her head and spoke rapidly. "Are you hungry? I am. What if I make dinner, and you open the bottle of wine we bought?"

She jumped to her feet, scooped up her sandals, and walked barefoot up the path toward the cabin.

Kang collected and folded the blanket, lost in his musings, following Cara at a more leisurely pace.

Welcome Home, Moon

July 2007
Seoul, South Korea

MOON BOUND UP THE STAIRS under the front portico of the Moon family estate, in high spirits, pushing through the front door. He dropped his bags in the foyer, bursting with good news and the eagerness to share it.

"Hello!" he called out happily. "I'm back! Where is everyone?"

The household manager was reading the newspaper in his small office off the kitchen at the rear of the house, reading glasses balanced on the bridge of his nose. He promptly removed the glasses, put down the paper, shrugged into his formal jacket and finished securing the buttons as he hurried to greet the master of the house, Moon Hyo.

Manager Park smiled broadly at young master Moon—as he had always thought of him—and bid him a warm welcome home. "I trust everything went well."

Moon nodded in answer to his devoted retainer. "Very well, thank you."

He glanced up the stairway, disappointed that no one had come to greet him. "Where is my family?"

Several members of the household staff peeked at Moon around the kitchen doorway. When he glanced their way, they fluttered out of sight like a covey of startled quail.

The manager replaced his smile with a firm set to his jaw and a troubled, solemn expression. "Consul General, Miss Sang Hee and her husband are staying at your apartment in the city…with your son."

"And my wife?" Moon asked stonily, sensing that an upheaval had occurred in his absence, for which he was not present to prevent.

"With all due respect, sir," the manager responded quietly, bound by convention and unable to speak freely. "This is a question perhaps best asked of Miss Sang Hee."

Moon surprised his sister when he presented himself at his apartment in Seoul later that afternoon. The severity of her brother's expression, his brusque manner, and the errand upon which he had come, promptly quelled Sang Hee's delight at his return.

Moon checked on his sleeping son, declined the offer of a chair, and paced before Sang Hee and her husband as they sat side by side on the couch in the spacious living area.

When Moon shot rapid-fire questions at Sang Hee about the events of the past week, she recounted them honestly, not sparing her brother.

"When you left Seoul without a word of explanation to Cara, she wanted to go home. To America." Here Sang Hee's voice dropped to almost a whisper. "Our mother had her detained by the police at the airport."

Moon closed his eyes and shook his head. His voice was edgy. "Our mother."

On that subject—testament to their mother's bitter and interminable duplicity and her knack for repelling the people closest to her—Sang Hee divulged a long-held secret. "Did you know that when our father was assigned as Ambassador to Singapore for four years that he took his mistress with him?"

Moon stopped pacing long enough to fix his sister with a disbelieving scowl.

"Our mother knew. I'm not sure she cared." Sang Hee clearly was reluctant to disclose what she had learned from an overheard conversation. "He may even have had children with the woman."

Moon stared at Sang Hee, speechless.

Struggling to cope with the current family turmoil, this erstwhile fact was something Moon did not need or care to hear.

His world—a world he had trusted to be immutable—was tilting on its axis, requiring every bit of his resilience to hold fast.

Sang Hee suffered through several strained seconds of her brother's silence. She smiled gratefully at her husband when he put a consoling and supportive arm around her shoulders.

"All of us were waiting until you came home," she divulged to her brother.

"Where is Cara?" Moon inquired—assailed at once by the sensations of betrayal, anger, and misery.

Sang Hee dropped her chin to her chest, unable to bear the anguish in her brother's eyes. "She was staying with Madame Chang, but after Madame left for a planned trip abroad, she disappeared."

"How long ago?" Moon asked in an atypically weak and reedy tone. "Two days."

"What if she's hurt, or worse?" Moon lamented with a raised voice, arms held out at his sides, palms up, to punctuate his point.

Sang Hee had never seen her brother behave so emotionally. She realized how badly shaken and frightened he was by Cara's disappearance and, despite everything that had happened between them, how much he cared for her.

Sang Hee soothed her much beloved older brother. "We have professionals looking for her, checking the hospitals and police stations."

Moon curbed his agitation. Neither his sister nor her husband were responsible for this situation. He was—by his pride, his resistance to share his plans with Cara. Because he could not bear the thought of failing again in her eyes.

Moon excused himself. Before he disappeared into his study, he remembered himself and turned to his sister and her husband. "Thank you both," he murmured humbly, "for caring for our son. We will both thank you properly when..." He shook his head as if to clear it—too preoccupied to think clearly. "When Cara is with us again," he concluded with more confidence and determination.

"We have loved taking care of our nephew, *Oppa*," Sang Hee kindly assured Moon. She placed a loving hand on her husband knee. "We are trying to have children of our own."

Moon's brother-in-law hung his head and blushed.

"We like it here, *Oppa*," Sang Hee confessed shyly. "It's peaceful and private. May we stay?"

Moon fidgeted with impatience and anxiety at the delay—at a conversation best undertaken at a more convenient and less urgent time.

Nonetheless, he smiled indulgently at his sister, newly emancipated and reveling—indeed, budding—in her independence from under their mother's thumb. "For as long as you like."

He softly closed the door of the study behind him, seeking assistance from a trusted and seasoned expert—one who had connections in law enforcement and a keen eye and ear on current events in Seoul.

Moon accessed a saved contact on his hand phone and, when the call went through, spoke imperatively to the private investigator who had assisted him with the location and surveillance of Cara after her three-month absence from Seoul following her physical assault.

What Moon learned only served to ramp up his apprehension.

Currently, the Seoul Metropolitan Police Agency was preoccupied with more than a mere missing person's case. The capital city had become the center of a struggle for supremacy among underworld rival gangs—a killing ground.

Judas

July 2007
Seoul, South Korea

THE SEOUL METROPOLITAN POLICE AGENCY was on full alert. The Agency enlisted every available officer from any department or adjacent district to work on the newly formed Emergency Organized Crime Task Force.

Once Jeun Ji-tae's feet had landed on South Korean soil, he and his dark legions declared full-scale war on local crime syndicates. Violence was erupting all over the city. The medical examiner's office was stacking bodies like firewood.

Some cynics in the political sector suggested a law enforcement stand-down. They theorized that, if these thugs killed one another in their bid for prominence and power, it would forestall commitment of law enforcement personnel and the heedless expenditure of tax dollars. The absurd scenario postulated that the agency—as the last man standing—would bat cleanup.

Ryu was pragmatic—no longer surprised by the lack of logic and common sense displayed by politicians. His superiors in the agency unanimously agreed with his admonition to ignore the edict.

His main concern was to protect Kang—which was why he had cleared his passage out of Seoul and offered a safe house for him to wait out the carnage. Ryu was determined to give Kang every opportunity to fulfill his mission.

Alexei Kosovskaia, the big Russian who had befriended Kang—owing to some shared history known only to them—entered the command center escorted by a Metro police officer. Security would remain tight around the task force perimeter.

Kosovskaia caught Ryu's eye. Although puzzled why the Russian had come, Superintendent Ryu waved him over.

Kosovskaia's attitude was confident and urgent. "Jeun and his men have gone after Kang." He assured an agitated Ryu, "They know where to look."

Ryu shook his head in disbelief. "How?"

Kosovskaia and a few of his most trusted men were waiting for Jeun Ji-tae as soon as he landed in Korea, disembarked from a private plane and walked across the tarmac to a waiting town car. They began surveillance of his movements and, with sophisticated covert listening devices, monitored his communications.

"One of your men met with Jeun outside Kang's apartment building after they ransacked his place. He must have overheard you speaking with Kang. He told Jeun where Kang could be found."

Ryu's brow puckered in disbelief. "One of ours?"

The big Russian nodded grimly.

"Point him out," Ryu encouraged him dubiously.

Kosovskaia scanned the busy command center with sharply focused, ice blue eyes. They came to rest on a middle-aged cop working at a desk overrun with paperwork.

Shim was a nineteen-year veteran, repeatedly passed over for promotions. His peers and superiors recognized his performance and dedication to the job was, at best, mediocre.

Kosovskaia pointed an accusing finger at the end of a long and stiffly held arm. When the man looked up, Alexei made the shape of a gun out of his hand.

"Bang!" he taunted with a sneer, firing the imaginary pistol.

The little squid nervously rose from behind his desk, as though considering making a run for it. His skittish eyes darted among his fellow officers who now looked upon him with suspicion and disgust.

"Hold him," Ryu gruffly commanded his men. "I'll deal with him later."

Ryu would initiate a thorough investigation of Shim's lifestyle and financial affairs. If he found any irregularities, he would make certain that Shim suffered the harshest penalty under the fullest extent of the law.

Ryu spoke to his second in command. "Assemble our SWAT team immediately. And arrange helicopter transport to Gangwon-do."

"Yes, Superintendent." His man sprang into action, barking orders to his team and using his hand phone to mobilize Metro's elite sharpshooter specialists.

"Tell the local district police that we will need transportation after we arrive," Ryu added to his orders. "Put all hospitals and medical emergency units in the area on standby."

He called after the Russian who was running for the exit of the command center. "Where are you going?"

"Got my own ride," Kosovskaia called over his shoulder. "See you there."

Superintendent Ryu would have stopped him—being a civilian and a man of questionable scruples when it came to forming alliances and abiding by the law. But Ryu realized that Kosovskaia could deploy his men immediately, whereas he first would have to obtain clearance and approval from his superiors.

Kosovskaia might prove to be Kang's best chance for survival.

열일곱

17
Strangers In The Night

July 2007
Hwacheon-gun – Gangwon-do

CARA RESTLESSLY TOSSED AND TURNED on the padded futon of the cabin's only bedroom. The air inside the cabin was stifling and muggy. She fanned her thin nightshirt against her body, cooling the moisture on her skin.

When she had sleepily yawned after dinner, depleted from the events of the last few days and relaxed from her one glass of wine, Kang smiled and insisted that she take the bedroom.

Cara rolled over to gaze out of the window. A storm was brewing in the distance.

She padded lightly across the front porch in her bare feet, floorboards creaking in soft complaint as she trespassed over them.

Kang sat on the wide lacquered bench that crowded the façade of the cabin, head resting against the clapboard siding, eyes closed.

Cara eased the light comforter she had found in the cedar-lined cupboard in the bedroom over his body, carefully pulling the edges this way and that to cover him fully.

He did not rouse.

She stood a moment and reflected upon his face in the fading light of evening. After so many years, at least in repose, she still thought him boyish and handsome.

Reluctant as she was to leave the cool fresh air and return to the suffocating heat of the cabin, she turned to go inside.

She drew in a startled breath when a warm hand grasped her wrist. Her head swiveled toward Kang.

The corners of his beautifully shaped mouth curved upward.

She shyly returned his smile.

He coaxed her backwards, his arms supporting her as he pulled her across his body, seating her to his right on the bench. He tucked the blanket around her bare legs that crossed over his lap, and encouraged her to lean against him as they sat together in the soft night air.

She was keenly aware of his arm circling her shoulder, the steady swell of his chest and, every so often, a tantalizing hint of his citrus-scented cologne.

After a time, Cara began to relax and enjoy Kang's tranquil company.

She glanced up at his profile, and then curiously followed his distant gaze.

The mountainous horizon roiled with ominous black thunderheads—arcing randomly with flashes of light in their billowy depths—rumbling threateningly. In their restless wind-driven march, the rainclouds shape shifted and expanded as they thrust toward the cabin, elapsed time between flash of lightning and boom of thunder narrowing.

Cara had witnessed her share of thunderstorms while growing up in Northern California. "Here it comes," she said in quiet awe.

"Are you frightened?" Kang inquired mildly.

He smiled at her brave denial when she faced him with large eyes and shook her head. His fingertips caressed her cheek, skimmed to her mouth, and outlined her lips.

Kang remembered the many times he had made love to this woman in his mind, remembered how he had expressed his ardor—sometimes tender and devoted, other times forceful and primitive—to bring her and himself pleasure. He yearned to do them all tonight—perhaps their one and only night together.

He craved to hear his name on her lips, spoken in a voice husky with passion, to have her burn in his arms over and over again from the flames he torched.

He kept a wary eye on her expression as he bent his head to kiss her mouth, his lips soft and searching.

He ran his fingertips to the hollow of her throat where he had seen the beginnings of the scar that marked her fused collarbone. He shifted the neckline of her nightshirt to view the consequences of his ambition.

When Cara self-consciously attempted to cover up, a determined frown puckered his smooth forehead. He captured her hand in his, staying it within his firm grasp.

He pulled Cara with him as he slid down the smooth finish of the bench from a sitting to a lying position, pillowing her head on his arm.

Once again, he pushed aside the fabric of her neckline. He took responsibility for the existence of the fine red six-inch scar by covering its length with gentle kisses, taking the remembered pain of it into himself.

Her shapely legs, arched over his, had come free from the coverlet. He gazed at the parallel scars on her left knee, faded over time, which remained from two reconstructive orthoscopic surgeries. He lightly ran his thumb over them.

His heart constricted in his chest when Cara looked away, eyes glittering with tears.

"Don't," she protested weakly, requiring neither his sympathy nor his remorse.

Kang took her chin between thumb and forefinger, turning her gaze back to his. He focused on her face, eyes darkened by guilt.

Cara shook her head, almost imperceptibly—discouraging the uselessness, here and now, of such feelings.

The low ceiling of blackened clouds overhead bumped impatiently against one another like harried rush hour commuters, fiercely grumbling in discontent.

Kang slipped his hand under her lower back and held her tightly, laying his cheek against her breast.

After a time, he felt Cara's soothing caress over the crown of his head.

Apology offered. Apology accepted.

He felt her body tense when he put his lips to her breast and began, through her nightshirt, to awaken the nipple he found there.

The moist warmth of his breath, the gentle rasp of his teeth through the thin fabric of her nightshirt, aroused her.

Thunder reverberated and rippled between their bodies as he deftly unfastened the buttons that held her bodice over her breasts, exposing them to his reverent gaze.

They stirred his blood, these generous, perfectly round and lovely white orbs—petite nipples and areolas a delicate pink—just as he had always imagined them.

"Beautiful," he murmured.

He relished the sweet scent of her skin, the suppleness of her breasts as he brushed his cheeks against them and grazed his lips over their velvety softness.

He wanted nothing more than to take her breasts in both hands and devour them. Instead, he cradled one in his hand, exploring it with his mouth and his tongue.

Cara's body flushed with heat, moisture rising on her skin.

Kang reached behind him to stroke the twin scars on her knee. His fingertips created a voluptuous tickling sensation as they skimmed down the inside of her leg.

Cara promptly put a trembling and cautionary hand on Kang's shoulder, unconvinced that having carnal knowledge of this man—more fantasy than fact—was wise.

Yet, he would not be denied. He heard her sharp intake of breath as he opened her to his touch and slid his fingers into the ripe depths between her thighs.

The fury of the storm, now directly overhead, engulfed them. Vicious gusts of wind mercilessly whipped every tree branch, every blade of grass. The evergreen-scented wind now carried with it the smell of ozone—like electrical wires that had short-circuited.

Kang murmured sweet Korean endearments to ease her apprehension—to assure Cara of his long-suppressed attraction to her—to reaffirm his desire for her.

He used his tongue in sync with his fingers, each mirroring the others' movements—licking her breast like luscious cream frosting from a cake, circling her nipple with his tongue and using his fingers in the same manner around her erogenous sweet spot.

Cara moaned deep in her throat, felt her hips involuntarily rise, responding to his touch.

The sky hurled white-hot forks of lightening to earth—over which the mountains stood watch like unflinching guardians—shattering the silence and filling the air with jittery anticipation.

Caught up in the vortex of an untamable nature, Kang held Cara's breast in his eager mouth, suckling like a hungry child, the strokes of his hand picking up the pace.

A shattering clap of thunder rattled the windows and shook the foundation of the cabin, vibrating the bench upon which they lay.

Cara arched her back, clutching fistfuls of Kang's shirtsleeves, and cried out—again and again and again—shuddering in ecstasy.

Kang took her in his arms and covered her mouth with his, seeking to capture her climax—to draw it into his body and share in her pleasure.

Large raindrops began to pelt the ground, lashing the lush woodland growth that surrounded them. It became a deluge—rain drumming insistently and noisily on the tin roof above their heads, cascading like a waterfall over the edge of the veranda's roof.

Kang pulled the quilted comforter over Cara's naked hips and buried his face in her neck, enjoying the moist and musky scent of her heated skin.

Finally, the downpour subsided into a gentle, steady rain.

"Kang Dae Ho," Cara crooned softly in his ear, voice dreamy and drugged with sexual release.

Kang smiled. It may not have been as he had imagined it—at the height of passion—but hearing her say his name like this—silky and content—was infinitely sweeter.

He carried her on his back like a child into the bedroom, her smooth white legs wrapped securely around his hips.

They leisurely undressed each other.

Kang lit a small lantern that replaced the darkened corners with a soft orange-red glow, and joined Cara on the padded bedding on the floor.

His smooth and eager hands moved easily over her body—skimming over her breasts, caressing her abdomen, rear and legs—intent on discovery. He playfully nipped the nape of her neck with his teeth, an earlobe, and the tender flesh of her inner thigh—Cara gasping in surprise at the arousing sensations.

He took his time entering her, holding back to make the experience more sensual. Enveloped by her warmth, Kang experienced the lightheaded euphoria of an intimate connection to her—of her acceptance.

Cara was adrift in a kind of dream-like, surreal enchantment. After all this time, she was with the man who had captured her imagination when they were both young—mysterious and never far from her thoughts—yet always just beyond her reach.

Was this just another fantasy? More provocative to her senses, certainly, than any she had experienced before. Yet curiously—surprisingly—without sentiment.

Kang choreographed an exquisite and erotic ballet—a *pas de deux*—dance for two. He gracefully partnered and balanced with her in adagio tempo—a succession of slow, soft, and lyrical continuous movements. In ways both provocative and new to her, he coaxed her to the precipice and then stopped, pulling her back.

He drew her onto his lap to face him. As she tightened and released her internal muscles—stroking him with her every upward movement—he closed his eyes, head thrown back, beautiful mouth parted in an expression of tortuous ecstasy.

Unable to hold back any longer, he circled his arms around her and squeezed the breath from her as he shuddered and released a growl deep in his throat.

Cara wrapped her arms around his neck, feeling the muscles of his body clench and unclench, tense and then release.

Moisture beaded on his forehead, shimmered on the smooth gold-tan skin of his body, droplets sparkling on the glossy strands of black hair framing his face.

Cara felt sated, as if she did not have an ounce of energy or a bone left in her body. She dropped her head on Kang's shoulder, embarrassingly indolent.

Neither of them moved, clinging to each other, heart rates once again slowing to within normal range.

He kissed her neck. "Say my name," he commanded quietly.

"Mmm," she hummed, charmed by his request. "Kang Dae Ho."

Her observance of etiquette after what they had just experienced together amused him. "Less formally," he encouraged her.

"Dae Ho."

He tightened his embrace. "Thank you."

"For what?" she murmured.

His skin was beginning to feel sticky. "I need to bathe."

Cara sat up to gaze into his eyes and offered languidly, "I'll wash your hard-to-reach places, if you'll wash mine."

He made her smile when he lightly ran his hand over her face.

He was a tease.

"You have a deal," he said in English.

Fight Or Flight

July 2007
Hwacheon-gun – Gangwon-do

CARA FELT A WARM HAND gently pressed against her mouth. Her eyes flew open.

Kang whispered in her ear, "Ssssh. Get dressed. Hurry."

It was still dark outside.

Spurred by the urgency in Kang's voice, Cara shook herself awake, took the bundle of clothes he gave her, and dressed quickly.

He came back for her minutes later and guided her through the unlit and shadowy cabin, to a mysterious opening in the floor now exposed from a displaced area rug.

Kang descended a steep set of narrow wooden steps, stopped and turned to offer his hand to Cara. She clutched it tightly as he helped her stumble blindly into what she first thought was a damp cellar.

Kang hurriedly centered the rug over the trap door and pulled it closed.

Only then did he click on the flashlight he carried, illuminating the enclosed space.

Cara realized with a twinge of uneasiness that they stood at the mouth of a long and narrow earthen tunnel. She became anxious when confined in close spaces.

The dank, sour smell of wet earth assailed her nose, calling to her imagination an ancient and musty grave. She pulled her sweater over her nose.

She heard skittering further down the passage. Rats?

She drew near to Kang for reassurance. "What is this place?" she whispered.

He kept his voice low. "The cabin has been in the Ryu family for three generations. They dug this tunnel during Japanese occupation. They used it occasionally in the 1950s."

He bent his head and started down the low-ceilinged tunnel. Cara kept up with him, huddling close to stay connected.

Kang reached behind him and firmly grasped her hand in his, giving it a squeeze of encouragement, and led her into the unknown and cloaked depths beyond the weak beam of the flashlight.

Once they cleared the foundation of the house, Cara heard water drip, drip, drip—saw shiny, wet rivulets running down the walls. The recent storm created puddles on the floor of the passage where, over the years, rainwater had worn grooves in the hard packed earth.

They splashed right through them, keeping up a brisk pace.

That suited Cara, the sooner out of this dismal and tight space the less anxious she would feel. She brushed away the cobwebs that clung to face and hair with a repelled swipe of her hand.

Kang stopped abruptly. An iron, gate coated with a rusted patina from the dampness, barred the exit. He turned to Cara. "I'm going out first and take a look around. I want you to stay here."

Cara opened her mouth to protest his abandonment of her in this confined and frightening place.

"This time I insist, Cara," Kang cautioned her firmly.

When she realized he awaited her compliance, she nodded numbly.

He cast his eyes upward and listened intently. Apparently satisfied they were alone, he removed the padlock from the gate and patiently tugged on it. Kang winced in irritation when the gate grudgingly opened, its hinges screeching in piercing protest.

"Why we are hiding?" Cara inquired before Kang pushed through the flimsy wooden door beyond the gate.

He brushed his knuckles against her cheek. "Again, I have drawn you into my life...put you in danger."

Kang took her in his arms, making her nearly breathless in his tight embrace. He kissed her deeply—as if it would be the last time.

Cara became apprehensive.

"I won't let anything happen to you, Cara," Kang promised with a weary voice.

He handed Cara the flashlight, eased the wooden door open and cautiously stepped outside, surveying everything within a 360-degree perspective. "Lock the gate and keep it locked until you hear my voice give you the all clear."

"Be careful," Cara encouraged him softly.

He held her eyes an expressive moment before closing the wooden door behind him. Once outside, he resettled some of the brush he had knocked aside when opening the door.

Cara secured the gate with the padlock as Kang had instructed and waited with trepidation, holding her breath, in the ensuing silence. She flashed the beam of light down the long tunnel, determined to keep an eye on any critters that may be lurking nearby.

KANG CREPT THROUGH THE WOODS, keeping low, climbing a narrow footpath overlooking the cabin and concealing his presence behind some dense underbrush to observe the hum of activity around the cabin.

There were about a dozen men swarming in and around the old cottage. Within the confines of the crossing beams of light from their torches, Kang saw that they were ransacking the place.

"Nothing, Boss," one of the men reported in Japanese to a man impatiently pacing out front.

Kang got a clearer view of his face when he turned in his direction. It was Jeun's son, Jeun Ji-tae.

How did they find this place? Kang silently cursed his luck, grimly acknowledging the probability of an informant in Seoul Metro.

"Look around!" Ji-tae ordered angrily, giving the messenger a shove. "Go on! He couldn't have gotten far!"

He wanted those journals found. He needed them found.

His laugh was bitter. His old man succeeded in fucking him even in death.

Months ago, he was the one who planted the seed of suspicion in his father's mind about Kang's allegiance. He was the one who sat in the front seat of his father's town car to observe Kang as he spoke with his superior in a remote location along the Han River.

Jeun had been satisfied—clearly pleased—with Kang's loyalty.

How Jeun Ji-tae hated Kang. In his diseased mind—taking no responsibility for his role in the failed relationship with his father—Jeun Ji-tae despised Kang for stealing his father's trust and affection, for usurping his rightful place in the organization.

He would find Kang. And once he was in possession of his father's ledgers, he would slit Kang's throat with the ancient samurai *tanto* blade presented to him by his crew as a declaration of their allegiance.

But before he killed him, Jeun Ji-tae would take a great deal of satisfaction in telling Kang about the fate of his men—slaughtered like pigs at their headquarters when they recklessly challenged his authority.

All of them brave. All of them dead. Including Kang's right-hand man, Yi.

Ji-tae walked up the wooden steps and entered the old cabin, taking a slow, observant look around. He walked to the center of the living area and stood on a three-by-five-foot hand-woven rug. Glancing down, he was curious why one corner appeared to be wedged in a crack in the floorboards.

What Kang witnessed made him swear an oath and steal back toward Cara. Cara. He had to reach Cara.

"LIGHTS OFF!" KOSOVSKAIA ORDERED HIS driver when they were in close proximity to Ryu's cottage. He gestured to a wide clearing on the side of the road. "Park in that turnaround." He spoke to his men through his wireless communicator. "Everybody out. We go on foot from here."

A dozen well-armed men poured from three full-size sports utility vehicles. Alexei Kosovskaia and his crew double-timed down the narrow dirt road, keeping low and in the shadows, to mask their arrival from any guards Jeun may have posted.

They approached the cabin silently, cautiously. Kosovskaia concluded that, by all appearances, the element of surprise was theirs.

Kosovskaia motioned with hand gestures to his men to surround the area and tighten the perimeter around the cottage. They had their instructions. Incapacitate first. Ask questions later.

THE LONGER CARA WAITED, THE more anxious she became.

When she heard the voices of several men outside, she clicked off the flashlight, leaving her in an all-consuming and cloying blackness. Her breath came in rapid, shallow huffs.

Although it was highly improbable that they could hear her, she pressed the back of her hand against her mouth, forcing herself to breathe through her nose.

The men spoke in hushed tones in Japanese. Cara could only catch the odd word or phrase. They were on the hunt—for Kang.

She hugged the wall, grounding herself with a hand against the damp earth. Something with many legs skittered across her fingers. She vigorously shook her hand in revulsion and sprang away from the wall.

She landed against a warm body mass.

She sucked in a horrified breath, shuddering in shock and fear. She leaped forward and whirled around to illuminate "the thing" who now shared the confines of the tunnel.

Dressed in black, his face appeared to be floating above her like a disembodied and grotesquely painted kabuki mask—barbaric and ghastly. His eyes were hooded and sparkling—without soul. His lips were parted and teeth bared—without humor.

His hand shot out to commandeer the flashlight. With a painful twist of Cara's wrist, he turned the light on her face, blinding her.

"*Yariman*," he sneered, calling her a slut in Japanese—or less generously, Kang's pussy.

Insult and anger overtook fear as Cara shoved the flashlight toward his face, connecting with a dull thud against the bridge of his nose. The sharp metal edge of the flashlight broke skin. Bright red blood—in garish contrast to the monochromatic background—leaked from the gash.

Furious, he knocked the flashlight from Cara's grasp. It crashed to the dirt floor and rolled away toward a sloping corner.

They began pushing and shoving each other—each scrabbling to reach the flashlight first—Cara to use as a weapon, Jeun Ji-tae to find his way out of the tunnel and coerce Kang out of concealment.

Cara jammed a sharp elbow into her antagonist's abdomen. He grunted in pain and cursed her in Japanese, viciously grabbing a handful of her hair in his fist.

Cara cried out in torment, eyes tearing with pain.

He reclaimed the flashlight. "Open the door," he ordered Cara, shining the light over the doorway leading outside.

Anxious to leave the oppressive confines of the tunnel and breathe the fresh air outside, Cara unlocked and opened the door, still powerless under Juen's unrelenting grip.

Jeun Ji-tae hauled her outside by her hair and took a wide stance in a clearing. "Call Kang Dae Ho," he growled. "Call your lover!"

Cara winced and bit back a yelp of misery when he shook her by a fistful of hair. She remained stubbornly silent.

"Call your lover!" he bellowed like a wounded fiend. "Kang! Kang! Come see what I have found!"

Jeun Ji-tae slid his *tanto* blade from its sheath attached to a belt around his waist. He held it to Cara's throat. "Now! Or your whore will be choking on her own blood!"

Kang rushed Jeun Ji-tae from his blindside and hit him low, knocking the legs out from under him. Ji-tae, the *tanto* knife, and Cara flew in opposite directions.

Cara landed hard, outstretched arms doing little to break the force of her fall. She rolled away from the two men wrestling on the ground, each trying to overpower the other—to survive.

Cara recognized Kang by his white shirt. With the light of the moon cloaked by tattered remnants of thunderheads, it appeared as if he were in a death struggle with a wraithlike apparition, as treacherous as the consuming darkness.

Jeun Ji-tae taunted Kang with words spoken only for his ears. Then he laughed—a cruel, joyless sound.

Kang rolled Jeun and knelt over him, repeatedly punching his face with his fist, venting his fury.

Jeun helplessly suffered the beating until his hand brushed against the cold steel of a blade under the leaf litter and forest slash on the ground. His hand closed around the hilt of the *tanto* blade. Once firmly in his grip, he swung his arm in a wild and desperate arc toward Kang's torso.

Kang stiffened. He looked down at the hilt of the knife, foreign and unforeseen, sticking out of his chest.

Taking the advantage, Jeun rolled and knocked Kang to one side. He grasped Kang by his shirtfront and hauled him to his unsteady feet.

He tortuously eased the knife from Kang's body. The sickening, sharp hiss of a blade sliding from a dense mass of tissue made Cara gasp in horror. She now comprehended that Kang had been stabbed—perhaps mortally.

Jeun slowly raised his arm, tang of the blade in a downward position, ready to strike the killing blow.

"Noo!" Cara screamed in dread.

Distracted for a split second, Jeun glanced her way.

Cara's brief diversion was all Alexei Kosovskaia needed. He stealthily approached Jeun from behind and, using his considerable body weight, swung a thick wooden club against the back of Jeun's skull. The club connected with a dull thud.

Unbelievably, Jeun swiveled to stare with astonishment at his attacker. Kosovskaia muscled him away from Kang and clubbed him once again for good measure.

After Jeun fell heavily to the ground, the Russian violently shook him, making sure he was unconscious.

Cara scrabbled on her hands and knees to where Kang was slumped. His white shirtfront became a lurid canvas for an abstract budding crimson blossom. She supported him with her body, trying with little success to stem the surge of blood. The flow began to dwindle as his internal organs began to shut down, his body valiantly attempting to fight the severed veins and arteries drowning his surrounding tissues in blood.

He was going into shock.

"Stay with us," Cara desperately urged him in a voice raw with fear. "Stay with us. We'll get help."

A stranger to Cara—and a little frightening owing to his bulk and crystalline blue eyes—Kosovskaia knelt beside them and thrust a clean silk handkerchief in her hand.

"Hold this against the wound," he ordered in English with a heavy Russian accent. He put his hand over Cara's and pushed down. "Press hard."

The metallic scent of Kang's warm blood filled her nostrils as it seeped through her fingers, making them sticky—roiling her squeamish stomach.

"Hang on, my friend," the Russian solemnly advised, gazing down at Kang with concern and the sorrow of intuition. "Your comrade Ryu is on the way with his police."

He offered Kang a brotherly and gentle pat on the shoulder. "In the meantime, you are laying in the arms of a beautiful woman, no?"

Cara smiled wanly at the Russian, touched by his evident fraternity with and expression of affection toward Kang.

How could this be happening?

Feeling helpless and knowing she could do nothing more, she comforted Kang—holding him securely against her body, whispering soothing words into his ear, reassuring him that help was on the way.

But would it be soon enough? His life was ebbing with each heartbeat, his spirit nearly all that remained in his earthbound form.

Cara felt a twinge of guilt. He had promised to keep her safe, and he had. But at what terrible cost?

Would his sacrifice expunge the stain on his conscience for hurting her so many years ago? For putting himself and his career before everything and everyone? Was his act of heroism meant to be his path to forgiveness and redemption?

Cara clutched him tighter, believing that a soul darkened with sin could be cleansed by unselfish and valiant deeds. "Thank you, Kang Dae Ho," she crooned softly. "Thank you for saving my life."

Unlike the act of dying romanticized in movies or television melodramas, Kang would share no poignant words of parting between his short, rapid breaths. No soulful exchange of glances, as he focused inward on the trauma disrupting the familiar rhythms of his body.

A brief squeeze of Cara's hand—or perhaps it was just her imagination. A final rasping breath released from his lungs. A trickle of dark blood seeping from the corner of his mouth and tracking over his jaw. A soft, cool brush of air against her cheek—a fleeting flutter—and then he was gone.

Kosovskaia and Cara came to the same realization together, staring at each other in utter disbelief.

In frustration and rage, the big Russian jumped to his feet and stalked to the unconscious body of Jeun Ji-tae. He gave him a vicious kick.

"*Mu`dak, b`lyad*!" he howled. You asshole fuck!

Ji-tae groaned in pain, clinging to life even as the last crystals of sand marked the end of his time on earth.

Ryu and a half dozen of his heavily armed men ran up the knoll. He exchanged meaningful glances with the Russian. Ryu pointed to Jeun and gruffly ordered his men, "Get that piece of shit out of here."

Jeun did not rouse or make a sound as Ryu's men dragged him down the hill.

Then Ryu became aware of Kang laying in Cara's arms. He fell to his knees next to them, attempting to glean any signs of life.

His answer was in Cara's eyes.

"*Aigoo*!" he huffed, overwhelmed by grief. "*Aigoo*!" He laid his hand on the shoulder of Kang and shook his head—disbelieving—cursing his luck and the circumstances, his late arrival, and the loss of a man he considered to be a dedicated cop, a long-time friend—a brother.

Acquittal

July 2007
Hwacheon-gun – Gangwon-do

"I'M SORRY FOR YOUR LOSS, Superintendent," Cara sincerely offered as they sat side by side on the front steps of his cabin. She strongly sensed that the relationship between the two men had been more than professional.

As confirmation, Ryu nodded glumly and dropped his chin to his chest.

Cara took in a sharp breath and put a hand on his arm. "I just remembered something."

Before they left his apartment, Kang called her attention to the safe in his bedroom closet. His eyes solemn, almost black, he asked her to speak to his superior at Seoul Metro if, for whatever reason, he could not.

Ryu's head snapped up. He gave Cara his full attention, eyes prying hers with many and varied questions.

"He said his bedroom closet in his apartment in the Itaewon District contains items of interest to you. In the safe behind the wall."

Ryu shook his head, tears glistening in his eyes. "I knew it," he whispered fiercely. "I knew Kang would do himself honor."

He jumped to his feet, spurred by a sense of urgency. "We will see you safely back to Seoul."

"I can give her a ride," the big Russian, Kosovskaia, offered as he joined them. He was curious—very interested to know about this American woman's relationship with his friend, Kang.

Law enforcement and emergency medical personnel swarmed in and around the cabin, yet only one man caught Cara's attention—standing in stark clarity among the blur of human forms.

She slowly rose to her feet. "Thank you, gentlemen," she said to Ryu and Kosovskaia, smiling wanly, "but I believe I have a ride."

They followed her gaze.

Moon.

Somber and composed as he stood in the center of chaos—among the loud voices and frenetic forensic activity—his watchful eyes never left Cara.

She felt the breath leave her lungs—her tense muscles relax—weak with relief.

He was here. He had come for her.

Moon approached them and cast an inquiring glance at Ryu. Ryu nodded, giving him permission to take Cara from the scene.

When Cara descended the steps, a blanket draped about her shoulders, Moon protectively curved his arm around her and guided her through the throng toward his town car. He opened the front passenger door for her and Cara slid on the seat without a word or a glance.

Moon anxiously observed her after he settled behind the wheel. She was staring out of the windshield as if in a trance.

"Are you all right?" he asked, voice strained with worry, his nerves as taut as a high wire. It had been a long drive. Too many hours in which to agonize about what he might find upon his arrival.

"My hair hurts," she responded vaguely.

Moon frowned. Was this more of her glib humor that he struggled to understand? He scrutinized her expression. No, she was serious.

He started the engine of the luxury car and slowly rolled down the driveway, their faces awash in the multi-colored swirl of lights from police cruisers, prisoner transports, and emergency medical response vehicles parked haphazardly on either side.

Cara looked on as the body of Kang, encased in heavy black plastic, was loaded into an ambulance. Following the stretcher bearing Kang's body, Superintendent Ryu grimly climbed into the back of the ambulance to accompany a fallen officer and his longtime friend back to Seoul.

Kang Dae Ho.

Cara had been relentlessly haunted by an unexplainable fascination for a man she barely knew. A man who made love to her as if she had been as much a fascination to him.

Over the years, they would encounter each other from time to time—each chance meeting frustratingly fruitless and ill timed. One meeting, she could never forget, proved harmful.

In her daydreams, she had molded Kang in the image of a man who would please her—whom she could easily love. No doubt, he had done the same with her. Destiny had benevolently intervened, sparing them both disillusionment—the sorrowful discovery of the defects in their inventions.

Kang Dae Ho.

Cara recalled the omen prophesied years earlier by a young fortuneteller in Sinsa-dong. *He is not to be yours in this life...but will wait for you in the next.*

"Be seeing you," Cara murmured solemnly as an emergency medical technician secured the ambulance doors.

It was time to let him go.

Then There Was You

July 2007
Gangneung – Gyeongpo Beach

NEITHER OF THEM SPOKE. NEITHER of them ready or willing to discuss a subject that was too fresh and raw—the outcome of which was too unpredictable.

At a crossroads, Moon pointed the car away from Seoul toward the east. Cara observed him with interest when an hour later he turned south onto the highway that paralleled the Sea of Japan.

Moon drove into a parking area along the wide stretch of Gyeongpo Beach and stopped the car. Cara smiled when he glanced her way, grateful to him for bringing her to the ocean. A place where it was possible to revive a tattered spirit and, just maybe, a tormented relationship. She slid through her opened car door, slammed it shut, and skipped down a slight incline to the sandy beach.

♪ "Emmanuel"
Chris Botti feat. Lucia Micarelli

Moon retrieved the blanket given to Cara at the fishing cabin, and the shoes she had shucked once on the sand, toting them as he traced her small footsteps. He hung back about ten paces to give her space.

Every so often, she would glance over her shoulder, as if reassuring herself that he was still there.

It awakened a memory in Moon of a similar walk upon their first meeting a number of years earlier—on a resort beach on Jeju Island. Moon grievously reflected on the pristine possibilities that awaited them—before they had yet to betray each other's faith and love.

Cara trudged across the sand, the calves of her legs aching from the strain. In the burgeoning light of day, she caught sight of the front of her clothes, rusted with blood. Kang's blood. She numbly inspected her hands. The creases in her fingers and the lines on her palms were stained red—like a macabre roadmap—destination unknown.

She stood at the tideline, facing the infinite and misty gray horizon that promised an imminent sunrise, enthralled by the gentle waves lapping against her bare feet.

Moon watched with apprehension as she began to walk toward the ocean, seemingly lured by the receding waves.

Come. Come with us, they enticingly beckoned Cara. *Come…join our primal and enduring rhythm…come be cleansed…released.*

Waist-high in the ocean, Cara raised her arms as if inviting—surrendering—to the oncoming break of waves. She allowed them to engulf her, to draw her down to the undulating serenity of the sandy bottom.

In disbelief, Moon lost his grip on the blanket and Cara's shoes and ran to the spot where she had just stood. He was stunned. Paralyzed.

Heart hammering against his ribcage, hands drawn into fists at his sides, he anguished over whether he should reclaim her from the unpredictable currents.

Is this what you want, Cara? To be free of me? To be free of this world? He squeezed his eyes closed and bowed his head.

Is this how it will end?

"Don't leave us, Cara," he begged in a ragged voice. "Come to me, please. I love you."

CARA FLOATED IN A SOOTHING and silent gloaming.

Blessed Mother, what have I become?

A sweet feminine voice—free of judgment—kindly assured her, *Wiser, I think.*

The clear, dulcet tone eased the heaviness in Cara's heart.

Will he ever understand me? Cara beseeched her spiritual companion. *Will he ever forgive me?*

That man?

Cara plainly perceived Moon anxiously pacing on the shoreline, racked with indecision and dread.

That man who is terrified that you will not return to him? Agonizing over whether he should dive into the ocean at his peril and rescue you, or allow you to accomplish what you seemingly desire.

Cara heard Moon's earnest entreaty. *Don't leave us, Cara. Come to me, please. I love you.*

Cara took great consolation from the crowning message imparted in her consciousness by her gracious guardian.

Relinquish yourself to the imperfections of love. For that is how love is—imperfect. Welcome every joy and fulfillment it offers. Safeguard and nourish it. For love is what keeps the human heart beating, and the soul replenished.

MOON WEPT TEARS OF RELIEF when Cara rose from the waves, keeping her feet under her in the swirling tide, slowly making her way toward the beach.

Cara held Moon's eyes with hers, pausing at the tideline to gauge his sentiment.

Moon noticed that she was shivering—from the cool morning breeze or apprehension, he was unsure. Smiling wanly, he held up the blanket and fanned it before her, encouraging her to accept its protection and warmth.

She walked toward him with restored purpose, pushed through the blanket into his arms, and began to sob uncontrollably.

Moon enveloped her in the blanket, clutching her tightly. "I thought I had lost you," he lamented, voice cracking in desolation.

Cara suspected that he was referring to more than her plunge in the ocean.

Moon rained feverish kisses over her face, tasting the salt of the sea on her skin. He soothingly rocked them in a side-to-side motion. "I thought I had lost you!"

SHIELDED FROM THE BREEZE IN a cove of wind-carved sand and driftwood above the tideline, Moon had cocooned them both in the warmth of the blanket. Cara sat between his knees and leaned back against his body, securely wrapped in his arms. They watched the rim of the sun—shrouded in a swirling haze—push above the horizon.

Cara sighed contentedly, burrowing into the warmth of Moon's chest. "Don't let go."

"I won't," he assured her.

She took the initiative, broaching the subject they had been purposely avoiding. "Is there anything you would like to ask me, Moon?"

His gaze took on a faraway aspect, his features tense. "No."

"I promise to answer you honestly, if you do," she persisted softly.

His tone was self-derisive. "We find ourselves here because of my lack of judgment."

"We both have made our share of mistakes, Moon," Cara insisted gently.

After a beat, she admitted softly, "I learned something over the last several days. Something that took me by surprise."

She frowned, continuing her ruminations aloud. "It's amazing how often I am caught unaware. Embarrassing, really. The more important the matter, the more mystified I am."

Moon smiled. "Is this a private conversation or can anyone join?"

Cara blinked, coming out of her reverie. "Sorry."

He prompted her with some hesitation. "What is it that you learned?"

Her eyes scanned every facet of his face, nothing impeding the clarity of her perspective. "I have never felt in another man's arms, the way I feel in yours."

Moon pressed a grateful and warm kiss against her temple. "How do you feel?"

She replied reflectively, "Like I am home."

"Wherever we are?"

Cara smiled. She had once told Moon that they could consider themselves to be home—wherever in the world that might be—as long as they were together. She was pleased that he remembered.

"Yes, wherever we are."

"Then, will you come with me to America?"

"America?" she confirmed in confusion.

She felt him nod his head. "I have been offered a professorship in the History Department at Yale University."

She gasped and popped up, pinning him with accusing eyes. "So, that's what you've been doing!"

"What did you imagine?" he inquired, unruffled.

She made a wry face. "You were being so secretive, I wasn't sure if you were fomenting anarchy or designing a bomb of mass destruction."

Moon shook his head, now relaxed enough to be entertained. "Always fanciful."

"Well, you gave me no inkling."

"I was studying for my credentials to teach in America, and earning my Ph.D."

"And your recent absence?" Cara questioned. When she had indulged her impatience and temper—succumbing to temporary insanity.

"Testing for my credentials."

She stared at him, incredulous, feeling more than a little foolish. If only she had known.

She relaxed and leaned back against him, at last appreciating and acknowledging the magnitude of his accomplishment. "Congratulations, Moon. That is quite an achievement."

Moon grasped her chin to lock her gaze onto his. "We have one more, very important, matter to discuss."

"What is that?" she asked in a small voice, wary of his stern manner.

"Cara, would you do me the honor of becoming my wife?"

How sweetly stated—so formal and respectful.

The first time Moon had mentioned the subject of marriage, when he was living in San Francisco, he had couched it by saying he wanted Cara to stay with him, so that he could spend the rest of his life with her—loving her. Technically, he had not asked her to marry him.

As always, Cara's response was direct and to the point.

"Do I have to marry you to go with you?"

Moon could just imagine the conservative New England response to their living in sin—given their mercurial and very public history—and having a son, no less.

"Yes."

He sounded adamant.

"Do you think we will get it right this time?" Cara questioned dubiously.

"We will start over in a country more accustomed to racial differences. Far away from my mother's interference and the obligations of my heritage."

"That sounds wonderful," Cara conceded dreamily.

"It does," Moon agreed with a contented smile.

She could not deny that Moon had worked tirelessly—done all of this—for them. This time, he was the one who had made the sacrifices necessary to begin again.

"Will you give me time to think about it?" Not that she really needed it. She was just testing.

"Yes," Moon affirmed, not fooled for a minute. "Until next Wednesday. When we leave for America."

"In four days?"

"Five days. Today is Friday."

She swiveled to kneel before Moon and sat back on her heels. Eyes wide and guileless, and with an unusually serious aspect, she declared, "I will agree to marry you."

He grinned in relief, reaching for her.

"On one condition."

Her resolve tested Moon's confidence. "Which is?"

"From now on, we will keep no secrets from each other," she decreed firmly. "We will share our thoughts and discuss our plans. Always." She extended her hand. "Agreed?"

Moon fleetingly contemplated his much anticipated future—a new culture, a new career, a fresh start with the woman he adored, and his son.

He was under no illusions that it would be challenging to overcome his natural inclinations—a lifetime of cultural conditioning. Nonetheless, to sustain his relationship with Cara, he was determined to accept and abide by any conditions she set—within reason.

He soberly shook her hand. "Agreed."

A Fresh Start

열여덟

18
First Day of School

September 2007
Yale University – New Haven, Connecticut

IN THE EARLY AFTERNOON ON THE first day of fall, Moon
walked into his inaugural class at Yale University—History 104
with his assigned teaching assistant close on his heels. He entered the
lecture hall and stopped short.

The hall appeared to have exploded with students. There was standing
room only—and not much of that. Clearly, the people jammed into the
room exceeded the fire marshal's posted maximum capacity.

Silence fell over the gallery upon his arrival. Moon slowly cast his
eyes over the students, and a nervous titter spread throughout the hall.
He took off his jacket and hung it on the chair behind the metal desk
at the front of the class, and took his time rolling up his white dress
shirtsleeves while walking toward the seats of the theater-style lecture
hall. He confidently stood before the throng of students, stance wide,
and put his hands on his hips.

One of the undergrads whispered to his friend in awe, "Jesus, he's
like the King of Siam."

After a pregnant pause, Moon observed dryly, "Well, aren't I
popular?"

The crowd laughed in relief.

Moon held out his hand for the class roster. His teaching assistant,
nervously hovering close by, promptly passed it to him.

Moon perused the list, and then glanced up at the sea of smiling young faces. "How many of you are registered for this class?"

Less than twenty hands shot in the air.

"And the rest of you?" Moon inquired, amused.

"We wanted to check out the man who left his country and a promising political career for the love of an American woman," one of the female students piped up.

Everyone laughed, but it was uneasy.

The corners of Moon's mouth curled in amusement. She likened him to a royal who created an infamous constitutional crisis in the British Empire when he abdicated his throne to marry his mistress—a commoner and an American.

"As far as I know," Moon quipped, "I am still welcomed back."

Another short laugh.

"That must have been tough, man," an earnest young black man, toward the front, commented with admiration.

"Have you seen my wife?" Moon inquired pointedly.

The young man nodded and grinned slyly. "Yes, sir. I have."

Moon smiled. "Then you must know the choice was not that difficult."

That brought forth a hearty laugh from the class, breaking the ice. A few in the class applauded.

"Why history?" a male student inquired from the upper decks.

Moon nodded thoughtfully, glancing up in the direction from where the question had come. "Since man's first footprint on this earth, his history has been written by his nature...lust, greed, intolerance, fear, ambition, arrogance, and ignorance."

He moved freely in front of the class, impassioned by the subject. "Each of us is making history by the decisions we make...shaping our collective experience in time. How we choose our leaders or blindly follow them, believe or worship, fear or distrust, love or hate. To understand history is to understand ourselves."

He glanced up from his discourse to acknowledge his students. "I personally find that fascinating."

Two rows up from where Moon stood, a thick-shouldered young man snickered and passed a remark about Moon's career change. "At least history is a more noble profession than politics."

Moon regarded him evenly. "Mr...?"

He shifted uneasily in his seat under Moon's steady gaze. "Freeman, sir."

Moon checked his roster. Mr. Freeman had registered for the class.

"I gather, Mr. Freeman, that you have little regard for politicians." Moon's observation was at the same time satirical and amused.

"That is correct, sir," the big red head endured.

"Even your president?" Moon inquired with interest.

"Especially my president," Freeman replied. A few of his classmates clapped.

Moon's gaze swept over his audience. "How many of you are old enough to vote?"

Nearly all in the audience raised their hands.

Moon nodded. "Who here is registered to vote?"

Less than half the hands remained in the air.

Moon was satisfied that he had made his point.

Freeman grumbled something under his breath.

"You have something to add, Mr. Freeman?"

"It doesn't matter if we vote. The Electoral College decides who will be our president. Until the office no longer takes millions of dollars to win, the grassroots of our country will never be represented in Washington."

A rousing round of applause and shouts of agreement from the majority of students in the hall.

Moon waited for silence. "Thank you, Mr. Freeman. While that sentiment is pessimistic at best, and flawed at worst, it was well thought out and passionately expressed."

Moon tried taking a different track with his impressionable spectators. "Have any of you noticed what the Oval Office does to the men who have served as President of the United States?"

"Made them rich?" someone sniggered.

"CEOs make far more with salaries and bonuses, I assure you," Moon stated. "No, I was referring to the way they age. They appear to age two years for every year in office."

A few students nodded in agreement. Others clearly had not given that a thought.

"They ride around in Air Force One, take vacations at Camp David, and kiss babies. How hard could that be?"

Moon keenly eyed the outspoken Freeman. "So, you think the job is easy?"

"Sure," he pronounced with arrogant lift of his square jaw.

"Please," Moon motioned for him to come down to the floor beside him. "Won't you join me, President Freeman?"

Uncomfortable now that Moon had called upon him to participate in some sort of charade, Freeman resisted with a smirk, "I can't act."

"Can you think?" Moon pressed dryly.

"Yes, sir."

Moon waved him to a chair that his teaching assistant moved to the front of the room.

Moon cast his glance over an intrigued crowd. "Who here believes that might makes right? That military intervention in a crisis is not only warranted, but strongly advised."

A young man looking like a recruiting poster for the ROTC raised his hand.

Moon smiled in satisfaction. "Please, join us." He dragged a chair next to Freeman. "Mr. President, may I introduce your military advisor."

A young woman's hand shot in the air.

Moon acknowledged her with a nod. "Yes?"

"My organization donated heavily to the campaign of Mr. Freeman. The President-Elect made us certain promises. It's my job to make sure they are kept."

"What is the mission of your organization?" Moon inquired with interest.

"Environmental protection."

Freeman groaned. "Give me a break."

Moon grinned. He hoped this young woman had signed up for the class. He motioned for her to come down. "Won't you join us, please?"

Moon surrounded President Freeman with members of his cabinet, his politically motivated detractors, a few constituents, and one environmentalist. He postulated a scenario in which the president had to react, call upon his advisors, and assure his constituents that he was capable of solving an imminent crisis. Admittedly, this task simultaneously required the president to attempt to keep everyone happy and refrain from antagonizing one another into a downward slide into chaos.

Moon anticipated the outcome.

It was chaos.

Reaching the breaking point, Freeman jumped to his feet and shouted above the agitated voices of his fellow participants. "Listen here! I am the President of the United States and my decision will be final!"

A stunned silence ensued.

Moon checked his wristwatch and smiled. "Congratulations, Mr. Freeman. It took you only forty-three minutes, seventeen seconds as the leader of the free world to crown yourself King."

The classroom erupted in hoots, whistles, applause, and loud laughter. A few wads of balled up yellow lined notepaper flew at Freeman's head.

President Freeman flushed red as he folded back on his chair.

Moon held up his hand for order. "Ladies and gentlemen enrolled in History 104, please read chapters one through three of your textbook before our next class."

Groans.

"Although we will be using a textbook, classwork in the form of participation in debates and discussions will be heavily weighted toward your grades. It is not my intention or preference to have you memorize and regurgitate names, dates, or events, but rather understand cause and effect—setting a course of action in motion, analyzing the possible outcome, and reviewing the consequences."

A question from the front row. "Do we still have time to sign up for this course?"

Moon deferred to his teaching assistant for an answer to the young woman's inquiry.

Moon's bespectacled and bearded young assistant consulted his class enrollment notes. "Uh...yes." He nodded. "Until Friday of this week at noon."

The class disbursed, students nodding to Moon or complimenting him on the excitement of the class, his teaching techniques, his brilliance, as they filtered out of the room.

"Splendid, Professor Moon." Dr. Emile Grant, the grandfatherly head of the history department, gave him a wink as he stood inside the doorway. "Or should I say Dr. Moon."

"I haven't received the official notice yet, sir."

"Bring your certificate to my office once you do."

"Yes, sir."

The Dean looked around the hall and frowned. "I think we need to get you a bigger venue. Perhaps the new auditorium."

When he departed, Moon dismissed his young teaching assistant. "Thank you, Mr. Garcia."

Gustavio Garcia grinned, considering his good fortune at drawing this wild card. God knows he had done his share of assisting phlegmatic professors who droned on and on, lulling everyone to sleep. "My pleasure, sir. I'm going to enjoy working with you."

When he also left, Moon collected his coat from the chair behind the desk. He glanced up, startled to see someone still seated against the wall on the top row of the lecture hall.

It was Michael Lee.

Michael leaned forward and put his elbows on his knees. "Impressive."

Moon modestly misdirected the compliment. "First day. I'm sure the class size will shrink."

Michael shook his head doubtfully. "I wouldn't be so sure."

Moon raised his brows as Michael nimbly skipped down the stairs to join him. "Did my wife send you to collect me?"

"She did," Michael confessed easily, without guile. "She doesn't want you to be late for your birthday party."

Michael handed Moon a copy of the Yale Daily News, the oldest published college daily in the country. An attractive photo of Moon with his arm around Cara graced the front page, a fanciful headline and lengthy narrative below it.

"*Aish!*" Moon exclaimed with a huff of air.

"Exactly," Michael murmured, enjoying Moon's reaction.

The Sweet Life

September 2007
Yale University – New Haven, Connecticut

Moon and Michael chatted companionably as they leisurely strolled through the pleasant, tree-lined streets rimming the campus. Fifteen minutes later, they arrived at a homey New England saltbox style house, chintz curtains blowing in the breeze through the double hung paned windows, the inviting scent of fresh baking coming from the kitchen.

Michael happily mused that the house could be a model for a Norman Rockwell painting—a slice of Americana. He followed Moon over a brick pathway around the house to the screened back door. They were just in time to hear Cara's raised and agitated voice coming from the kitchen.

"Regalo Michael Moon! Stop feeding Missy your father's birthday cake this instant!"

The two men stopped and exchanged smiles.

They heard Cara wail, "Look at this mess!"

Missy, the family dog adopted from a collie rescue organization, bolted through the screen door that slammed behind her—sharp muzzle frosted with butter cream icing—and ran around the corner of the house to hide in the bushes.

Moon shot Michael a perceptive glance. "I think you had better rescue your godson."

The men entered the roomy farmhouse-styled kitchen to find a destroyed birthday cake on the kitchen table, and a soon to be two-year old boy caught red-handed with the evidence all over his chubby cheeks and hands.

Michael scooped him up in his arms on his way through the kitchen. "What do you say we get you cleaned up?"

Moon quietly approached Cara as she stared with dismay at his ruined birthday cake. He placed a consoling kiss on her cheek. "Hi."

She looked up at him, tears of frustration threatening to spill over her lower lashes. "Hi."

Moon did a three hundred and fifty degree scan around the kitchen. It was a disaster.

Three layer cakes—or rather, three attempts at layer cakes—sat side-by-side on the countertop. He cocked his head, observing their tendency to lean—lopsided to the right, to the left—with layers both thick, and thin. Some were pale, others on the verge of scorched.

He pulled out a chair from the kitchen table and swept Cara onto his lap. "How was your day?"

"Funny," Cara objected weakly, head bowed. "It's your birthday, Moon!" she lamented.

He was touched that she had put so much effort into his celebration. No one had ever done that before. "I know."

"I finally got your cake right, and now look!" She gestured to the cake that looked like a bomb had gone off in the center. "It's ruined!"

"You worked hard," Moon conceded, trying not to laugh. "I can see that."

"Yes."

"You kept all of them," he observed curiously.

"I thought maybe later we could take them down to the homeless shelter," she suggested vaguely.

"Let them eat cake," Moon quipped, aware that he had taken liberties with the often-misquoted statement questionably attributed to the young Queen of France, Marie Antoinette.

"I love history professors," Cara rallied. "They're so clever."

"No, no. I think it's a good idea," Moon granted quickly. "We'll take the cakes and the leftovers from our dinner." God knows, Cara cooked enough for an army. "I'm sure the people at the shelter will appreciate it."

She seemed mollified. "How was your first day at school, Professor Moon?"

"Interesting. I think I'm going to need a bigger classroom."

Cara grinned. "Charismatic. That's what you are…charismatic."

"More so a curiosity," he stated flatly, pointing to the copy of the *Yale Daily News* that Michael had thrown on the table. "Both of us, actually."

"Is this our fifteen minutes of fame?" Cara queried gaily.

"Don't you think we've had our share?" Moon noted acerbically. He pulled her head down to plant a kiss on her lips. He grinned, enjoying the weight of her on his lap. "By the way, in a week or two, I will be Dr. Moon."

"Oooh, really?" Cara squirmed with pleasure. "I love playing doctor."

Moon smacked her backside. "Behave yourself." It was so like Cara to start something he wouldn't have time to finish. "Our guests will be arriving soon."

She grabbed two fistfuls of his hair and hung a long, deep kiss on his mouth.

When she pulled away, Moon was as inflamed as his soon-to-be-lit birthday candles.

Satisfied with her handiwork, Cara purred, "*Saengil chukahae,* Moon." Happy Birthday.

Inspired, Moon grabbed the back of her neck and drew her head down to give her a reciprocal kiss.

"You two need some private time?" Michael quizzed, entering the kitchen. He carried a sparkling clean little Regalo in his arms.

He passed Regalo to his father as Cara vacated his lap. Moon grinned when his son happily snuggled against him, clutching his disreputable gray bunny rabbit.

Cara wrung out a clean, warm washcloth in the kitchen sink, went to the back door and called, "Missy!"

When the Collie came on the run, Cara led her into the kitchen. She squatted in front of her and cleaned the remnants of Moon's birthday cake from her regal and delicately boned muzzle.

"Poor thing," Cara murmured fondly. "I wouldn't be a bit surprised if you barf up what Regalo fed you. Tsk, tsk."

She stood, satisfied that Missy was presentable for their guests. "Take a break, girl."

The Collie circled several times and contentedly curled up on her comfortable cushion in a secluded and quiet corner of the kitchen.

"Would you drive me to the bakery?" Moon asked Michael, who had settled in a chair opposite him at the table.

Michael looked perplexed, glancing at Cara. "Sure. Why?"

"Psst," Cara hissed at Moon. When she had his attention, she opened the refrigerator door to reveal an elaborately decorated bakery cake, unharmed, on the top shelf.

She struck a pose as Moon stared at her in wonder. "A girl scout is always prepared," she preened without shame.

He and Michael laughed, appreciating her dramatic flair.

"What have you heard from the United Nations?" Michael inquired of Cara.

Cara had contacted the Training and Outreach Coordination Department at United Nations Headquarters in New York City to introduce herself and her credentials, hoping to have an opportunity to provide her services to South Korean and Japanese delegates and visitors to the U.N. After a thorough application process and interviews with several recruiters within the Department of Training and Outreach, she was included on the on-call interpreter roster for special conferences and events.

"There is a week-long conference scheduled next month," she replied, smiling contentedly. She was looking forward to seeing some familiar faces.

Michael tilted his chin at Moon, questioning how he and Regalo were going to manage in her absence.

"Housekeeper," Moon replied confidently.

"Ah," Michael responded.

"Moon was the one who encouraged me to restart my career," Cara interjected, passing a loving glance in his direction.

Acknowledging her family responsibilities, she would only work part-time. That decision was prophetic and now upheld by yet another compelling reason. After a recent visit to the doctor for fatigue, Cara was stunned to learn that she was seven weeks pregnant. Much as she had coped with her first unforeseen pregnancy, she took the news with a kind of pragmatic, albeit bemused, acceptance.

She had waited to tell Moon until this evening—after Regalo was fast asleep, Michael and Mairet had retired to their guest suite for the night, and she and Moon were alone.

"When is Mairet arriving?" Cara asked Michael, running water at the sink.

He checked his wristwatch. "I'm picking her up at the train station in twenty minutes."

Cara turned from the sink, wiping her hands on a tea towel. She took a long moment to survey all that was right and good in her world, and give thanks for her many blessings.

She was still a bit incredulous that she had set down roots—the family, the rambling house, the loyal dog. Now that mobility, either upward or outward, was not in her foreseeable future, Cara's only stipulation to Moon while they were house hunting was that there be plenty of room for family and friends who wished to visit.

Sang Hee and her husband, having vacated the family estate to leave her mother stewing in a broth of resentment and betrayal, were now permanently ensconced in Moon's apartment in Seoul. Sang Hee happily reported that she and her husband were expecting their first child in early summer the following year. She promised that once the baby could comfortably travel, their family would come to New Haven and introduce Moon and Cara to their new nephew and Regalo to his Korean-born cousin.

Cara's parents were coming for a ten-day stay in a couple of weeks and were anxious to see a New England fall and the Moon's newly purchased and remodeled four-bedroom home.

In his senior year of high school, Franco had scored well on his SATs and was applying to Yale University for the following school year. Moon was doing what he could to assist and encourage him through the daunting and arduous process.

Michael seemed contentedly diverted by his new relationship with a brilliant young woman who worked for the FBI. Cara took an instant liking to Mairet McCarron from their first meeting. She was clearly devoted to Michael.

Moon was affably engaged in his chosen profession and new environment. He was relaxed, lighthearted, and loving to Cara and little Regalo.

Moon had recently bestowed on the toddler his Korean name, Man-Young—meaning ten thousand prosperous years. Moon Man-Young.

Cara was touched that Moon had included the surname she had assumed when employed by the Chang Agency.

"Perfect," she pronounced with supreme satisfaction, grinning at the three males and one collie who shared her life. At this moment—this precious moment—everything was just perfect.

photo: Nicole Cherie Dove

R. L. Lee calls the beautiful mountain wilderness
of Northern California home—
a place to stretch out, gaze at a pristine sky, and dream.

OTHER BOOKS
BY R. L. LEE

*All My Love,
from The Land Of Morning Calm*
Book 1 of the Cara Youngblood Moon Novels

Mira Loma

www.ingramcontent.com/pod-product-compliance
Lightning Source LLC
Chambersburg PA
CBHW030400180626
46812CB00005B/1866